The
CABLE DENNING
MYSTERY
SERIES

by
James P. Alsphert

James P. Alsphert presents

LOVE ME
OR
KILL ME

**A
Cable Denning
Mystery**

**BOOK
2**

Published 2018 by Movies of the Mind

Printed in the United States of America

First printing, 2018

ISBN-13: 978-1-64056-013-0

MOVIES OF THE MIND
www.moviesofthemind.net

CONTENTS

Prologue: "And the Walls Came Tumbling Down"

CONTENTS CONTINUED

Prologue

'AND THE WALLS CAME TUMBLING DOWN'

<u>All in a Day's Work</u>

It was one of those days. From my first cup of coffee to my last cigarette, it was a non-stop whirlwind. It started while I was minding my own business doing an errand downtown, when I heard a lot of sirens and then some shooting. A local bank on Figueroa was being held up. I saw the lone thief dart out of the bank with a female hostage. I drew my .38 and pursued the rather tall man. He ducked down an alley with his hostage, just before 6th Street. I was hot on his trail when a cop car screeched in after me and forced me to stop. I told them I almost had the robber and that they were stupid as hell to stop me. Just then, Lieutenant Keith arrived in an unmarked car and when I told him the situation he yelled something about having the patrolmen's badges and sent me on my way...with the promise of himself and two other cops right behind.

Years of experience had taught me how to figure these guys. So the first thing you ask is, up or down? A guy on the run cannot remain ground level too long. So will he hide in an attic somewhere, the top of a building, in a Ferris wheel cage at a carnival—or find some subterranean hideout where he could hang out and release his hostage without giving himself away or killing her. What was close by? Then I spotted it. The City of Los Angeles had been excavating for a new sewer-line branch on the other side of 6th Street near Spring Street. It was to intersect with the main sewer channel that eventually snaked into the Los Angeles River and down to the sea.

I ran until my breath all but quit on me. Once in the corridor of the main sewer, I climbed down a few iron ladder rungs to its water level. There were concrete walkways on both sides of the main channel. Sure enough, I picked up two distinctly different shoe prints heading toward the river. *These* were the moments I lived and breathed for! When the threat of danger is high, the time gets tight and there's a need for quick thinking and action and just maybe at the other end of the pursuit, there's a damsel in distress to rescue. Just before the place where the sewerage channel plunges forty or fifty feet straight into the L.A. River, I caught up with them.

He'd heard the echo of my footsteps and was lying in wait for me when I came into view of his gun sights. He fired wild and the woman screamed. I ducked behind a large cement pillar. "Hey, copper! Can you...can you hear me? Throw your gun out and the lady here doesn't get a bullet with her name on it."

"Look, you idiot, I didn't run all the way down here to give up my weapon. You send the woman over to me nice and safe 'n sound like, and I'll give you a chance to escape. Remember the game 'hide-and-seek'? I'll start counting to one hundred once she's over here with me. By the way, how much dough did you get away with?"

I knew I had to distract him as best I could. "How in the hell should I know? I didn't stop to count it! Why would you wanna give me a chance to escape, copper?"

"'Cause I ain't a copper, just a private investigator—probably not even a good shot," I sort of stretched the truth.

"Maybe I know you—what's your name?"

"Denning...Cable Denning..."

"You ever a cop?"

"Yeah, once upon a time—are you gonna hand the lady over or do I come out shooting and we both hope for the best?"

I heard the sound of sirens echoing and bouncing up from the river. "Where in hell am I gonna go, Denning? I could jump down the water chute to the river...yeah, maybe that'll work."

"No it won't...it's gonna be crawling with cops in about ten minutes."

"Why are you giving me a break—wanna share of the dough?"

"No thanks. I guess today's just your lucky day. Send over the lady."

"Any tricks and I kill her, Denning."

"I doubt that, Mister. I don't think you've got it in you."

"Oh, no? Don't push your luck, ex-copper."

Then in the subdued light, I saw the woman come out and start walking. As she made her way toward me, I kneeled low and kept my gun trained on where I figured the bank robber might be. "It's okay, lady I've got you now," I whispered as the shivering woman grabbed my arm. "Okay, I'm starting to count now..." I moved her out of harm's way, completely behind the cement column. "Now, stay low and quiet, lady...and don't talk," I whispered to her.

Just then, he made a break for it and went running toward the filthy waters of the city sewer system. He was never found.

Sometimes you get lost. Sometimes life deals you out a bad hand and you lose your way. Then you find yourself in a place that goes beyond what you can handle and you dwell in a twilight world like a zombie, the walking dead...fated to numbness without real feelings inside. You kind of forget why you're in the world, if you ever knew. But maybe even that doesn't matter. So what does? Maybe something deep down identifies you with yourself—but you can't be sure, because who is *self, anyway*? A man—a woman—a sexually acquired personality and maybe, if you're lucky, flavored with some semblance of character and likeableness? Who really knows? At some point you find yourself sitting at your desk in the dead of night...your finger circling the rim on your gin glass and your eyes become fixed on that red glow eating its way up your cigarette...leaving just the dead ash behind—and you ask...in the end, *who really gives a damn*?

So I walk the streets, listening to that distant music in the land of my head, where memory or something close to it plays ping-pong with my emotions, and a desolate, lonely sax plays somewhere beyond the next hill, over there. I was still pretty raw as I walked up Bronson Avenue toward the park and that music was tearing me apart with every step I took. It was like a melancholy blues—that haunting reed playing *The Man I Love* with a forlorn sadness, tracing all the hurt places in my damaged psyche, pouring its eerie call into the sky for a woman now deceased, the girl who didn't quite make it to become my December bride. But God, that woman could sing, and it was that young, beautiful woman who sang it for *this* man, the crumbling quiet man who walked the trail to the top of the incline. She had only been gone a few days, but each one of those days seemed like an eternity to me and I fought tooth and nail to avoid walking into the muck of death and guilt and all the shit we pile on ourselves when finally the chips are called in and you have to face yourself. It was the advent of Honey's death that began a lifetime trait of learning how to avoid…finding ways to compartmentalize so the left hand won't have to know what the right hand's doing.

It was late October, and a slight chill wafted through the little dells of grass, brush and oak trees. I sat on a little hill up by the Bronson Caves, tossing small rocks onto the road below. A few hikers and daily walkers passed by and greeted me with a nod, but I barely noticed. An old man with a cane came along and struggled his way to the end of the box canyon, where the road ended. He rested there for a while and then started back. He stopped in front of me, and appeared to be checking me out. "It's rattlin' through the sky, it is—this new beginnin'. So why is it you're a-mopin'—sittin' there like a dead toadstool? If somethin' be a- happenin' yesterday, well then, let it…yesterday's gone, it is…and it ain't comin' back nohow. If 'twas money, you'll be makin' more of it—if it be a woman, never grieve beyond what your heart can take—if it's your job, sure a new one'll come…and if it be God who's a- pesterin' ya, tell him you'll be comin' home soon enough anyhow." He drew quiet and seemed to be squinting to see me at

5

all. "Life's about just gettin' on with it, lad. Humph! You're too young for that kinda worryin'. Me? Ha! I pulled my bayonet out of the belly of my own kin in the Civil War, I did. And for what?"

I grew a little impatient with the lecture. "Well, I do appreciate your advice, pop, but I really would like to be left alone, if you don't mind."

"No ya don't! The young never appreciate the old—and do ya know why? 'Cause ya gotta learn wisdom for yourself, through your own experiences. But seems to me you're stuck in the past, boy. Hell, at my age I got a right to be spendin' my days in memory and regret—but not you—no, sir! You gotta tell the world you ain't done yet, tell 'em jus' cause ya fell down, it don't mean that ya ain't gettin' up, shakin' your fists at the sky and saying, 'Today is mine! And it's all I got!' The mill cannot grind with the water that's already passed through it, son."

He hesitated and looked at me with old blue eyes, now covered with milky white lenses. The old man was almost blind! "How...how did you know I was sitting here when you can't see?"

"Who says I can't see?—impertinent ingrate! You see here? These orbs on either side of my nose—what makes you think I can only see with *them*? Ah, but the eye in the middle here," he said, pointing to a place in the middle of his forehead, "she sees the colors...of your so-called *humanity*." He coughed and then spat on the ground. "Yep, I saw your dark colors, but underneath that...ha! a rainbow of goodness, lad. Come on out and live, son, the journey's short enough as it is—" He

6

coughed and spat once again and hobbled away, tapping his cane against the red rock road.

I got back to my office and sat down at my desk, rummaging around a bunch of papers. I had lost several clients because I didn't have the will to work most days. I lit up a cigarette, took a big drag and kicked back in my comfy chair. I noticed I was trembling. I got up and clicked on my little box radio. The announcer on radio station KFI made it sound like all hell had broken loose. He was broadcasting from a remote location near the new Los Angeles Stock Exchange—that was currently under construction—and kept repeating that sixteen million shares of stock had been liquidated in the past few days and the financial world was beginning to collapse. Radio Corporation of America, General Motors, U.S. Steel, Goldman Sachs and hundreds of others had taken a bath in the market place, losing 40% of their value. It was October 29, 1929, and a massive sell-off precipitated what was only the beginning of the "Black Tuesday" legacy, which was to hit bottom by 1932, losing 89% of its stock value. Suddenly it dawned on me—that's what Crazy Jack had been talking about—it wasn't the pigeons up there on the ledges of the skyscrapers, but men jumping from those precipices to their deaths below, men whose speculation, greed, lust for power and money, had collapsed the house that Jack built.

And speaking of Jack, the terrible thing I realized in the epiphany of that moment was that Crazy Jack had consistently warned me to get Honey out of the *Bella Notte* club. Well, I didn't heed his warning—and now she was dead—my *'golden throat'* was dead. I turned off the radio. Why should I give a shit about what the rich and powerful do to amuse and destroy themselves? I went back and sat at my desk, opened the bottom right drawer and took out a full bottle of bootleg gin. I drank for what seemed like hours, slowly fading away in a stupor. The phone was ringing, but I ignored it. Then my world started spinning and I passed out...sliding limp and crumpled, out of my chair to the floor below.

How long I lay there I can't say. Eventually I crawled to my bedroom and boosted myself onto my rumpled old bed. There I collapsed, neither living nor dying, lost in oblivion...descending into a dark nothingness.

CHAPTER 1

'OUR LOVE IS HERE TO STAY'

One day I awoke to see the most beautiful face I'd ever known looking down at me. She was smiling and had flashy brown eyes and lovely, shiny black hair. Her pearly white teeth glistened in the subdued light, her lips were warm and inviting. I thought I must still be dreaming. Beauty like that could only exist in celestial dimensions, far from the ugly chaos of man's demented idea of what a world of simian creatures should look like.

"Oh, mi hombre bonito—despierta, mi amor!" Adora Moreno cooed. The beautiful vision stood above me. I could hardly speak. My mouth was dry and my eyes almost glued shut. I felt my face. It was still there, but I had grown a beard and moustache. Adora laughed. "Ay! You look like *un hombre muy malo, sí, mi desperado!"* God, I loved this woman! I reached for her, but I was too weak and my arms fell to my side. She kneeled on the floor by my bed and stroked me with a warm washrag. *"Bienvenido, querido.* Welcome back, my *pobre* beloved. I am here..."

Again I tried to reach for the beautiful young thing. "Adora...Adora..." was all my mouth could manage as I again lost consciousness. In the days that followed, I discovered this devoted angel of mercy had come to live with me. Day and night she nursed me back to health, sleeping on the floor on an old blanket she found in my musty closet. Finally, perhaps three or four weeks later, I was able to sit up and take in some chicken soup she

9

had prepared on my little hot plate. I took in a deep breath and gazed at my caretaker. "Yes...you...thank you, beautiful Adora," I said on that day. Then all of a sudden I began to think of practical things like money. "There's...uh...there's some dough hidden—out there—under the table lamp on my desk...get it..." She went out and came back with a small wad of money. "How much is there? I want you to use it—you have no money—how could you buy groceries and take care of me at the same time?"

"Shhhh...!" she whispered. "You do not worry, *mi amor*." She counted the money. "Seventy-two dollars."

"Take it. Spend it on what we need."

"Okie-dokie," she tittered with a smile. "You are boss man. *Yo soy tu esclava*—I am your slave, my love."

Slowly I recovered and began to pick up the pieces of my life, thanks to my luscious and intelligent Adora. She had left the travel agency to her mother and sister and essentially spent her days and nights with me in my dingy little quarters. One day I had the guts to bring up past events. "You knew...I mean, about Honey?" I asked, carefully measuring my words.

Her eyes were soft as she came to sit on the bed beside me. "Sí, Cable, I read it in newspaper two days after. It was so *horrible*. I am truly sorry...I know you love her very much...but you must heal now..."

My eyes misted a bit just remembering about my perished *'golden throat'*, the spunky, gorgeous young blonde from the country who made good in the big city. "I got lost, Adora. I'm still not sure where I am—or for that matter, *who* I am. I've let everything go, haven't I? Do I have a business anymore?"

10

She smiled and said with a little tease in her voice, "Oh...I donno...I answer *el telefono* calls and tell your customers I am Mexican cleaning lady and you are gone away. But that you come back soon. And I keep good *registros* of everything. You can build again, Cable. I will help."

I extended my arms to her. For the first time since I'd drifted into the land of oblivion, I felt my beautiful Adora fall onto my chest. We lay there clasped around each other for the longest time. "Adora...there is no way to repay you...except with love...I've always loved you...I've always been in love with you...always..." I said, kissing her hair.

"Oh, *mi amor*!" she cried and held me even tighter, letting go of some of those tears which must have piled up through the many weeks she had looked after me. She slowly moved her face to my lips and once again I felt the inexplicable magic of her kiss. Every part of me responded to her and I could feel I was coming back to life, coming back to the world, coming back to love.

Bringing in the Sheaves

Adora and I spent Christmas of 1929 at my mother's. It's hard to describe how joy and pain can mix together when the past is being pulled out of you like an old festering sore that needs healing, while the future holds brightness and hope like a shiny new train pulling into the station, or the stockings of red and white hung from my mother's Christmas tree. I guess it helped a lot to observe how Mom and Adora chattered on together, as if they were old friends with deep affection for each

11

other. I sensed a warm closeness between the two women and wished I had someone like that in my life still. Mario Angelo's death left me bereft of such a privilege. Mario and I had spent endless Christmases together and played as youngsters with the crude but new toys our parents could afford. I remember having a wooden dump truck with wooden wheels—and one year Mario got a B-B gun and shot up a whole shelf of Mason jars in the shed, for which we both got into trouble.

Being in love with a woman changed a perspective of mine. The one that said you're always in control of your life and you call your own shots. Adora made me see what a powerful role the female principle played in a man's life, especially when both of them felt the same and found it hard to be away from each other. Was it a growing process or a weakness, I wondered? Or was it the fervor of youth when the fuse of sexual desire and excitement burned so bright? The few men who had influenced me in my formative years were tough as nails, independent—and thought women were born for cooking, sewing, cleaning and the birthing and rearing of children. Romantic love wasn't an issue, only the practical everyday demands of survival figured in their equation and tenderness was a sign of a weak link in the chain of a young boy's development. But I do remember my Dad drunk as hell holding my mother in the middle of the floor, dancing with her, laughing his big belly laugh and smiling at her as he spun her around the room. He hadn't been afraid of affection for his mate, nor did he shun me in that department, often coming into my room in the middle of the night, his breath smelling of Irish whiskey, his speech slurred. "I love ya, son!" he'd say. "And you're old man is a rootin', tootin', shootin' son-of-a-bitch on wheels!" Then he'd hold me in his arms and slobber a big kiss all over my cheek. I was half-afraid and half enjoying it as the over-stuffed galoot embraced me. Sometimes my mother would look on, smiling, but I sensed she was there just in case the old boy got a little rough with the heir apparent of the Denning clan. But when I was very small, I seemed to recall a day when something died in my mother and she seemed to shrivel and a light went out in her. So when Dad kicked the bucket, she may have missed his bigger-than-life sparkle, but I was never sure her grief was all about my father. But I missed him. Sometimes I cried when I walked through our little house listening for his wonderful, resonant voice. I think I missed his big bear hugs, too, even if he reeked of tobacco and whiskey.

It seemed to be a time of bringing in the sheaves, as our early Christian background would have said—that time of harvesting what one has sown so far in this life. What did I have to show for my almost thirty years of existence? Since joining the police force, I'd seen the underbelly of the world, that seedy dark side of humanity where almost anything and everything can—and does—happen. Maybe I thought I was a knight in shining armor drawing my sword and dispatching evil wherever I found it. Those who were such a scourge on society were a kind of vampire, draining the blood of the hard-working and the honest, whether they lived in a mafia stronghold or at city hall. If they were lone killers, they were easier to find and bring to justice. It was the hidden corrupt ones that were harder to weed out.

The tangled web of their miscreant dealings had deep roots and without a roadmap became confusing to the knight who had pledged himself to vanquish that enemy. Mario Angelo was one that died for that cause. Maybe someday I would, too, but I knew it wasn't today and I had some kind of magic on my side, something I sensed lived inside me, as well as beside me, and saw me through some pretty dangerous scrapes.

I had gone out to the little patch of garden, that we called our backyard. Adora came out and put her arms around my waist. "I am so happy, Cable. *Feliz Navidad.* All I need is here...with you and your mamma. I care for her, as *mi hermana.*"

"Yeah, I can see that, babe. We should get *your* Mom and sister together for New Year's, huh? That way it would be three babes and one guy. My kind of odds."

She laughed heartily. "Oh, you...I am not *una mujer celosa...pero,* I am beside you, *mi amor, porque tú eres mi corazón...*"

I turned to look at the woman standing beside me who had no clue that her beauty could have easily outshone any movie star. Yet her humble and simple nature didn't make any such demands on her ego. She would be contented in a barrio or a mansion, for her heart would live the same way no matter the trappings of an increasingly materialistic world.

We went inside. The Christmas meal was simple and the three of us made the best of a quiet day. But both women knew the grieving inside me was not yet over. Honey had been gone a little over two months and some raw places kept erupting in me like scathing magma pouring down the sides of a volcano into my gut. It still hurt like hell. But the worst was yet to come that day. My mother had turned the radio on for some Christmas music, but not all stations played the seasonal variety of pap which was traditionally served up on that day. The Great Depression had only just begun its slide into financial ruin and some radio stations preferred to play the music of the he and she world, perhaps thinking it would boost the sinking national morale. Because, after all, romantic love was the last remaining starship of hope in a world fragmented by greed, right? Suddenly Honey's version of *It All Depends on You* came wafting across the airwaves. Both my mother and Adora looked across the table at me. I froze and closed my eyes. I got up and excused myself and went back outside. But this time I went out the front door, and down the steps onto the familiar streets of my youth. It was a place where brawls were fought on the sidewalks, where gangs would kill over some territory nobody would ordinarily care about.

Someone had considerately turned the radio off, but too late. I was still crumbling inside. Sometimes realities are deceptive, like when you think you're over the flu but it comes back, only this time like gangbusters and all but prepares you for a pine box at the local cemetery. The most terrible place for a memory to be, is in an idealized world of "what ifs" and imagined perfections. Then the measuring stick becomes that which can never be justified in the living, breathing everyday world. I would have to find a way not to idolize Honey Combes or see the vision of a beautiful blonde woman in a red-sequined gown under a bright spotlight singing her heart out at the *Bella Notte*, singing before adoring audiences to loud, raucous applause—singing to *me*, Cable Denning, ex-cop-gumshoe from the tough side of the tracks, now at twenty-nine years old, a cinder nearly burned down to the core of his paltry existence.

Adora and I hugged my mother goodnight and we went to my ramshackle office to sleep. I felt bad that my beautiful lady had to put up with living conditions that at best could only be described as *basic*. But she never complained and slept beside me in quiet repose. She helped out with office work as best she could. The oncoming economic depression helped the bottom to fall out of service businesses like mine, and only the well to do could afford my services. After all, I wasn't the local grocery store. Food, rent and utilities were the basic necessities of 1929. All that aside, I knew my life would have to change. I was made with an instinct somewhere in me, a strange siren that called to me in the night—nights that summoned me to my senses and created change and transformation. I knew I would have to build up my business. So...where would I start other than a bolder print in the yellow pages of the phone book?

New Year's came in with a bang. Adora, my mother and I attended a small get together at *Todo el Mundo*, their little travel agency on the ground floor of the Pico House near the Pueblos de Los Angeles area. Adora's mother and sister, Elisa and Flora, hosted us along with a few other neighbors. There was one who stood out, in particular...a Señor *Antonio Vargas*. He was about six-feet tall with a very well-groomed moustache and dark, wavy hair. His eyes were that flashing kind of dark-brown, he spoke with a definite Latin accent and you just knew he was thinking lots of things while he pretended to be enjoying the party. Earlier in the evening he hit on Adora, who politely gave him the brush and pointed over to me as the man she was with. He deferred but kept an eye on both of us the rest of the evening. By the midnight hour Señor Vargas had mysteriously disappeared and when we began to clean up after the party, Elisa came out of her bedroom alarmed, saying it had been ransacked and things had been strewn all over the floor. Immediately, I put on my private detective hat and put two and two together. This guy had been looking for the *God of Our Fathers*, the famous *Fen de Fuqin*, now safely in the hands of its rightful owners in the land of the *Cave of the Seven Truths*. My earlier adventures with good vs evil nearly cost me my life and did take a terrible toll on some of the characters in the drama orchestrated by a sinister so-called "Order", the *Oculus Pyramis Mandatum*. I knew they would never quit. Whoever "they" were carried a big stick and controlled the world from a secret backstage doorway.

We helped Elisa and Flora clean things up, took my mother home and by two-thirty in the morning January 1, 1930, we were in bed, snuggling. Frankly, I don't know what I would have done without that exquisitely beautiful woman's love and warmth. If one were to be religious and had a bent toward the spiritual unknown, it was almost as if God had sent an angel to be with me because my loneliness would have been unbearable and I may have quickly drunk and smoked myself to death. In a way it reminded me of that Al Jolson song, *Sonny Boy*, the one Honey sang to me that night at the *Bella*

Notte. "*When there are grey skies, I don't mind the grey skies, you make them blue, Sonny Boy...Friends may forsake me, let them all forsake me, you'll pull me through, Sonny Boy...*" It was Adora's constancy that pulled me through. I knew that being in love with someone is the riskiest business in the world outside of walking into a burst of bullets from a Tommy gun. But I had risked it with Adora, and so far I was winning. I just hoped that she got enough out of the relationship to fulfill her, besides the bedroom and our day-to-day companionship. Maybe, ultimately, love is both the risk *and* reward in the same breath. Who knows?

On New Year's Day we awakened early and made love in a torrent of pent up passion. Then we slept again. Adora made our first cup of coffee and I stayed in bed looking at her curvy naked body jostling about the small room. I was thinking of a new song I'd heard recently and thought it catchy. Adora had heard it on the radio as well and hummed it a few times. I was looking at her as I began humming to the tune. "I don't remember all the words, doll, but I wanna sing to you."

"You do?" she asked, raising her eyebrows and smiling. She came over to join me on the bed. "Ay señor! I think we need a bigger...uh, how you say—*la cama*—the bed is too *pequeño* for our love making."

"Yeah, you're right. 'Cause I'm really a romantic dick deep down inside, you know—that is, aside from being a *private* dick."

She tittered. "Ay...sí...you are my private dick, no, señor?"

"Sí, señor," I answered. And then I began to sing in my morning baritone. "*Stars shining bright above you,*

18

night breezes seem to whisper, 'I love you,' birds singing in the sycamore tree, dream a little dream of me..." Then she joined me. *'Sweet dreams till sunbeams find you, sweet dreams that leave all worries behind you, but in your dreams whatever they be, dream a little dream of me...'* "Once again." *'Dream a little dream of me...'* "One more time..." We repeated the last phrase and she fell into my arms, bursting with the sunshine this love had brought into both of our lives. After all it was a gift—and no one can keep a gift like that, it was on loan and there was no payback date—just the certainty that it could not last forever. "Happy New Year, babe," I said—holding my Adora.

CHAPTER 2

THE CURSE OF NEPTUNIA

It was about eleven o'clock on January 11th and I was sitting at my desk, figuring out what to do next, when the phone rang. "Yeah, Cable Denning here."

"Mr. Denning. My name is *Benedict Royce*—you don't know me, but you come highly recommended. I...I would like to have a private conference with you about a very, uh.....delicate subject."

"A conference, huh? Well, Mr. Royce, my doors are usually open roughly from ten in the morning to—well, whenever I get tired of hearing the gripes of human beings beset by their problems."

He laughed lightly. "Humor is very important, I would imagine, in your business. But it is not possible for me to come to you. If I pay your fee, would you be kind enough to come to my home?"

"Well, if it isn't too far—yeah, that can be arranged. But I don't have an automobile, Mr. Royce. I'm still hoofing it or taking advantage of our most convenient electric trolley system here in L.A."

"I see...would it be convenient if I sent a car around to pick you up? I—I, uh, live in the foothills above Pasadena."

This guy was evidently well heeled and I needed the dough. "Yeah, that'd be fine. When do you want to, uh, arrange our meeting?"

"This afternoon, if possible, say around two o'clock?"

"Can do. So, uh, I'll, uh, expect your car about an hour before?"

"Yes. Thank you, Mr. Denning. If you'll please wait downstairs by the curb, my man can easily identify you if you'll describe yourself."

I laughed. "Well, Mr. Royce, that could be a challenge on any given day, but ordinarily I wear a trench coat, a light-brown fedora, stand about six-feet and probably will be smoking a Lucky Strike."

Again, he chuckled. "That sounds...uh, fair enough, Mr. Denning. I'll look forward to meeting you. Thank you again for changing your schedule to accommodate me."

"No problem, Mr. Royce. Business has been kind of slow since the stock market decided to go south for the winter."

"Until then, Mr. Denning."

He hung up and I could have done a jig. I needed that kind of money in the bank. I was down to the last thirty smackers in my pocket and nothing in my bank account. Maybe old Gianinini would give me a loan, but I'd read in the papers that Bank of America had suffered some losses back in October of last year. Well, all I could do was hustle and hope to the gods that enough dough would come my way to take care of February's bills.

Adora was spending the day helping her mother and sister at their travel agency. *Todo el Mundo* was suffering along with the rest of us, as people simply didn't have the extra cash to take that trip to Ohio to visit Aunt Martha. Only the rich floated above the financial waters during this fateful year of 1930. Hang on to your hat, Denning, I told myself—and call upon those money angels who pour out the greenbacks from Nirvana or wherever they operate from.

21

As Benedict Royce had promised, a huge black limousine drove up in front of my joint on Franklin precisely at one o'clock. It hadn't occurred to me that it might be a trap set by my old nemesis, the *Oculus Pyramis Mandatum*. But it was too late and I was packing my .38 close to my chest just in case.

We rode for about an hour and when the limo turned into a paved road with a couple of large pillars at the entrance, I knew I was in for a glance at the top of the heap in this old world. Soon we approached an imposing large estate, the kind with fifty rooms and eight fireplaces, manicured trees, shrubs and lawns and two flights of stairs leading up to the main entrance. The chauffeur let me out and indicated I should walk up the concrete steps to the entrance. I did so and used the brass knocker, which was in the shape of a dolphin. The usual stuffy Englishman greeted me with a perfunctory smile after looking me over. He must've thought I came from the costume department at a local movie lot. He led me to a large drawing room. From floor to ceiling, the damn place had more books filling its shelves than the downtown library. Soon another man entered and motioned me to follow him. We walked down another corridor until we stood at a huge white door engraved with a pair of golden dolphins. What was with this guy and the fish world, anyhow?

We entered, and standing in the middle of the room was a rather tall, slightly over-weight man with a mostly baldpate, only silver sideburns and not much else remained atop his head. His eyes were steel blue, his mouth pleasantly curved up in a welcoming smile. He was dressed immaculately. "Mr. Denning. I am indebted to you for coming all the way out here to meet with me." He came over and shook my hand. His grip was large and warm. "Please come over here to my sunlit window and sit with me."

I walked with him and sat opposite the man on a large, over-stuffed chair. "Thank you. It's good to meet you, Mr. Royce," I said, looking out onto the vast grounds that surrounded the estate. "What do you call your place here, if I may ask?"

"*Neptunia*, named after the god Neptune. You know, sea and air and all. I've always been very fond of the oceans of the planet and the endless abundance that the salty waters of the earth seem to contain." He snapped his fingers as a butler entered. "What would you like, Mr. Denning—I always imbibe around this time in the afternoon."

"Well, truth be told, I'm an English gin drinker—but with Prohibition and all—"

"—say no more, Mr. Denning. We have the finest imported English gin—can't beat the Juniper berries from the south of England, you know."

"Yes, thank you. I'd—I'd, uh, settle for that just fine."

He studied me. He glanced at the hat in my hand, my rumpled trench coat and scuffed brown shoes. "I can see you're a man of the world, sir. Your business no doubt takes you to the less desirable ports of call in our fair city of Los Angeles, would you not say?"

"Yep, you got that right. Most of my work is weeding out errant husbands, wives, lovers and miscellaneous violators of our proper moral codes. So I snap Kodak photos of those who have trespassed, in compromising positions and show up in court with the evidence. It's usually about money, Mr. Royce."

He smiled quaintly. "Dear me, what people won't do for—for—uh, emotional fulfillment, even at the risk—"

"—I think we can call it by its real name—good old sex someone isn't getting at home. The restless heart is a dangerous weapon, I've discovered, Mr. Royce."

"My, my...yes...so I've read. Sounds to me as if you've read a bit yourself? I'm an avid reader. Always have been."

"If you mean have I read more than *The Wizard of Oz, The Great Gatsby* or *Huckleberry Finn*, the answer is yes. Even though I tend more toward non-fiction."

"Ah, a man who likes *fact*, an admirable quality, indeed. Speaking of which, may we get down to the reason I requested this conference this afternoon?"

"By all means, Mr. Royce. I'm...I'm all ears...but first, I do have one question. You mentioned I come to you highly recommended. Your discretion permitting, I'd like to thank that person if you don't—"

"—ah, but my discretion does *not* permit. Suffice it to say your credentials are experience and excellence in getting the job done. I hope you understand."

"Yeah, sure. Okay, on with it."

"Oh, one more thing before I begin, Mr. Denning. Would you be kind enough to surrender your firearm to Henry, my butler, before we commence—knowing that such things are even present in my company makes me uneasy, if you please. And, if you would be more comfortable, feel free to take off your overcoat and give it along with your fedora to my man Henry, as well."

I got up, took off my trench coat, fumbled for my .38 and handed them over to Henry. He bowed, thanked me and exited with my belongings. "Okay, Mr. Royce. Anything else before I relax with this fine drink of gin Henry just delivered?"

"Yes, there is one more item." He reached into his breast pocket and took out a sea-green envelope. He offered it to me, so I got up and retrieved it from his hand. Then I sat back down. "Go ahead, open it, Mr. Denning. This is to show my earnest confidence in you." I opened the envelope. I thought some dough might be forthcoming, but when I took it out and counted seven one-hundred dollar bills, I was rather surprised, to say the least. "Are you sure you have *that* much confidence in me?"

"A crisp new hundred dollar bill for each of the seven seas of the world. And, as I said, you come highly recommended. May we proceed?"

"So, how may I be of assistance to you, Mr. Royce?"

"As I said, what I have to share with you is of a very confidential nature. Nothing I say must ever leave this room."

"Confidence and truth are two big items on my list..."

"Excellent. So...here it is, Mr. Denning. I am a very, very wealthy man—most likely the richest man in all of Southern California. But money isn't everything, and of late I fear for the safety of my two lovely daughters and my beloved wife, Mathilda."

"I'm sorry to hear that. But please continue..."

"My two daughters couldn't be more different—as if they had different parents. My eldest daughter, Eden, went rather wayward in her teenage years. Now...she, uh, is well invested into business—but a business that does not carry my stamp of approval, if you know what I mean."

"No, I don't know what you mean. Would you care to be more explicit?"

"She runs a bordello in North Hollywood. It is one of the most exclusive and her clientele come from the very elite of our community—some of them married pillars of society."

"So tell me something new, Mr. Royce. That story's as old as the hills and twice as boring."

"To you, perhaps...but to me it is simply appalling, disgusting and of course puts my family in a bad light. It is common knowledge that Eden runs the thing and makes a lot of money."

"Well, that part could be commendable—at least she doesn't depend on you for support as so many children of the idle rich do."

"In a way, I wish she did—err...*would*...it is irritating for me to deal with this embarrassment."

"And the other daughter—has she fared more to your taste?"

His face lit up and a warm smile crossed his lips. "*Zephyr*...ah, my little prize. Pure and good, mysterious and intelligent, remote and warm—that describes my little sea urchin pretty well, I put it to you, Mr. Denning. Just being in her presence makes me proud of her."

"So, if I'm not mistaken, what I'm hearing is a fairly large dose of partiality here. Of course, it isn't unusual for a parent to have preferences in their children. I was an only child, so I never experienced—"

"—but I love my family equally, Mr. Denning. And all of them are at risk. It is not just simply a matter of financial considerations, or the risk of losing property or investments—but *life and death*, sir. It is for this that I implore you to hear me out."

Suddenly the man was running scared inside. He tripped across something that had evidently bothered him daily, but maybe he had learned to shove it down deep for a while. But when it came up for air, I could tell fear had gripped him like the hand of the ol' Grim Reaper. "Please, continue, Mr. Royce," I said as I sipped on my fine gin.

"Somehow I need to conceal my family—steal them away during the night, deliver them to a safe island, or some sanctuary, not easily accessed, where they will be undetected and untraceable."

"So far, I get it. You want to get your family out of the U.S.—someplace where whoever's chasing you in your nightmares, can't get to. So how do I figure into your concerns?"

"Well, that's a touchy one, Mr. Denning, and one I earnestly hope you are willing to undertake. You see, none of them will listen to me per se. But if *you* perhaps could speak to each one of them in my stead, fully representing my wishes, it might make the difference."

"Why can't you hire a lawyer for that? You gotta remember, Mr. Royce, I'm just a gumshoe who used to be a cop at one time, who carries a .38 because we live in a dangerous world—"

"—that's precisely why I cannot hire an attorney for the job. You're tough, Denning, you've got the guts to take the bull by the horns, so to speak. You're trained in

27

dealing with the dark side of things, the violent threats that back a man up against the wall, and the kind—"

"—who threatens you while using your family for collateral. So, if I may ask, Mr. Royce, what is it you know that they—assuming there is a 'they'—don't want you to know?"

He sat back on his large over-stuffed chair and took out a cigarette. I came over and lit it for him. "Thank you, Mr. Denning. I think I'm going to like working with you."

"Whoa! Wait a little minute here, Mr. Royce. I haven't said yes yet. See here? I've still got those seven hundred smackers right in this envelope here on the table. I might be brave and all and know how to handle a firearm, but I'm not into suicide—at least not this year. And you didn't answer me—what do you know that they don't want you to know?"

He took a big drag on his cigarette and let out a big stream of blue smoke. "Well, you see, I know too much, Mr. Denning...much...too much...I—I personally don't mind dying, if it comes to that. But not my girls. I've been married to the same lovely woman for thirty-three years. Through her, I sired two exquisite daughters—albeit different as night and day—yet equally my flesh and blood. Love isn't about approval in this world. Love is only about love, which must include acceptance."

Royce made me think a lot of things in a very few seconds. "Yet you must somehow have been involved in a business so dangerous as to have it come back now and bite you in the butt, if you'll pardon my frankness. Did you consider that when your girls were growing up?"

He looked down at the floor. "Money and power are equal corruptors—partners like a double opiate—and pretty soon you're hooked. You're also young and ambitious and getting richer by the day. Maybe one doesn't consider the price to be paid for such folly when youth runs through your veins like injections of pure gold and you can never picture yourself older than thirty—ever."

I was angry. I had seen and known this type of man before. Only they came with different faces. They were Ravna, Frank Laggore, Jack Dragna—ambitious men who would've bulldozed granny down for that extra bit of power and that next dirty dollar. "Guys like you make me laugh, you know. Twenty years of betting against the spinning roulette wheel and suddenly you've got a conscience because now your family is threatened—and maybe for the first time you realize you, too, are expendable. Was that what you wanted, Royce? The corruption of greed and avarice—do you want your children and grandchildren to become that, too!" I boomed at him. "And if they don't mold themselves after the upstanding model of their *pater familias*, then the other end of the coin is a life threatened—you and your family become fugitives, forever running from the bad guys, their footsteps always a few paces behind you....until one day—and you'll never know what day that will be—they've caught up to you and bang! bang! it's over and everyone's dead. You know why? Because if I'm guessing right, this whole thing wasn't about money for them, either, but something far more sinister and secretively powerful, and if it fell into the wrong hands could cause these powers that be, a mighty inconvenience, Mr. Royce. And they can't let that cancer spread, now, can they? They've got to nip it in the bud—right away, as soon as it's decided you have become a risk or are derelict—or who knows?—maybe you're on some timetable of theirs.....bam! at a certain age pop goes the weasel right out the window and six feet under!"

Royce had turned white as he stared at me. I knew no one had ever talked to him like that in his life. But I took the risk at that moment because I was hedging the bets in my favor. Finally he spoke. "This...this is precisely why...why you were recommended to me, Denning. You've got the guts to wrench it out of your craw and spill it here on the table in front of us. You see, you've crossed over a line of personal risk and danger. I would have killed a lesser man than you for verbally lambasting me the way you just did. But as you said, truth is truth—isn't it?...and it neutralizes the moment. *I've got to have that kind of man on my side*. I'll pay you whatever it takes if and when you deliver for me. And when you do, I'll be there for you."

"*Yes*...can be a terrible word, Royce. Its implications can pursue you the rest of your life if you make the wrong choice. I stand at that crossroad right now, here, with you..." I took out a Lucky Strike and lit it up. "You see, as you probably already know, I've been down this road before with a whole crew of motley, dangerous people, all after one thing, all willing to kill whoever they need to in order to get it. Men without conscience or consideration, respect or principle. So, when I mention panic button words like *God of Our Fathers* or *Oculus Pyramis Mandatum*, neither of us will be surprised now, will we, Royce?"

30

He remained calm. "No...we won't be surprised. So now you've discovered my dirty little secret. Now you know that I have sold my soul for a mess of pottage. But what I cannot bear is that I made the same deal for the souls of my beloved wife and two young daughters." He got up, walked over to the window and looked out at the handsome landscape. Then he turned. "Please...help me, Denning. I beg you...I don't know where else to turn. I have pretty well run out of options."

"Well, it's kind of nice to know I was last on your list," I said with a hint of sarcasm in my voice. "It's too bad, isn't it, that sometimes we're allowed to speak for the destiny of other souls?"

"It's a downright tragedy. Will you help?"

"Oh, by the way—not to change the subject—but while I'm taking mental notes, you didn't mention what your youngest daughter, uh—"

"—Zephyr..."

"Yeah, Zephyr. Both of your daughters have very unusual but catchy names."

"*Catchy*? Is that how you see them? Believe me, that wasn't Mathilda's or my intention when we named the girls. Anyway, she lives in a seashell."

That one bowled me over. "Uh...could you clarify that one a bit for me?"

"Well, from the moment Zephyr was born, she had an affinity for the sea. She loves sea creatures. She even has a favorite dolphin she plays with on a regular daily basis. Everything from her diapers to the wallpaper delighted her as long as it had an oceanic theme. We tried traditional clothing, monograms with lambs, little bears, fairy tale characters and the like, but she cried upon having them in her surroundings. Then one day something curious happened. When she was barely walking, maybe a year and a half, we took her to the beach for the first time. The minute she saw the water she lit up and started cooing in a strange language that was all her own. She ran for the water and Mathilda and I grabbed her. But she began to weep the most heart-wrenching tears you ever saw—so we stayed with her as she continued toward the surf. Unafraid, she walked into the water, smiling, laughing, and calling out to some invisible world in her imagination. Fearlessly she braved the waves and walked deeper and deeper into the water until she began to swim! Her mother and I were shocked. And for the best part of the afternoon she stayed in the water, happily frolicking and speaking to her invisible playmates. Or maybe they weren't invisible, I don't recall."

"No sharks?" I asked, lifting my eyebrows. I knew every once in a while a great white or tiger shark would take a nip out of a swimmer around those waters.

"Just dolphins...or...or as I said, *make believe* playmates."

Something he was saying didn't resonate quite right with me. He stopped and took a deep breath, looking at me as if he were *expecting* a retort of disbelief. "I have this feeling there's more to it, Mr. Royce."

"Oh, yes, there's more alright. Just as Mathilda took her hand to lead her out of the water, a most peculiar thing happened. From out of nowhere a young dolphin appeared. Now, the beaches around Malibu have never been known to have a native species of dolphin. Zephyr tugged away from my wife and embraced the little dolphin, placing her cheek right up close to its eye! Both Mathilda and I knew at that moment this was no ordinary child."

I put out my cigarette in an ashtray on top of a little round table. I got up and put my hands in my pockets, looking down at the seated Benedict Royce. "Quite a story, Mr. Royce...quite a story."

"But you don't believe it..."

"On the contrary, I've seen places and dimensions the ordinary guy wouldn't think about in a lifetime. So your Zephyr comes across as unique and plausible. You say she lives in a seashell?"

"Yes, I built her one in a little cove the family owns above Malibu. She lives there quietly, bothers no one."

"What about schooling, education—that kind of thing—not to mention social skills? I'm sure you don't want an *idiot savant* on your hands..."

"That's another strange part about the puzzle of my daughter—she's fully educated. It's as if she drew the '*knowing*' out of the air or something. They say some people are born fully conscious, whatever that means. Anyway, Zephyr is as smart and alert as anyone could be."

"Now *that* may be a little far-fetched, Royce. But for now, let's assume all that you tell me is true. I'll need a little time to think this thing over—and if I accept—now remember, I'm saying *if* I accept, we'll have to have a little game plan, right?"

"Yes. But you need to consider that time is of the essence."

"What's the matter—your ghosts getting closer?"

"You might say that."

"I'll tell ya what. You keep your little green envelope with the seven hundred greenbacks for now. That way you won't be able to say I had a good time on your money until I've earned some of it."

"As you wish, Denning. Oh, and if you should happen to decide favorably within seven days, I will give you a five thousand dollar bonus—simply for your expediency."

"Sounds like a good deal to me." I got up to go. Henry brought my hat, coat and gun and I donned them. "There are a few pieces of the puzzle that don't quite fit, but I'll mull them over—and we'll go from there. In the meantime, you might think about how you're going to prepare the female members of your family for a smoking, drinking, skirt-chasing young gumshoe who calls it as he sees it."

Again, Royce chuckled. "You do have a way with words. Where did you get that clever patter from? It's rather musical, I'd say."

"Thank you, Royce. I'm not sure. Maybe it comes from the fact that I truly enjoy good music. I'm a sucker for a smoky dive, a good band and a knock-out doll in a low-cut green sequined gown singing her little heart out underneath a spotlight."

"That might make a man's blood pressure rise. I see what you mean. Some people get their emotional nutrition that way."

"Now who's clever with the words? Say, I like that. May I use that phrase if the occasion comes up?"

"Certainly." He approached me and shook my hand. "Remember, seven days with a 'yes' answer and you're five grand richer. And here's my private phone number.

Call anytime. The sooner the better..." He handed me a sea-green business card with a fancy phony business name on it. *Zerotrope Publishers* and a telephone number was all it contained.

I thanked Mr. Benedict Royce and left. On the car ride back I kept thinking about things, especially how hackles were going up and down my neck thinking about how life threatening to my person the next footsteps I take might be. Also, the odd disposition of young Zephyr left me with a kind of funny feeling. After all, it wasn't every day I was likely to meet up with some babe who might be half-human, half-mermaid.

An Evening in Eden

When I told Adora about my very bizarre new potential case, she was excited and could hardly believe anyone *had* that much money, let alone offered it to me. I considered the 'yes' from her court and three days later made it for myself. 'Yes,' I would take on the case. I called Royce and he was anxious and delighted at the same time when I told him my decision. Right away he ordered his car to pick me up. Immediately upon arriving and being escorted into his presence, he gave me the original seven hundred dollars plus the $5,000 bonus. Well, at least the man delivered on his promises. Now I was rich, now I could afford that little cottage for Adora and her mother and sister I was planning on surprising them with some day. I also planned to pay off Honey's wedding ring, which I kept in its original little grey velvet box in my top dresser drawer at the office. I couldn't see burying it with her corpse. It would just sit there while the moldering body turned to dust.

Mathilda Royce was a decent woman, a bit nervous and unfulfilled I suspected, but intelligent, beautifully groomed and very nice to me. She was rather tall and slender, with tastefully tinted hair that gave her sophistication instead of age. Her voice was decidedly British Isles, somewhat low and muted and she made sure she was close to you when she spoke so she wouldn't have to raise her voice. Our first private audience was awkward, because her husband wanted to stick around until I suggested I fulfill what he hired me for. "So, Mrs. Royce," I said after Benedict Royce departed. "I'm sure you know why your husband hired me. And if you have any questions about my role here, I suggest you address them up front."

"Well, I'm never quite sure what Benedict is up to, but I suspect it has something to do with his work—and it's simply not safe for us to remain state-side. Is that what you policemen might call, 'getting the drift?'"

"Yes, Mrs. Royce, that's sounds pretty close. Are you willing to uproot until this thing blows over?"

"Blows over? Oh, you mean comes to an end? I hope so. But I will miss my garden club meetings, bridge on Saturday evenings—and my newly found sport of golfing during the week. Have you ever golfed, Mr. Denning?"

"No, ma'am, I'm afraid not. It's a bit time consuming for a simple street-pounder like myself. You know, I'm too busy chasing naughty lovers and nasty killers and all those kinds of things."

"Oh, dear...Benedict always says I'm too insulated from the real world out there. It is violent, isn't it? But you know, I never tell him, but I read murder mysteries a lot—and some of them are pretty racy as well—if you know what I mean," she said, a tad embarrassed.

"Oh, yeah, I do know what you mean. So...are you willing to go peaceably to a carefully chosen new location—a special place to live with a brand new life style? Plus, I'm sure you understand, I can't divulge its location, just in case you're caught and pumped for information—that you won't have, of course."

"Pumped? Does that mean I will be sexually assaulted?"

I chuckled. "No, it means some bad guys might want to twist your arm or something to make you tell them where you and your daughters are going."

"Oh. I see. It all sounds so...so *cloak-and-dagger*, you know, Mr. Denning. Well, I don't suppose it can be any worse than what it is already—I mean, this pressure and all Benedict threatens me with. I hope to Heaven you won't take me to a cold clime—I distinctly cannot stand cold climes. I have a bit of arthritic pain in my fingers, you know."

Benedict Royce told me he had purchased a small island in the Caribbean a mile or two off the waters of Nassau, Bahamas. I thought a person could do a lot worse than that, for God's sake. "Well, sounds to me like you're the easy one, Mrs. Royce. What's your guess regarding your two very different daughters—who I have yet the privilege to meet?"

"Eden is just impossible. Stubborn, skimming over life like a board game—she likes to be in control of—of *everything*. When she speaks, she whispers and hisses like a snake, a sneaky snake. Very subtle, that one. And I suppose you are aware of what she—she *does* for a livelihood. I was never so embarrassed in my life when I found out—"

"—so how do you think I can persuade her to exit California and let someone else run the flesh shop while she's gone?"

"I don't know. Eden is Eden. Now our Zephyr is a different story. Of course we'd have to build her a seashell house—but it can't be in a cold land—cold climes simply undo me. And poor Zephyr would perish in anything under seventy degrees. That's why I insisted on the Bahamas—so pleasant, don't you think?"

"Yeah, you could do a lot worse, Mrs. Royce." I could see Mrs. Mathilda Royce was a fine woman, if a bit off center, but I also knew she couldn't help me with the daughters any more than she had. "So you'll convince your daughters they've got to get out—and soon?"

"Oh, I couldn't do that—at least not personally. I think Eden thinks me rather weak and ineffectual—while Zephyr—well, Zephyr lives in a different world, Mr. Denning. I'm not sure how to communicate to her that she may be in danger. She lives without fear. The guesthouse above Zephyr's seashell is maintained by a Mr. Crickle, an old English gentleman we're all so very fond of. He watches over our little girl most ably."

So I was on my own. I said my good-byes and when I got back to my office in the mid-afternoon, I decided I'd jump on top of things right away, so I called Eden Royce at her place known as *Hollywood Highlands Manor*. She came to the phone. "Hello, Miss Royce. My name is Cable

Denning. Your father hired me to represent him in a matter I need to discuss with you. When will you be available."

"Oh......! Well, uh...I'm available most all of the time, Mr. Denning. Daddy mentioned you were—uh, young and handsome. And you're not an attorney, are you?" Her voice was soft and breathy, as if she was having sex on the phone with you and you didn't know it.

"No, ma'am, I'm just a private dick plying his trade on the streets of Los Angeles. You know, trying to make an honest living."

She snickered at the other end of the line. "Private what? I'm not too sure I heard you correctly."

"Oh, that's short for private detective. I know what you're thinking—and in your line of work, I suppose every dick *has* to be private, huh?"

She giggled. "Oh, you are funny, Mr. Denning. Denning...first name Cable? I'll call you Cable. Yes, I would like to meet you. Daddy is so persuasive about you. He promises me you'll be *good*...and a girl like me always insists on *good*—matter of house policy."

"Yep. I get it. You can call me Cable if I can call you Eden, Eden."

Oh, certainly. Fair play, you know, Cable—gets a girl a lot of—of special favors. But I know you're not com-ing...coming over to see me for any special—uh, *favors* now, are you?"

"We just need to talk, Eden. What about early this evening?"

"Well, the girls are pretty busy this evening. But since I am the...the *proprietress* of my own establish-ment—I don't—I don't indulge much in sampling the benefits of—of...my...trade...so I will be open—I mean my *'Amore Inn'* will be open for you—say, around nine o'clock? And as I always say, Cable, *the amore in the bet-ter...*"

I laughed heartily at this character. "I'll be there, Eden. And thanks for not putting me off."

"Oh, Cable, just hearing your voice, I don't know what girl would ever want to put you off—I think it would be far more enjoyable to put you *up*—for the night. Don't you?"

I could tell the gal was a tease. But there was some-thing I liked about her. "Yeah, well, I'm afraid that con-versation is about all you're gonna get out of me, as I said. See you tonight about nine."

Eden Royce's establishment, known privately as the *'Amore Inn'* went under the respectable name of *Holly-wood Highlands Manor*, a seemingly legitimate 'board-ing' school for young women. Modeling, acting, dance and musical vocal arts were taught at the place. In 1930 booze had to be brought in from the rear of the joint by one of Jack Dragna's 'distributors' under the guise of a milk delivery truck. The building was a well-groomed four-story affair, located west of Ventura Boulevard where the coast mountain range began its ascent, giving "*Highlands*" its legitimacy. It could have been a little Hearst Castle, twinkling there in the night, and it was fairly isolated in a clump of Cypress and Palm trees, its red terracotta shingles nestled in among the verger. The bottom story was devoted to the pursuit of the theatri-cal arts, while the upper three housed the women, and deluxe rooms where they could entertain their male customers. Men were allowed only after dark. Thus, it appeared, no neighbors complained, and since the mayor and half of his board of supervisors frequented Eden's happy manor, no legal complaints were filed—or if there were, they would conveniently disappear into a "backlog" of dusty files. I had to hand it to Eden Royce— it was a great way to make a fast million bucks while attending to the lusty needs of the well-heeled male population of Greater Los Angeles.

Having no car, I had to take a taxi from Ventura Boulevard, where the orange streetcar line ended. I noticed the 9:00 p.m. traffic to the joint was brisk and I was but one of the many patrons swinging around the circular driveway. I paid my taxi driver, walked up to the massive mahogany door, and used the knocker. And speaking of which, a brunette with extra-large knockers greeted me with a smile and lipstick so thick and red you could paint a dozen fire engines with them.

"I'm—I'm Cable Denning...here to see Miss Royce?" I said.

"Yes, Mr. Denning, Miss Royce is awaiting you. If you will take the elevator to the fourth floor...please turn left when you get off and walk straight ahead. You'll run right into Miss Royce's suite."

"Thanks," I said. Got to the fourth floor and turned left. The carpets were red and plush, the wallpaper was a flocked mass of Italian-style angels in red and gold, blowing horns and otherwise frolicking. I came to a pair of large white doors. I knocked. A blonde dish opened it. She looked me up and down, until I felt like I was under a microscope. "Eden Royce, I presume?"

Eden Royce was about five-foot four, warm blue eyes, a very sexy pair of lips and smile, a cute button nose and a body that wouldn't quit, from her toes to her very bleached blonde hair. She had a rhythm when she spoke, as if she did so with her entire body. I found it very intriguing. "Cable Denning, I presume?" she said mimicking me.

"Yep, it's me. Quite a joint you got here."

She extended her hand in the most feminine of ways. I took it. "Thank you for coming all the way out here to see me...and I am happy to meet you—handsome young men always make me happy—especially...how did you say on the telephone...when they're *private dicks*."

We both laughed. "Good to meet you, too, Eden," I said surveying the plush room with lots of reds, yellows and warm indigos splashed about. "I can see I'm in the wrong business."

"Well, from what Mother tells me, Daddy has paid you handsomely to watch over little old me and my— my crazy little sister. So, perhaps you'll make out...just fine. Would you like a drink?"

I said yes and she brought me the same brand of English gin that Benedict Royce had served me. "This is good stuff," I said as I toasted her. "Won't you join me?"

"I don't drink alcohol...it fades the face away, you know. I want to be...comely...and remain attractive all of my life, Cable. Oh....I can't stand people who neglect their bodies. All of my girls—uh, students, are required to take rigorous calisthenics." She stretched her chest out and raised her arms so one could see her nipples rise to attention. She offered me a chair, then sat opposite me. "I understand, Cable, that Daddy wants you to bore me with some pressing…matter."

"I'll get right to the point, Eden. Your father feels you're in danger if you remain in California. Plain and simple."

"That wasn't the kind of pressing I was hoping for, Cable. But continue on, Daddy warned me it wouldn't be pleasant—at least at first. But what if—what if the sun was a woman? Would that change things? We already know there's a man in the moon, right?"

I didn't know where the dame was going with this. "I'm afraid I don't follow, Eden."

"Everything is so…*male* in the world—don't you think? What if our source of life—the sun—were female? Wouldn't it be a gentler world? And the old man in the moon could fight on his desolate—terrible cold world all he wanted."

"Well, that's a novel approach, I must say, Eden. I never thought of things that way." I was beginning to think all the women in the family might have a screw loose somewhere.

"Perhaps you *should* think outside of the patriarchal box…soft, warm, living, breathing beauty…the female sun would bring. After all, she's the one who gives life, isn't she?"

"Yeah, I guess you're right at that."

She got up, came over to me and took my right hand. "If I may be…so bold…" She looked into my palm. "This is the hand that gives out…to the world. Oh, look. Poor man—already deep lines from birth…beset you…violent experiences." Her soft warm fingers tracing my palm felt good. "Your life line is short, but exciting—oh, I like

43

that, Cable...I'll bet you're a very...exciting man to the fairer sex...shall we put you to the test?" she implied in a sexy cooing tone. Then she simply slipped off her garments and turned her back to me. Now I knew she was crazy. The parents had forgotten to tell me that part. "What would it take, Cable...for you to want to see the nude *front* part of me?"

I was scrambling for words. "Eden—I didn't come here for fun and games—despite the fact that you're a very desirable woman. We should get to the business at hand—you know, the stuff I came for?"

"Can't we just play for a few minutes? This could be...the way I get to know someone...what kind of a man are you, really?"

"Alright, but you'd better put your clothes back on. I guess we can, uh, continue the palm reading. I was beginning to enjoy it."

"Later. Right now, I'd like to get to know you better. You see...I believe if we join our bodies, I will know whether I can trust you or not. I always pick up the right vibrations in intimacy...can you...help out a damsel in distress? What more can I do...to show you...my intentions are...sincere?"

It was even hard looking at the backside of this dish, let alone imagining what the naked front display might be. "As tempting as you are, Eden, legally I'm your father's surrogate here—and I'm supposed to be about the business he hired me for."

She came over to me, gently took the drink out of my hand, placed it on the table beside my chair and pushed me softly back into the cushions. "Surrogate—is that something you suck on?" she purred in the sexiest of voices. She turned all the lights off except for one lamp burning low in a corner. Then she turned to face me. Her body was exquisite, white as a penguin's breast and supple as hell. "I promise you...if you enjoy me as much as I feel I'm going to enjoy you...I will be clay in your hands...and you can do anything...anything you like to me—or with me."

Shit! I thought to myself. What a compromising position I was in. It was one of those situations where you were damned if you did and damned if you didn't! She approached me like a cat, stealthily. I took a big breath and awaited her assault. She slid onto my lap and brought her lips to settle quietly on mine. Actually, it felt good and I could feel the babe had a very needy, sincere place in her. "Why...why do you want to do this, Eden?"

"Because I need to trust you, Cable...besides...I love the way you talk—and look. I'm beginning to think you're a man who's a *man*—and I must have that essence in me. Do you understand? So many men...are pansies, wimps...not you...I can feel it...you live in danger—and I...am dangerous. A perfect fit..."

She began unbuttoning my shirt and before I knew it I was naked with this enchantress on her spacious maroon bed with shiny satin sheets. I could tell she was sexually starved and she was not in the habit of partaking in this kind of intimacy. Her babble was mostly all talk, because underneath it all she was a frightened little girl, who probably buried some terrible nightmare she experienced long ago. Her lovemaking was expert, yet sincere and she reached an orgasm with great moans and sighs and begged for me to release into her.

45

When it was over, she lay there next to me, spent and smiling. "You okay?" I asked for a want of anything else to say.

"Oh, Cable....you are wonderful. You just helped me release tons of—of anxiety that had been building and building in me...for weeks..."

"What is it that has you running scared? I see it in your dad, too. Your Mother seems to be elsewhere."

"Oh, Mother is capable of blanking everything out. Not me." Then she went back to her slower, seductive voice. "But right now...Mr. Denning...private dick...I am cancelling out the world...with you...and you know what, handsome?"

"No, pretty doll, tell me."

"I'm really, really happy. I haven't been happy for a long time. It's your presence. Even if you don't live very long in this world...you were stuffing...a lot of quality into me a few minutes ago. God, Cable, now I smell of you...that wonderful male essence smell." She breathed in deeply. "Do you know what it feels like to have a man's juices combine with yours—and to feel a part of him all over?"

"No, I can't exactly say I've experienced that, Eden. Remember, I'm the wrong sex for it." No wonder she ran a bordello, she was so damn sexually fixated.

She giggled and threw her warm body onto mine, putting her arms fully around my neck. "Stay with me, Cable. A week—a month...I've plenty of money. We can even go away—"

"—I can't, doll. You've forgotten why I'm here. You said it yourself, your Dad paid me big bucks to *help* you get away—and I've got to stay on task here, babe." I was

46

also thinking of Adora and her beautiful sincere eyes, that glowing heart that made me always want to come home to her. "And besides, there's someone in my life I care a lot about."

The corners of her mouth turned down. "Oh...there always is...isn't there?" Then she rolled off the bed, put on a robe and lit up a cigarette. She dropped all the pretensions of her affected, seductive voice. "Oh, well, I'm a fair actress anyhow, aren't I? I fooled you for a few minutes, you know, pretending to desire you and all, enjoying your manhood, faking an orgasm—I'm pretty good, huh?"

"Yeah, you could've fooled me, kid," I said, full well knowing she had pretended none of it except her phony vamp-like voice. "I was really into you—if you'll pardon the expression—and felt the same from you."

"All a sham, I'm afraid. I'm the great pretender, Mr. Denning. I'm many personalities all rolled up into one. At least for a man, that can be exciting. So I'm an expensive whore with selective tastes. Big deal." She took a deep drag on her cigarette. "Truth is, I enjoyed you...but I've got to reject you—pfft! out of my life. Do you know why? Sincerity kills me. I can't stand honest, truthful lovemaking. And yours was, Cable Denning. It hurts too much."

"Tell me...what the hell happened way back there somewhere in your youth that scarred you inside, Eden?" I asked, getting myself dressed. "I sensed that same thing from your father, mother—and the same feeling also stalks the hallways of *Neptunia*. What about your sister? Is she also warped along with the rest of you?"

47

"Warped, Cable? Warped? Ha! Zephyr has been out to lunch since the first day she almost drowned in the ocean at Santa Monica. I was four years old and there. I saw the panic, the brain damage later. My mother and father denied it, pushed it away, made up some insipid story about her being native to the sea world and supplied my sister with all the fantasies her drowned-out little brain could desire—to keep her out of a nuthouse."

"Okay, that takes care of Zephyr. What about you? What happened to you that you shrivel away when I bring it up?"

"Well, I can't say it, detective. Not even to myself. So, please.... leave it alone, if you don't mind."

Whatever it was, the same pervasive evil seemed to infect the whole family. But in the end, none of it was any of my business. "Okay, doll, I'm sorry. I didn't mean to push you."

She came over to me as I was putting my trench coat on. "I *do* think you're handsome—and I *do* feel your essence still on me right now. Normally I'm a more careful girl. But I let you because I wanted you."

"I wondered about that. But I guess that's a woman's prerogative, isn't it? I mean, who she lets in and who she doesn't..."

"Suffice it to say I don't let *anyone* in very often. And as far as moving away to some strange land and starting over on my father's whim.... forget it, Cable."

"I think it's your father's *fear* that drives him, Eden, not a whim. He's running scared, or haven't you noticed? Your keeping me in the dark about what happened way back when, makes it harder for me to do my job. I hope you understand that. Okay, so I work with a handicap. I'm used to it. You know what they say, 'you can lead the horse to the water, but you can't make him drink it...' I think that's you, young entrepreneur. I don't know what has to happen to shake your house, but I don't think it's today. Maybe your sister will be more co-operative."

"Good luck," she said rather harshly. "You may as well try and catch the wind, Mister—and after all, that's what her name means—*soft, summer wind.*"

"So it has nothing to do with the sea, then?"

"Nope. Not a thing. My Dad's fabrication—and my mother went along with him because she's my mother and a bit ditzy in the head herself. Not crazy, just a flitter bug. You know why? Because my Dad stopped making love to her right after we were born. He always reminded us girls as we grew up that sex was solely for procreation—and when that was over, well, find something else to do. So guess what I did?"

"You opened a whorehouse."

"Yep, only a clean, classy one would do for me, Mr. Private Detective. Hell, U.S. Senators often frequent my Place when they're in town."

"You're a lot tougher than I thought, Eden. But I also know when you made love to me, just for an instant, I felt a wonderful, warm woman surrender herself, actually *feel* she was being made love to and some light came through the dark."

"In your imagination...ask anyone who knows me, Cable. I'm as tough as nails and twice as mean when I'm crossed. You were looking at the frosting on the cake, not the insides."

"I don't think so, kid. I've kicked the can around the block a few times." I took a big breath and extended my hand to say good-bye. For an instant she lost herself again and came crashing into my arms, hugging me like a little girl who just lost her best friend.

"I wish I was someone else, Cable!" she whimpered.

"I'm—I'm not my brother's keeper, Eden. Nor my sister's savior, nor a knight in shining armor about to rescue the damsel."

She was crying as she backed away. "Don't ever offer me just your hand, Cable. I don't know what you do to me—or whether it's that you're a good person and I know it—or whether it's your damn fancy patter, and you weave a spell with the tone of your voice. But I do want to hear it again someday...soon?"

"Thanks, Eden, but I can't guarantee that. Benedict Royce hired me to do a job and I'm on it—the best way I know how." Her flipping back and forth bothered me, as if a polarity switch kept alternating inside her from hardness to tenderness.

"Good-bye, Cable. Let me know how you make out with the other family members. And, oh, I thought I'd warn you—Zephyr has been known to not speak a word for days on end."

I left and as my taxi drove away into the night, I was thinking how crazy this world was and how damaged people get when some ingredient in the love barrel is left out and we grow up crippled. People are haunted by their own ghosts. I suspected Eden Royce was no exception. Sure, I had lots of ghosts shoved down deep inside me, those places we all like to avoid because when they erupt all hell breaks loose and our emotions make us

50

sick. At thirty years of age, I had more than my share. The thick calluses that had grown around my psyche from a rough childhood of fight or flight posed as a double-edged sword for me. On one hand they insulated me from the hard knocks most people can't tolerate—but on the other, they hardened and numbed me, forced me to look into the eye of evil and the diabolical.....sitting there in the hearts of men and women who have stepped into the shadows.

CHAPTER 3

THE GIRL WHO LIVED IN A SEASHELL

It was late when I walked up the steps to the landing. Suddenly I heard a shriek coming from my office. It sounded like Adora's voice. I drew my .38, got out my key and came bursting in through the door. Adora was backed up against a wall on the far side of my desk while a short little creature was trying to calm her with arm gestures. It was Toggth! "Adora! It's—it's okay, babe. I know him." I went to her and took her into my arms to calm her. She was trembling. "It's alright— Toggth and I have had a few adventures together. He was looking for me—and he, uh, doesn't enter or leave using conventional methods."

"Ay! Tuve mucho cuidado, entonces—yo soy temeroso, querido!" she exclaimed, out of breath.

I left her and approached the little creature standing quietly a few feet from us. "Toggth! It's good to see you, but you really can't just appear and vanish in my office anymore. Adora's living here with me until we can get a little house somewhere..."

I looked back at Adora. This was news to her. I had been thinking about getting us a little place with the dough I had received from Benedict Royce. Maybe even invite her mother and sister to join us.

"I'm sorry, Cable, I did not know." Then he looked sympathetically at Adora. "Please, excuse my frightening you. I assumed Cable was alone and—"

"—Adora, this is Toggth. He's sort of an overseer for Lei-Tao. Remember, the Chinese gal I had the adventure

52

with in San Francisco when you kidnapped me on the train?" I snickered.

"Oh.", was about all that my beautiful lady could say. Being a lover of danger herself, she stepped forward and offered her hand. "I am glad to meet you, señor. But you sure *me espantaste*—make me afraid."

The gentle Toggth took her hand and soon Adora settled down. "I am delighted to make your acquaintance, beautiful lady," he said, pouring on the charm. Then he looked up at me with those warm little orange eyes of his. "Cable, we need to speak. In confidence." I asked Adora to take the little box radio and go into the bedroom. She smiled gently at Toggth and left with the radio under her arm.

"Yeah, my little lady sure got a start, you little son-of-a-gun, you. But I am glad to see you nevertheless. I think of you now and then. How's Lei-Tao doing?"

His face saddened. "She has gone back. A new one will take her place. The lotus has returned, Cable."

"You mean for another fourteen thousand years or so?"

"Perhaps. Depends on the wellbeing of the *Fen de Fuqin*."

A place in my heart sank. I had become attached in a strange way to the exquisite Chinese Red Dragon Lady. "Well, just about now I wouldn't take a bet on the safety of the precious capsule—there've been a lot of stirrings from you-know-who since Ravna got a few unexpected bullets in him, fired by the flying priests."

"Yes, Father Tortelli and his 'Holy' accomplices. But, as you know, others will come. Their supply of demons appears endless."

"So...what can I do to help? It seems our fates are kind of tossed together in this terrible grab-bag."

"The man who has hired you...Mr. Royce...was very high up on the human side of the *Oculus*. But he objected to something they did to him and his family many years ago—and he has since become an unwanted participant. His usefulness to them has come to an end."

I was surprised—but not really—that Toggth knew about Benedict Royce and his family. "Well, I guess I've got no secrets from you now, do I, Toggth?" I laughed. "And you keep turning up like an old song with bad lyrics." I lit up a Lucky Strike. "So whatta we gonna do?"

"I suggest you fulfill your pledge to Mr. Royce and remove them from the soil of the United States as soon as possible. That island opposite Nassau in the Bahamas might be a good place to begin. But you might also have to move them around from time to time—elsewhere..."

"How in the hell do you know about all these things, Mister? Crap, I'm barely on top of them and here you're coming out with all this stuff like you were reading it from a notepad."

"I guess I am, sort of. Anyway, the first thing is to see to the family, in my opinion. And please, don't get involved with the daughters like you did Lei-Tao. Your presence in her life almost extinguished her lovely flame. Have some boundaries and propriety, despite your youth and drives."

I was rubbing my chin thinking of this evening's sexual encounter with Eden Royce. "Hmmm....yeah, that's good advice, Toggth...I really felt bad about Lei-Tao—passing the baby off and all—poor Ginny Fullerton had no clue."

"It wasn't a baby, Cable—at least not in the normal sense. It was Lei-Tao's insufficient attempt to bear you a human child as a token of her love for you. But it was doomed from the start. It was incinerated."

I winced a little. Even if the fetus, whatever it was, got destroyed promptly after Ginny's delivering it, it was still a part of Lei-Tao and me. Why in the hell did it bother me? Crap, it was a monstrosity! Or was it?

"I see," I said looking out the window at headlights passing below.

"Just so you know, Cable. I cried...the little girl inside the pod was beautiful. She glowed with an iridescence even in death. Her hair was shiny black, her little eyes a warm brown like her mother's."

"Please...Toggth...let's move on. I don't think I can take too much more of this."

"Sorry, Cable. So...get the family to the Bahamas as soon as you can—or you may not make the journey in time." He hopped up on my comfy chair behind my desk as I stood, still looking out the window, smoking. He took a deep breath and let it out. "Unfortunately, we are not going to be dealing with humans from this point out. There is a relentless, ambitious creature, completely without conscience, as you might know it, who heads up the earth section of the *Oculus Pyramis Mandatum.* So far, they've sent only humans to do their dirty work, but even the aliens do not know how to access the *Fen de Fuqin*. There are safeguards to prevent it from being stolen again. Now they will do *anything*—kill *anyone*— to get at it."

"I've—I've always had this question, Toggth. If these guys are so brilliant and advanced, how come they don't know what the *God of Our Fathers* contains? It seems to me they could have decoded at least some of it by now—even the phony had the right symbols on it, right?"

"Wrong...I duplicated only parts, Cable, so that it could not be decoded. I also confess to taking out the golden etched parchment inside, that *really* contains the secret of life and enables the *Tone of Creation*. It was painstakingly copied from the original parchment thousands of years ago."

I raised my eyebrows. "You? You removed the tablet from inside the capsule? No wonder they were pissed when they tried to figure the damn thing out!"

"I couldn't risk it being in their hands, Cable. I substituted it with some worthless replica. Believe me, there was no other way."

"Yeah, I believe you—but the trouble is, *they're* gonna believe you too when they put it all together and come hunting you down like a pack of ravenous alien wolves."

"So that's where you come in."

"Me? Now, wait a minute Toggth. I'm having problems here just buttoning my shirt in the morning. I'm a human...remember me? The guy who makes lots of stupid decisions and can't keep it in his pants?"

Toggth smiled. "I enjoy you, Cable...I always have. Your honest, bumbling ways endear you to me." Then he drew serious. "At some point they are going to come for you. They will probably attempt an easier way first, like arrange a private meeting with you. If that doesn't work, they'll come, as you say, like a pack of ravenous wolves."

"Oh, that's comforting. So now they're gonna descend on *me*, probably kill me when they don't get what they want—"

"—that's precisely why they won't kill you. You're the only one they know of—human that is, because they surely do not know about me—who knows about the *Fen de Fuqin*. Remember, you have seen it in the Blue Light of Noda. They are relentless with details. Every tiny little thing you know or have experienced with the capsule they will want to know and cling to every word you care to share with them on the subject."

"Yeah, that's swell, you little pirate, you. So you're gonna leave me holding the bag at the eleventh hour, is that it?"

"No, Cable, I would never do that to you. You will *lure* them to a certain spot on the map when the proper time comes. It will be a trap. We of the other dimensions have not been idle. And don't get any preconceptions this is to save earth people, per se—but rather to save the *inner mechanisms of harmony* that allow your three-dimensional world to function. That...is what the *Fen de Fuqin* is all about, harmony and balance."

"So when does all this happen? You know the last few months haven't been exactly an emotional picnic for me, you know I lost—"

"—yes, Cable, I'm sorry you lost someone dear to you. I must say, however, that exquisite female creature waiting for you in your bedroom is truly extraordinary. I'd keep her if I were you."

"Thanks, Toggth. I appreciate that. And I think I will keep her." I went away from the window and sat opposite him in my client's chair. "So let's get on with this show—have you any idea what a weight it puts on me, never knowing when the other shoe will drop?—"

"—timing...*timing*, Cable. That's the secret. I will keep you informed. In the future, remember they will haunt you for your memory of the *Fen de Fuqin* and attempt to access it from you through whatever means are at their disposal. Right now, I suggest you perform your paid-for task and secure the Royce family as best you can. I must go now."

I got up and bent down to hug my little creature friend. "Thanks for coming, Toggth, even if you scared the crap out of Adora. But I think she'll like you."

He waved at me and disappeared before my eyes. I grabbed a bottle of gin out of my right drawer and poured. Then I went into the bedroom. Adora lay on the bed listening to the radio. She seemed content just lying there awaiting me. She sat up when I entered. "*Mi amor*, everything is—is hunky-dory, no?"

I sat on the bed and took her into my arms. "Yep, everything's hunky-dory, babe. Toggth and I had some business to discuss. Some loose ends, that's all."

"You talk about *nuestro casa*, *mi amor*, our house somewhere?"

"Yes, Adora...I hate it that you have to live in this hole of a place. I thought with the money I make with the Royce case we can afford a nice little house—you know, to rent at first and maybe later to buy. Whatta ya think?"

She held me tight. "Oh, *mi querido—te adoro*! *Gracias*, Cable, for thinking of me—*us*." Then her nostrils picked up an odor from my clothes as she sniffed. She backed away. "You have been with another woman...I can smell, Cable..."

"Yeah, I can't lie to you. It wasn't even intentional—I mean, I had a slight altercation with this blonde babe who owns a bordello—and is one of Royce's daughters. Well, it turns out, she was very seductive—and she told me if...if I'm going to convince her that she has to leave the country, she needs to trust me and be more familiar with me. One of the—the, uh, ways she said she had in doing that was to—to, uh, bond with me physically. And being that I kinda wanted to cut to the chase and get through to this stubborn woman—I—I, uh, well, you know...I'm sorry, Adora, you know I would never want to hurt you in any way."

Tears came to her eyes but she didn't cry. She sniffed them back and took a deep breath. Instead of rising to temper—which she had every right to do—she quietly put her head on my chest. *"Mi querido*, you know I give my heart to you. Do you give your heart to me?"

I knew I hurt her. Sometimes truth is more painful than little white lies. But what else could I do? I adored this beautiful young woman and to lose her would all but destroy whatever decency was left in me. To tell her the truth was to keep things pure and straight between us. "Yes...doll...whatever is left of my heart belongs to you. I swear it." I stroked her radiant black hair. "Men are weird creatures, Adora. More times than not they're driven by their balls and not their heads."

"But I want your balls, too, *mi amor. Pero sólo para mí. Por qué?* Why do I have to share you with another *mujer*—some woman who cannot love like I love you, Cable..."

My heart felt heavy and I held her tight. "Babe, I swear to you, I will be true to you—as I have before to-day—I mean, I don't even think of being with other women other than looking—just *looking* at a pretty face, a pair of nice tits—or some fine gams now and then."

"Gams? What's those?"

"Legs, hon. You know, just legs..."

She took in a deep breath and exhaled. "You promise? I want to belong only to you, Cable...and I want you to belong only to me. Is that *justo?* Fair for both of us?"

"With a love like yours, Adora, yes, yes, and yes! I am sorry I was so stupid. I only want you, doll. You're the best I'll ever have or know."

She gave me a little smile. "When can we look at some little casas, mi amor? I am not so sure I want *mi madre o mi hermana* living with us. What will happen when I scream out with *mi placer*—my pleasure when you make love with me."

"Then you'll make love with me again—sometime—even if I don't deserve it?"

"Oh, sí, señor." Then she smiled a teasing smile. "But I donno...I have to practice first—*pero*, I do not know who to practice with. Do you know some *hombre muy malo* who will make me...good lover...?"

When a guy's in the doghouse with the woman he loves, it really matters, I was discovering. Her touch, her breasts and womanhood had dominion over you, and like a fly to flypaper, I was drawn in, hypnotized by this beautiful young woman's smile and demeanor. "Yeah, I know a *real bad hombre* you can practice on—but what if you like him better than me after a while?"

"*Entonces, señor Cable*, you will just have to accept it," she chortled. "I think I start now…! But first, *you* go take a bath!" We both laughed as she fell onto my chest, happy to be in my arms again. Nothing stays the same. But I knew one thing, that as long as we lived, I vowed to myself that day, I would never stray from this rare and exceptional woman. And I didn't.

Zephyr

Of course, the Royce's beach cottage had to be in the ritziest part of Malibu. Standing on a bluff a few miles north of the wharf, stood a light sea-green home with off-white trim and a black shingle roof. After Honey died, I had sold her Packard to a clothier I knew. He always said I could borrow it if I ever needed to since I practically gave the car to him. At the time I was grieving so, that I couldn't have anything around reminding me of Honey. But on this day, I decided to drive, and even though I had no driver's license, I zoomed along Highway One until I bumped down the stone-filled driveway leading to "*Royce Cove Cottage*", as the sign read near the mailbox at the highway junction. I parked and walked up to the front door. A cool northwest wind was blowing the wind chimes into a tangled frenzy as a bent little man with thick reading glasses greeted me. "Yes?" he said, as he looked me up and down.

"Mr. Crickle? I'm Cable Denning, Mr. Royce probably called—"

"—oh, yes, Mr. Denning. He was very clear. You are to have run of the house and invite Miss Zephyr up—if she'll come. She hasn't been up here in months, though. I hear the folks may be traveling abroad soon?"

I was a bit confused. "Mr. Royce said I was to have run of the house? But I'll be here only a short while—and most of that will be spent talking to Zephyr."

He smiled a knowing smile. "Oh, you'll be here a while, Mr. Denning. It isn't as easy as all that, you know, corralling Miss Zephyr."

I asked Mr. Crickle for instructions regarding the exact whereabouts of Zephyr's seashell house. He pointed to a trail and I descended the bluff to the sandy beach below. In a little cove, set about twenty feet above the tide line sat a gleaming white mini-castle in the form of a seashell! It appeared as if a cavern had been built into the rock, then the structure built out from that. Only a rope ladder was visible, so the quaint little fortress was easily defensible, and no one had access to the seashell house unless they were invited and the rope ladder dropped for them. But today it was down and whoever occupied the sea-house may not have been in. I approached the place and looked up. I called out. "Zephyr! Zephyr Royce! I am a representative for your father. I would like to speak with you. Can you hear me?" I waited and paced around the sands for a couple of minutes. Then I repeated my calling out to her. Nothing. Only the sound of the northwest wind, the shifting, restless sands pulling along dried pieces of seaweed and an occasional call of a seabird could be heard.

I sat down on a rock and tried to light a Lucky Strike, but every match blew out before I could light the end of the cigarette, so I gave up and decided to just plop in the warm sand and think of what next to do. Then suddenly

I saw her. Rising up out of the sea came a delicate, perfectly shaped young woman—totally nude! I tried not to look but it was impossible as she moved toward me. She had dark auburn hair, was perfectly proportioned, possessed diminutive features, flawless tanned skin, lovely firm breasts and a very small pubic area. I called out to her but she paid no attention to me. Nor did she speak to me. I got up and followed her to her rope ladder. She turned quickly to look at me, to make sure I wasn't going to attack her. Her eyes were light green and glowed in the early afternoon sunlight. She put her hand out to stop me from proceeding any further but again said nothing. Then she began ascending the rope ladder. "I'm—I'm a representative for your father, Miss Royce. I really need to talk to you—in person without all the sounds of nature pounding at my ears. Will you come up to the cottage when you can? I'll be waiting there until after dark. Then I have to go home. Okay?"

She kept climbing and when she reached the little landing deck in front of her seashell house, she pulled the ladder up, not even looking back down to see if I was there. How rude! I thought. After all, I drove all this way out to see her—and bam! the whole thing's a bust. I went back up to the cottage, asked Mr. Crickle if there was any booze around and he pointed to a whole cabinet stuffed with liqueurs, scotch, wines, Champagne, vermouth and my favorite—English gin! I fixed myself a nice half-glass of the stuff and sat down, feeling dejected, on the sofa. The afternoon sunlight was warm coming in through the windows. In fact, without the wind, it was downright enjoyable. I called to Mr. Crickle who was making himself some lunch. "So...you watch after her...what's the trick? I promised Benedict I would talk to her."

"There is no trick, Mr. Denning. Zephyr comes like the wind, and goes like the wind. She speaks rarely, and then only if there is just cause. She minds her own business, has no friends, is self-educated, daydreams a lot, but spends most of her time under the sea."

"Under the sea? How does she breathe, for God's sake?"

"Zephyr is extraordinary. She has gifts...gifts very few possess."

"How did she come by them?"

"I don't know. Some kind of abnormality in the recipe that makes up a human being at conception, I suppose."

The sunset was lovely and I watched the huge red ball sink behind a fog bank that looked like it might be on its way in for the night. I didn't know what to do. Seems like I was having a hell of a time with the Royce girls. First Eden and her stubborn and feisty manner set me back, and now Zephyr's mute approach made her inaccessible to me. Mr. Crickle had retired for the evening and I was getting myself prepared to drive back to the city when the front door opened and in walked this enchanting little creature. She couldn't have stood more than five-foot two and wore a very thin green slip. Those glowing green eyes looked me over like an eagle checking out its next meal. "Hello, Zephyr," I said in a non-intimidating voice. "I'm glad you came. Will you listen to me if I tell you something very important?"

She walked slowly to a couch opposite my chair and sat quietly, her hands folded together. She nodded her head slowly up and down. "Now...before I go back to Los Angeles tonight, I need to make it clear to you that your father thinks it is dangerous for you to remain here by the sea, or for that matter, remain in California. He has purchased an island in the Caribbean Ocean, in the Bahamas. He seems to feel if you remain here, your life will be threatened—or simply put, possibly worse— you and your family may end up dead."

She was looking for something in my eyes. Apparently, she found it. "What is your name?" she finally spoke, her voice was fresh and feminine and very soft. "I am Zephyr."

"Cable—Cable Denning. Yes, I know yours. I've met all your immediate family, beginning with your Dad. I met Mother—she seems the most co-operative. Your sister, as you might guess, is stubborn and a little married to luxury." I looked at her and smiled. "And you? What about you, Zephyr? Do you know anything about the looming danger?"

"Water...water..." she replied. I had no clue.

"Water? Are you thirsty?"

"Water...tears...sorrow...eyes."

She looked at me as if she was looking *through* me. "Sorrow in my eyes? Is that what you're trying to say?"

"Pain. Sorrow, anger." She twitched her head and turned it into her left shoulder in a quirky way. Then she straightened herself, got up and walked toward the door. I went after her and grabbed her arm to stop her. She spun around and slapped me hard across the face, her green eyes wide and fearful. "No!" she cried out. The sound of the ruckus brought Mr. Crickle out of his room in his robe. He sized up the situation.

"Are you okay, Zephyr? Did he hurt you?" Then he glowered at me. "I'm afraid you'll have to leave, Mr. Denning."

"Not so fast, buddy boy!" I said. "I come with my own set of credentials and this family's as dysfunctional as a French tank!" I looked at the still livid Zephyr, trembling a few feet from me, frozen where she stood. "You forget what I get paid for, both of you. Now, whatever it takes to communicate what I came here for, is however long I'm going to stay, got it? Now, you can call the cops, but I know most of them. And I don't think you wanna do that because they're worse than me. And another thing, even if it takes you packing your bags along with Miss Priss here and getting into my Packard—sooner or later we're leaving this cozy little beach hideaway."

"My, my," Mr. Crickle said, stopped in his tracks by my firm little speech. He looked over to Zephyr. "Perhaps we should try and behave civilized and sit down, all of us together and listen to Mr. Denning. If it's as urgent as you suggest, then perhaps we should take heed."

Crickle urged Zephyr back onto the same seat she occupied before our altercation. He sat to my left. I lit up a Lucky Strike and blew the smoke in Zephyr's direction. "So...now...I repeat...your father and your employer have sent me to get you, Zephyr, out of here—and, as I perceive it, this includes you, Mr. Crickle, inasmuch as you seem to have a pacifying effect on young Zephyr here."

"Fiona," the young woman blurted out.

I looked at Crickle, puzzled. "She believes that to be her genuine first name, although her birth records do not bear that out."

"Oh," I said, looking at the lovely young woman, now somewhat settled down. My right cheek still smarted and I was rubbing it when Zephyr got up and came over to me. I put my arms up to guard myself for fear she'd hit me again. But she gently grabbed my wrists, lowered my arms, closed her eyes and bent down to kiss my cheek. The touch of her lips against my skin was soft and deep. She backed away with her eyes still closed. My reddened cheek felt better. Then she slowly opened those green orbs of hers and smiled faintly at me. "Uh....thanks, I assume that to be an apology?"

"Love..." was all she said. Then she sat back down.

"Agreed, Zephyr's ways are bizarre, Mr. Denning," Mr. Crickle commented. "But they're sincere. In kissing you just now, she has accepted you. That's how she functions, simply, directly."

Zephyr was still smiling at me, her eyes fixed on mine. "No touch...touch...now touch...feel...," she intoned quietly.

"Thanks...I guess..." I cleared my throat and put my cigarette out in an ashtray by my chair. "Now, Zephyr, I'm sure your parents thought carefully about the selection of this Caribbean isle in paradise. Especially for you, warm water, lots of sea creatures—you know, the kind of things that make you happy."

"Sea...fish...dolphin children..." she muttered.

I looked at Crickle. "Dolphins seem to be her children...or perhaps closer kin than us humans. Her preoccupation with the sea seems to have begun at birth."

"We take the train to Florida. Then we board a tramp steamer for Nassau. All of this must be done secretly and without drawing attention, so as to not alert the sleeping lions. Once they are stirred up, I think the crap is gonna hit the fan and we'd better be out of harm's way. So, is everything understood? *Royce Cove Cottage* and Zephyr's seashell house will be properly closed up. But to keep snooping eyes and ears out, it will not be sold immediately."

"Swim...my dolphin children wait...*Lexie*...take *Lexie*, my child."

Again, I raised an eyebrow and glanced at Crickle. "I've not seen the creature, but she maintains she swims with him every day. Now, oddly, there was a time in her life none of us can explain. Let me see...she's twenty-six now...when she was nineteen or twenty, a strange anomaly occurred. Zephyr kept rubbing her stomach and indicating she was expecting a child. Her protective ferocity prevented us from taking her to a physician, so we kept our eye on her. Indeed, her stomach did grow and we assumed she had somehow been violated by a young man and was pregnant. Then one day she simply disappeared. All of us were beside ourselves with trepidation that she had drowned herself in the sea because she perhaps did not wish to bring the child to full term. We even called in the police, search parties, everything we could think of. Mr. and Mrs. Royce were devastated, for as you've learned, Zephyr is their favorite—and poor Eden, although the eldest, was always left behind in the running. Then, as mysteriously as she had disappeared, one day Zephyr came up out of the sea healthier and happier looking than ever. She glowed and tried to communicate to us she had had a 'sea-child' and they swam together every day and frolicked in the calm, cold waters of the Pacific Ocean. No one has ever seen her so-called child, but it keeps her occupied and sane, I guess. So...that's the dope, as you Americans might say, Mr. Denning."

Again, I was quite taken with Crickle's story. I glanced over at Zephyr. "So...uh, Zephyr...how do you propose we take your dolphin child with us to the Bahamas?"

"Swim...Lexie and I swim...swim fast together..."

I chuckled. "That's impossible, kid—you'd have to swim the length of the Americas to Panama, then take the canal into the Caribbean until you reached the Bahamas. That'd take months...and you probably would be eaten by sharks or killer whales along the way—they love seals and dolphins particularly well, I hear, not to mention lovely young women."

"Perhaps we can place 'Lexie' in a tank and ship him with us when we embark in Florida," Crickle suggested, humoring Zephyr.

"Well, we gotta figure this thing quick, whatever you decide. I've got to go now, but I'll be back in a few days with specific info and some tickets. I suggest you two get ready to depart, Mr. Crickle."

I got up to go. Zephyr stood up as well and followed me to the door. I shook Crickle's hand and started for my car. Just then, Zephyr darted over to me, grabbed my hand and pulled on it. "Lexie—see Lexie!" she insisted. The fog had come in and I stumbled down the embankment with her in the darkness, her hand firmly in mine, pulling me along. We reached the sea and dashed for the shoreline. She dragged me into the very cold water, shoes and all. I was up to my chest, fighting off small breakers when she stopped and uttered, "Stay!" to me. I just wanted to go home to Adora and get out of these damn wet clothes!

Then I saw something that I never imagined I'd *ever* see. In the semi-light of a half-moon peaking in and out of the fog bank, a chattering little creature came up out of the sea with Zephyr. "Lexie...Denning..." she said with a happy smile. "My child, Denning...Lexie, my child..."

I don't know why, but I was fighting to hold back tears and trying like hell not to whimper like a baby. Something deep in me had been touched and I couldn't figure it. "Well, I'll be—I'll be a monkey's uncle. I'll never doubt you again, Zephyr." I glanced at the sea creature who seemed to be about five feet long, maybe two feet wide and chattered incessantly. I put my hand out. He came up and I petted his head gently. "Hello, there, little guy. I'm...I'm pleased to meet you," I said, still trying to control my emotions. Lexie cuddled up against my leg and his energy felt good. Then another unexpected thing happened. Zephyr approached me, and with her palm gently touched the cheek she had struck earlier. Then she bent her head toward my face and kissed my cheek just as a larger wave engulfed us and we lost our footing and under the wave we went. Suddenly I felt her lips clinging to mine, holding me with all her womanly passion and strength, her body pressing into my cold and numb chest. She pulled me up for air. Lexie was still jumping and chattering away. "Love..."she whispered in my ear against the sound of the sea. She hugged Lexie and he disappeared under the waves. Then she took my hand and pulled me to the shore.

Should I live to be an ancient storyteller, this one had me puzzled. Yet there it was before me, real as earth and somehow as right as rain. I told Zephyr I had to go home to Adora and get out of these wet clothes. "Adora?" she asked me.

"Yeah, Adora's my partner, my love...someone who lives with me."

"Zephyr lives with Fiona? Zephyr like Fiona. Maybe like Adora. Meet Adora?"

"Yeah, why not, if you like. I'll bring her before we ship you out with Lexie. You had better ask Lexie if it's okay if he's stuck in a tank for a few days. First, we gotta ship him by rail to Florida. Then we'll load him aboard the freighter. Zephyr, does your family know about Lexie? I mean, not even Mr. Crickle has seen Lexie, right?"

"You believe...no one else believes." She reached up and touched my face again. "Love...face...love...Denning." she said hesitantly, as if I wouldn't approve.

"Yeah...*now* I believe, Zephyr...and so will everyone else when they see your beautiful sea-child. I can feel it...Lexie's a pretty unique fellow and he'll be a big hit."

She smiled and hugged me good-bye. I struggled up the trail in my wet clothes and knocked on the cottage door. A sleepy Mr. Crickle answered. "Yes. Oh...I thought you'd gone, Mr. Denning..." Then he saw my sopping wet clothes. "Oh my, come in..." He went to a closet and fetched me some dry clothes. "I'm certain Mr. Royce wouldn't mind."

71

When I had changed into other duds and stood there in the middle of the room looking like a damn clown with clothes much too big for me...wearing no shoes—Crickle, trying to stifle a smile, said, "I take it Zephyr wasn't through with you."

"Lexie exists, Crickle," I said. He raised his eyebrows in surprise.

"Indeed? That is a sight yet to be experienced by my person, Mr. Denning. Are you sure you haven't fallen victim to Zephyr's fertile imagination?"

"Yep. She's on the level. You just have to *believe*, she tells me."

"Hmmm...well, we'll see...we'll see..."

I thanked him for the clothes and I left. As the Packard roared along Highway One, I was recalling the crazy day and evening. By the time I reached my office and tip toed in, Adora was already asleep. When I put the bathroom light on and she saw my very strange costume, she started. "Cable! *Qué pasa aquí?*"

"Well, babe, you wouldn't believe me if I told you. But I'll tell you anyhow...I met Zephyr Royce today. First she was a bit distant, even a little hostile...and slapped my face. Then when Mr. Crickle, her overseer, informed me she was *really* odd, we arrived at a better place—especially when she led me to the beach below her seashell house, dragged me into the freezing Pacific Ocean for a gander at her 'child', a playful little dolphin named *Lexie*. There...now that was *my* day—how has *yours* been?"

She sat up in bed, the sheet falling off her nude body, exposing those wonderful breasts I loved so well. "*Extraño, Cable*—do you drink gin with strange girl? *Ay, lo-*

co, señor, loco!...you are always in crazy things." She lay back on the bed, looking up at the ceiling. "*Este día es por mí?* I go to *Todo el Mundo*, read ads for rent places. I find one, Cable. Will you come look with me, *por favor?* I am happy to be in new casa with you, *mi amor*."

Obviously my strange day's events were of little interest to Adora. But I think the busy little woman in her was planning on that honeymoon house we'd share together. After all, it was fair. Most women needed domestic roots, not a business office with the phone ringing and weird people popping in to dump their marital problems all over the desk. I showered and got into bed with my beautiful lover. We were both tired and soon were asleep, contented, in each other's arms.

CHAPTER 4

WRAPPING TROUBLES IN DREAMS

After we found the perfect little house on Argyle off of Franklin Avenue for $35 a month, we decided to really celebrate and go dancing. My little Latin lover was decked out for the evening and looked like a million. I had bought her a red satin outfit with white shoes and gloves. The blouse was a little too low-cut for my taste, but Adora had nothing to hide and I let it go at that.

I'd heard about a huge dance hall at the very end of the Santa Monica pier...sometimes referred to as the *Pleasure Pier,* called the *La Monica Ballroom*...a pretty popular place for dancing with great dance bands, but had never been there. I read that it was the largest on the west coast and at its opening in 1924, 25,000 people converged on it and were accommodated. Now that I had a little extra dough, I thought I'd take my lady to dinner and dancing in style. We took the Pacific Electric red car through Beverly Hills right to the pier. We walked by the now famous carousel and arcades and a wooden roller coaster and we could see the massive La Monica with its Spanish-Moorish palace look with 3 towers at each corner topped with minarets with the façade walls molded into decorative curves. As we approached the entrance there was a bill with the names of that night's entertainment...but only one name jumped out at me. "Well, I'll be damned...look who's singing here at the end of the

Santa Monica pier...if it isn't Misty Sheridan! Whatta ya know about that?"

Adora looked at me in surprise. "You know *esta mujer...esta* Misty?"

"Yeah, she was singing in a club I was in a while ago. She's pretty good, too."

We walked into a lavish ballroom...very ornate with the look of French renaissance. The biggest dance floor I had ever seen. All wood and lit up with a brilliant chandelier. The orchestra was playing and folks were already kicking up their heels. We were seated near the dance floor. It wasn't as crowded as I had expected. Maybe the Depression having its effect. Our dinner was good, my lady and I danced some of the evening, but it wasn't until Misty Sheridan launched into *Wrap Your Troubles in Dreams* that I remembered how much I was in love with Adora Moreno. *'When skies are cloudy and gray, they're only gray for a day'*, the song said, *'so wrap your troubles in dreams and dream your troubles away'*. Even rich people couldn't compete with love when you're lucky enough to have it—and life can get mighty lonely if you don't have someone to keep you warm on those nights when memory and regret haunt you like an looming specter.

So I told my Latin princess how much I adored her that night and she cooed and purred all over me while we danced, ate or sat in a booth drinking and simply enjoying each other's company. I had met Misty Sheridan when she worked at the *Café Montmartre* on Hollywood Boulevard a year or so ago and I liked her voice and style. Her personality was smooth ...professional. You just knew she smoldered inside with a certain brand of sexuality. Her hair was reddish, her skin white and eyes a friendly blue. She had a great figure and wore her gowns as tight as the law would allow.

Misty had just begun a song called *After You've Gone* and suddenly I realized I became trapped in an emotion that kept pounding me to bits as if I were a piece of abalone on a cutting board. Suddenly, Honey had invaded our amorous time and was saying, 'How could you, Cable—come see another singer! Aren't I the love of your life? Cable, I'm not gone. I'm right here, right here...can't you feel me?' The lyrics to the tune, *'After you've gone and left me crying, after you've gone, there's no denying, you'll feel lonesome, you'll feel sad—you'll miss the best friend you ever had...there'll come a time, now don't forget it, there'll come a time when you'll regret it...your heart will break like mine and you'll want me only...after you've gone, after you've gone away...'* I turned away from Adora, fighting off tears. She picked up on it. *"Mi amor, qué pasó?"* Then she put two and two together. *"Ay, qué lástima, querido. La canción sin sonrisa—pero triste.* It is Honey, huh? *Tu recuerdos...*I am sorry, Cable." She took my arm and cuddled her cheek to my shoulder.

"I'm—I'm sorry, babe. I wanted us to have a good time. I—I didn't see that one coming. Memory can be such a crappy return trip—let's pay the check and go home. Make love to me, doll, tonight...so I can forget."

"I will always make love with you, señor—but not because I help you forget. *Pero, porque t'amo.*"

I left Adora by the hatcheck girl and went to put a fiver in Misty Sheridan's tip jar. She saw me and approached. "Thank you...say, don't I know you? You...you came in one time at the last place I sang—"

"—yeah, good memory...Cable Denning." I extended my hand. "We did meet several months ago when you were singing at *The Café Montmartre*. I told you I'd come see you again someday."

"Are you alone?" she asked, checking me out in an approving manner. "I could stand a drink with someone I can talk to."

"Well, I'm sorry, Misty—but I am with a lady and we're on our way home. Maybe some other time we can have that drink."

She looked around the room, scanning the women, I suspected. "I would say the most attractive woman in the room—besides me—is that beautiful dark-haired Latino gal over there..."

"You just won a kewpie doll, lady. Congratulations."

"Thank you...I'm just not so sure who's the luckiest—you for having her to take home with you—or is she damn lucky to have you to take her home? I see a lot of people. One always wonders about things like that—how two people come together and what attracts them."

"If I recall right, you warned me off that night I came in to hear you. Weren't you the one who said you weren't into *men*?"

She smiled at me, her warm green sequined gown revealing in all the right places. "Yes. It's true, I did tell you that. In fact, I still have a female lover—the same one. But I've been wanting to be, uh, more *adventure-*

77

some lately. Trouble is most men are boring. But I saw something in you that night I never forgot."

"It's a big front...women like my patter because I've got a big mouth and fair vocabulary."

"That might be part of it, Mr. Denning—"

"—Cable, remember, Cable..."

"Cable...but I'm guessing you've done some things or seen some things in your life that set you apart. Am I getting warm?"

"Just chalk it up to *mysterious*, doll. And maybe a little living on the edge kind of lifestyle that private dicks do—like walking a tightrope in the dark with no pole."

She laughed. "Private what? Did I hear you right?"

"It's an old joke I pull on dames all the time. It's short for private detective, that's all. Any other intimation is censored," I joked.

"Damn, I'd sure like to get to know you better." She looked back over to where Adora stood, patiently waiting. "Are you serious with the little Mexican number?"

"Yeah, just about as serious as someone like me can get, I guess."

"Then I'm glad for you. Not too many couples are happy these days. Depression and all, I guess. Even the business here is really down." She took a deep breath and sighed. "Well...if things change—or you ever change your mind, I'll be singing around somewhere...maybe we can have that drink..."

I said goodnight to Misty Sheridan and Adora and I headed out for the streetcar stop. "You like that sexy red-hair lady? You make love to her—she knew you, Cable, I can tell..."

"No, babe. Like I said, she was singing in a Hollywood club about a year ago and I came in one night. She remembered. That's all."

"Oh," she said, a little tentative about my answer.

"You know, sweetheart, I'm glad you're a little jealous now and then. It makes me feel wanted. I feel the same when other men look at you in that way. I guess people are rather territorial, aren't they?"

"Terri...who? Oh...sí...I think I know what you say—*exclusivo*."

"Yeah, babe." I stopped and took Adora Moreno in my arms. "I never want you to think again that I'll be anything but true to you, kid. You're my woman, and I'm your guy—and that's all there is to it—comprendo, señorita?"

There in the middle of the sidewalk she grabbed me and held my head until her lips were smashing into mine, back and forth, wet and warm and I could feel her temperature rise and when we finally got back to the cottage, I had this feeling I had the most sensual girl in town in my arms. Love like this could never be bested in this crazy world, I thought at that moment. Count every minute as precious, Cable, I told myself. Love her, be true to her and never let her go!

The next day I was back at *Royce Cove Cottage* with the train and steamer tickets needed for Zephyr and Mr. Crickle, along with a hefty allowance for *Lexie*, the dolphin also known as Zephyr's "sea-child." It was early afternoon and when Crickle opened the door, it was a glum face that greeted me. "Mr. Denning...I have sad tidings. I'm—I'm afraid I didn't tell you all, the other night. Zephyr has a disorder known as split personality. My beautiful mermaid of the Pacific has gone away—Lord knows for how long—and Fiona has taken possession. I suggest you do not go to the seashell house. It will be in vain."

"I don't know about you, Crickle, but I have a job to do here—and I'm doing it! So, if you're not packed, do so immediately. When I return I'm gonna have Zephyr in tow, toss you both into my car and whisk you off to *Neptunia* for a final meeting with Mom and Pop Royce. Is that clear? Let me put it another way, if you're not coming, you're *dead*. Plain and simple. I leave that final decision up to you."

I left old Crickle shaking in his boots and made my way down the trail. I trudged across the sands until I stood underneath the seashell house. "Zephyr!" I called, "It's Cable...Cable Denning...I've come for you and your things."

A very pretty facsimile of Zephyr Royce appeared about thirty feet above me. "Miss Royce isn't in today, but come on up, whoever you are."

Damn—that's all I needed—some crazy babe who jumps in and out of her personality skins! I climbed up the rope ladder. She was dressed in a fine yellow robe with nothing underneath. Her face had changed so that a rather erotic smile fell across it. Or maybe it was some kind of impertinence, like her sister, Eden. "Hello, again, Zephyr. I sure as hell hope you're ready. I got winded just climbing this damn thing."

80

"Have we met?" she asked, checking me out like it was the first time she'd ever seen me. "I informed you that Zephyr Royce is not in today—and I have no idea when she might return."

"What about her dolphin buddy, Lexie?"

"Oh, that's it. She's probably out swimming with him. It's okay to have a pet, but I told her all that salt water simply isn't good for the skin. She'll grow old before her time."

Now I thought *I* was going nuts. If the two women were twins, they couldn't be any more different in their personalities. I looked her over. She had the same nicely tanned body, the same nice green eyes and her nipples stuck out through her yellow robe. Yep, same girl I saw walk nude out of the ocean. "So what's your name—if not Zephyr?"

"I'm Fiona—the only sensible one—and the only reason I let you up here is to be able to push you down if you get fresh or something."

"Look, lady, I'm in no mood to play your little psychological games—I have tickets here for your departure on a midnight train to Florida three days from now. If I have to hog-tie you kicking and screaming, I will get you back to your folks at *Neptunia*. So what's it gonna be?"

She frowned. "I hate insistent men. You think you'll get your way with me, don't you?" She took her robe off and bared her totally nude body to me. "Tempting, isn't it? Well, you can't have any. Know why? Because I am an *untouchable*—and I do not kowtow to lower folks—"

81

"—I'm gonna touch you alright, Miss Untouchable, with a rope, chain or whatever I can find in this eagle's nest of yours to bind, tie, gag or otherwise confine you from escape or further movement!"

I grabbed for her but she ran into the seashell house. I was in hot pursuit as I bounded in but suddenly a frying pan or something hit me on the head and I went down for the count. Sometime later I could hear a flock of seagulls flying by, cackling their familiar calls. I was lying on a carpet in Fiona's nude lap! She was petting my head. "So sorry...Fiona...did this..." My vision cleared a bit and I could see the disposition on the face had changed and it was that of Zephyr. "Calm you...you good for Zephyr...love...Lexie says...he like you...me, too..."

"Zephyr? Is that you? What happened to your terror of a sister?"

"Fiona bad...I come back...for you...feel love..."

I sat up. "You—you need to put some clothes on. We've gotta get out of here, kid. Grab what you can and let's get up to the main house." She was cooperative, mainly because I think she liked me, but also because I think she sensed danger and I would be able to protect her and her "sea-child" a lot better where we were going.

We descended the rope ladder. When we reached the sand, however, I spotted three ornery looking men running towards us around the bend by the edge of the rocks to our south. I took Zephyr's hand and at the same time realized it was too late for Mr. Crickle—they had gotten to him and time was running out for us as well as we ran down the beach. Zephyr pulled me along a spit that led into the tide line and we sped into the surf. She pulled me under and we swam in the murky waters, with me following her toward a huge sea stack in the distance.

I was out of breath and had to surface. As soon as I did I heard gunshots and bullets riddle the water just inches from my head. I took a big breath and shot under the water again. Bless her soul, Zephyr had waited for me and we continued toward the sea stack. Since the sun still shone brightly, we could see down about fifteen feet or so. She led me into an opening in the sea stack and suddenly we were in a huge cavern, only half of which the tides of the ocean could reach!

Zephyr pulled me up on a deck of rock. I was seriously out of breath. "Thanks, babe—too damn many Lucky Strikes and booze lately, I guess. Are you alright?"

"Yes." She nuzzled her nose into my neck, kissing it gently. "Both okay...Lexie smart, go under waves..."

We were in a fine mess. The train and boat tickets were now a soggy clump in my pocket, I was trembling from the cold water, more than likely Mr. Crickle was dead, the goons who were after us probably either burned or flattened the tires on my borrowed Packard—and I doubted that I could swim out of this cavern back to the shore. "What are we going to do, Zephyr?" I asked, feeling defeated as hell.

"Love..."she said quietly, looking down into the surging waters below us. "Love is good...like ocean is good..." Then she looked at me with those wonderful green eyes that were housed in that gorgeous little nude body of hers. It seemed to me we were up a creek without a paddle. The only light in the cavern came from the restless, shifting ocean water below us, but it was mid-afternoon by now and I knew when the sun set in a couple of hours, we would be trapped in a hopeless pitch black tomb. I also realized Zephyr could easily dive down into the waters below and swim her way to freedom. If I perished here in this crypt of rock, so be it. But something kept telling me my number wasn't up—not quite yet.

"You go ahead, maybe you can go for help, kid. I don't think I can swim out of this hole and back up to the surface in one long breath. I almost didn't make it *in*to this dank hole."

"Zephyr stay with Denning...not leave..."

"Well, if we're gonna die together here, we might as well be on a first-name basis—*Cable*—call me Cable. But I think you should get out of here."

"No...stay," she persisted. So I grabbed her by the shoulders and looked into those green eyes barely glowing in the subdued light of the cavern.

"You're just as stubborn as your damned sister. Now, look, Zephyr—get out of here, now! Go and try to find some help."

She looked at me, her eyes widened at my touching her. "No! Stay! I stay with you, Cable...!"

"What the hell happened to you and your sister that made you so strange and incorrigible? Hell, what do I have to do to kick you out of this deathtrap we're in? I'm freezing and as my body temperature drops, it won't be long, I'll probably just drift off to sleep and that'll be it, lady. So, go—and go now!" Again I nudged her with my trembling arms and again she resisted. By the time I had scooted her half way down the escarpment toward the water, she turned on me and hit me hard on the chest. Then a wild look came into her eyes.

"I told you I hated insistent men!" boomed the voice of Fiona. "If you touch me again, I'll—I'll kill you!" I drew back, shocked that the gentle Zephyr had once again turned into the monstrous Fiona. But even if these were my last breaths on earth, I would still do my best to save the poor, confused little creature.

"Look! Whoever you are, you're getting outta here—understand? I don't want your death on my hands when I leave this old world and I sure don't want to be choked to death by you...while I'm sleeping my last sleep into oblivion."

"You are stupid, like my father! You never understood—ever!"

"Never understood what, Zephyr? What *happened* when you were a little girl that split you in two? Yeah, I might be stupid, kid, but I'm not that stupid. You've got to bring it up and spit it out—that's the only way you're ever going to become whole in this screwed up world—face it, Zephyr—face whatever chased you so deep into yourself that you can't find your way out!"

"Never! Never! Never!" she shouted as she jumped up and started to climb the rocks above us, clamoring like a little crab to get hold of the jagged edges. I tried to grab her ankle, but I tripped and lost my footing on the uneven floor of the ledge. Fiona/Zephyr fell several feet, hitting her head as she tumbled over the edge, and went splashing into the water fifteen feet below us! Instinctively I dove in after her, hitting the cold water like it was a block of ice. She was stunned from the fall and bleeding from her scalp. I felt terrible and there seemed to be no way out of this nightmare we were trapped in. Suddenly I heard a chattering behind me and Lexie the "sea-child" appeared with his happy perennial smile. He flipped his tail at me and somehow I got it that he wanted me to grab it. I reached for Zephyr's arm and with my other hand, latched on to Lexie's tail. He let out a series of chatters as if he was telling me something. I took a deep breath and he plunged into the murky waters with me in tow, while I held on to the stunned Zephyr's arm. The little creature was fast and powerful and we zipped down into the abyss and then headed straight up for the light above us. Soon we burst up to the surface and I gulped for air as I pulled Zephyr's limp body closer to my own until I held her head in a clench above the water so she'd be able to breathe. The little magical Lexie continued to pull us toward the shore. He took us in as far as he could, and when I was able to catch my breath, I lugged Zephyr's wounded body out of the surf to the safety of the sands above the tide line.

I quickly looked around, the thugs who shot at us earlier had gone. Lexie continued to stand by, circulating just enough in the water to keep his body submerged. I was still trembling from the cold and exhaustion, but I began to pump on Zephyr's chest, put my mouth onto hers and blew some air into her lungs. The blood had stopped running down her face and she opened her eyes. But these were different eyes looking at me, the same green orbs but someone else lived inside them now. As her vision cleared she looked up at me and smiled. "Cable...it's me! Zephyr! I can...I can speak...freely now...like I've been dreaming, but I remember you—"

"—that's great, kid! Welcome home!" In that moment I realized by some miracle the knock on the head had somehow finally merged both of her personas into one perfectly whole and lovely young woman. She lay there beneath me, her naked body heaving new air into it, her countenance calmed and at peace. She reached up, threw her arms around my neck and hugged me. "So, is—is, uh, Fiona gone now?"

"No, Cable. I love her...she's here, inside me...she was always my first name. I was born *Fiona Zephyr Royce*." Then she got a puzzled look on her face. "But something happened—"

"—don't try to think about it right now, kid. Right now we've got other fish to fry—uh...pardon the expression." I looked around. There was perhaps an hour before sunset. "We've got to get you off this beach and to safety. Can you walk okay?"

"Yes. But I can't leave Lexie."

"I wasn't planning to. That little guy saved our lives. We owe him. Can you go tell him we'll be back for him? We have to find a way to transport him to the aquarium aboard the train."

"Yes." She ran into the water and embraced the chattering happy little creature. She spoke to him and soon returned, grabbed my awaiting hand and we ran up the trail to the beach house above. We got to the top of the hill and I asked her to hide in the tall grasses until I was sure the coast was clear. I was still freezing from the dripping wet clothes and the oncoming cool of night. My .38 was still in its breast holster and I took it out. I crept closer to the house. The front door was open...always a bad sign, I reminded myself. I did find Mr. Crickle's body slumped over one of the living room chairs. He'd been dead only a short while. There was no sign of anyone else. I rummaged through the closets until I found enough clothing for both Zephyr and me to wear. The Packard was still in the driveway. I checked it out and it was untouched...the key still in the ignition. The thugs must have left in a hurry, which also bothered me. What other *death assignment* might they have yet to perform this night?

I went back for Zephyr and we dressed there in the grass because I didn't want her to see Crickle's corpse. We ran quickly to the Packard and I started it up and soon we were roaring down Highway One. "How are we going to save Lexie and Mr. Crickle?" Zephyr asked, that wonderful soft note of concern in her voice that was so characteristic of her.

"We've got enough dough to get a tank truck to the cottage. A couple of us can put Lexie in a blanket sling and carry him up to the tank. Then he'll be safely transported to a boxcar in downtown L.A. Of course you and I will accompany him." Then I took hold of her delicate hand. "But I'm afraid it's too late for Mr. Crickle, Zephyr. Whoever it is that's trying to kill you got to him first."

"Oh, no!" she whimpered. "Not Mr. Crickle! He never hurt a mouse! I knew him since I was—" She began to cry and turned her face toward the window to conceal her tears.

"—we have to let it go, kid. There'll be lots of time for grieving later on. Right now we've gotta stay clear headed and make sure you and your family are safely on that train in a couple of days."

She squeezed my hand. "I'm frightened, Cable. But as long as you're here, I feel better, at least. But what about my sister? Were you able to persuade her to come with us?"

"Nope, not yet. But we're working on it. I'll drop you off with your folks, then head over tonight to see if I can rope her in."

"She's very stubborn. She's like I was—in a fog—and more than one person—"

"—yeah, so I've discovered. Well, she's not any more stubborn than Fiona was," I kidded her.

She giggled. "Yes! You're right! I must have been horrible."

"Well, let's just say you were persuasively *unpleasant*," I said.

"Cable...even in that haze I was in, I could hear your voice. And I can remember using the word *love*—and I meant it. With you, I mean."

"Thanks, kid. You're a swell little lady." She grabbed my hand and squeezed it.

"You are the only man...I've...ever known...Cable...I have been afraid to touch anyone—especially men."

"I don't blame you there, Zephyr. Men, including me, seem to have this one preoccupation—you know, wanting to seduce anyone with nice tits and who wears a dress."

"I'm not sure I know what you mean," she said innocently.

"Forget it. It doesn't really matter."

As we approached *Neptunia*, hackles started to form up and down the back of my neck. My intuition was coming in loud and clear. I found a little indentation by the side of the road a block or so from the estate and pulled into it. I told Zephyr to wait but she wouldn't stay without me by her side, so we trudged through the grasses and oak tree thickets until we came to the back of the house. Indeed, I had seen a large green touring car parked immediately outside the front entrance and was taking no chances. Those ruthless mugs could be waiting inside, guns cocked. We sneaked quietly in through the back door, found the stairwell and Zephyr led us upstairs into the private quarters of her childhood. Everything was dead silent. She took my hand and led me into her bedroom. She excused herself to go into the bathroom and I waited quietly with my .38 drawn, not even knowing whether or not it was too waterlogged to fire. Quickly and like a sprite on wings of air, Zephyr dashed out to check on things, leaving me helpless to defend her. Soon she returned and told me the coast was clear and there was no one in the house. "What about the car outside?" I whispered.

"It's Daddy's. I'm so worried. But if Mother and he are safe, I think I know where to find them."

"You do?" I asked, raising my eyebrows.

"Yes, Daddy had built a secret hideout in the house. I don't know why. I think he was afraid of something for many years. He did it to protect us, I think." Then she noticed the shabby way we looked.

She took my hand and we went back into the bathroom. Quickly, before I could recover myself, she stripped me naked, did so herself and led me into a large, warm shower. I must admit it felt good as hell—and twice as warm. Zephyr's little naked body rubbed against mine as she took a bar of honey-colored soap and began to wash me down. "*Sweetheart* soap," she purred, "since I was a little girl Mother always made sure Eden and I washed with it. I love the smell."

When she got to my private parts, though *she* was uninhibited about it, I contracted a half-erection, which did not go un-noticed by the comely little sea nymph. She seemed to focus on the area for an extra long time, watching it rise there in the hot, steamy shower. I could see her instincts come to life. "This…is okay? What's happening, Cable? I have so little experience with men and—"

I cleared my throat. "—well, not really, kid. It's a man's way of getting sexually excited before he penetrates the female's—genitalia."

"I'm sorry, Cable. I don't understand. But…I think it's causing me to experience something…between my legs. Like a hot, throbbing, opening—"

"—Zephyr! I'm sorry, kid, but we have to stop this. Please. Thank you for washing me—and you'll forgive me if I don't do the same for you—but that would be tempting the fates, and I'm sort of promised to a beautiful young woman. I've already broken my promise once—and I don't want to do it again. Can you understand that?"

"Yes. But that doesn't stop what I feel. But I respect you, Cable, an awful lot."

"Now that you're completely you again, young lady, someday you'll meet someone who's good for you and right for you."

"Young lady? How old are you?"

"Almost thirty."

"Well, I'm twenty-six, Cable. I must ask you, please don't call me 'young lady.' I'm a woman, barely younger than you are."

"Yeah...I guess you're right. I sometimes feel a hell of a lot older than I actually am. Maybe I've just lived too damn much life—"

She put her hand to my mouth. "Shhh...!" she whispered. "I think I hear something." She turned the shower off. We got out of the shower, grabbed a couple of towels and quietly began to dry off.

"You do know what my instinct was when we were in the shower, don't you?" she continued to whisper. "I have never felt anything like it before...and it felt so good..."

"Yeah, it's called being human, that's what humans do—they're sexually on most of the time—natural breeders, you know."

"What does that mean?"

"Forget it," I said, winking at her. "I'll tell you someday."

We sneaked totally nude into her bedroom. She led me to a walk-in closet where she quickly dressed into clothing she hadn't worn in years. It still fit pretty well, I thought, even though it might have been a little tight here and there. That didn't make it any easier on my libido, which seemed hard pressed to ignore this lovely little woman's womanly curves. She asked me to stay put and ventured forth into the rest of the up-stairs. Soon she signaled for me to come. We went into what must surely have been her father's room. There she fit me into some rather awkward clothes until once again I looked like some vaudeville clown. Even the shoes were too big for me.

"Now...follow me," she said. She led me downstairs to a fireplace with large wooden panels on either side. Then she pressed a stone on the hearth and the left panel swung open like a door and we entered quickly. She pulled a lever and the panel closed. We made our way down a narrow passage until we came to a flight of descending stairs. We went down, cautiously. Suddenly we were in the most comfortable quarters one could imagine, a large room decorated with wonderful gold leaf framed pictures, a dazzling chandelier hanging from a twelve-foot ceiling. There before us stood Mr. and Mrs. Royce and Henry the steward of the house.

Both parents called out and Zephyr went running into their arms. When they heard her articulate speech and noticed her relaxed mannerisms—the new-found Fiona Zephyr Royce—they were jubilant. They thanked me profusely, and registered sadness at the murder of Mr. Crickle. I updated them as best I could and they sent me on my way to retrieve the one remaining daughter. Zephyr accompanied me to the front door. She hugged me. "Cable, I think I felt my first pangs of desire tonight. I want to thank you for making me feel so many wonderful things. I wish it were me you wanted and loved—but I respect you so much—that I know if I were that lady you love, I would want you to be true to me."

"Thanks, Zephyr...you're okay, you know. The journey ain't over yet, kid, hang on to your britches—there's a bumpy road ahead."

"Please don't call me kid, Cable. I'm a grown woman capable of everything healthy, grown women are capable of, okay?"

"Yeah, sorry again...*woman*. I'll—I'll, uh, try to remember that. You know, old habits die hard and all." I walked down to the Packard and roared off into the night.

CHAPTER 5

TIE ME UP, HANG ME DOWN

It was very late by the time I reached Eden Royce's *Hollywood Highlands Manor*. I knocked and some cute little thing in a blue robe came to the door. "It's too late, Mister. Business hours are over for the night."

I must have looked like Dusty the Clown standing there in Benedict Royce's over-sized suit. "Look, lady, I'm Cable Denning, I've been hired by Mr. Royce to—well, what the hell!" I pushed the lady aside and went for the elevator. She followed me and pulled at me all the way up to the imposing doors to Eden's suite. I knocked. There was a rustling inside and soon Eden Royce came to the door. But before she could speak, a rather distinguished looking older man came out of her quarters and brushed past me, not saying a word.

Eden Royce looked at me. "Business is brisk tonight, isn't it, Mr. Denning? Are you here to bore me again—or make love? If the first, you can go home right now. I charge more to be bored—if the latter, it's three in the morning—I charge triple after two. So what will it be?"

I pushed the door aside. "Stop the games, Eden. We've gotta talk now." She motioned for the little dish in the blue robe to go. She closed the door and turned to look at me and snickered. "Have you been in a theatrical production? Now, don't tell me...Barney the Bum—or maybe Pete the Clown...? Has anyone told you how ridiculous you—"

"—Crickle's dead, your sister, father and mother are holed up in the secret chamber at *Neptunia*—and frankly, I'm surprised you're not dead yet."

She looked at me, checking my eyes out. "Yep, you're telling the truth alright. So what do you want me to do about it? Life is good for me here, business is the best it's ever been, I'm rich and still beautiful and I fuck who I want when I want to—including you. What else *is* there, Mr. Private 'Dick'?"

"Oh, there's the little matter of your life hanging in the balance, Eden. Whoever's trying to bump off your family shot at Zephyr and me earlier this afternoon, after they killed Crickle. I have this distinct feeling you're next. Now, what's it gonna be—come with me—or end up in pieces in the cemetery of your choice?"

"Oh, you are soooo melodramatic, Cable Denning. I told you once—and I'll tell you again—I'm staying here to rake in the dough and fuck my little brains out when I get the notion. By the way, you were the best I've had in a long time. Anytime you want to have a love-hate rematch, just whistle."

I'd had enough of this broad. I turned and started toward the door. She chased after me. Suddenly she was affecting her sultry, sensual voice again, the one I'd heard on the telephone the day I first met her. "Please, Mr. Policeman, stay with me awhile. I'm—I'm all *worked up* from that poor rich slob you met on the way out. He can't perform with his you-know-what, so he likes to lick me all over. So...now I'm ready for a *real* man—what do you say, big boy?"

"I've been there with you, Eden, and as pleasant as it was—you're a cheap dame with lousy taste—including me. I'd be the last guy I'd pick for a good roll in the hay. You know why? Because I'm sexual, hard-driven, treacherous and hard-living! I drink, smoke, chase skirts all over town and hang out in dingy, smoky nightclubs late at night, hanging on to every word of some pretty doll in pink sequins singing a favorite tune. Existing like that leaves you with a mixed taste in your mouth, lady, the one that says life stinks and every once in a while if you're lucky, you find someone decent and loyal—someone who's capable of real love—and she teaches you there's more than screwing under satin sheets in your penthouse here, but that plain and *simple* still works in this world. I cheated on her with you and I've been trying to get the taste out of my mouth ever since."

Eden Royce stood there still holding my arm. Then, all the wind had gone out of her sails and she dropped it along with her phony voice. She walked away, then turned back to look at me. "If this woman could ever love a man, it would be you. But unlike your mysterious lover, I'm not capable of *being someone*. You see, I'm a non-entity who picks up identities along the way, Cable. I'm a saint on Sundays and a whore on Wednesdays. I'm a businesswoman on Tuesday and a contributor to charity on Friday afternoon fundraisers. Look at me, do you know who I am? I don't. I can't change, ex-copper, because I have nothing to change to. Tell my Mother and Daddy I'm the lost sheep who didn't come home—and let it go at that. Good night, Mr. Denning." She turned and went into another room. I put on my hat and left, feeling I had failed at my last task in securing the safety of the entire Royce clan.

When I got back to the office, for the moment I had forgotten Adora and I had a cottage together. It was past four in the morning. But I knew she'd worry, so I called. "Hola! Cable! You okey-dokey, *mi amor?*"

"Yeah, it's me, babe. I had quite a day and I'm here at the office. I think I'll just plop here for the night. I've got to get the Royce family up and away tomorrow, capture and contain a happy little pet dolphin, and shift the folks around until it's time to depart. I promise I'll be with you tomorrow night. The night after, I gotta take the train with them to an undisclosed location. Sorry, babe, but I'll be gone for a while."

Her voice seemed sad. *Lo siento, también, señor.* I miss you and want you, Cable. *Por favor*, come home *pronto, mi querido."*

"I will, babe, I promise. And when this thing blows over, I'll take you away for a couple of days, how's that?"

Her voice lit up at the other end. *"Promesa? Entonces, cuando, cuando, cuando, mi amor?"*

"We'll discuss it tomorrow night. I love you, Adora Moreno," I declared, feeling all the feelings possible for me to experience in this world, with this beautiful woman. "Do you still like the cottage? Are you happy there, Adora?"

"Oh, sí, Cable. Mucho. Only you are missing."

We hung up and I crashed on my bed. But as soon as my head hit the pillow I began to dream. Since I was a kid I've been good at dreaming. Maybe it was a way to escape a dismal, tough childhood. It was one of those dreams where everything got mixed up. I was walking on San Simeon Point with Honey and we could see Hearst Castle above us on the hill, the fog parting to reveal the gleaming white towers in the morning sun. It was like that day we had walked amongst the sweet smell of Eucalyptus trees. She was happy and her honey-colored hair was blowing in the morning breezes, her blue eyes smiling at me. Then suddenly I was standing in front of her grave, looking down into the dark abyss where her coffin lay, before the final shovelfuls of dirt sealed her away from me forever. I heard her beautiful voice calling to me and then it turned into a song...a song that haunted me from the first time I'd heard her sing it at the *Bella Notte*. Her soft, sexy voice was singing those poignant lyrics of Irving Berlin's *What'll I Do?* and she was reminding me how far away we were from each other. "*When I'm alone with only dreams of you, that won't come true, what'll I do?*" she concluded. Then her arm reached up from out of the grave and she pulled me to her, and I felt myself floating down into the darkness to join her. Suddenly I felt a tap on my shoulder and it was Crazy Jack asking me for a cigarette and telling me I mustn't go down there, I mustn't succumb to the darkness of the dearly departed Honey Combes, I must fight to keep on top of things, fight to go on living and breathing and loving—and vanquishing the bad guys who made up a disproportionate part of the world...guys who would sell out their mothers for the next buck or bid for power. I was crying and Crazy

Jack took his dirty sleeve and wiped my tears. Then suddenly I was ripped out of the dream.

It must have been ten or so in the morning when I heard a persistent banging at my office door. I put on some pants and stumbled into my office. I ambled to the door. "Yeah, who is it?"

"Cigarette! Cigarette! Jack! Jack see Cable! Open!"

"Crazy Jack?" I asked, still in a fog from my dream.

"I don't know! I don't know! Let Jack in. Cigarette!"

I opened the door and let my old disheveled little friend enter. Crazy Jack was one of those leftovers that society had already written off. No one knew whether he was truly crazy or a man so gifted with psychic powers, that even he became overwhelmed by them, and so appeared to people as a misfit, subsisting on Skid Row, a wandering derelict forgotten by most of the world. But I'd seen Jack in action...heard him predict with deadly accuracy, events the average Joe Blow had no clue about. "Damn, Jack, you were just in a dream of mine—how the hell?—"

"—Cigarette! Cigarette!" he demanded. So I went to my desk, opened a fresh pack of Lucky Strikes, took the first one out, gave it to him and tucked the rest of the pack into his vest pocket. I lit his cigarette for him. He took a big drag and settled down a bit. "Crazy Jack not see Cable—long time. Blonde girl gone now...dark girl Cable love...go now, go out, leave...danger come fast! But I don't know! I don't know!"

"Not again, Jack. You know, it seems ever since I've known you you've been warning me about the next impending disaster about to come crashing down on me like a summer thunder storm." I took out a cigarette for myself and lit up. "Yeah, it's been a while. In fact, I was going to pop in on you and get your drift on the Royce family thing I'm involved in just now. Can you pick them up or something? Can you get them outta town safely?"

He did an unusual thing. He grabbed my wrist and closed his eyes. He was always trembling, so the feel of his nervous body went rankling through my own. "Go now. Warm water fish girl...save...okay. Other girl...danger...big man, die. But I don't know! I don't know!"

"Crazy Jack! Hell...I wish we could have an ordinary conversation here. I always get bits and pieces from you. How am I supposed to figure it out—I mean, when you toss me all this shit on the installment plan?"

Just then there was a knock at the door. Since I was in only a pair of pants standing there with a crazy man from Skid Row, I cleared my throat and spoke authoritatively. "Yeah, who's there?"

"It's me, Cable, Daddy and I are waiting for you down below in the moving truck. Did you forget? You know, Lexie and all?"

I opened the door and there stood the young and comely Zephyr Royce. "No, babe, I—I just over slept, that's all."

She looked at me, a slight smile on her lips. "I didn't remember so much hair on your chest. Did you grow some last night?" she kidded me.

"Oh, by the way, this is Crazy Jack—Jack, this is Zephyr Royce, the—the *fish-girl* you were describing."

Zephyr was more prepared than most people to accept Jack as she found him. "Hello, Crazy Jack—pleased to meet you—are you a friend of Cable's?—he's certainly a friend of mine—I mean, sort of a new one—"

"—I don't know! I don't know!" came Jack's standard reply. He looked her over. "Pretty fish-girl—pretty baby boy, fish boy!" he exclaimed. "But I don't know! I don't know!"

I thanked Crazy Jack, got dressed in a flash and soon Benedict Royce, Zephyr and I were down at the beach looking for Lexie. We had prepared a blanket-sling for him and when Zephyr found him and explained what we were going to do, the reluctant little dolphin allowed himself to be carried in the sling up to a small tank in the back of our rented covered truck. As fast as we could legally drive the large truck, we drove to a freight terminal in East Los Angeles. There we found a specially assigned boxcar that had "Royce" written on the outside. I immediately told the yardman to erase it—for sure, it would be a dead giveaway to the thugs who now sought us out for their next killing spree. When Lexie was safely in his cozy tank, Zephyr remained with him and a small suitcase she had taken for miscellaneous items, including a few stinky fish to feed Lexie on the long trip to Florida. I promised I'd be back tomorrow evening by the time the train was scheduled to depart. Zephyr hugged me and then on an impulse, kissed me strongly on the lips. "That's what I felt like doing in the shower last night, Cable. I'm—I'm still pulsing down there...you know..."

I smiled sheepishly at her and left. Benedict Royce drove me to my office. He parked the truck and turned the motor off. I cautioned him to be extra careful when he gets on the passenger train tomorrow night and Zephyr and I would see him and his wife when we arrived two days later. "I don't know what you did, Cable, but whatever it was, you brought my daughter back to me." He reached into his pocket for an envelope. "Just a token of my esteem and respect for you, young man. And although you failed at bringing Eden back with you, I'm sure you did everything in your power to persuade her."

I took the envelope without opening it. "Thanks, Royce. It's been a bumpy ride, but it isn't over yet. Eden's got the same split personality Zephyr had when I first met her. She's stubborn as hell."

He reflected. "Just like me in my youth. Zephyr had always been somewhat favored by my wife and me, but we still love Eden and want her home—I mean, her new home. Are you sure there's no way to bring her to us?"

"Yeah, I could hogtie her and bring her in fighting, kicking and scratching. But you know, Royce—"

"—please, call me Benedict. We can dispense with the formality of last names at this point"

"Sure, why not? When I was a kid, I never knew the last names of most of the boys I played with. Did you? But as far as Eden goes, you can lead the horse to the water, but you can't make her drink it."

"No, I suppose not. She's a grown woman with her own mind. I...uh... didn't play with friends much in my youth—more or less a loner. May I ask what brought about the integration of Fiona and Zephyr, and so, the miraculous return of my daughter?"

"Far as I can figure, a bump on the head. It seems she was changing back and forth faster than a light switch. When I pursued her in the ocean cave, she fell on the rocks, and hit her head. Lexie saved us and when I gave her artificial respiration on the beach, she came to as a different girl."

"Thank goodness, Cable, and many thanks to you." He took a deep breath and checked me out. "I...I, uh, think Zephyr's in love with you. You may as well know, it's doubtful she's ever known a man. Please be gentle with her. She has no idea how cruel a man can be when it's just for sexual pleasure—"

"—I don't need the lecture, Benedict. Eden told me about your proclivity for sex only for procreation. So I know your stance. Just don't mess with my preferences—or your daughter's. As far as I'm concerned, she's safe with me. I have someone I'm in love with, and that's not about to change because of your lovely little sea-daughter."

"I'm thankful to you, Cable. See you in Miami?"

"Yep, day after tomorrow. Now, you and your Mathilda stay low...down in your little hideout if I were you—and is there a phone there—just in case I have to reach you?"

"Yes, same number as upstairs. Okay, Cable—we'll see you in the land of swamps and grapefruit." I got out of the truck and made my way up to my office. I opened the envelope Royce had given me. Five thousand more bucks! I was becoming the most independently wealthy private dick in L.A.! I took out the dough and tucked it away in a secret compartment under my comfy desk chair.

I sat at my desk, reveling in the events of the past few days. I was also looking forward to being with my Adora tonight, when the phone rang. "There's a warning bell in a familiar cave...you will die anyway, but I wouldn't hurry it if I were you...get off the Royce case." Then he hung up. I sat there suddenly shaken out of my good luck feelin'. When something like that happens, all the other bad things that you've shoved away, come rushing out of their little corners to remind you. I was thinking of two things Crazy Jack had sputtered when he woke me up this morning. *'Other girl danger...big man die...'* he'd told me. I was sure he was talking about Eden Royce and her father. But how was I to save them? And now I had to figure out what that warning phone call was all about. The only other caves I knew about other than the one in the oceanic sea stack, were the Bronson Caves, up in Griffith Park. I grabbed a flashlight and had just started for the door when the man I had sold Honey's Packard to showed up and insisted that I return the car immediately and that I was no longer privileged to borrow it. I gave him the keys and suddenly I was without wheels again.

I took a cab up Canyon Drive to the Bronson Park gateway. It was early November, 1930, and it had just rained. The perfume of decaying weeds, bushes and leaves filled the afternoon air. I walked briskly up the trail toward the caves. When the world smelled this good, it was hard to feel that anything could be wrong with it. And, you know, maybe there wasn't anything at all wrong with the *world.* It was *people* that caused the shit to rain down on this poor, unsuspecting plan-et. Who could imagine that a group of errant apes with brains too big for their britches would violate the highest and purest codes of a beautiful planet? I was thinking of the poison gases used in World War One, the war to end all wars, I was told. But I doubted that. The money was too good, the power too intoxicating for war-mongers, politicians, the restless rich and the discontented, psychopathic criminals that ran the world. No, someone would conjure up a new war, a new super-criminal would emerge under the pretext of doing good for his people and a new dictator would be born to snuff out yet another generation of hope-fuls, intending to fulfill the idealistic vision of a perfect world.

I approached the caves and took out my flashlight. There was no one around, so I entered the larger of the two entrances. One branched to the left, so I took it and followed it through as it wound around to the other side, checking out the sides of the walls for any-thing suspicious. Young lovers came giggling through and greeted me. I smiled faintly and they went on their way. The wind was blowing through the caves and I thought I could hear a small bell somewhere. I continued to search. Nothing. Then as a stronger breeze swept through the cave and the bell rang loud-er, I followed the sound to near the main entrance. The bell was ringing right above my head, hanging around the neck of a very white and dead Eden Royce! Someone had used mountain climbing pitons and spiked her to the top of the cave and hung the bell around her neck so it hung about six inches below her body. I felt ill as I stood there in the restless breezes, looking at Eden's limp body and blonde hair hanging down. Another brutal, senseless murder by a diabolical sect of thugs bent on ruling the world. For a last time, I looked up at Eden Royce's lifeless, body. In that moment I was reminded somehow about the three pigs who had different choices on how to build their houses before the big bad wolf would huff and puff and try to blow their houses down. Well, Eden's had been the house built of straw and they nailed her—literally.

I made my way down the hill, took the streetcar back to my office and called the police. I told them only of the discovery and nothing about my knowing the woman or my implication in the case.

When I reached the little cottage Adora and I shared, I did my best to put on a happy face. But she was sharp and saw that something bad had happened that day. "*Qué pasó, mi amor?*" she asked in her always sympathetic voice.

"Oh, nothing much … just another senseless murder of a young woman who wouldn't listen. They killed the eldest Royce daughter."

Adora put her hand to her mouth. "*Ay, Cable! Qué horrible!* Why do you stay in such a terrible business, *querido*? One day soon…maybe it is you who will not come home to me…I would not live then, my love…"

I took my lady into my arms and I cried gently on her shoulder. She understood that even the toughest of us in this world have places that haven't yet grown that impenetrable callous. She comforted me, fetched me a glass of gin, undressed me and took me into the shower with her. She caressed me, licked me, sucked me, and finally took me into our new double bed and made love to me. For a while it worked, I could push away the personal connection with the Royce family and realize I was my own person, a distinctly different being in a cosmos of twinkling little lights known as human hearts and souls. Or maybe some beings didn't have souls. I don't know. Or maybe we all pretended we had them and in the end, when the chips were down, we reverted to the savage brutality of survivalist, battering and punching our way to be the fittest. And in the end the strongest ape won. Take away love—and what was left?

Finally, with Adora holding me tightly I drifted off into a restless sleep, knowing full well that tomorrow I would have to face the Royce family again, and one by one, tell the story of the little piggy who had refused to build a stronger house and perished at the hands of the Big Bad Wolf.

Early the next morning I joined a sleepy Zephyr in the freight car with Lexie smiling out of the glass aquarium at me. "What kind of a night did you spend?" I asked, checking out the straw pile she must have slept in. "Did you eat it or sleep in it?"

She laughed. "I like your sense of humor, Cable. No, I slept in it but had to go to the bathroom outside—without being seen—which is very awkward. And it wasn't a very pleasant night without you—"

"—thank God," I kidded her, looking around the boxcar. "If I've got it right, the train is supposed to pull out about 10:30 or so. We've got a little time, want to grab some breakfast somewhere?"

"No, Cable, I can't leave Lexie. Can you get us something for the trip? I've got two sandwiches and a jug of water."

I went off to find a café or diner. I did find a yard-man poking his head in and out of boxcars. He saw me coming. "You're on railroad property, buddy, whatta ya want?"

"I'm with the Royce box car—bodyguard." I flashed him my private dick I.D. He checked it out. "Hell of an expense for a lousy little fish, don't you think?"

"Oh, you know, pets for the rich...there's no limit to what exotic animals they may come up with. Next time it could be a giraffe, then you'd really have a hell of a job poking a hole in one of your boxcar roofs," I joked, ribbing the hapless, gruff man.

"Yeah, I suppose. We'll be delayed. The streamliner coming in from the east is late about forty minutes."

"Oh, thanks for telling me. Is there a diner or something around here where we can grab some breakfast to go?"

"Yeah, it's called *The Switchman* and it's two blocks down, go left on 11th. You'll see it on your left. Make damn sure that tank of water is secure before we hook you to the train and pull out of the yard. Is it just you and the girl?"

"Yeah..." I said and thanked the man. I found the café, got some fried potatoes and eggs and started back to the boxcar when I noted a very shiny, black sedan parked about a hundred feet from the track.

Those hackles went up on the back of my neck and I quickly dodged into an alleyway that led to the next block over. I crept along the front of the buildings until I was near the tracks again. Three goons were sizing up the boxcar with Zephyr and Lexie in it! I was out-sized and out-gunned. What could I do? Then I watched in amazement as a small switch engine came puffing up toward the still-detached boxcar. We were not scheduled to be hooked up to the main train for another hour or so. The small engine stopped and a brakeman hooked the couplers. The boxcar door was open about two feet or so and I saw Zephyr peak out only to be threatened by a gun pointing at her, obviously telling her to stay inside and keep out of the way. I had to think fast!

I ran back down toward the little café and found a phone booth. I fumbled in my pocket for the Royce's number. I dialed and it rang at the other end. "Yes, hello..."

"Benedict, some of your ghosts just showed up at the rail yard. I think they're kidnapping the boxcar with Lexie and Zephyr in it. Now, I don't know how, but I've got to tail them and find out where they're taking her. If it's just to kill them, they could've done that already, right in the damn boxcar. But I don't think that's their plan. I've got a feeling you might know, Benedict—if so, you'd better come clean just about now—because I don't think we've got a lot of time here."

"Oh, Lord, Cable—I think I do know! Where are you? I'll come meet you."

"There's a little café called *The Switchman*, 11th and Pacific. Oh, and there's one more thing." I steeled myself, because somehow I never got used to being the bearer of this kind of bad news. It wasn't easy to tell a parent—even a neglectful parent—that one of their kids just got killed by murderous thugs, and they were the reason for it. "Uh...brace yourself, Benedict. They got to Eden. I found her body hanging upside down in the Bronson Caves yesterday."

There was a long pause. I realized in that moment a new reality had to sink in to Benedict Royce. Maybe for the first time in his life, the man used to dining at the Ritz while dancing the two-step with aliens had to face up to the shit he'd created and now he could literally call his fortune *blood money*. "Eden...? Oh, no...no...not Eden...! I was just thinking of a way to make up to her—" he said, his voice trembling.

"—well, guess what, Royce—it's a bit late for that! You should've told her that dark truth you're still hiding up your sleeve, long ago and given her the choice—because either way, you lost her a long time ago."

He ignored my comment. "That's—that's why the police were here, at our door last night. Mathilda's upstairs. I don't know how I'm ever going to tell her... When the police came, we didn't answer...why didn't you tell us about Eden last night?"

"I was pretty beaten down myself, Mister. You see, I happened to like Eden in my own peculiar kind of way. She suffered from the same malady her sister got cursed with—only she expressed it with a different kind of rebellion. Frankly, I was pissed because I knew you and your wife had written Eden off your 'care list' years ago and you judged her life style because of your own sexual hang-ups. Well, now, guess what? It's too late for any of it, Benedict, and Eden won't have a chance to heal the horror that filled her psyche and damaged a lovely young woman who might've had a chance in this world, for a piece of happiness. She wasn't a bad person, Benedict, just warped by something you allowed to come slithering out of the bag a lotta years ago. Now it's come home to haunt you—and unfortunately, your wife as well. So don't push it if you're not on my list of favorite persons today, Royce."

Again there was that pause when you just knew someone at the other end of the line was falling apart and trying to think at the same time. "I'll...I'll see you in a few minutes...I'll be in the green touring car with Henry driving."

"Yeah, okay..." I hung up, disgusted at humanity, from all angles.

I rushed back and stood in the shadows watching the boxcar with the switch engine sitting there steaming like a dragon at rest, awaiting the next order someone would give. But who was calling the shots and what was it they forgot or neglected to do before they killed the whole family off? A half hour went by. The yard boss came around to check on the gunmen who stood by, loitering. He admonished them and they shot him where he stood. They dragged his body under a train on a parallel track and returned, continuing to talk together as if nothing had happened. Amidst the seven or eight tracks and awaiting freight trains, it was unlikely anyone had seen the yardman get it. But I got it. I got the complete lack of conscience these demented creatures carried like a badge—but of cowardice—and an unforgivable aggression on a society that was still on its knees, fighting its way out of a deep economic depression. So far, 1930 wasn't any better than the previous year and the economy kept sinking with soup lines and ever increasing joblessness. Oh yeah, there were always those who would profit from the travesty. Those whose lives hung out in that shadow-land Royce's so-called 'associates' found so inviting—and profitable. For them, it was okay to fiddle while Rome burned, because they and their kind held the keys to the empire of greed, lust, power and money. And after all, that's what made the world go 'round, wasn't it?

Reach of the Transeo Terra

Benedict Royce picked me up in front of *The Switchman Café* and we drove around the block until we faced the boxcar Zephyr and Lexie were imprisoned in. "Now it's truth time, Royce. Frankly, I'm tired of the bullshit you've been feeding everyone for the past umpteen years—your wife included. So tell me what happened way back there when the girls went haywire, so a lot more people don't die, okay?"

Royce asked Henry to leave and we sat in the back seat alone, looking at the boxcar in the late morning sunlight, its Tuscan red paint standing out from the other dull colors Southern Pacific splashed on their rolling stock. "I was young and ambitious then, born into wealth, pre-possessed of exceptional I.Q. and I had a penchant for the unusual, particularly numbers and financial mathematics. I was recruited by an organization that promised me position and additional wealth—a kind of ground floor opportunity, you might say."

"Who and what was the organization?"

"You already mentioned it. The *Oculus Pyramis Mandatum* was composed of the richest, most influential men in the world, I was told. Financiers, bankers, and Wall Street geniuses who made the Rockefellers seem like school children. They mandated fiscal policy in developed countries throughout the world and could make or break a nation if they really wished to do so. They had two other branches, I later discovered. One was a group called *Oculus Metus Vires* and they were the enforcers of policy, established by the order. Anyone breaking those codes was dealt with most harshly."

"Yeah, like killing someone on a whim for disobedience, eh?" I said, a tad of bitter irony in my voice.

"The third branch was called the *Oculus Transeo Terra*. This was the scientific experimentation branch, so I was told. In truth, it was the spawning ground for bringing through alien beings into physical human form so that they could live among us undetected. Their goal was to keep the earth people unsettled, in a state of chaos and uncertainty, taking advantage of an earlier visitation by other beings who had *turned down* certain genes or coded segments of the human makeup, making them less than they really were. But they needed a marine-type of human being who could

114

be submerged for a long period of time, swim swiftly—yet possess all the mental faculties of a human being—as a spy. So I was given a most unique opportunity to help them accomplish this by allowing my young daughters to participate—so they said."

"Oh, I can't wait for this one, Royce. You son of a bitch—you really did it, didn't you? You sacrificed your daughters—"

He put his hand up to stop me. "—that's not all, Cable. Mathilda was pregnant with our son. The Order *requested* that they take the fetus before he was born and modify him with hormones and gene splicing applications from my two daughters. They made me slip Mathilda a potion that would induce false labor and anesthetize her at the same time. At first I vehemently opposed any such notion. But they threatened me and said if I wanted to continue a prosperous life at *Neptunia*, it would be best for me to consent. Otherwise they would eliminate me and my family."

Benedict Royce was shaking and I gave him a cigarette and lit it for him. But that didn't stop the shaking. "So you sold out your family, thinking there was no other way to save them..."

"Believe me, there was none. Not only that, but they can read your mind within twenty feet or so. So whenever I had an audience with them, they could read my fear and hesitation and remind me just how vulnerable my position was."

"So, let me guess. They doped up your wife and rushed her to a secret lab where they operated on her, removed the fetus. Then she was told she had lost the child—when in truth those bastards were engineering a brand new little species of fish boy—how am I doing so far, professor?"

"Yes! That's exactly what they did! How did you know?"

"Oh, I've had a little experience at one of their laboratories—one that would have resulted in the procurement of my family jewels. You don't have to be an extra-terrestrial alien, just use common sense."

"Good God, Cable. And you escaped?"

"Not really. You see, some good Samaritans came to my rescue at the last minute—and pow! the bad guys were dead and I was home kissing my girlfriend good-night."

"And no reprisals?"

"Nope. Not yet. Maybe I knew too much—and maybe I still do. Anyway, back to you. So they drug and extract vital genetic components out of your girls, and that modified them in some undesirable ways—"

"—the result was multi-tiered, but essentially the operations caused a rift between right and left brain lobes, and a personality disorder developed in both girls. Eden went the way of defiant rebellion while Zephyr seemed brain damaged on one hand and her Fiona persona emerged, becoming aggressive and articulate. But only Zephyr was modified to be the marine overseer for our son—who, most horribly of all—was modified and suspended in some huge test tube until he was fully formed enough to exist as some misfit marine creature."

"Oh, I don't know," I said sarcastically, "he's kind of cute, don't you think?"

Royce ignored me. "*Oculus* was expanding and they needed someone like Lexie who they could perform secret experiments on."

"So what happened?"

"Lexie was a failure. They told me they'd keep an eye on his progress. But they never did. Lexie was the first of a long line of experiments—and failures. Subsequent marine 'sea-children' were born more obedient and efficient, I've heard. But I've never seen any."

"Why did Eden and Zephyr consent to the operations?"

"They didn't. Like their mother, they were drugged in their sleep to be compliant. Days later they awoke in their own beds, aware only that time had passed. Nothing more. I was the only one who knew the whole story."

"Well, isn't that nice? All these years, Royce, you kept those deep, dark secrets—even from a wife you couldn't have sex with anymore because you felt guilty tearing her family apart and any more children born to you might have meant more experiments—isn't that right, Mr. Upright Citizen?"

His eyes welled with tears. "Yes...yes..."

"And you sloughed it off as some high and mighty moral stance about sex and procreation—when all the time it was greed along with a good dose of fear that drove you. Then you waited through the years for the other shoe to drop, but you didn't know if, when or how any of it would happen. It was like *swimming on Mars*, awkward and alien, but you thought maybe if you did your job well and remained a cog in the big machine, they'd forget about you—and their failures with your offspring. But they didn't, did they? They knew that little Lexie was unique and the telepathic connection between him and Zephyr had deeper roots and they wanted to dissect them. So you opposed it, but what you didn't realize, Royce, was that you came with an expiration date stamped on your forehead, *'look at me, dupe and dummy'* for the company store."

"Yes, it's true, Cable...it's all true..." He sobbed a little as he looked out the window and then across to the hostage boxcar. "Zephyr—Zephyr is the most precious thing in my life. If—if I lose her—"

"—you should have thought about that before—a long, long time before, Mister. For all we know they'd have all been safe on some desert island by now—and Eden might bitch some, but at least she'd be alive! And what about your son? Have you ever bonded with him—or at least tried to communicate with him? How do you know he wasn't hungering for your love all these years—the father he never had?"

Royce put his face into his hands. "I—I was embarrassed, ashamed to call him my son...a chattering little dolphin boy with a permanent smile...I couldn't find a way in to him—"

"—you mean you didn't *want* to find a way, Royce. Why does Lexie deserve less love or consideration than Zephyr—or your now dead daughter, Eden? She was starved for love, would have given almost anything to be held by you—or her mother, for that matter." I had a feeling it was all going in one ear and out the other.

Just then the little switch engine began pulling the Tuscan red boxcar further back into the crowded freight yard. Royce looked alarmed. "Oh…they're moving…we've got to follow them—no matter where they go—we've got to save Zephyr. I couldn't bear it if she—she—"

"—don't get your shorts in an uproar…we'll bide our time a little longer. They've got to switch the boxcar to something on rails they've already assigned." I put out my cigarette in the sidearm ashtray. "By the way, when you first called me you said I came 'highly recommended,' so who *did* drop my name in your ear saying that I'd be highly qualified for the job at hand—because I'd like to shoot him."

"A plant who is not the same kind as those who associate in the *Oculus*, but nevertheless he's an alien who seems to get along in human form quite well. His human name is Joe Lorena. He used to work for a crime syndicate here in the city. Something unpleasant happened and he went underground, where I met him. He had committed himself to a kind of 'detoxifying' or re-training program. I was there for some mental and emotional therapy because of what I was dealing with before I called you. It was Lorena who told me to give you a call."

"Tell me you're not one of them."

"I'm not one of them. ' Underground' is a safe house for aliens who need correcting—voluntarily, of course—and most of them are pretty nice guys and gals."

"Men *and* women?" I asked. It suddenly dawned on me that I had never considered the fair sex in the alien equation. "How can you tell a female alien—"

119

"—they're moving, Cable. What—what are we going to do?" Benedict Royce sputtered. "Don't lose them!"

The switch engine pulled the boxcar containing Zephyr and Lexie to another siding. I knew I had to move now—and fast. "You stay here—or better yet, get Henry and get the hell out of here. Have him drive you back to Mathilda, in the hideout—and sooner or later you've got to tell her about Eden. Maybe it's a good time to help her heal some of those deep gashes she endured because of your ego and selfishness all those years."

Royce made a face like a little boy having to face a severe spanking. "Yes...I guess you're right. I've got to save what I can, since I made a ghastly mess of everything else."

"Money and power ain't the end-all-be-all, pal." I looked him over. "I guess you're sort of experiencing that. If I had the time or inclination, I'd rub your nose in it." I opened the car door. "Watch your back and keep your phone line open." I closed the door and walked away, not sure how I was going to handle this new development.

Somehow I had to get those murderous bums out of the way, rescue Zephyr and Lexie, and the three of us hightail it for—for—for where? I had no idea. I glanced back over my shoulder to see if Royce had left yet. But the light-green touring car remained where I'd left it. I crept through the lines of freight cars until I spotted the little switch engine and the Tuscan colored boxcar. I made a run for the car, but they must have been waiting for me because I heard three shots ring out and I dove for the gravel deck and rolled under a boxcar opposite where Zephyr and Lexie were kept captive. There were three thugs, two of which now stood guarding the boxcar. One of them was creeping around in back of me, hoping he'd hit me with one of his three shots. I poised myself, aimed and rolled out from under the car just in time to fire point blank into the man's chest. He got off one round into the air and fell. Now I had the other two coming at me. I blasted one before he could get a bead on me and he fell, mortally wounded. The remaining killer was mad as a hornet, but he left his post and ran around to the other side of the boxcar to obtain better cover. I ran towards the boxcar that held the precious sea-child but the thug came out firing. I dropped to the ground, but he wasn't shooting at me. Benedict Royce had a concealed weapon and came around from behind a group of small buildings firing away at the gangster! But Royce was a bad shot and he took two bullets in the chest, and staggered to the ground on his knees. I took advantage of the situation and discharged two of my last three bullets into the angry thug. I hit him in the skull and he dropped like a sack of Irish potatoes. I ran to the door of the boxcar and yelled to Zephyr and she quickly slid open the door. But life is funny and in the flurry of things the one man I thought I had killed staggered to his feet and fired his .38 at all of us. One bullet shattered Lexie's glass tank and the water poured out of the boxcar along with glass and a wounded Lexie. I turned and dispatched the remaining gangster with my last slug. I knew the little dolphin boy could breathe oxygen, so I wasn't worried on that account. But a large piece of glass was stuck into his side. Zephyr flew off the boxcar to help her father and we both dragged him to the Tuscan boxcar. The engineer of the switch engine had fled to call the cops, I assumed.

There is always something strange, that when in the middle of chaos and calamity, there is a quiet, an eerie hush that comes over the scene. Royce staggered to where Lexie flopped on the deck of the boxcar. "Son...my son," he cried. He was bleeding pretty bad and I didn't think he had too long to go. "I'm so sorry...I was ashamed of you—because—because I was ashamed of—of myself...I never got to say...*I love you*, because I didn't know....what...what to feel...."

The little creature flapped his tail. I hopped up onto the deck of the boxcar and checked out the piece of glass stuck into Lexie's ribs. I started to pull it out. "Little guy, I owe *you* my life...this might smart a little—so hang on!" I ripped the broken shard out of the dolphin boy's body and he winced and let out a little yelp. It looked like I got it all out.

"Oh, Cable—no!" Zephyr quavered.

I ripped my shirt off and dabbed Lexie's wound with it. He seemed okay everywhere else. I looked into his warm, soulful eyes. "I think you're gonna be just fine, young one," I said pityingly. "We'll get you back into some sea water and you'll heal in no time."

Barely able to stand, Benedict Royce bent into the boxcar and embraced the little being. "Forgive me, son...at least...even though I'm dying... I—I can still tell you...I wanted to love you, son...but I—I didn't know how..."

Lexie snuggled his snout into Royce's chest and let out what must have been one of those indescribable sounds, that traveling across the universe can define joy and sorrow at the same time. Police sirens sounded in the distance and I knew this chapter was over. No, there would never be a family reunion on some small island off Nassau. This was the end of the line. Benedict Royce breathed his last breath holding his sea-child son. Zephyr held her father and I held on to her as the police came to haul us off and sort out the body count and mystifying nature of a very active morning in the life of Cable Denning, P.I.

And so ended the Royce case. Lexie recovered just fine and Zephyr returned with him to her seashell castle, there to frolic with him in the waves for the rest of her days....or so I was told in later years. For whatever reasons, the *Oculus* never bothered to check *Royce Cove Cottage* again and the Royce family faded from memory along with their nefarious plans. Eventually as she grew old, Mathilda Royce sold off *Neptunia* and came to live in the cottage at the cove. She was never told that Lexie was her son. Sometimes it's hard to put together, but far as I can figure, the maternal bond between Zephyr and Lexie probably came about to compensate for neither Mathilda Royce nor her husband showing parental love for their hybrid offspring. Nor did I discount what the *Oculus Transeo Terra* did to psychically bond the wonderful, energetic little sea-child to his sister, Fiona Zephyr Royce, who was as soft as the gentle west wind, and above all, I would never forget.... she was the girl who lived...in a sea-shell.

CHAPTER 6

GOR THE HORRIBLE!

1930 seemed to be whizzing by like a boomerang that zips over your head but never comes back. My business was flourishing, despite the rotten economy, Adora and I were getting on great and as far as my nemesis was concerned, all appeared quiet on the western front. The Royce case had pretty much worn me out for a while, so some smooth sailing felt good for a change. There was no way to tell at the time, but it was the calm before the storm—and just around the corner all hell was about to break loose from its fiery confines.

Some nights I would still sleep at my office to give both Adora and me some space once in a while. She enjoyed having her mother and sister over for Mexican coffee and tortillas, babbling a hundred miles an hour in Spanish. Sometimes they would spend the night with Adora. It may have been my imagination, but I had noticed Adora seemed to be losing weight. Some mornings her skin seemed sallow, her energy more listless, her breasts beginning to sag, as if some of the life in them had been drained away. Something just seemed odd to me. But I let it pass and got on with things, the way normal people are supposed to do, we all get older, right? But actually, that crazy music that played in my head whenever I was alone with the world, was a haunting reminder that I wasn't "normal" and would never be "normal," whatever that meant.

Once in a while I missed walking down into a dive and hearing some dish singing great tunes while people jabbered, laughed, drank, smoked and propositioned each other—a life style I could get used to, I thought. But after Honey, the taste kind of went out of my mouth and so I figured the straight and narrow might let me live a little longer. But you never know about these things. Life has a tenuous vise-grip, holding you there in the darkest areas, squeezing your throat just enough to keep you aware of it. Then, at any time, the Great Decider can come in for the kill, apply the pressure and bam! —your whole world changes for good.

It was about 8:30 on a Tuesday night. I sat at my desk preparing some papers for a court hearing, puffing on a Lucky Strike. A half-filled glass of gin sat opposite me. But I was still thinking about the *music*—that lonely sax weaving haunting melodies through my soul, making me remember what beauty is all about. Beauty is a falling oak leaf in Bronson Park, an ocean view, an exquisite smile, an Irving Berlin tune that transforms the moment, or some doll who looks too perfect to be a human woman. And since I met Joe Lorena and Benedict Royce, I'm not so sure that some of those dishes weren't aliens! I was mulling all of this over when the phone rang.

"Yeah, Cable Denning here."

"Cable, it's me, Zelda—how are you?"

"Zelda! Good to hear from you. Oh, I'm fair to middlin'—how about you? Gees, it's been a year or so? Whatever happened to those plants you were supposed to decorate my office with?"

"You wouldn't believe what I've been through. After I finally found a nice place to live—I mean, *us* to live— my plants and all, I met this guy, and just like you said, I found him among the white coats in an experimental laboratory. Botany, of course. He was researching this and that, stuff my Dad had done years before. Anyway, I kind of went for him, Cable. We dated for about three months without having sex. You know me, Miss Cautious. So when we decided to move in together so he could help me pay the rent at my new place, he sits me down and tells me he's a fag—a damn homosexual—and that he'd like to experiment with me, a woman, to see if he might like it. And that would make him bisexual—and that I couldn't stomach."

"Tough break, kid," I said, feeling for the little nondescript, bookworm.

She drew a big breath and let it out. "So I broke my heart, licked my wounds and here I am—talking to you, my old friend. Still want some plants?"

"Yeah, sure, the place looks a bit barren. Adora just hasn't got around to—"

"—who's Adora?" Zelda's voice suddenly grew stiff and cold.

"Uh....well, someone I met, Zelda. Life goes on, in case you haven't noticed. I grieved a long time, and actually wouldn't have made it through without this young woman's assistance. So...there you have it."

"Oh." Again, her voice was aloof. "Well, I hope you're both happy, Cable." Then she got over that bump in her road. "I've always thought the world of you. I know you know that. After all, you were the only man who ever took me out dining and dancing—"

"—yeah, and helped you get sloshed," I laughed.

"But I loved getting sloshed with you, private detective. When can I come over so you can help me upstairs with the plants?"

"Where do you live?"

"I—I just moved in at Argyle Apartments. I'm sort of your neighbor. I'd love to see you, Cable—I've missed you...and whenever I would think about you and—and...well, you know...I don't—"

"—it's okay, Zelda. You can say *Honey*, because love doesn't go away that fast, doll. She's still singin' in my ear, you know, sometimes late at night when nobody else can hear."

"I'm glad to hear that, Cable. The longer she's gone, the more I realize how much I loved her. She's still kind of with me, too. So that makes two of us. When can I come over? How about tomorrow—I've got some time off from that horrible, boring lab while they're rebuilding some project or something."

I looked at my calendar. Crap, it was already November 22—in a few days Thanksgiving would signal my least favorite time of the year, that obligatory desert between Turkey Day and Christmas the merchants called *the holiday season*. "Let me see...tomorrow's Wednesday...what about late afternoon. I've got a few things to do earlier in the day."

"Sure, swell!" she said with her old enthusiasm. "Maybe we can go out for a drink or something...it's been a long, dry spell, Cable."

"Well, I don't know about going out, but I can offer you some fast company and cheap gin for your trouble."

She giggled. "That'll do. I really like the fast company part. I'll see you tomorrow with a station wagon full of plants."

We said good night and I hung up the phone. Then I picked it right back up again and rang the cottage. I wanted to check in on Adora. She seemed okay, but a bit tired. She said she was glad I wasn't with her tonight because she had begun her period two weeks ago and was having terrible cramps tonight. I asked if I could help and she said a couple of aspirin and a hot bath would take care of it. I told her I loved her very much and we said *buenas noches*. That Cable Denning intuition was working overtime as a prickly, strange feeling ran up and down my spine like a bad dose of electric therapy. For about three months, Adora's behavior had been changing and I sensed her health didn't seem quite right. It wasn't that she didn't have the warm, giving love and harmonious demeanor she'd always had, but she had difficulty in accessing it—centering in on her old and wonderful self—not to mention how incredibly sexual she was naturally prone to be. I thought I would get her to a doc for a thorough checkup.

Finding Goldilocks At the Teddy Bear's Picnic

It was a cold February. 1930 had whooshed by and now it was already 1931 and the country was sinking deeper into a Depression that had already lasted longer than it should have. This was a prosperous country with untold natural resources. Someone somewhere had

128

pulled the wrong strings. Or had they intended it to turn out that way?

Wednesday brought in a fresh rain from the northwest. It was early afternoon and I was finishing up a court prep-case when I heard a light knock at my office door. I got up and went to open it. "The door's usually open, lady," I said as I took a double take at a babe who knocked me to the floor before the first round bell as she entered.

"I—I didn't know," she said in a low, breathy voice. "I took a chance you might be in—you are Mr. Cable Denning, are you not?"

"Yep, that's who I woke up as anyhow. Please, come in. What can I do for you?"

"I'm—I'm looking for a private detective to assist me on a very important—and personal—matter."

"Well, that's me, lady. *Important* is my specialty and I'm incredibly discreet when it comes to personal matters," I bragged, having a little fun with this young dish who stood about five-four, had wonderful hazel eyes and a warm smile, reddish hair with a stylish grey-felt hat. Her face was petite with carefully plucked eyebrows, an almost orange-red lipstick painted on a pair of inviting, puffy lips and she wore a fine off-white gabardine skirt and jacket with a dark blouse underneath. She also wore very loud and shiny red leather highheels. *That* stood out to me. Something didn't quite fit, but I couldn't put my finger on it.

"Thank goodness you said that. You just don't know who to trust these days. Living in such desperate times. I mean, a woman could easily get accosted simply— simply crossing the street, now, couldn't she?"

"There's an old theory, Miss…"

"…Miss Mapleton—Sarah Mapleton."

Standing above her, I extended my hand. "Pleased to meet you, Miss Sarah Mapleton." She took my hand and clasped it tightly. I could feel fear running through her and her hand was very cold, kind of like the hands you hold at the local morgue when you're checking out a bracelet tag. "As I was saying, I've got this theory that *we attract what we fear*. It's kind of like, oh, say…a law of attraction…an automatic given in this newfangled pop-up toaster world we're increasingly tossed into."

"I see what you mean, but I'm not much of a believer in myths, fairy tales and old home-spun remedies. I'm more at home in the world of facts and those things I feel we can verify—shall I say—scientifically?"

"Yeah, I get your point, but don't you think there are *layers* of aspects to us—unknown things we can maybe only guess at?"

"Forgive me for saying so, Mr. Denning, but you speak most strangely and I must ask you to refrain from philosophical discussion if we are to associate."

I got a little miffed at the uppity character wrapped up tight in this good-looking gal. "Well, then, Miss Mapleton, perhaps it's best that we don't start now—associating, that is."

"May I ask why you say this?"

"Because your sophisticated prattle, haughty manner and stiff-upper-lip approach may not be compatible with my slightly more—if I may use the term—lenient viewpoints of life in this swirling cosmos we dwell in, Miss Mapleton. Therefore, I suggest you seek your private dick elsewhere."

130

"What did you say?"

"I said, I suggest you seek your private dick else-where...are you also hard of hearing—or did something I said offend you?"

She seemed flustered. "I...I'm not sure. You mentioned a certain phrase that, uh, *may* have seemed offensive to me—"

"—*private dick*, Miss Mapleton, short for private detective, not necessarily in capital letters. Are you one of those puritanical sweethearts brought out on Sunday mornings to parade after church so as to convince the local gentry into believing that if such a sophisticated young woman can attend the land of mythologies, then so can they?"

She looked indignant and got up to go. I followed and opened the door for her. She looked at me, the blurry-eyed detective from too many gins and Lucky Strikes the night before, my hair slightly disheveled, wrinkled trousers a bit too baggy and my white shirt open at the neck with no tee shirt underneath a crumpled grayish suit jacket. Her eyes flashed, her lips rubbed against the lipstick, her solid-looking bust stuck out. "I've never been so insulted by a stranger in my life, Mr. Denning. But I do have one question. Why on earth would you badger me with such silly questions and comments— I'm twenty-five years old, have traveled the world and consider myself fairly well educated, socialized and civilized. And you, probably with hardly a grade school background, uncouth manners and a very cutting, judgmental manner—why would you say these things to me and lose a potential client... completely out of keeping with Mr. Lorena's—" She stopped, slapped her hand to her mouth. Yep, she'd said too much. That slip of the tongue had cost her the whole ball game.

"Well...it seems you answered your own questions, whoever you are. You alien things who try to impersonate humans have it all wrong. You need a lot of practice, lady-thing—or whatever you might call yourself. Ha! Ice-cold hands and bright red high heels—a dead giveaway, Miss Mapleton. And your language syntax isn't quite down yet. A few hundred years and you might get it. I could feel it in my gut when you came in the room, real human women don't quite behave like you just did. I ought to give you some lessons."

Her eyes were misting at not only having been discovered, I thought, but being humiliated by a mere human. "You'd do that for me? I mean, teach me directly—as one human to a not quite human presence?"

"Well, I don't run a school for alien education here, you know...but if I had the time—and since you guys are here in full force anyway, salt and peppered throughout our world societies—I thought I'd bone you up a bit, you know, catch you up to snuff."

I handed her a tissue from my desk and she wiped her eyes. "Thank you. I'm sorry...I—I didn't mean to be rude to you, either. But you have to admit you are a bit hard on your new clients—"

"—I don't remember accepting you as a new client. Even rough guys like me that come out shooting first, have to have protocols to go by. Example... how dangerous is this possible case to my well-being?"

She reached into her purse and took out a long, slim dark cigarette. I lit it for her. She coughed. "I'm—I'm not used to your tobacco products—or alcohol. It disturbs the chemical balances that are still transforming in my body."

I looked her over. "Well, I must say it's a hell of a body, Miss Mapleton. Whoever put you together had some great concepts."

"Thank you, Mr. Denning. I think I perceive a slightly softer side to you, after all."

"Just a ruse, lady. I don't quite trust aliens yet. At least not the violent kind who are big on violence and short on conscience—not even if they're the Joe Lorena type. Do you know what I mean? I get the feeling your kind must think we humans are pushovers, pre-conditioned to dwell in a limited mental cubicle the size of my fountain pen. Well, guess what? Some of us can think standing up, feel with intuition the rotten breaks beings like you are bringing to our population, all in the name of do-gooders—'Yeah, let's help the poor dumb bastards out, feed their faces, wipe their butts but most of all, learn their ways so one day we can take over'. Isn't that sort of how it goes, Miss Mapleton?" I had worn myself out already and I'd only just started! I left her standing there and went back to my desk, opened the upper right-hand drawer, got out a bottle of gin and poured myself a tall one. I looked up and she was still there, just staring at me, in retro-shock. "Would you like a drink Miss Mapleton—I mean, before you leave?"

"No thank you, Mr. Denning. I told you, we can't drink your—your alcoholic beverages. It makes us deathly ill. I'm surprised it doesn't destroy you—with the quantities you must consume—"

"—maybe we all destroy ourselves in different ways, lady. Can you stand there and say you have the perfect life with the perfect positive attitude without ever wanting to commit suicide because one day your brain suddenly starts malfunctioning and life adds up to a pile of crap?"

She surprised me, walked back toward my desk, and stood opposite me, checking out my eyes. "You are truthful. I like that. Maybe I should hire you, after all. To answer your question, no, I have never felt what you describe. When we are shape-altered into human form, we are given serums on a regular basis to keep us subdued and—and..."

"—compliant—I think that's the word you're searching for in that little alien dictionary you keep in that pretty little head of yours." I took a deep breath. "So why did Joe Lorena send you?"

"He didn't send me. Rather he recommended you as someone who might help me find *Goldilocks*."

"Who?" I asked with an incredulous smile on my mug.

"Goldilocks—a sister alien also in attractive human form."

"Oh, why didn't you say so?" I said sarcastically. "I deal in lost sisters with the name of Goldilocks every day or so." I took out a Lucky Strike and lit it. Then I sucked in a big drag, let it out slowly and sat down in my comfy desk chair. "Maybe we should start all over, Miss Mapleton. Won't you sit down?"

She did so. "Thank you. I really wanted to leave, but something told me I shouldn't."

"It's called *intuition* here on earth—what's it called where you come from?"

134

"Oh, I'm really from *here*, Mr. Denning. I was what you might say a test tube embryo. My male parent was a *Sens Parafactor*—like Mr. Lorena—and my mother a movie actress—all human."

Now I was putting it together. Lorena and his species were still working with the hybrid breeding process—the one that early on cost the life of his beloved Honey Combes' biological mother. Joe Lorena had told me they'd perfected things in the ensuing years and since Honey was half and half, she was also one of those lovely creatures born sterile. She was actually thinking of trying to have our baby with her father's alien expertise down in some secret lab somewhere. Only Honey got killed near the apex of her comet-like career by a savage lunatic, a guy by the name of Frank Laggore. Now the rest was history. But the past seemed to be coming back to haunt me as I sat across from the gorgeous auburn-haired beauty. "So you guys are still integrating with *homo sapiens erectus*, eh?"

"Homo erectus—who?" she asked innocently. "Isn't that part of the male sexual organ mechanism, I mean, a process when—when it fills with blood and swells, allowing—"

"—yeah...that's erection...but, well, we're not talking about that, Miss Mapleton. *Erectus* in this case refers to the evolving species that finally were able to stand up—erect, if you get my drift."

"Oh, I understand now. I am scientifically trained, synthesized molecular components—but I am not very socially skilled—despite what I said about traveling the world." She looked down at the floor. "That wasn't entirely accurate. Most of the traveling added up to little more than transferring to underground laboratories in other countries."

"I still think you're a mighty attractive woman, at least in appearance, no matter who else you might be under that delectable skin of yours."

She smiled as if she'd heard it for the first time. "Do you really feel I'm attractive as a human female? Thank you, Mr. Denning. Mr. Lorena has told me I remind him of someone beautiful he once knew, but most of my own kind look at me in disgust and see me as a misfit—not really belonging to either species completely."

"Well, believe me, lady, I think you fit just fine and in all the right places—and bet you'd be a hot number under the sheets."

She wrinkled her brow, seemingly confused. "Under the sheets? I'm—I'm not sure what you saying..."

"Eh....skip it...just a rather crude way of saying you'd be pretty wonderful to make love to—with that soft skin and pretty smile of yours, not to mention some of the unmentionables, like lovely, warm breasts—"

She started unbuttoning her blouse. "—would you like to see my breasts? To see if they are mentionable, I mean, worthy of what you say would be acceptable—"

"—no! Please, Miss Mapleton. I'm—I'm afraid it would distract us from the task at hand. But thank you anyhow." Phew! I was beginning to feel my masculine temperature rise and I knew I had to get off the subject pronto. "So where do you currently work, if I may ask."

She buttoned her blouse back up. "In an underground laboratory..."

"I see. Seems like a lot of things go on...*underground*. So why doesn't a dish like you have a million guys pant-

136

ing for you at the door? If I were an available guy, I'd be doing my best to get your clothes off and invite you to hop in the sack."

Again she looked puzzled. "Hop in the sack?"

"Yeah—look—I'm sorry. I'm not being very professional here. I think we should, uh, get back to business." I ground out my cigarette in my overflowing ashtray and sat with my hands folded, looking at the strikingly good-looking young woman. "So, tell me. What's your story, Miss Mapleton? Everyone has a story, you know. That's part of what I do. Listen to stories and get paid to tell entertaining yarns about the perversity of the universe—not just earth people anymore—but all of us, spread like peanut butter and jelly all over the bread of the cosmos."

"Each race of beings has its peculiarities, I suppose. But I think there are some essentially parallel qualities all creatures share, no matter where they come from."

"Your story, if you please, Miss Mapleton? I'm not an all-day lunch counter and I have a lady coming with a whole bunch of houseplants in a little while. I have to figure out where in the hell to put them."

"I like the way you talk, Mr. Denning. We could eschew the formality. Will you call me Sarah? I look at you and see someone who only *seems* not to care... but *is* caring. Is this not so?"

"Just your story...please, if you don't mind....you can call me Cable if you like—just not on Wednesdays."

"But *today* is Wednesday."

"There you have it, Sarah. Today it's Mr. Denning."

She tittered lightly. "Yes, okay...I apologize. Now, what I came to you about—*Frieda Goldilocks*. The *Three*

Terrible Bears have taken her on their picnic—and I'm very frightened."

Now I was beginning to think this dame had a major screw loose. "I have a feeling we aren't talking about the same 1800's British fairy tale we non-aliens grew up with."

"Well, partially, Cable—uh, Mr. Denning. The fairy tales are universal and thus serve as codes to describe both entities and events. For example, a *picnic* is where something is devoured—and my poor Goldilocks will be destroyed unless we can get to her first."

"Whoa, wait a minute here, Nellie. What do you mean *we*? I hope you don't expect for a minute that I'd endanger both myself *and* my client...on some terrible, 'devouring' picnic, trying to save the life of one of your alien companions, do you? So let me get this straight. Goldilocks is a code name for an alien sister—real sister or the other kind?"

"She is my own blood. My father and mother had just the two of us. I am eldest. Her birth name is also Judeo-Christian. Rebecca."

"Now I am aware of the original story, that before a pretty little thing named Goldilocks came into being, young comely babe and all—there was an old witch or crone as the invading visitor—and the three bears were indeed pretty mean dudes, none of the pap served up to children later, as Mama, Papa and Baby Bear whose porridge had been sampled—or devoured, such as in your case. How am I doing so far?"

She smiled at me and unconsciously grabbed my hand across the desk. "Yes Mr. Denning! You're so perceptive." She quickly withdrew her hand. "Oh, excuse me. Americans would say I got—got—got—"

"—you got carried away, Sarah. But why did your parents give you Judeo-Christian names? Seems to me they'd be more like *Quarka & Masissia* or something."

"The vibration of the name, its roots and history also help define the pathway of the intelligent being, sensitive enough to tune into the destiny impulse behind the name."

I marveled at my luck in this world. Why did all the whacko jobs come to me for help? "Now it's getting pretty deep in here, kid. If I hear you right, the destiny is in the name...so if that logic follows, the three big bad bears are some pretty rough players in this story, huh?"

"It's a lot more than that." She leaned on my desk and lowered her voice. "Sarah...my namesake, was Abraham's half-sister, dangerously beautiful. When Abraham married his half-sister, he had to protect her constantly from other men. But it was not always possible. One day Abraham and Sarah were traveling in a caravan, with Sarah safely hidden inside of a jeweled chest. At the Egyptian border, the caravan was stopped by three foreboding men, as large as bears, who demanded that Abraham open the chest, thus revealing the radiant and lovely young Sarah. The evil bears lusted for Sarah, vied for her favor by wagering large amounts of money to have her for their own. But a light from the heavens struck them down and the caravan proceeded to Egypt. But the devil upon hearing of the event, vowed to avenge his cruel and lustful minions. At a very late age, perhaps in her eighties, Sarah conceived Isaac, a child who would be sacrificed to avenge the

139

thwarted evil doers. Sarah lived to be 127 years old, and it is said her beauty shone brightly until the day she perished from the earth."

I was a sucker for a good story and Sarah's was as good as any I'd heard in quite a while. "So...now we've got the three bears *reincarnated* in the here and now, but they're not going for you—but rather Rebecca? Something doesn't make sense here...care to explain?"

She leaned back and took a deep breath, a youthful excitement upon her face. "The name Rebecca means to *tie or bind* and Rebecca was born very psychic, like a clairvoyant or prophetess. But that is a difficult role, for a prophet is never at peace, but riles herself as well as the populace into often disturbing action. At fourteen, Rebecca was married to Isaac and later sacrificed him when a cloud hovered over her tent and said she must be free. But it was difficult for her, because she was expecting twins when the vision above her tent appeared. During a very hard child birthing, a dark and mysterious man came to her, calling himself *Midrash*. This creature said he was the *devil* and was giving the new-born twins, Sarah and Rebecca, to his dark angel brother, *Gor*. These were the twins the young mother gave birth to, although during their mortal existence, they went under other names in order to escape capture by Midrash".

"Did ol' Midrash ever catch up with the girls?"

"No, they were able to escape by shape-changing into twin brothers. And history only records that Rebecca gave birth to Jacob and Esau. Over many millennia, the twins reincarnated several times. But when my sister and I were given the original names of Sarah and Rebecca, Midrash discovered us and has pursued us ever since. Now, he's so very close...I can feel it...." She said that trembling a little.

It was so hard to tell in this frickin' universe who was on the level and who wasn't. "So, if the devil...in the form of Midrash...failed, what happened next?"

"Before Rebecca died at the age of 120, Satan promised to give Gor Rebecca *and* her twin sister in a subsequent life." She stopped and looked intensely into my eyes. "That life...is *now*, Mr. Denning."

"And the three bears are the hired henchmen to get you and your sister to this *Gor* character?"

"Yes." She paused. "Do you have a restroom?"

"Well, it's in pretty bad shape, but you're welcome to use it—through that door, past my lumpy unmade bed—and there it is."

She excused herself. Suddenly it was very quiet in the room, but in my head I could hear the music coming out of the *Bella Notte* and Honey was singing '*What'll I Do?*' and my head was clanging out that certain insanity when a man who is perfectly happy finds himself attracted to another babe. Honey's song was right on: what'll I do with this dish? What'll I do when she walks out of my office and I'm once again alone with just my thoughts? And maybe like the words to the song, when I'm alone with those dreams of you that won't come true—what'll I do? Ha! Do a Cable Denning deep breath and put one foot in front of the other and keep walking straight ahead. No detours. Yeah...well...I knew when the babe walked back out of the powder room I'd be willing to go to bat for her and her sister. That was the way I was made.

141

Sarah Mapleton came back into the office and sat once more. "I felt a bit hot. Is it warm in here—or is it me?"

I looked at her. "Alien hot flashes," I laughed. "You know, you gotta watch that. It'll make you old before your time." I glanced at her. Something had changed. Then I noticed she had taken off her brassiere while she was in the bathroom and her nipples were now protruding through that thin dark blouse of hers. "Getting back to your Biblical riddle—first...supposing I do work for you—do you have any money or do I work for trade? And second....do you know where to begin—in other words, what clues do we have to go on?"

She giggled. "Trade? I assume that is selling myself physically in some manner to pay for your services?"

I laughed back at her. "Yeah, something like that. But really, truth be told, Sarah, I really don't do business like that. So put your mind at ease and let's examine that other avenue, the one that's got the green stuff wallets are so hopeful to contain."

"Yes...even though I might tell you...your first suggestion wasn't without merit...Mr. Denning...but I would be a failure, even at that, I'm afraid."

"Why is that so, if I may be so bold as to ask?"

"I'm *untried*, inexperienced in the ways of human women—I mean sexually. I'm sure a man like you requires seasoned women with lots of passionate assets to keep you satisfied and entertained, pardon my boldness..." She looked at me with those warm, hazel eyes. "But again, I may be wrong. I have no idea what human male desires are all about. All I ever get when I'm out of the underground like today, are—are stares, whistles—

some rude man even pinched my behind and had the nerve to tip his hat and excuse himself! But few men ever speak to me, like I'm unapproachable or something."

"Ah, yeah, it's that vibration you were talking about. You exude the inaccessible goddess, the kind of woman a man dreams about but wouldn't know what to do with if he had her standing naked right next to him. It's the formed ideal in the sexual head of man—and although his natural commandment is to breed with every woman who will spread her legs for him—he's suddenly thrown onto the altar of helplessness and sacrifice when the goddess enters the scene. You see, she isn't supposed to be just screwed and left—no, she's designed to represent the unattainable, the ideal to which men would aspire to find spiritual oneness, mating, bonding, happiness in the heavens of bliss beyond the mere he and she world—that place where lovers go when two are not only as one, but *equal*...where the divine feminine is counter-balanced with the power of the positive masculine. Both need each other, but must not fall helplessly into the pit of delusion that someone else is needed to make you complete or bring you to Nirvana when the role is called up Yonder. Intimacy is a boundless sharing, a kind of 'let's do this thing together and neither of us rule over the other, but couch ourselves in the nest of the perfect moment, where bliss and sensation explode into a new fireworks neither have ever experienced before.' "

A new look came over the face of Sarah Mapleton. She licked her moist lips and I could tell she had been moved by my rant. "Would *you* know what to do if a goddess stood before you?" she purred in a very warm, sexy voice. "As I said earlier, you have a way with your voice, Mr. Denning, that makes a girl, uh...feel things..."

"I don't know. I'm not a prophet. I'm just a guy with a big mouth and maybe sometimes a lot to say. You be the judge of that. But I can see where this is going, Sarah, and I can tell you right now, it ain't professional, nor is it the way I prefer to carry on with a beautiful potential client who happens to enjoy my speech patterns."

"Where is it going, in your opinion," she said, again her voice slow and low.

"Right into my bedroom if we keep this up."

"Is that so bad? And, oh, by the way...I've got lots of money...we print your United States money in a special underground depot in another state. So, I always have lots of one hundred dollar bills."

"I think we need to call it a day, Sarah. After all, I am human and there's another thing I need you to know. There's a cottage a few blocks over...in that cottage is a beautiful Latina woman whom I happen to adore. I don't want to trade her off, if you know what I mean."

"I think that's admirable, Mr. Denning. Loyalty or fidelity of that nature is rather rare, I would imagine. Especially if you *love* her, as it sounds you do. So, even if I were interested, I guess I came too late. I would dearly love to find someone like you one day. " She smiled and looked out of the window. " To be initiated into physical, emotional, sexual love by someone like you...yes, that would be like sunlight...pouring into your heart and body at the same time, wouldn't it?"

"Yeah, that's kinda how it feels, Sarah. I wish for you to find someone like that, too. This time we've had together today has been—well, it's been rewarding...and educational."

"Educational? You mean I didn't attract you beyond *educational?*"

"Well, I didn't mean it like that. Of course you did. I told you earlier, if things were different, I'd be crawling up between your legs and licking every square inch of you on the way up—hell, you're a rare babe—and they don't come along every day, you know. Sometimes I—"

She was breathing hard and holding her chest. "—please don't speak like that! It—it makes it worse for the person at the other end, the one who doesn't have someone to go home to. Do you know what that's like? Day in and day out watching your young years dissipate behind a test tube or microscope?"

"Yeah, I think I know what it's like to be lonely, un-fulfilled. You know what I did for years?"

"What?"

I closed my eyes so I could paint a picture for this lovely young thing sitting opposite me. "I walk the streets late at night until my body can feel the effects of the day wear off, and the cool air of the sea reaches enough inland that I can feel it on my face. Then I walk down into a noisy, half-lit dive where happy people are drinking, smoking, talking at each other there, standing in the sawdust...and the smells fill your nostrils. But then...then the real thing you came for opens up like a flower taking you away to a different dimension—the *music* comes pouring into you like refreshing drops of fresh rain and grabs you by the heart and tears you apart until your tears turn to joy and laughter and the hot whiskeys have made your head spin as you look up

145

at some cute dish singing her little heart out up there on the stage in the dirty spotlight with a fine band behind her. That's when I go away, Sarah, that's when I fill myself up, stretch my arms to a new place I've never gone before as people hold each other dancing and applause fills the room when the babe in the red sequin dress has finished her best song for the night."

Sarah Mapleton was crying, real tears ran down her face as I handed her a tissue. "Will—will you take me...some night when you go, Cable—uh, Mr. Denning?"

"Cable's okay now, lady." I chuckled, "I think Wednesday's about half over anyway."

Her voice was soft as she wiped her tears. "Okay, Cable. You know, it's so strange, but I was thinking as you were speaking that I didn't come here today just to hire a private detective. I came here to get discovered by someone. You...you...discovered me today, Cable Denning. So...will you take me one night to your favorite cabaret?"

"Yeah, Sarah Mapleton, I will. You know why?"

"Why?"

"Because you'll appreciate it, you *will* be discovered—but you got it wrong—not by me, but by *you*. Music is a magical road to self-discovery. When you let it take you over, it guides you to those special places you haven't triggered inside yourself yet. And when it happens—bingo! you're a new you! Trust me on this one, my little alien friend."

She seemed pleased. "Oh, am I your friend, Cable? Doesn't it usually take a lot longer for friendship?"

"Maybe not always, Sarah. Sometimes, it seems like there are people just born knowing each other. You

146

seemed strange when you came in this afternoon. But that was because I sensed you weren't like me, you were a different being trapped in a body that looks like my kind. But like you said, down deep we all share the same basic things in the universe—smiles, talk, beauty, art, music—love…"

"Can you love me, Cable?" she asked and almost bowled me over.

"Can you love *me?*" I said, reversing the equation.

"I already do. Love is something new to me. I mean, yes, I love my mother and father, some relatives, some associates, my dearest and loving sister, Rebecca. But if you're a woman and suddenly you love a man, it's really, really different."

"Thanks for that, lady." I glanced at her. I could see a beautiful young girl in the beginning bloom of her womanhood. I could also tell she was falling in love. I pitied her for that, for I knew with a guy like me, at best it'd be a day at the carnival, lots of excitement with laughter and cotton candy at the beach—and at night when the Ferris wheel spun us high above the lights of the crowded midway, and she would bring her lips to mine and we would kiss in the dark—her whole world would come alive for a moment or two. Then it would all go away, and in the morning when I watched her put her clothes back on, I would know the rest of the story…and things would end, not as they began, but as a sad whimper of love's agony, like the song of that lonely sax that kept drifting through my head, a haunting refrain, a naked melody hung on beauty and hope. But that was the way of love between man and woman, a short love song sung at last in the recesses of a broken heart. And maybe someday when the healing was complete, love would knock again at her door, and this time she'd know...

"So...shall you take my case, Cable?" she said, bringing me back to the moment. "I can't imagine trusting anyone else to find Rebecca and bring her back to us."

"I'll have to know a lot more, kid. But for now, let's say we've got a deal—when can we meet again?"

"How about tomorrow? I've got a few days off. How about noon?"

"Yeah, sure. Then we've got to roll up our sleeves and catch the devil in his lair, okay?"

She smiled as she stood up. I walked her to the door and opened it for her. She reached into her purse and took out five crisp one hundred dollar bills. "Yes...I'd like that...will this do to start the wheels turning?"

I looked at the dough as she handed it to me. "Oh, yeah, and then some, young lady. By the way, how old are you?"

"Your years or mine?"

"Take your pick."

"It sounds better in your years. I'll be twenty-three earth years next July." Then she glanced at the money in my hand. "Perhaps you can spend some of that illegal tender taking me out to show me one of those magic nights you were talking about—the one with all the music and atmosphere? Would you dance with me? I've never danced...I've watched others...but I think I would like it very much. I'm sorry, I've lived such a limited life compared to you, it seems—"

"—forget it, Sarah. Just live today. We'll let tomorrow take care of itself, okay?"

Surprising me, she tiptoed up and kissed me gently on the lips. It felt cool but sincere. "Thank you, Cable Denning. I'm very happy...to have met you. Tomorrow, then?" With that she left and I turned around and went to my desk. I got out that bottle of gin, poured myself another tall one, lit up a cigarette and sat back, marveling at how quick life changes, like a kaleidoscope of colors, filtering through my life. I took a big breath, looked at my watch and realized in just half an hour a highly energetic Zelda would be popping through my office door.

Sure enough, at 3:12 p.m. Zelda Blodgett walked in. But I hardly recognized her. She had lost at least fifteen pounds, no longer wore glasses and walked with a poise I did not recall! "Cable! It's so good to see you!" She ran to me and we embraced.

"Damn, kid, you look great! Maybe it's my imagination, but do you look younger than the last time I saw you?"

"It's been at least a year or so, Cable. When I decided to get involved with Clark, I thought I'd have to compete with the other girls in the office—and I won him—even if he did turn out to be queer!"

I laughed. "Well, good things sometimes come in surprise packages and his presence in your life made you improve yourself. Now, you're loaded for bear and ready for the next young bloke to walk in the door and romance you."

She let go of my arm and walked away. "I wish it were you doing the romancing. You're the only man I feel good with, I mean, who I know is a real *man* and likes girls the way guys are supposed to like girls."

"That's the luck of the chips, I guess, Zelda. But damn, I sure don't want to lose you as a friend. After all, we go back a ways now."

She examined the room. "You live here, don't you?"

"Yeah, sometimes. But Adora and I have a cute little cottage a few blocks away. I'm there more than here these days."

"Oh," she said, her voice a little pre-occupied. "So...where do you want the plants?"

"Crap, Zelda, I don't know a lily from lavender—why don't you pick three or four places in the office here and put whatever you want wherever you want."

She glanced in the bedroom. "How about a floor plant over by the window in your bedroom. I think it'd jolly it up a bit."

"Sure, why not? Do you still plan on watering them? I probably can get to it once a week if I'm here, but sometimes when I'm on a case, I'm gone for days at a time—can't guarantee your lovelies will be taken care of."

"How do I get in?"

"When I'm not going to be around for a while, I'll leave a key under the rubber mat out in the hall."

"Aren't you afraid someone might take it, break in and steal your valuables?"

I snickered. "Look around, Zelda. Do you see anything worth stealing? Almost everything in here I got from junk stores in the first place. Except my box radio."

She came over to me and smiled into my eyes. "You know, Cable, I think I've always loved you for one main

150

reason. And it wasn't the reason Honey loved you for, I'm sure. I fell for you because the little boy in you is so cute and honest. You're not afraid to show the world you're not rich with money, but rich in character and spirit. No matter who we are or what we become together, that's what I'll always like about you."

I was humbled by this zesty little lady. She told it like it was from the hip, from that place in her own honesty, the one that tells you life isn't fair, but sometimes we're lucky to meet someone along the way who's essentially good and fun to be with. "Well, thanks for that, Zelda. I'm truly touched. I'm also sure you can recognize that in me because you're kind of in the same boat."

"Not really...my family is pretty well to do. I live simply, that's all. I don't have a lot of needs. The only thing I really think about beside my job at the lab, is that I don't want to be lonely anymore. I don't want to wake up in an empty bed in the morning and pretend to reach for someone who's not there." She raised her voice and walked closer to me. "I want to live out a full life, Cable, have a baby or two and take walks with my husband on the beach on Saturday mornings."

"Don't look at me like that, Zelda," I kidded her. "I've seen that look on your face before. You're still wondering if Cable Denning is healed up enough after a year or so—and just because he's got a dame in his life he happens to be in love with—is there room for me in there somewhere, by virtue of some miracle?"

She looked down at the floor, scuttling her shoes. "Yeah, something like that, I guess... So help me with the plants, Mister Detective, will you?"

We went down to her nice new "Woody" Model A Ford wagon and hauled up the green things my little friend wanted to aerate my office with. When we were finished, I offered to buy her a coke somewhere at a soda fountain, but she declined. "Well, how about a rain check, then?"

"You see...my trouble is, Cable, I fantasize too much. I build things up in my imagination, hoping against hope that by wishing, at least part of them will come true. But they never do. Do you know what it's like to come home after work, sit and have a drink alone while you're listening to the radio about someone else's love affair? I'm twenty-four now and they say a woman is old at thirty these days. I have an aunt who's a schoolteacher spinster. I know she's shoved all her happiness down deep inside her because Mr. Right never came by. And right now, I'm following in her footsteps. Sure, I'm more attractive than before and I've worked hard to keep myself looking good and in shape. But what good does it do when nobody notices? I'm okay looking, but there are so many other young women who are—are beautiful compared to Plain Jane me."

I listened intently to Zelda's plight. I was sure thousands of young gals felt the same, sandwiched in between that twilight zone of almost a contender, but not quite. If men looked for integrity, intelligence, education and basic goodness, Zelda would win hands down. But they don't. Instead, most guys check out looks, tits and pussy first and last. "I don't know the answer to that, Zelda," I said. "Beauty is in the eye of the beholder. Some young guy is bound to see you...I mean, really see *you* sooner or later, kid. Don't give up."

152

"Why can't it be you, Cable?"

"Even if we dared to go in that direction, Zelda, at best it'd be a passionate love affair—the kind you hear in the radio heart-throb songs—and when it was over, you'd have none of the things you just mentioned you longed for. Stay my friend, believe me, you're a lot safer—and happier in the long run. You can't risk losing yourself to some guy who drinks too much, smokes excessively, still chases skirts in his head—and happens to be with a knock-out babe who he goes home to at night. They aren't your kind of odds, Zelda."

"No, I guess not..." she said, her eyes a little misty. Then she brightened up. "I will be your friend—just because there's only one Cable—and I never want to lose him."

We hugged good-bye and I thanked her for the plants. I closed the door behind me and took a big breath. This had been a weird day, any way you sliced it! Maybe tomorrow would be a little less hectic. But I doubted it. With one Sarah Mapleton, her missing sister "Goldilocks," better known as Rebecca Mapleton, and some vague but looming characters called The Three Bears---obviously bent on a voracious evil thing called a 'picnic,' I had this nervous feeling tomorrow promised to be a corker!

Saturnalia and The Purple Mists

That night I decided to be with Adora. Even though she'd told me she had been feeling bad, I chose to be at her side and to comfort her. When I got into bed with her that night, her beautiful but now pale face greeted me with incredible love. I held her without a word through the night. The next morning I asked her to dress because I was going to take her to a doctor's office. An ex-client's father was the son of a man who once said if I ever needed a specialist, I should call on him. I had no clue as to what he was a specialist of, but I called ahead and got Adora in early that morning. She had cramped a good portion of the night and told me she was still bleeding profusely.

"*Mi amor, muchas gracias* for being with me last night. I know I am no fun for you *este momento*—but I get well soon. *Promesa!*"

As I smoked out in the hall outside the doctor's office, I thought all kinds of things, not the least of which was my lover's health and well-being. What an irony! Here we were, the two happiest people I knew for the past year—and now this strange malady that seemed to be increasing in intensity. When the doc came out after giving Adora a series of in-office tests, he looked grave and took me aside as my Latin beauty dressed. "Your wife is quite ill, Mr. Denning. It appears her loss of blood is symptomatic of some deeper disease. Unfortunately, I must submit the blood samples I've taken to a laboratory and it will be a few days before we know what's what. But I've given her an iron tonic to build her blood back up a bit. Give her as much lean meat as she can handle. Also, she must rest and have no stress. Be with her as much as you are able, but of course she will not be able to participate in any marital intimacies at this time. Be patient. I will call you. Do you have an office number I can reach you at so we may speak confidentially?"

"Yeah, doc." I scribbled down my office number just as Adora came into the waiting room. She looked drawn. "Hey, babe, we're gonna build you back up with iron, steak and a lot of me!" I said.

"*Me sorprende, señor*—but it makes me happy..." She looked sadly at the doctor, as if the two of them knew something I didn't. "*Gracias, médico* Gilbert..."

I got her home just in time for me to leave to the office to meet up with the unique Sarah Mapleton at noon. "Now, are you sure you're okay until I get back?"

She looked up at me with those soulful dark eyes of hers as I lay her head down on the pillow of our bed. "*Sí, mi querido. También, ten cuidado en este día*, my love. Come home to me. You hold me last night and I sleep better. *Ah, dormir...sí, dormir...te amo, my Cable*..." Soon she closed her eyes and I got to the phone immediately and called her mother. I told Elisa the truth and asked if she would please watch over Adora during my work absences. She happily agreed and that made me feel a lot better.

Just as I got into the office, the phone rang. "Yeah, Cable Denning here..."

"Cable—Cable...this is Sarah Mapleton. I'm sorry to call you so late, but something terrible has happened. Can you meet me downtown at the Bard's Eighth-street Theatre? You know where it is?"

"Yeah, what's up, Sarah?"

"I can't tell you over the phone—please know it's important—and come just as soon as you can!"

I hung up, dashed out of my office and took a street-car to Broadway and Seventh. I walked from there to

Eighth. It was one of those huge show houses planted in the Merrick Building, a department store popular in the 1920's. There was talk that it will be renamed the *Olympic Theatre* in honor of the coming 1932 Los Angeles Olympic Games. The box office had just opened and I noticed the marquee as I approached the Merrick Building's Eighth-street entrance. The movie house was showing a William Powell and Jean Arthur film called *Street of Chance*. I kind of felt like every street from now on would hold a dark secret and plunge me into something that no sane man would take a chance on. But it was the stuff that made the blood rush through my veins.

I inquired at the box office for Sarah Mapleton. The lady seemed stumped and directed me to the manager's office just inside the theatre. I guess she knew I wasn't going to sneak in for a free ticket. I started for the manager's office when Sarah spotted me and took my hand and we all but ran downstairs, onto a landing, past the restrooms and to an elevator that stood at the far end of that corridor. "I sure hope this is worth missing lunch for," I quipped. "Or better than the movie upstairs."

She squeezed my hand. "I'm just glad you're here, Cable Denning." She seemed nervous. I had no idea this elevator descended twelve floors beneath the theatre! We got out at Floor-12 and the minute I stepped onto the concrete something hit me hard and I went out like a light.

When I came to, it was as if The Three Bears had been playing hardball in my head. A greenish glow emanated all around my blurry vision and I was being dragged feet-first down a long corridor into a strange golden contraption, shaped like an egg but with doors that parted from the middle out. Vaguely I recall it being another elevator that seemed to go even further down, only real fast, and my stomach began heaving Mozart's *Requiem* as we rushed toward what I thought must be the center of the earth. I tilted my head around looking for Sarah Mapleton. But it was just me and the lousy Three Bears. It occurred to me in a silly sort of way that I might vomit on them and by the time they cleaned the barf off their hoodlum clothing, I'd be gone. But who was I kidding? I was too damn hazy to even sit up! By the time we got to the bottom of wherever we were going, I was shaking and probably as white as a ghost. I felt like warmed over shit and my head was throbbing the main drumbeat to *Stars and Stripes Forever*. As soon as we landed, a rather serious appearing nurse shot me in the arm with a needle big enough to be used as a straw in a soda at Squibb's Drug store. I hurt like hell, but soon I was smiling as the stuff took effect and again I lost consciousness.

I thought I had either died or been transformed into something or someone else. I felt good as I awakened to a cozy little cottage with only a glowing fire in the hearth. I could think straight, my breathing was clear and my head didn't hurt. I sat up. It felt great. Then a soft, feminine voice gently called out to me. "There is a magic to fire light...in this cottage in the hills by the sea, time loses its meaning...the fire light holds you in its presence...all unpleasant things are suspended, and you can be anything, do anything, go anywhere the heart desires—with whomever you desire...you are at last...free...but when the first lamp is lit, time resumes and you are caught once again in the helpless, mortal state of meaningless nothingness...*for the passions that thrill love, and lift you high to heaven, are the passions that kill love, and let you fall to hell...*" Then she scooted on her knees closer to me. Her red-amber eyes glowed like coals from the fireplace. "For an earthman you are fair, primitive, rough—but possess the heart and spirit of *Those Who Remember*. Welcome...I am Rhea, also known as *Saturnalia*." She was a tall babe with electrifying red hair that ran to the bottom of her spine and glowed in the firelight. Her skin was exquisite and almost as white as chalk. Her body was equally endowed with marvelous curves and shapely breasts that stood out high and proud. Her toes and fingernails were a bright orange-red, more or less matching her shiny, long hair. She wore a diaphanous gown with lots of see-through places and a wonderful flower essence poured forth from her body, drifting into my olfactory senses and all but entrancing me.

"So...the first thing someone's supposed to ask is, where in the hell am I?" I said, realizing my voice was in fine fiddle.

"Does it really matter?" she murmured. "Mortals are always either leaving something or going to something else. What about here? Now?"

"I don't think we're made that way, Rhea or Saturnia—"

"—*Saturnalia*—please, at least pronounce my name right."

"Yeah, okay...so *where am I?*"

"In a beautiful little cottage by the sea—any sea—does it matter? You are with me, mistress of Cronus-Gor. He is also my husband, lover and I've born him seven children—all of whom he devoured."

I was thinking fast. I *must* be dreaming—yeah, that was it! That shot the nurse gave me when I fell out of the elevator. I couldn't act surprised, I had to go along with the dream—this drug-induced fantasy—until I could get out at the other end of it. "That—uh, that's a bit unusual, don't you think? Aren't you a little disturbed that your lover ate your kids?"

"*Karma*...just karma, nothing more. It is the *ravenous picnic* to which only the children are invited. Cronus-Gor isn't all dark and evil—just *mostly* dark and evil—and add to that...bad tempered. He fought with his son Zeus, for dominion of the earth—and lost. But I stayed with him. Every twenty-nine of your years I change my mind, but he always persuades me to stay. So I go into another phase of my self."

"I see," I said, thinking I must be sitting at the table of the Mad Hatter's tea party. "I'm but thirty years old—compared to you, I know so little—I need a little help now and then so I don't bump into the wall. So what am I doing here? I—I, uh, suppose I'm a prisoner of yours?"

"Thirty, thirty-thousand, three-hundred thirty thousand. What is the difference?—the *self of your self* is timeless. You're only a prisoner if you suppose it in your mind. What does your mind suppose? That's the most important."

I thought I'd better try to grab the upper edge of the conversation. "Ha! What does my mind, or my imagination suppose? Well, to tell you the truth, a cozy cottage with a nice, warm fire, a doll like you—you can guess what a man like me might be thinking."

"Oh, yes, you *desire me*, human male animal. I like that. You *can* have me—for a price. Isn't that how it always is? There's always a price to pay...isn't there?"

"Hmmm....let me guess. It's something I've seen, maybe touched, knew a little about—it was probably gold, fairly small, contained priceless knowledge and—"

"—oh! that almost gave me an orgasm! You are soooo perceptive, whatever your name is—do you have a name?"

"Doesn't everybody?"

"I guess I never thought of it concerning lesser beings. But I like your *sass*...stimulating—even if somewhat assuming."

"And I like your *ass*...so that makes us even, right?"

"Not quite. You see, sex is a *bonding, uniting pleasure* experience for me that quite exceeds your low and base standards of momentary ejaculatory release. I pity human females. They have barely begun and you selfish, petulant males are already finished, thinking about the next mammoth hunt with your crude jokes and spears."

I was having fun in this dream. "I wouldn't put it exactly like that, lady. You see, primitive *is* basic, instinctive, solely for the procreation of the species. Only more advanced folks get the drift of sensual pleasure as an ongoing recreation. And you know, even then it can get boring."

"Aren't you bright and revealing, whatever your name—"

"—Cable—just call me Cable. Since you don't have last names, neither do I in this little dream fantasy you're creating here for me."

"Oh, but this is no fantasy, Cable. For example, notice you have not seen Sarah or Rebecca, have you?"

"Well, I've never met Rebecca and I barely know her sister, Sarah—"

"—just as well, for she's in the mists already."

"In the mists?"

"Yes. Cronus-Gor insists on abundant spraying of the purple mists on a nightly basis. You see, the First Age of your planet was *gold*—and your species stole our phrase and called it *The Golden Age*. But, as I said, after I gave birth to Zeus and he defeated his father in vying for dominion over the earth, there appeared a legend that he and Zeus had been fallen angels in previous incarnations—and rather than father and son—became what you might call *Devil Brothers* together. But soon dissension caused a rift—you know, the usual rivalry between siblings, etcetera—very boring to me, actually." Then she looked at me in the flickering firelight. "May I kiss you now—to test your male prowess?"

I did a double take. "How in the hell can you want to kiss me in the middle of a really good story—that I happen to be enjoying?"

"Because I'm selfish that way. I am an impulsive goddess. Saturn is my home planet. I was born a Titan. Millions of years ago Cronus-Gor stole me from my native planet and mated with me. For the first several hundred thousand years I hated him, fought him, scratched him, bit him—and when he ate seven of my children so they wouldn't compete with him, I was beside myself with grief and anger. But then he made me a goddess—and eventually I forgave him. It's all *karma*, Cable, just fucking karma."

"You're a little rougher around the edges than I thought *yourself*, Rhea. So am I to meet your husband-lover or whatever he is?"

"To be sure. I'm the 'soften-him-up' crew. I'm supposed to lull you into thinking this is a dream, fantasy or whatever your little head is supposing at the moment. That way you won't go completely crazy when you learn the truth that you're not dreaming and that Cronus-Gor really does want something from you—which you have already most generously confessed you know quite a bit about. You see, when Zeus tired of ruling over the little earth people, he left this dimension. My Cronus-Gor at last got his wish and now rules over your pretty little blue planet with his obedient minions."

"So now we're getting down to it, aren't we? Now I get it—your Cronus-Gor is the real brains behind that *Oculus Pyramis Mandatum* so many humans have already died for, or been beaten into submission as victims of his selfish will and been tempted into material riches to the point of unstoppable greed, lust and power-mongering."

"Bravo! As your kind would say. Actually I have incarnated a few times. In the scope of *your* memory, I loved Verdi and Rossini—got a little soppy at Puccini—adored the crazy Beethoven, the struggling Schubert, the insane little genius child Mozart—and on and on. But your race went downhill musically from there. Except for some Chinese folk music, maybe."

"Hey, now you're trotting on sensitive soil, babe. I happen to be a fan of Gershwin, Berlin, Porter and a few other famous guys who made their own brand of great music in our little world down here—or *up* there or wherever in the hell we are."

"*Hell*...that's a good one, Cable...I think I'm going to like breathing you in during an evening of the purple mists."

"And there's another thing I'll defend on any planet or in any dimension, lady—you talk about atmosphere? Saturn here, Jupiter there, on Mars or the Moon, titans, gods or goddesses—heaven or hell, there's nothing like stepping down into a crowded nightclub late at night when the blue smoke fills the room, people are happy and drinking and talking to each other like life really matters—that something makes sense other than the day to day shit out there in the factories and sweat shops. Then a beautiful babe comes onto the stage in a red, knockout gown glittering with sequins and lets us have it with a song that makes us laugh or cry or clap or jump or shout or dance! That's freedom, Miss Saturn, that's a kind of happiness you purple people eaters can never compete with. You know why? Because long ago you concluded that coveted power was happiness, limited interaction born of revenge and hatred, power-mad demagogues and mistresses like you who have every name in the book except *love*. That's the one you forgot. And without that...you've got nothing on us humble, groveling humans...because every once in a while someone gets through the golden ring and experiences real love, the kind that doesn't tarnish in the halls of the gods, but stays clear and free and simple...that a touch...just one quiet touch...is the whole world..."

My hostess had tears in her eyes. "Now I *have* to breathe you in, Cable...I *have* to have you swirl 'round me in the purple mists until all that you ever were or will be...shall be part of me, too..."

"Good luck, Saturnalia. You'll also absorb the rotten part of me, the violent, negative cynic, the guy who smokes, drinks too much and chases skirts, and one who has enough balls to taunt the gods by striking out against the subjugation you and your kind have caused. You want to absorb that from your purple mists?"

"You never know..."

"Humans have it tough enough—they didn't need your other-worldly chaos, confusion and domination turning them into half-awake zombies battling over territory, a sexual pecking order and power for a place in the sun."

She smiled a wry smile at me. "By the gods, Cable, I love the way you talk. Will you be my pet muse? I could implore Cronus-Gor to spare you—after you've given him what he requires—and you and I could dwell in perpetual bliss."

"Naw...I wouldn't want you to put yourself *out* for little ol' me. Somehow I don't think I'm cut out to be one of your minions, lady......"

"—well, I could always put you *in*...I have this feeling you would be a fabulous lover, a wild, passionate animal, bent on conquering me."

"Dream on, doll—take me to your leader and let's get this shit over with. I've already missed my lunch and

I'm getting a bit ravenous. I don't suppose you have any of your kids hanging around I could eat?"

She laughed. "I sure like you, Cable. Are you positive you won't consider coming away with me after Cronus-Gor extracts what he wants from you?"

"Yeah, I'm not the 'kept' type. Besides, I suspect there won't be a hell of a lot of me left—depending on your boyfriend's methods of *'extraction'.*"

"So never say I didn't offer you perpetual life as a pleasure model for my court. Perpetual life is better than mortal life—but not as good as *immortal life.*"

"What's the difference? I can't imagine hanging around in bliss for the next million years or so screwing my brains out with ditsy dames like you. What's the point? Remember that mammoth hunt you were talking about? Well, men like me have to do that regularly as clockwork as their *in-breath* of life, then resting in the arms of a babe when he brings home the bacon, tusks and all. So, perpetual, immortal—what the crap difference does it really make—if you're happy and doing what you want to do in this or any other life?"

"There's a big difference. You see, perpetual life is *renewable*—you must be eligible to be renewed after so many thousands of your years—or be thrown by *Thantos* into Oblivion. Titans, such as I was, are renewable— but gods and goddesses are *immortal*—they can never die or perish or be thrown into Oblivion. We are the Privileged."

"Well, pardon my dust, oh holy one—and pardon me if I don't give a rat's ass about any of it. Let's just get on with it and introduce me to this piece of work you call Cronus-Gor. I'm glad you don't go around introducing

165

yourself as Mrs. Cronus-Gor. That definitely would *not* win you a popularity contest."

She chortled. "Oh, it pains me at the thought of ever giving you up! You're such a refreshing treat. I don't know how beings like you slip through the veil to become three-dimensional, let alone mortal. I'm positive you're from somewhere else. If I weren't the jealous type, I'd tempt you with *Persephone* or *Thea*, but they'd want to steal you away for themselves. You see my dilemma..."

"Oh, yeah, of course...so I'm asking you again—take me to meet that son-of-a-bitch who's fucked up my earth world."

"Oooo...aren't we so angry and judgmental? As I told you, Cronus-Gor is only *mostly* dark and evil—not all. He might even drink and laugh with you. Depends on the day. Or he may delight me and vaporize you instantly into the purple mists! Then...I'd...I'd have the memory of your essence with me—indefinitely!" She giggled and if I didn't know better I would've sworn she was demented. But somehow she wasn't. It was all just a way for her to amuse herself in a world beyond the perpetual, the world of the immortals, those who never run out of time because they don't *live* in Father Time's constraints. And for Rhea-*Saturnalia*, her uniqueness must have forced her to keep that part of her psyche creatively alive—or else she might truly go nuts.

"Well, if he vaporized me right up front, then he wouldn't get any of the good stuff—you know, the *Fen de Fuqin* stuff."

She went white. Her face grew taut. "What did you say?"

166

"I said the *Fen de Fuqin*," I said, checking out some trepidation in those red-amber eyes. "That...seems to bother you...doesn't it?"

"I know what it is, but I've never heard it called that before. You must have known one of the immortal sisters—those who guard over it. No one knows where what you speak of is kept. The immortal sisters are *Asian* on your plane of existence. They are a very old race. Did...did you come into contact with one of them?"

I knew she was pumping me for points with old Cronus-Gor, so I kept zipped up about anything having to do with *Lei-Tao* and in that moment realized what a risk she had taken whisking me off to the *Cave of the Seven Truths*. Not even *these* immortals knew where the original *God of Our Fathers* was! Although I still have to say the tantric sex was great and experiencing it with her burned into me a memory I will always cherish. In fact, just thinking about that crazy Chinese lotus dame made me a little homesick for those innocent, daredevil Cable Denning days back in '27 when a naïve cop still more or less believed that the police were supposed to be on the side of law and order—and the bad guys weren't. Well, it all got muddled up somehow.

I ignored her question. "How about letting me see your dearly beloved. I'd like to know what odds I'm up against here."

"See? I have never seen Cronus-Gor..."

I could've dropped my teeth. "Never seen him, yet you had seven children by him—what is he, a big drop of oozing pus or something?"

"*Eight* children. I sneaked a girl by him. " She walked away from me, then turned back to face me. "No...he's

167

just never—never been visible. Some gods stay form-less...a kind of nebulous energy presence."

"Saturnalia, you mean you're standing there telling me you've been with a man—uh—creature or whatever he is—and enjoyed his sexual favor, yet never seen him?"

"I'm afraid that's how it goes, Cable," she said, giving me a rather naughty smile. "There are so many, many dimensions compared to what you're used to in your little three-dimensional pretty blue planet."

"So how will I know where he—uh, is...when I'm talking to him? How do I know he won't wallop me when I can't see him?"

"You'll know...he's quite an excellent conversational-ist. He prefers those he has audience with to *imagine* what he looks like—and he often likes the varying de-scriptions. It entertains him." She approached me and put a soft, feminine hand on my shoulder, then squeezed it. "But I can see *you*, Cable, and I far prefer looking into my lover's eyes than closing my own and experiencing only the sensations."

She took my hand and we walked out of the cottage into a strange, dark land. The land was dusky and flat, the sky an unfocused steel gray, and there was no land-scape except pulsing, glowing little rocks on a trail we walked on. Soon we saw what seemed to be a huge white granite tower in the distance. "What's that?" I asked, marveling that the tower extended to what seemed like many hundreds of feet into the air.

"Even gods die, eventually, Cable. You see, that is the *Tower of Eternity.* Every ten thousand of your years, a little bird flies from a long distance away, and alights on top of the white tower. There he sharpens his beak with one stroke to the left, and one stroke to the right. Then he flies off again, to return in another ten thousand years. When the tower is completely worn away by the little bird sharpening his beak, then eternity will end— and all of us will die."

I tried to get my mind around what Rhea-Saturnalia was saying. No one could comprehend that, I thought. "Well, judging from the thickness and height of the tower," I joked, "that'd be quite a spell from now, I'd say."

"Yes..." she commented. We continued on our way. In the distance, there existed a place where some kind of sun or bright light penetrated an opening in the otherwise dull sky. It shone upon what appeared to be a marvelous golden castle of some kind. When we got closer, I couldn't believe how immense it was. I'd guess it was probably five football fields long and wide and grew to the sky with one stunning black tower that rose at least two or three hundred feet from the ground floor.

"Well, this sure beats your cabin," I crackled.

"Oh, I don't know. I love my little sanctuary." Then she stopped walking and turned to look at me. "Will you kiss me good-bye now?"

I was taken aback. "Good-bye...?"

"I'm not invited. Only you are." She came closer and put her arms around me. "Hmmm....oh, this feels so good...Cable...sometimes, just sometimes...I wish I were a mortal woman, able to feel all the terrible emotional risks mortal women must take with a man."

"Risks?"

"Yes, like the risk of loving...being so different and all. We all live in different worlds, you know. It just appears we come together in physical union. But you cannot feel my joy or pain—and I cannot feel yours. So the experience is exclusive to each of us. If you'll let me kiss you now, I will feel new things I've never felt before—but you'll not feel them—because your feelings are *your* feelings."

"I guess...uh... I guess it's okay—plant one on me..." I said.

Ever so tenderly, Saturnalia fit her lips onto mine. A shot of electric something went down to my toes and I could feel my face flush. "Whoa, lady, what brand are you carrying?" It felt damn good.

"Good-bye, Cable Denning...if I stay any longer, I shall wish to go with you, to the land of mortals—and careless, fatal love..."

Just then I heard a man's voice calling to me. "Sir, are you okay?" He was standing over me and I was in a small office with movie posters plastered all over the walls.

"Uh...yeah...where am I—and who are you?"

"I'm Bob Brown, the manager of the theatre here. The janitor found you at the end of the lower corridor beyond the restrooms."

Suddenly I realized I might have dreamed the whole thing! "Was there...uh, a girl with me—pretty young thing by the name of Sarah Mapleton, about five-four, hazel eyes—?"

"—we found *you* on the floor, detective, and no one else. I took the liberty of checking out your identity in your wallet. Mr. Denning, right?"

"Yep, that's me...but no girl, huh? And there's no elevator that goes down several floors beneath the one you found me on?"

"No sir. Was she in your company when you entered the lobby of the theatre? I saw no one. Do you wish me to call the police?"

"No, thanks...in a way I *am* the police in this case."

"Of course, I understand."

I thanked Mr. Brown and left the theatre, more perplexed than ever. Did I or did I not meet the comely little half-alien in that theatre—and did we not take an elevator ride deep down into the lower sanctums of the building? Was I pummeled by The Three Bears or not? Did that nurse shoot me with something that put me into the land of Saturnalia? I knew one thing for sure. Sarah Mapleton *did* come into my office yesterday before Zelda Blodgett marched in with her plants.

How could I have dreamed the whole damn thing? Some answers had to happen soon, otherwise I would start believing my mind was going. I took the yellow and green car toward Hollywood. I was worried about my Adora and had to get home to her.

Egrets That Die in Springtime

The late afternoon air was smelly and stagnant. I thought to myself, if I had gotten to my office by noon and down to Bard's Theatre by one—and it was five-thirty now—that meant I had dreamed the whole se-

171

quence from the time Sarah Mapleton grabbed my hand and we started for the elevator that didn't exist—at least not in this dimension. It had all seemed so real—from the fireplace in the cottage, Rhea-Saturnalia's voice, our conversation, the description of this *Cronus-Gor* character—walking on the bleak landscape towards the golden castle with the magnificent obelisk—the thousand-foot granite tower where the little bird came to sharpen his beak every ten thousand years. Where did all that come from?

I got off the streetcar and crossed the street. Just then I felt a gun in my ribs and a rough man's voice said, "Keep moving, buddy, toward the alley—over there."

I did as he said and we turned off the main street into a dirty alley where a garbage truck was picking up the trash along the narrow corridor between buildings. "Uh...you don't need the gun, buster. I'm not gonna turn around and bust you one—"

"—shut up and keep moving," he persisted. As we approached the garbage truck, the stupid thug hit me hard on the skull and I went limp as he and the garbage truck driver tossed me into the trash. Then I lost consciousness.

When I came to, I was on the floor of some large room where everything from floor to ceiling sparkled with gold flecks, lighted by some invisible florescence. My head hurt like hell and the whole area around my right elbow felt numb. I must have banged against something. Then a dark, commanding voice spoke. "Did you know...more Egrets die in springtime than any other time of year? It seems the parents build the nests

172

over water...and cruel little chicks, usually the pesky first-born, force the weaker chicks out of the nest into the water below. There, many creatures ravenously devour them. Quite tasty, I hear."

As I sat up, my gut did a series of somersaults and I knew I was in *his* presence...the creature-who-would-be-God...*Cronus-Gor*. "It's been a long chase, hasn't it? Like the Egrets, it's always been the survival of the fittest between us. Why don't you come out so I can see you?"

"Gods are never seen, Denning. Human brains are so deficient that I can cloud your mind from ever seeing me. Let me assure you, I am *very present*...and do not fool yourself, it has *never* been a contest between us—only *you* run the risk of not surviving."

I carefully felt the bump on my head. "Well, one thing I can say, you're a hell of a lousy host. I could use a couple of aspirin and a hefty jigger of gin just about now." The room had an interesting reverberation to it and our voices echoed back and forth.

"You were dealt with harder than I instructed. I will provide what you request."

In an instant those very same items appeared in front of me as I sat on the floor. "Well, I'll be damned—are you a magician?"

"Ha! Like children's play toys—transubstantiation of molecular substance. Energy becomes moldable clay in my hands."

"Let me get one thing straight. I didn't dream going to the theatre with Sarah Mapleton—or meeting your dearly beloved, Saturnalia, right?"

"You may call me *Gor*."

"Alright...Gor. What about those sisters, Sarah and Rebecca Mapleton?"

"They have already enriched the *purple mists*. Rhea informs me she would be most grateful if I presented you—as a gift to her—in the form of that which is breathed in nightly before any other mode of repose can take place, the *purple mists*."

"I see. And you have no conscience about simply killing two young women and reducing them to this—this horrible *'mist'* you and your significant other keep talking about?"

"Conscience signifies *guilt*—and since I have no moral code to concern myself with as you and your earthlings do, then taking vital life has no more significance to me than stepping on a bug."

That was rather one sided, I thought, but my head began to feel better. "That's something I always wondered about. What is existence like without conscience or any kind of moral code?"

"Law and order is established in the universes, not by gods or goddesses—and *humans* are uniquely unqualified to bestow a modicum of fairness upon themselves or other creatures, due to their self-delusion and corrupt nature."

"Hmmm...so I take it your opinion regarding humans is kind of low on the totem pole of the cosmic hierarchy?"

"Humans are abominable, deceitful and treacherous...that is why it is so easy for me to manipulate them. Their weaknesses are always the same: greed, lust for control and power—which in your world society translates to financial accumulation."

"You are right on that score." I cleared my throat and looked around the gold room. Strange lighting that slowly changed color every few minutes emanated from seemingly nowhere and filled every corner. The room had high ceilings and smelled pleasant, sort of like a faint wisp of a billionaire's expensive after-shave lotion. "So, let's get on with it, Gor. We both know why I'm here and why I'm not dead yet, right?"

"Ravna failed me. Your dealings with Lei-Tao and her little overseer, Toggth, led me to believe you know where the *Fen de Fuqin* is hidden—for I know it functions to keep the equilibrium in the balance of things. It would be better for me to have it for safe keeping..."

"You see, Gor, you're as rotten as the rest of us—just singularly more powerful. But your bottom line is still power, control, greed, lust—I mean, look how you stole Saturnalia from her happy home planet?"

"She told you that?" There was a silence. "Gods take what they claim as theirs—who would contest me?"

"Another god, maybe more powerful...but it really comes down to the big question, *'just because you can, should you?'* And creeps like you hide out in some smoke-screen disguise so no one knows you're just as corrupt as the next guy—or god, in this case."

"Silence!" his voice filled the cavernous room. "The *Fen de Fuqin*...where is it? Take me to it or I shall apply tortures to you so hideous that even I wince at the very thought of the pain they inflict."

"Yeah, I've had a go at your style, Gor—a little underground lab where Ravna and his little bulldog surgeon got it. They were gonna start by de-balling me, you know—then just in the nick of time I was rescued. I'll bet that one disappointed you."

"I hate priests. Your mythological creature churches maintain an arsenal of well-trained men and women because they want what I want...only they are primitive compared to me...and the Order..."

"Ah, you must be speaking of Father Carlo Tortelli and his flying priests. Well, they sure saved my ass! I'd be ground up meat destined for alien dog food by now if it hadn't been for them."

"Enough talk, Denning...you have a big mouth with very little to say. I have decided that mortals are ultimately useless, helpless little things. I will begin torturing you tomorrow. But before we do that, I invite you to spend your last sane night watching the *Eve of the Purple Mists*."

Something he said scared me a bit. "Last *sane* night, did I hear you say?"

"Yes...the nature of the torture will unfortunately alter your brain waves and normal cognizance will be permanently disturbed."

"Hmmm...I see...if that's the case, then how in the hell are you gonna extract the location of the *God of Our Fathers* out of me?"

"Once the brain is softened, if you will, all that information will come 'dripping out' of you without your consent and we shall be able to view all of your life's outstanding experiences. A form of brain control, which as I said, has unfortunate side effects." Then Cronus-Gor dismissed me. "Tomorrow then, Denning. I hope you shall be co-operative."

"Don't count on it," I mumbled half under my breath.

The room began to dim and I was led out into very spacious quarters where I bathed, rested somewhat and donned a thin gold robe that was accompanied by a pair of golden slippers. They were solid and I thought of Dorothy from Kansas. What if I clicked the heels together as she did the ruby slippers? I had escaped to the Oz books as a child and thought of L. Frank Baum as the kindly grandfather I never had as my bedtime story teller. Yet I felt these slippers had magic in them. What a silly fantasy, considering I was on the verge of having my brain sucked out by some alien "god" who was on a power trip.

As I was sitting on the edge of my bed contemplating my fate, suddenly a shadow flashed across a curtain outside my room. Soon someone walked right through the wall and approached me! It was Saturnalia dressed in a knock-out night gown with a thin gold belt. Those solid, ample breasts stood to attention for me and she came right up to my face and kissed my nose. "Well, don't you know better than to enter a strange man's room without knocking?" I chided her.

She attempted a weak smile. "Cable...listen...I don't want you to have brain damage—I want you whole and real when Cronus gives you to me—because your impairment will affect the potency of the purple mists when I breathe you in."

"Oh, that's swell—you come rushing in here like on a secret mission to tell me I'd best be in good health so you can kill me tomorrow or the next day as you inhale my essence through your nostrils? Yeah, that makes me feel a whole lot better!"

"I really wish you could be my lover. But Cronus is such a stick-in-the-mud about things like that. The last time I tried with some handsome Urantian, he hung him upside down. His toes stretched until his body reached clear to the floor! And he smelled terrible."

"You know, Rhea, I kind of like you, but I'm not really interested in your past lovers, the night of the purple mists—and I don't look forward to being lobotomized tomorrow. If you don't mind, I'd like to be alone."

"You can't. Cronus has ordered me to escort you to an *Eve of the Purple Mists* so you can see first-hand how wonderful it can be."

"Wonderful for *you*. For me, it's previews of coming attractions, lady. By the way, where in the hell are we? How come one minute I'm in this cozy cottage with you, then we're walking toward this palace or whatever—and zap! I'm back in L.A. where nothing on the bathroom floor of that Eighth-Street Theatre is the same as I recall it the first time—and now I'm here after getting clubbed by one of your hubby's goons and tossed into the back end of a garbage truck! And by the way—again—where is *here*?"

"*Induced illusion*. Cronus will never tell. You *are* in Los Angeles in this dimension—the one you're used to—but Cronus calls his *Oculus* Order together by summoning them to Fifth Street and Alvarado where they're picked up and blindfolded until they reach here. I know the way to 'here,' but I have to come from the other side to get here. I know it sounds confusing—because it is, even to me...you see, I can flip from dimension to dimension. In fact, I'm going to have to put you to sleep to get you to the *Eve of the Purple Mists*—because that's in *my* dimension, where my cute little cottage with the warm fire is."

"Look, lady, I don't want any more shit shot into my veins. And I told you, I don't give a rat's ass about your purple mists thing. Leave me alone." As I said that, I felt a pin-prick stab to the side of my neck and I was out.

Saved By the Bell of Sorrow

Somewhere I was hearing a lonesome sax playing *Yesterdays* while a church bell rang from a steeple in the distance. The music wound through me like ribbons of color, hitting my heart like the bumpers on a pinball machine. In these semi-conscious minutes between conscious life and oblivion, there is a wisdom that creeps into you like a knowing cipher—singing out its silent song to what's left of your brain and will—to continue this insane existence we call 'life'. So, even if you go there involuntarily, it bubbles up from a part of you that must still be alive, maybe part of memory and regret, joy and pleasure, hope and aspiration, dejection and hopelessness.

When I awakened, Saturnalia was looking down on me and smiling while her fingers stroked my cheek. "Whiskers...tactile stimulation, Cable. Feeling your manly growth travels from my fingertips right up my arms to my breasts and down to—to you-know-where."

Looking at this dish as I awakened by the warm firelight in her cottage, I was thinking how grand it might be to experience another kind of manly growth with this babe. Overlooking her obnoxiousness, there was still a hell of a lot of voluptuous woman there. I was lying prostrate on a comfortable sofa, looking up at her. "Feels good, babe." I took a deep breath, trying to figure out where I was or what hellish experience I might be in for next. "So, is this my *night of ecstasy* with you before the axe falls tomorrow?"

"How I wish. I told you I can't be your lover. Cronus would punish me terribly. So now it's time to walk the *purple rainbow* and experience the marvelous mists."

"So, what about Sarah and Rebecca Mapleton? Will I be breathing them in?"

"That was yesterday. No, a whole new group of essences is in the air tonight. I know that one of them is a famous dancer Cronus personally chose. He wants me to dance. I love the motion, the rhythm. Do you like to dance, Cable?"

"Oh, yeah, just regular nightclub stuff—not ballet or anything."

"I'd like to do ballet as well. I love the fresh, free motion of moving every part of my body to its maximum pleasure expression. During your nineteenth century, I would swirl and twirl around the back of the theatre in Russia while the orchestra played Tchaikovsky's *Swan Lake*. I have always seen myself as the poor, ill-fated swan."

"Why would you say that?"

"I don't know...just a silly feeling."

"Alright, kid, take me to the celebration of the purple mists. I'm sure there's no way out of it."

Then she bent over and kissed me on the lips. "I can't let you perish, Cable." Then her expression and voice grew serious. "Listen carefully. Cronus can hear our thoughts if he chooses to. He sees them as mental pictures, our own visualizations. So, when I tell you what we're going to do, please try not to visualize it. It would jeopardize everything. Think of something or someone else."

"How about seducing you?" I kidded her.

"That would be worse. Think of some happy child-hood memories, a forest, the sea. Anything but what I tell you, okay?"

"Okay...I'll do my best."

She pulled me up until I was sitting. Then she sat next to me. "We will experience the purple mists. Then *on the way out* of the rainbow, I will take your hand to a dimensional exit I know about. You must trust me and walk through it, no matter what. Do you understand?"

"Yeah, babe, thanks, I do....but what about you? Are you coming?"

"I can't. It would be too obvious to Cronus. He's a lot smarter than both of us put together."

"I wouldn't be so sure about that. Every creature has its flaws...there's a weak crack in everyone, Saturnalia. I suspect your abductor-husband-lover is no exception. You know, a lot of guys I've known put up a pretty good smokescreen, but once you penetrate it, you get to see the chinks in the armor."

"I hope you're right, Cable. We must go now."

We walked out of her cottage. There was what looked like a stone outhouse with a door. We entered into it and descended a bunch of stairs. At the bottom we were suddenly in the company of many of the titans, gods and goddesses privy to this experience. It was a puzzle why I was allowed to experience it. But I guessed old Gor thought this was my last night—and it had been his wife's wish. A deep purple glow filled a large chamber as we entered. In front of us the participants were suddenly sprayed or coated somehow with a purple substance that seemed to glow from their bodies. As crazy as it seems, we then actually walked up a purple rainbow that was as solid as the earth. We crested the arch and descended into a large theatre-like room with very comfortable seats. Each seat contained a pair of goggles and, as Saturnalia explained to me, were to be used as enhancers so we could see the essences in the mists more clearly. We were silent as she helped me mount my goggles. Then the room went dark and a wonderful music began, coming from nowhere and everywhere at the same time. Then the auditorium began to fill with glowing purple mists. They whirled and swirled slowly from what seemed the floor of the edifice. The area of my solar plexus began to vibrate and my temples began to throb. I found myself breathing hard and fighting myself to inhale. My body was not taking to the experience too well. My instinct told me to breathe minimally, but I could still feel the essences of other beings floating around in confusion, lost from the bodies they so recently had inhabited. Somehow I knew it when the essence of the dancer Saturnalia had told me about appeared. She seemed to recognize me and wished to enter my solar plexus, as if she felt it the only safe haven. I let her in, but refused all others consciously.

Saturnalia seemed to be enjoying the experience immensely. She rocked back and forth slowly and at one point took her hand and grabbed my crotch, as if she was having some kind of very sexual fantasy with who- ever was entering her at the time. This whole process lasted for about a half-hour or so and then the soft lights came up. We took off the goggles and waited until all others had exited the auditorium. Then Saturnalia led me to a pitch-black panel in the wall near the beginning of the purple rainbow ascent. It measured maybe ten feet tall by three or four feet wide. "Click your golden slipper heels together twice and walk through it, Cable, now—and whatever you do, don't visualize it and...good luck."

Crap! So L. Frank Baum's ruby slippers trick wasn't original! I wondered if *he* had gotten a glimpse of other dimensions in order to write such fantasies as the Oz books. I turned to look at her and whispered. "I can't leave here in a purple robe and golden slippers, lady— can you do something about that?"

"Oh," she said and waved a hand over me and my original Cable Denning clothes, fedora and all, appeared on my body. Except for the golden slippers, that is.

"You're not coming?" I asked.

"I can't. I have to go back. When Cronus discovers you missing tomorrow, there will be all Hades to pay. And I'm sure he'll summon Thantos to hunt you down. Go now, quickly!" she said. She pushed me and I went through the wall like a hot knife through cotton candy.

I found myself in the middle of traffic in downtown L.A. with sirens wailing, horns blowing and people on the sidewalks. It was business as usual, shopping, eat- ing, selling something or pandering on a busy street corner. I shook my head back and forth to clear the cobwebs from my brain. I was relieved to find that my golden slippers were once again my Thom McCann's and I set off to get home to my pale little señorita!

I took the yellow and green streetcar and got off near Franklin and Argyle. Elisa, my lover's mother, was sitting in a comfy chair reading the newspaper when I entered. "Hello, Elisa. Sorry I took so long. Got into more than I expected—same old story, I know—"

"—why did you not call, Cable? Two days we worry. Adora is getting weaker. You must stay with her. She needs you."

"Yeah, you're right—and I intend to do just that. But still have to make a living, so can you come over when I need you to cover for me?"

"Of course, Cable, *sin duda*. But now, go to her. She cries for you. Never has my niña been so in love."

I thanked Elisa, gave her carfare and she left. I tip-toed into the bedroom where my reclining little señorita lay quietly. I approached the bed. She looked so pale, wasted, as if all life was draining from her. I wanted to cry because it hurt so much, but I knew I had to keep it together. She opened her eyes to half-mast and looked up at me, a faint smile coming across her lips. And so I smiled down at her. "Sorry I was gone so long, my beautiful lady, but you know this old gumshoe life—"

"—where have you been, *mi precioso*?"

"Well, I went on an unexpected trip, babe. Anyway, I'm back and what can I get you?"

She smiled again. "You...just you, Cable. You are all— *todo y todo*—I ever wanted *en mi vida, querido*..." Then her voice trailed off as she coughed and covered her mouth with a weak hand. "*Ay, salud!* When I get well...*yo*

184

no escondo mis deseos femeninos! My lusty woman…will have you…*pronto, mi amor.*"

I sat on the edge of the bed next to her. "*T'amo, Adora,*" I said as I held her hand and tucked it into my chest. I was exhausted. I undressed, took a shower and quietly slid into bed with my beloved Latina. She awakened long enough to put her arm around my waist and her head on my chest. In that position I fell asleep secretly praying that my healthy energies would siphon off into her as we slept and she would awaken in the morning, fresh and horny as hell, like my old Adora.

Two days later I was knocking on the door of Crazy Jack's dilapidated apartment house, marked *#408*. It was in the worst part of town at the Panama Hotel, on the 4th floor—a rundown four-story dump located in *Hell's Half Acre*, the center of skid row, near the corner of 5th and San Julian Streets. He was the only one I trusted with the prophecy stuff. Jack never wanted money, just cigarettes and had come by his gift naturally and probably in his less than "normal" mental state had little awareness of it.

He wasn't home and I wandered the streets looking for him. Often he hung out in the neighborhood where the down and out, forgotten souls of humanity dwelled. There was the smell of cigarettes, booze and urine all mixed together as I walked down Los Angeles Street. I cut through an alley to intersect with San Pedro when my eye caught something vaguely familiar. There, leaning up against a wall, looking completely spent and deteriorating, sat an old lady. But it wasn't just any old lady. Her fading reddish long hair and torn golden dress clued me in. I went up to the elderly woman. "Saturna-lia?" I gasped. How could this be? Just three days ago she was this devastating dish, the goddess Rhea-Saturnalia, wife of the head of the *Oculus Pyramis Mandatum,* Cronus-Gor!

She looked at me. Her face was covered with boils but there was no mistaking those red-amber eyes of a once magnificent and beautiful Titan of Saturn, her native planet. "Cable...Cable..." she whispered. "I've been talking to you...silently...I have wished for you to—"

"—how in the hell did you end up here—looking like that?" I inquired, staring at her in total disbelief.

"Punishment, Cable, punishment...Cronus discovered my—my complicity in helping you escape—so he took away my goddess status, ripped away my Titanic powers and reduced me to this common mortal woman...rife with misery, disease and old age. Cronus said he read my thoughts—that I wanted to be with you—so he granted me my wish, but not as the beautiful goddess you knew and desired, but this rotting old hag."

I bent down and got on my knees in front of her. "Oh, God, Saturnalia. I'm so sorry...it was me—my fault, if it weren't for—"

"—no, Cable. We all make decisions for ourselves..." She snickered an ironic laugh. "Besides, it was pretty boring...being...being an immortal. Too many lies inside of me, things I concealed, other things I tolerated—just to be an immortal goddess. But...do you know...what I learned from...from all of it, Cable?"

"No, babe, tell me...what did you learn—maybe it'll teach me a thing or two about this insane universe."

"You've got to stick to who you're born with—*that* person. I wasted nearly a half-million years to discover that. So, don't—"

"Cigarette! Cigarette!" a voice called out behind me. I spun around to find Crazy Jack looking down at us.

"Hello, Jack, I was looking for you...went to your place...do you, uh, do you know this woman?" I asked him.

"I don't know! I don't know! Cigarette!" I straightened myself, took out a Lucky Strike from my pack, gave one to Crazy Jack, lit it up for him and put the rest of the pack in his dirty topcoat jacket. It was a ritual I always performed for him. He smiled nervously, which was his way of saying 'thanks' and then looked down at Saturnalia. "Not human...strange lady...not human—but I don't know! I don't know! Confuse Jack!"

"Yeah, I—I understand, Jack. I've known her from—from another dimension. We had a couple of adventures together—are you sure you haven't seen her before?"

"I don't know! I don't know!" He started to tremble a little, as he always did when he was the least bit distressed. He puffed away almost angrily on his cigarette. "Satin Latin lady...gone...Cable...you love satin Latin lady...she goes whoosh! Away! But I don't know! I don't know!"

That statement of Jack's hit my heart like a sledgehammer hitting a cow's skull at the slaughterhouse. I knew it was true. But not until now did I confess it to myself that my Adora was not destined to remain in this world too much longer. Crazy Jack knew it—and somehow I knew it. "You always come up with the doozies,

Jack." I looked back down at Saturnalia. "What about this lady—what can we do for her?"

"Not real...not real lady!" he stammered. "Come—come—come from up *there!*" he said, pointing to the sky. "You must leave—leave her—but I don't know! I don't know!"

"He's right, Cable. Cronus is using me as a tracer...to find you. He can see through my eyes if he wants to. Go, good mortal, it's okay....but there is one more thing I want to say to you..." Again I bent down as the ugly old lady whispered in my ear. "I wish I had taken the risk to be...be your lover, Cable. If I was to be...demoted and perish...then I would have preferred that—that ecstasy...with you..."

"But I thought you told me once you were made a goddess you couldn't die....that you're an immortal..."

"We are *all* immortal, silly man. I lied...because it was good to feel...different. Cronus' punishment is to this *body* I inhabited for so long—perhaps too long.....go now, don't worry about me...see you again sometime...some other life, perhaps...."

I looked sadly at the unique lady who had befriended me and saved my butt from a terrible fate at the hands of her ego-mad lover. "Maybe, Rhea Saturnalia, you never know...even if I believed in it, I wouldn't know where to find you."

"Oh, don't worry...I'd—I'd find you..." Then she summoned me close to her and she took my arm. "Will you please check on...on my daughter now and then, Cable?...I've had to transmigrate her...to Earth...to keep her safe...from her father..."

"Daughter...? Oh, yeah, the one you told me you sneaked by Old Mean Puss, your god-husband, or whatever. She's where?"

"She's safe...for now...in a little town called Cambria Pines...here in California. It's—it's up the coast—"

"—yeah, I know where it is. I had cause to visit William Randolph Hearst's mighty Moorish castle in San Simeon not too long ago. We passed through Cambria on the way."

Her words were labored. "I'm so glad...I will be indebted to you, kind man. Her name is *Cassiopeia*, Cassie for short—ha! a constellation of the night sky—named after Andromeda's mother. She is staying with a beneficent alien by the name of Arthur Beatle. He hasn't adjusted too well to the earth ways...but he blends in quite well...and he's built a nifty little castle...of his own...on a hillside in Cambria. It's called *Nitwit Ridge*, right above the *Sunset Motel*." Her hand trembled as she looked at me with those intense eyes only a distressed mother could have. "I trust you, Cable. Please...?"

"Yeah, alright, I'll drive over there one of these days and check up on her. How is *she* adjusting to planet Earth?"

"By the gods, Cable, she is so beautiful—I fear for her getting involved with lesser creatures than herself. You know, men..."

I took exception to Saturnalia's attitude. "Yeah, I know, *men*...what—you immigrate her here and then proceed to put down the very people she has to deal with?"

"Well, you know how awful...some men can be..."

189

"You oughtta know, you married one—or had children by him or however you define your relationship."

"Please...we are not talking about me, but about my daughter, Cassie. My body will disintegrate...within a few weeks and I will leave it. I can't go to her like this—look at me! She'd run...she remembers only a young mother as pretty as she is. No, I could not bring such a heavy weight upon her."

"So, instead you're putting it on me." In a way I resented her request, for it put an obligation of responsibility on me I really didn't need just about now. I took in a deep breath of resignation. "Okay...what does she do—I mean, does she work to support herself."

"She doesn't have to...but she does. I gave her money she...she has secretly hidden away and uses it at her discretion. She works behind the counter at McKay's Pharmacy in the older part of town."

"Well, once again I let somebody else talk me into—"

"—you'll find her rewarding...and intelligent...way ahead of her years...and of course, like all my family lineage...quite good at prophecy...she's probably a very good...*Seer.*"

I kissed her on top of her dirty grey-reddish hair. "Let's hope I don't get the wrong girl—they'd throw me in the slammer." I smiled at her. "Well, here's lookin' at you, kid..."

As I walked away, I turned once more to look at the lady who saved my life....and left, with Crazy Jack following me. "So, Jack, can you pick up anything on her husband?—he's some greedy god who wants everything his way...that lady, Saturnalia, that was his wife and she got punished for helping me out. Damn, that makes me feel like shit, Jack."

"I don't know! I don't know! Bad thing come—run! Oh...!" He held his head with one hand. "Street turn to gold—you grow old! But I don't know! I don't know! Gold piece keep safe—they come, pick you up! Cable, run!" He was trembling as he spoke, his head shaking in a tremor.

"One more thing, Crazy Jack." I had to pump him before he disconnected into his own lost world. "What do you see around the corner of 5th and Alvarado? Any strange people congregating, disappearing?" I was thinking what I was told about the *Oculus* "pick-up" co-ordinates at that intersection.

"I don't know! I don't know! Cigarette! Cigarette!" the nervous man replied, looking away from my eyes. I lit another smoke for him.

"Well, if you see or hear anything, you know where my office is, Jack. Drop in and see me sometime."

"I don't know! I don't know! The Hook come deadly! The wizard run—but I don't know! I don't know!"

I left Crazy Jack scratching my head. Maybe he was finally going over the edge and the poor fellow was losing the connective tissue that made the brain function with some semblance of coherent behavior. I boarded the streetcar thinking... *this* had been one hell of a day!

CHAPTER 7

DEATH BECOMES HER

As the days peeled away into months, Adora became weaker and at least three medical reports confirmed, my love was afflicted with *leukemia*—a complicated disease of the blood. The doctors we visited didn't know a hell of a lot about it, only that they called it the "White Blood" disease. A research doctor at a local university told me privately it was called *hematological neoplasm* disease, an attack on the lymphoid system.

We spent a dismal New Year's Eve 1931 with Elisa, Flora and my mother sitting at my lover's beside. The disease was progressive, we were told. White blood cells increasingly began to outnumber the red ones, and the malady had its beginnings in the bone marrow. The particular type of this virulent disease she had, was a death sentence and all I could do was to keep her as comfortable as possible and make sure she got her daily injection of painkiller. But the pain of it was slowly killing me, too. I didn't know what the human capacity for heartache and suffering was, but I was about to find out.

The pall of death can sometimes have its own beauty, and my failing sweetheart glowed in those last days with a pallid and ghostly appearance. Her loving eyes and sweet voice never changed, nor did her bravery in facing an imminent demise still in the bloom of her young womanhood. "How's the pale princess today?" I would say, trying to cheer her up.

She'd smile at me and look at me with those liquid brown eyes. "*Ay, mi amor... soy una buena princesa...*I wait all the days...*por mi príncipe*. Are you not my prince, *querido*?"

"You bet," I would say. "For now and forever, kid. How about if I go out for a banana milkshake, your favorite?"

She would laugh. "Ha! At least ten of them!" Then she would draw serious. "*Pero,* I have no *apetito—no tengo hambre, gracias.*"

Then I would come to kneel on the floor next to her bed and take her hand. It was fragile and white as the painted wall above her. "So if you don't want to eat, kid, how about sailing around the world with old Cable Denning here? I've always had a yen to ply the seven seas—I might even make a good sailor—you think you'd be—be, uh, a good first mate?"

Then she'd look at me and her eyes would brighten. "I am always your first mate and I will go with you anywhere...*dondequiera*..., my love..."

"Well, then, that settles it," I would say. "Tomorrow I'll drop by a first-class travel agency—hmmm....I think it's called *Todo el Mundo*, downtown. What do you say?"

"Don't make me laugh, Cable...I am too *debil*—too weak, my love. *Pero...es verdad?* You take me sailing—to—to *Catalina*?"

I lit up. "Yes! Yes, señorita! When do we go?"

"*Ay, estúpido! El médico* will not let me go..."

"Hell with the *el médico!* If you want to go...we'll go..."

"*Verdad? Con mucho gusto con te, mi amor.*"

The next day I called Elisa and her sister Flora and told them of Adora's wish. They thought I was crazy but if it was what she wanted, they would arrange it. I told

Adora and she was excited as hell. I thought something that stimulating might even bring her around. Stranger things...........? So we planned to rent a sailboat—with a motor aboard just in case my sailing skills petered out—and I would sail us smoothly across the briny blue Pacific, traveling the twenty-six miles to the island of Catalina. This was Wednesday. We would take our grand adventure on Saturday. All of us were excited.

In the afternoon, a great fit of depression overcame me and I had to get out of that environment I came to hate...that stifling house of sickness and impending sadness and death. I called Elisa and she came to watch my lover. I took the streetcar as far as I could and walked the rest of the way up to the caves at Bronson Park. It was late afternoon and as I walked, I recalled when I found Eden Royce's corpse suspended from the ceiling inside one of the caves. I never entered them again. I climbed the loose shale hill above the caves and came to rest atop a hill next to an old sage bush. Far in the distance I could see a fog bank come rolling in from the sea and knew the cool breezes would start up at dusk as the damp messenger would invade the park. It was one of those days when you find yourself reviewing your life, daring to look in all the corners and crevices and sweep out what doesn't belong anymore. I would be thirty-one pretty soon and it seemed I had lived three hundred years already. Life is funny, it was like a kid from the rough side of the tracks would always have it rough, no matter how hard he tried to shake it. If he was born poor, struggling and tossed into the arena of hard knocks and violence, that feature would haunt him all his life and stick with him, a curse attached to his hip like a birthmark. As close as I thought I'd come to breaking out of it now and then, somehow I was always ripped back into making a living listening to the raw sewerage of peoples' lives and that streak of deception and violence all humans contain and are prone to when the cards are stacked to deal you out a bad hand.

Just then a pleasant, warm voice called out from behind me. "None of it's as bad as you make it out to be, Cable. Just be open to change—and change *with* it. You are not your sister's keeper—nor were neither you Lei-Tao's, Honey's nor Adora's."

I spun around to see a little man with warm eyes and a pleasant smile. "Toggth! You son of a gun! Where did you come from?"

"Where do I always come from? Nowhere and everywhere..." He reached his hand up to my shoulder and squeezed. "I can feel your sorrow, Cable. But you must let it go. This earth life is not just about romance, excitement, money and adventure—but about *lessons well learned so you might discover what you came for. Remember...remember...*" Then the little creature sat beside me. "Do you remember, Cable? So few do..."

I hugged Toggth as we sat together. "I am glad to see you, little fellow. It's been a hell of a road since we saw each other last. Crap, the thing I remember most in the last three or four years is *loss*—Mario, Honey—now Adora—"

"—but what have you *gained?* The mosquito fish is born in the season of the mosquito—balances, Cable, nothing is ever lost without gain somewhere—look for it. Life, death, death, life...a cycle..."

195

"Yeah, but you don't have to die, like Lei-Tao. That has a definite advantage, wouldn't you agree?"

"Well, like Lei-Tao, one day I shall choose to recycle. We all do. We cannot stay forever in the same form. It gets boring. Nevertheless, the *reality is never the physical body* but the entity *aware of the animation of that body*. Amongst the Chinese mortals, the 'dearly departed,' as you might say, are given a ritual send-off, where they are washed, blessed, dressed and cleansed of all earthly trespasses, made up like Lei-Tao in a Chinese Dragon Parade with rouge, lipstick, colored face powders—but it is for the *spirit's* honoring that this is done, not for the body in itself. The tradition has become corrupted along the way. So remember, your physical body is never your reality—or shouldn't be, in any case."

"Easy for you to say," I laughed. And it *was* easy for this little guy to slough off death. That was because he never felt emotion the way humans do. Especially when we come to love someone. But he was reading my mind. "Those balances you're talking about, I'm not seeing those lately—"

"—*attachment* becomes dependence upon another, Cable. Love, but don't become attached. Free the other person and in the same moment you free yourself. Desire binds us to the post.....grinding in the dust of futility—tied to ancient habits that the *body* dictates. It is never your true heart or mind that dictates that you should become unhappy because you love someone—or lose them. It's all temporary. Everything. Nothing is as permanent as change..."

"All well and good for you to say, Toggth. But you're not down here in the sewer trying to clean out the

196

pipes. After a while the dirty world kind of rubs off on you. And you find yourself stuck in a squirrel cage of repetition, making the same mistakes over and over—"

"—that's the whole thing! *Lessons*, Cable—*remember what you came for*! Let go of all the rest and things will work out perfectly."

I had to change the subject. "So...to what do I owe the honor of this visit?" I said, looking at him a little sheepishly, trying to ignore that everything he was saying, was giving me a case of the heavies.

"Your sorrow awakened me from a tidy little sleep back at the *Cave of the Seven Truths*. I'm certain you realize that after your escape from Cronus-Gor, your days here may be numbered—and shortened. *If* he gets hold of you, he will extract the information you harbor in your memory of the golden capsule. I think I told you I gently confiscated the gold-etched microfilm and hid it. But, of course, we must not allow anyone to discover the whereabouts of the original *Fen de Fuqin*."

"Pretty sneaky guy, eh?" I laughed. "So that makes you an accessory in this crime of The *Seven Truths*, doesn't it?"

He chortled and slapped me on the arm. "Ha! You got me there! Being Protectorate over the Protectorate can be tricky!"

"So who took Lei-Tao's place over-seeing the precious *God of Our Fathers*, etcetera, etcetera?"

"Oh, a beautiful creature named *Kwan Ling*." Then he looked at me with a certain narrowing of his eyes. "But you...shall not meet her. I cannot afford another Protectorate to fall in love with a mortal."

197

"Aha! At last, the chinks in your armor, eh? Well, you won't have to worry about that. I've—I've got my hands full these days..." I was thinking about Adora and Saturday's navigation of the Seven Seas.

"At any rate, you must be extremely vigilant. As I said, you don't want to end up like poor Saturnalia. Gor will use all the powers at his disposal to track you down and pounce."

"So why hasn't he come after me like gangbusters already?"

"He's biding his time. He doesn't want to make the same mistake twice. *Saturnalia*, much like Lei-Tao, betrayed certain trusts. And you saw what happened to her. No, he does not wish to miss the mark this time, Cable...so beware."

It was getting heavy and I had to change the subject again. "Is Lei-Tao still a lotus seedpod—or whatever?"

"For many thousands of your years yet to be. Relevant time is different in different dimensions. All is relative."

"So...can you help me avoid this Cronus-Gor piece of shit? Like you said, I know sooner or later he's gonna come down on me like a hoard of locusts on a fresh grain field—and bam! it'll be over."

"Well, it's a little more complex than that. Gor is an immortal, as you've already learned. He is alien to your plane of existence. Secretly, like other visitors, he is compromised breathing the earth's atmosphere. If you can get him to exhaust himself with excitement that causes heavy breathing, he will have to go away for a while to replenish himself."

"Hmmm...." I thought this might be a breakthrough. "Ha! that's a rich one. What about all the other alien helpers and mortal goons that form the *Oculus*? Talk about remembering, I remember a few weird encounters already—not the least of which was the Royce case. And these guys play for keeps. In one of the caves below us here, I found the body of Eden Royce, crucified to the ceiling—"

"—death, life...life, death, Cable—I remind you, they have value only as part of the cycle in the fabric of existence. They mean little in and of themselves."

"Well, to me they have a lot of meaning, buddy. I just happened to be wired that way. You know my whole thing, Toggth, *truth* and caring are part of my make-up, not to mention beautiful babes and great music in a smoky club. Gor or no Gor, that's the kind of air *I* like to breathe."

He chuckled. "I would like to attend some of your musical activities sometime—may I accompany you one evening?"

"Sure, why not? But right now, I've got to attend to Adora...I'm taking her sailing this weekend. I don't know...how long..."

"I understand, Cable. It is so difficult for humans to see beyond attachment, habit, sexual practice and expectation. I'm very sorry you were *turned down*."

"Turned down?"

"Chemically, genetically altered. Some of what you originally had has been 'spliced' out of you, if you will. But, let us not discuss it today. One day you will encounter it again. Be patient. Let life grow on you in a positive way. In the meantime, I will watch your back, as you say, and warn you of Gor's next line of attack. And it will come, Mr. Smart Detective, oh, it will come…" He squeezed my hand and then he was gone—poof!—just like that, into the ethers. The approaching fog bank was beginning to move my way…as the sun set behind it, a cold chill went through my bones.

A Place in the Sun

The rental agent made sure I purchased a lot of insurance that morning. An inexperienced landlubber chancing the high seas was no laughing matter for *Oat's Maritime Rentals*. Captain Oats was a big guy with burly hands and hair pouring out of his chest like an eagle's nest stuffed with straw. His voice was rough and deep. "Sailin' ain't no cheap trick, Mr. Denning. No laughin' matter any way ya slice it! Endin' up in Davy Jones' Locker would also put a black eye on me happy customer's record, you know. Are ya sure, now, mate, you can go that twenty-six miles and back again? For seventeen dollars more, you can leave the vessel at the dock in Catalina and take the ferry back home and I'll pick it up later."

I thought for a minute. Elisa and Flora were sitting with Adora outside on a bench. "Well, since this whole thing's setting me back some big bucks anyway, maybe you're right. We'll make it a one-way ticket, then. Thanks, Captain Oats, for the suggestion."

"I'm thinkin' we'll both be feelin' the better for it, mate." He handed me the receipt papers and the keys to the motor on the seventeen-foot sailboat. "Now, she's all gassed up. You be crankin' that motor a few times after primin' 'er...but once she's flooded, you gotta be waitin' a wee while afore she'll go again." I saluted the Captain and left.

It was a marvelous day. The morning sun had just peaked up over the eastern mountains and the sea was calm. It was so clear that we could see Santa Catalina Island's two thousand foot peak in the distance. Hell, no compass necessary on this voyage! I thought to myself. Just keep your eye on the piece of rock out there in the briny blue.

Elisa and Flora helped me get Adora safely and comfortably aboard. They hugged me and made me promise I'd call the minute we got back. Both of them felt a lot better about me nixing the return trip on the little schooner. We cast off and I can still remember Elisa, Flora and Captain Oats waving from the dock in the morning light. Some images get snapped inside your brain like a photo image taken on my trusty old Kodak. And I just remembered I had forgotten my camera back at the office.

Elisa had suggested turmeric powder as an anti-seasick agent. So both Adora and I tolerated a teaspoon of the stuff before we left. It was bitter as hell and dark yellow like curry. I checked out the gas engine part of the boat first, because I knew I couldn't rely on my sailor's skills in maneuvering the jib and sails. So we glided out of San Pedro harbor under power. Adora was seated close to me with a white tire around her little, shrinking body. Life preservers were a must and mine hung on the mast. A mile or two out we looked at the diminishing coastline. "How does it feel, babe—to be out in the

201

beautiful blue briny?" I asked her, checking out her smile and disposition. I could always tell if she was faking it. But she appeared calm and genuinely happy to be free of the confines of her bed and the cottage.

"Oh, Cable—*tengo animación, querido!* I am excited to be here! *Gracias, mi muchacho pobre. Voy a recordar este día, señor Denning.*" I will remember this day all my life...to love you for it, and to say you have been *el amor de mi alma*...the lover of my soul...and....and my heart. I...I would live for you all the days....longer....if I could...*este día*, this day....tomorrow....and the day after....the day after...forever, *mi amor.*"

I left the throttle for a moment and came over to embrace her. "Adora...I love you...in case I never say it again like I mean it now...I want you to know...I love you more than I've ever loved anyone..." Feebly she threw her arms around me and dropped her head onto my chest. That snapshot in eternity was one of the most beautiful moments of my lifetime and one I would never forget, no matter what lifetime I would be living—or what would happen beyond this day.

At the same time I hated myself for resenting this lousy rotten break in our lives—maybe feeling sorry for myself—even though I knew Adora must be enduring the impossible. A young woman filled with vitality and gentleness, warmth, beauty and sensuality one could never measure, felled by an unexpected killer. It was like having a Frank Laggore, a Ravna or a Matrangas living inside of you, waiting to pounce when you're not looking. And I knew that's how the killer struck my dear Adora... slow and deadly. I was thinking of what Saturnalia said that strange day when I woke up in her cozy cottage by the fire. *'For the passions that thrill love and lift you high to heaven, are the passions that kill love and let you fall to hell...'* For some reason that stuck in my craw like life's supreme irony. *Really* finding a partner, someone who fits like hand-in-glove in your life and in your bed—and bam! it all shatters like when a storm hits and there on the floor lay the broken shards of a storm window, sparkling like little diamonds of happy yesterdays...reminding you that it can't be put back together....the glass is broken—and somehow you've got to find the guts to throw it out with the memory and the regret, like Toggth said. Somehow I had to learn to let it go. But I didn't know how. I was in love with Adora Moreno, the only doll I ever allowed myself to really feel that with. I had committed myself and crossed the threshold, and there's no turning back from that, no matter who else comes in or out of your life—a one-time love is a one-time love. And so now it was like our own passions had turned against us, the tide was going out and we were being abandoned and Hell was just around the corner...*'for the passions that thrill love and lift you high to heaven...'* Well, at least I'd known that in my lifetime. Adora had set the standard for what love ought to be between man and woman in my book. And she was the best.

We were making good time with the gas engine doing about fifteen miles-an-hour, so I decided not to be the brave sailor, hoist the sail, and risk getting hit in the head with the jib. About half way to Avalon, my lady complained of a headache. I didn't have a damn thing to give her except the turmeric and drinking water we had brought aboard. I gave her some of each. She made a bitter face but took it down like the good little scout she was. "That's my girl," I said, comforting her as best I could with one hand on the rudder wheel.

About two hours later we arrived at the little docking port in Avalon, the only town on the island. Adora seemed to be getting worse. I didn't know if it was seasickness or what, so as soon as I tied up the boat, I went into a little registration office. "I've got a sick lady, is there a doctor here in town?"

A matronly woman told me she'd phone ahead and instructed me to go up a block and turn left. The doctor's house and office were about five doors on the right. But there was no one to watch Adora. I went back to the dock and jumped into our little sailboat. "Babe, I—I want you to be seen by a doc, real quick. I'm gonna run up to the next block and fetch him, if I can—or do you want me to carry you there?"

"You go...I wait here." Then she looked up toward the sky with a beautiful expression in her lovely brown, glowing eyes. "When I go, Cable, I want to be *un pája-ro*—a seagull, who skims the water and glides...oh....*sí, señor Denning, yo quiero estar un pájaro*!" Then her gaze went to my eyes and a wonderful knowing smile fell across those luscious lips I had kissed so often. "I am having a beautiful *vision*, my love, I dream I am floating....not like *esta vida*...this life has been....oh, so *muy triste*, until you come---my okie dokie lover *hombre muy malo.*" I took her hands. She looked back out toward the endless water. "And now I am light....no more *contesta*...no more fight to live, *mi amor.* I am in a land of *muchos colores*, many colors....*pero* we cannot hold on to what we love today, Cable.....we cannot hold on to our

204

cuerpos, our bodies....they are....what you say? Amor, our love cannot be given....but it is...uh....uh..."

"—loaned Adora, just for a while—"

"—Sí! We loan our bodies, no? Maybe I even loan my heart to you, my man. Oh...*mi* handsome *hombre.* I loan that to you, also." Then she looked at me with such longing, I had to turn my eyes away. "I love *your* body, *mi amor,* it has given to me too much pleasure—much excitement...*sí....mucho* fulfillment. Now like the pájaro I will fly...to a new land...I will make a happy nest...for us...and when you come to be with me, my beautiful se-ñor, I will be like *la luz de la luna*...all lighted like the moon for you." She winced in pain. "*Ayi!* You...you go now...*por favor...*I will be okie dokie Joe."

I leaned over to kiss her and told her I'd be right back. I couldn't face what she had just said, so I ignored it. Just then a little creature stepped out of the vessel's cabin. "Don't worry, Cable. I will see to her while you're getting the doctor."

"Toggth!" I exclaimed. "How in the hell did you—oh, never mind, I know how you—"

He beamed at Adora. "—and this is the exquisitely lovely lady that has had Cable all a-twirl these many months."

"This—this, uh, is Toggth—remember that day in my office when he so frightened you?"

Adora's gentile manner made me choke up. She was no longer afraid of the little man-like creature and smiled her best smile. "Sí, I remember, *también, con mu-cho gusto, señor Toggth.* I am pleased to see you once more..."

"As I am you, sweet child." He looked back at me. "Get going, Cable, what are you waiting for?"

I scrambled up the deck ramp and ran down the street. It was a half-hour by the time I was able to rustle up Dr. Ingle and brought him to the dock huffing and puffing after exercising his short little legs all the way from his office. He did a double take on Toggth, whose hands were holding my señorita's head. Adora seemed to be enjoying it and some color had returned to her face. "*Ay, médico, gracias* for coming. This is Toggth, who watched over me while Cable—"

"—young woman, let me examine you," the doctor said matter of fact. Toggth backed away. "Perhaps all you have is a case of sea sickness. A lot of folks get it on their way out here, especially in rough seas." He did the usual, and after a while approached me. "I think the young woman has been quite ill, from all appearances. But I can detect nothing. She said she is not in pain or discomfort at the moment. But all the same, I'd get her to the mainland on the next ferry—at two-thirty this afternoon." I thanked Dr. Ingle and tried to pay him but he insisted that Adora's beauty was payment enough and went on his way.

I turned back to look at Toggth. "You let the guy see you...isn't that a bit unusual for Mr. Hide-and-Conceal?"

He came forward to me, looked up with understanding yellow-amber eyes. "I have taken away her pain for a while. That's why the doctor could find nothing." Then he took me aside and whispered softly to me. "Her heart will stop soon—and then she will transition, Cable. I know I cannot tell you to prepare, but *prepare.*"

"Hey, you *dos hombres—qué es su secreto?*" Adora was feeling better and I could tell she liked Toggth a lot.

"Oh, Toggth was just telling me he did some healing work on you, do you feel better?"

"Sí. Señor Toggth take away *mi dolor*. I am good now," she said in a perky voice. "Even I have *apetito*— shall we eat something, Cable?"

"Sure, babe, if that's what you want. I'm delighted, I mean, you haven't eaten anything except soup and medicine for a long time."

We thanked him and bade Toggth good-bye. We found a little diner not far from the dock. My lady was weak, but with me holding her hand she could manage a slow walk. There was an interesting expression on her face, like a far away look you have when you know you're going to take an exciting journey somewhere. By two-fifteen we were on the ferry heading back to L.A. Adora was feeling a bit chilled, she said, and wanted to sit inside and watch the ocean go by from there. I stayed with her until I was dying for a smoke. I told her I'd be right back. "I miss you...*para siempre, mi amor* ..."

I tried to fight back the tears, but my eyes misted. "Damn it, Adora—it's hard enough! Please...don't hurry things along...I can't think of it, my love—I just can't."

"*Lo siento*, Cable. You go *fumar*. I rest here...okay, Joe?" she said with a forced smile. I could tell the pain was coming back.

I wrapped my coat around her and went out onto the deck and lit up. Whatever in hell possessed me to want to take her out to Catalina in her condition? She seemed to enjoy the idea of it. It was probably beyond her limits now. I felt so alone, even with my ailing beloved just beyond those doors, resting. Life deals us so many unanticipated cards. How could I have known the love of my life would turn to jelly from the inside? But I also knew I needed to spend every minute I could with her. I tossed my cigarette overboard and went to rejoin my beautiful lady.

When I got in, she seemed to be resting and her eyes were closed, a soft smile crossed her lips as if she were dreaming of something wonderful and far away. I sat next to her. "You know, babe, I'm thinking we need to take a little more fresh air now and then...what do you think? I should take you to Bronson Park and we can sit on a bench..." Just then I realized how still Adora seemed to be. I felt her arm. It was limp. I pushed in on her wrist with my thumb to feel a pulse. My beautiful love was gone. There, of all places, amidst the chattering passengers, noisy ship engines, the hum and vibration of the wood and metal, my beloved left this world. I sat back next to her warm little body, pressing my lips together so I wouldn't start bawling in front of all those people. So I took her hand and held it, so no one would notice. Not until we got into port.

Mors Vertit Unum Page (Death Turns a Page)

Adora Moreno had died on March 29th, 1932—on Honey Combes' birth date! It's a sorrowful thing when only ten people attend your funeral. My mother stood on one side of me while Elisa and Flora Moreno stood on the other. A few scattered friends and acquaintances filled out the rest of the group. But the big surprise to me was the gentle and understanding face of Zelda Blodgett. She had gone through my travail with Honey and she knew my grief would be all but unbearable. I recalled how she held me on the bed that night Honey was killed. She did so maternally. Yeah, sure, she had romantic designs on me in her own little mind, but she overcame them in that moment. And I liked her for that.

I was thinking also of my mother. Many years ago with me holding her hand, we were burying my father. The burly bloke had another soft spot in him besides my mother. He loved music and when he was drunk enough, he would sing songs at our piano in the parlor, my mother playing for him. His favorite song was an old folk tune entitled *Roses of Picardy.* Even as a child I could feel love's regret when he sang the lyrics that stuck out to me most: '*And the years fly on forever, 'til the shadows veil their skies...but he loves to hold her little hands and look in her sea blue eyes...and she sees the road by the poplars, where they met in the bygone years...for the first little song of the roses...is the last little song she hears...*' Now, my dear Adora had heard her last little song and I am reminded of the sadness my loving mother must have been feeling in that hour.

The priest spoke the funeral mass in Latin there at the gravesite. He was a lovely old Irishman with a twinkle in his eye, as if he knew something the rest of us didn't. But his ending remarks were hard-hitting and I took my mother's hand when he went into my heart and tried to rip it out. Because I was thinking, how many times can we watch someone we love get lowered into the ground? How do people do it? Maybe they turn off. Maybe they have a faith of some hereafter, or that after all, as Toggth said, all is cycle and re-cycle and nothing ever really dies. But, damn, it goes away and leaves you with a hole torn in your heart.

"God does not always choose for us the life we think we want," the priest began. "His mercy and love, although sometimes incomprehensible, brings us to the truth of our lives, nonetheless. We come to the earth as guests, children of Him who gave so much and asked for nothing in return. If Mary wept for her crucified son, God rejoiced in the lifting of our sins by his sacrifice. *'For God so loved the world that he gave his only begotten son...'* May we say that for our sister Adora, who in being released of the flesh, may stand consecrated and unjudged beside the Lord. May God be with Adora always, and with those of us who are left behind with immeasurable sorrow from which there is no release except the passing of time." He rang his little hand bell and the altar boys did their thing with the incense. "May you walk with the Lord all your days..." He uttered some more Latin stuff and that was that.

I could not watch as they lowered Adora's body into the damp, cold earth. I had to think she wasn't there, anyway. I watched a red-tailed hawk circle majestically in the sky over the cemetery. Maybe now, in this perfect time when something comes to an end with unmistakable finality, she was up there—in the sky—happy as she was that day when she said to me on the little sailboat, "Cable, I want to be a bird...a seagull, floating over and swooping down to skim the water...without a care..." Well, maybe on this day she got her wish, maybe life *does* go on in many forms—who the hell knows?

I went up to my mother and told her I'd take her home. She insisted she would prefer to take the street-car home alone. She comforted me and I could tell her own sorrow was great as she and Adora had shared a deep bond. Then I hugged Elisa and Flora. They asked us to come to *Todo el Mundo* for a cup of coffee and a roll. But I told them that just now there were too many memories there where Adora and I met. Now it seemed to be many years ago. But it wasn't. We had lived and died within a short space of time, love and life rising to its highest place—then like the ocean's tides...life ebbing...leaving the shore behind, naked and lonely. The rest was like a song that would keep playing on inside me, haunting the places that we felt were safe, but weren't—you have to keep walking with that tune in your ear because some day you'll have forgotten it— and the worst thing we can do in this life, in my opinion, is to forget love.

Zelda came up to me and embraced me. She didn't say anything, simply took my hand and walked with me to the streetcar stop. Finally, she looked up at me. "You know, Cable, I knew I would come, even though I didn't even know your lady. And I thought of things I would say to you. But I saw your face, like the day Honey died and I held you. That's all I wanted to do...just hold you, say nothing, be nothing. I am so sorry. I can only imagine what you might be feeling. Twice in your life, you have lost so much..."

I squeezed Zelda's hand. "Thanks, Zelda, you're okay, lady. Now I have two gravesites to visit. Will you come with me sometime when I don't have the guts to go alone?"

"You bet. I'd go anywhere with you, Cable. You know, I'm rather like my plants, feed and water me a little, and I'll give you a lot of growth—and maybe even look pretty for you."

I smiled at the attractive young lady who had become my friend. I took a deep breath. "Well, Zelda, somehow I gotta pick up the pieces and get on with it, I guess. I'm not sure what for. But I'm glad you're my friend...come by soon...your plants need watering."

Don't Send Me Flowers

Affording an extended trip, and leaving my business for a few days was no easy task during the crippling economic depression that was tail spinning well into 1932. I had a feeling the bottom hadn't been reached yet, either. Taking care of Adora's medical bills, the extra expenses to keep the office and renting our little house pretty well drained my finances. The Royce money was almost gone. Plus my mother's monthly pension, after my father's death, from the steel factory where my father had worked, came to an end when the factory became victim to the 1929 crash. It seemed almost everyone was going belly-up these days. So now I was also supporting my mother, even though she took in ironing when she could. But hell, even mothers don't last forever and mine was starting to show the years of wear and tear life had bequeathed to her.

To pay for my journey I decided to try and sell the diamond ring I had bought for a wedding that never quite took place. I hated to do it—take Honey's only remaining physical link to me and pawn it for the going market price. Those days, pawnshops and jewelry stores were often tossed together. Such was the case of Abe and Golda Sachs on lower Broadway. Don't ask me why, but Jews seemed to be the money exchangers and merchants of the world. Especially in gold, silver and precious gems, they were not to be bested.

I liked the Sachs. So, this one day I came in with a heavy heart to sell Honey's ring. The shop was neat but cluttered at the same time. Everything from accordions to banjos hung from the walls. They had a "new" section of rings and neckpieces where I had originally purchased Honey's ring. I walked in with a semi-smile, trying to make the best out of a rotten situation. "Hello, there...anybody in?" I asked, not seeing a soul stirring about.

Soon a little old lady with intense bright eyes and straggling grey hair came out. "So what is it you want— we're not buying today. Too much inventory gives my husband a headache!" she said with a very decidedly thick accent. "So you want to buy—or what?"

"No, actually I bought this ring here." I took the little velvet box out of my pocket, opened it and showed her the ring.

"Nice piece. Oy vey! I remember you, a year or two ago. You're the handsome policeman, right? What happened? The girl got cold feet—what?"

"No, she died—before we got married." I said that still not quite believing Honey was gone forever. "I won't be needing it. I was hoping you could give me something for it. I paid a little over a thousand and paid it off some time ago. You can check your books, to see

213

that I'm paid-in-full. I'm in a kind of tough spot just now—"

"—I believe you! Abe does the books. I think he was happy the day he got your money order to pay off the ring. I remember now, he was scratching his head as to why he gave you nine years to pay the ring off! The wife really *could* be dead by then!"

Abe Sachs came out. He was stout with wisps of white hair on his temples. The rest of his pate was shiny bald. He wore gold-rimmed glasses and had thin lips and intense blue eyes. "So what's going on here, Golda?" He looked me over. "Ah, the newlywed policeman, eh? You came to return the ring already? What's with things not lasting these days? Last week a lady came in to sell her wedding ring. The husband ran off with the house-keeper—you figure—women and men...you're cursed if you do and you're cursed if you don't."

"So *you* did, Abe. Are you sorry now? Huh? Such a thing! You should be glad that I stayed all these years to hear you complain." She looked at me. "He complains about everything—from his lumbago to the property taxes and the guys up there in Washington running the country into the ground, he says."

"Ya! That's right! Into the ground! First you work yourself to the bone, making a decent living. Then they come and take it away with taxes? Such a thing I don't need!"

I felt I had become lost in their conversation. "I—I, uh, would really like you to consider looking at the ring. I'd sell it reasonably—"

They ignored me because I knew they were really into it just about now. "—and another thing—if you

214

don't feed people and offer them jobs—they die! They *die*! We knew enough rough times in the old country, why should we come here to live it again?"

Mrs. Sachs seconded her husband's voice. "Mrs. Beinberg—a nice Jewish lady—runs the shop next door. She and her husband are closing the doors next month." Then she glanced at the ring. "So how could we afford to pay you anything for the ring—take it out of our life savings?"

"No, I was just hoping—hoping you'd be able to give me some dough to get out of town with. You see, since I've seen you last, things have gone pretty rough for me—"

"—who hasn't got it rough, Policeman—" Abe Sachs interrupted.

"—Denning, Cable Denning's the name..."

"Mr. Denning. Denning...that's not a Jewish name—you're a Mic from the Irish side of the tracks, ya?"

"Yeah...that's right...grown up with a silver spoon in my mouth and a knife in my ribs. That kind of tender loving care..."

"So all of life is a fighting, Mr. Denning. You fight to be born, you fight to stay alive, sometimes you even fight to die! Such a thing it is. Don't complain if you can still walk, talk and breathe and you don't ache all over. What do you expect of life—a golden Cadillac with a mansion overlooking the ocean? Ha! Look at us here, slave labor, day in, day out—and what do we get for it? Old age—that's what we get! I get lumbago and my wife gets old, ugly and worn out—"

"—Abraham! Why is it all the time you insult me in front of customers? So I'm not perfect—but I'm all you

215

got—don't forget that. I also gave up my life for you and suffer through every day hearing you complain. It's too hot in the back, my leg hurts, those damn gentiles, why doesn't God give me a goddess? How much money I spend on the rent—even if I haven't bought anything for myself in twenty years! How much do you hear me complain, huh? How much? What am I, the doormat or what?"

Abe Sachs ignored his wife. "So you should want I buy your ring back? And why should I do that? I'm not a good Samaritan, you know. I'm in business for *business*—the kind that *makes* money."

Mrs. Sachs was calmed down a trifle as she looked up into my face. "So you were saying you had tragedy or something in your life? Such a time comes...when you need rest from the world. I listen to the radio to get away from that *nudnik* over there. Music calms the nerves, opens the heart, you know." Then she looked at her husband. "He's a wounded man, my husband, such a thing that he should live to not regret his life and what tradition and every day brings." She smiled a little at me. "Abe, this man is hurting—needs a kindness—give him something for the ring."

Abe Sachs gave his wife a dirty look and turned to me. "Supposing Golda has a point—we can't always be in the game for money—after all, there's family and possessions, then there's business and acquiring possessions—and *then* there's money—which permits the family and acquiring of possessions! Such a thing I can't understand in the world—does nobody get it? Money makes the world go 'round! Without it we might as well be beggars on the street." He nodded his head vigorously at his wife. "Kindness, now you're asking...I should be so lucky to have you as my wife" he said, recalling Golda's earlier statement... "Do you know, Mr. Denning, after forty years she barely cooks and sews? I have to go to Mr. Weiss, a tailor down the street to get my pants to fit. And always, I'm finding dust on the furniture. Look at this place. Look around. The French horn up there—hasn't been dusted in years!"

"Abe! You should be ashamed for yourself!" said Mrs. Sachs. Then she looked me up and down. "How old are you, Mr. Denning?"

"I'm going to be thirty two in September."

"You see, Abe, such a young man—he deserves a fresh start."

"You should worry about a September birthday in April? In Latvia only the girls celebrated birthdays. Boys had to be men—and soon. Take it from a guy who knows, Denning, don't worry about the birthdays!"

Golda was tapping her foot on the floor. "What about it, Abraham? Forty years and you think I don't know you?" She winked at me.

Abe Sachs was thinking. "Most I can give you is two-hun—"

"—five hundred!" Mrs. Sachs cut her husband off.

Abe Sachs frowned. "Okay, okay...five hundred but not a penny more—I'm paying here, way above whole-sale! I should praise the day I can sell the ring for that. Five hundred dollars in these depression days is like two thousand a couple of years ago."

"Thank you, Mr. Sachs. I'll take it. I won't forget it. If I make it big someday in the private detective business,

I'll come back and double your money. I promise," I said, trying to be as conciliatory as possible.

"Don't promise anything...in this life, young man. Nobody wants the burden of something promised weighting down the mind. You should want success? Don't think about getting rich. Think about getting happy—like me. Abraham and me fight like tooth and nail, I even pushed him once into the street when we were young. But no horse and buggy was coming, so I went out, took his hand, and brought him back home. Then we made love—and everything was okay for another day or two."

"Golda! What's with the telling about our love life here? Have a little respect for our private business. Besides, who wants to know about two old Jews making love when they were twenty-five?"

"I'm interested," I said, enjoying this battling couple. "I've always marveled at what keeps a man and woman together so many years."

"The patience of God," Golda Sachs responded.

Abe Sachs didn't reply and went to the back room. He soon returned with a medium-sized black metal box. He opened it and took out a clump of money. He counted out five one hundred dollars bills and tossed them at me across the counter. "Here...sign this receipt for the ring. I gave you money, you gave me the ring, I give you the receipt. Oy vey, I still don't know how I'm going to sell it for even that amount. You know, Denning, I'm buying back a used item. But it's in such good condition, maybe I can place it among the new jewelry. Maybe I'll recover some profit that way...maybe even you'll get married again some day soon and you'll buy it back for

218

that special gentile lady. Or have you ever seen a nice Jewish young lady you might fancy? I hear gentiles and Jews sometimes get along better than Jews and Jews."

"I don't think I'll be marrying anytime soon, Mr. Sachs. But I hope you get your price." I signed the receipt and started out the door with my five hundred smackers. "Thanks again..." I said.

Golda Sachs followed me out onto the sidewalk. "Young Denning...some lessons come by pain—such a thing we cannot avoid. But keep your eyes straight ahead and they will see the good side of life. There is one, you know. Even after all you've lost." She came to me and hugged me. She was whispering. "Now...if *I* was one of those young Jewish girls Abe was talking about, I would definitely lift my skirts for you." She giggled. "Good-bye, Mr. Denning. And good luck."

I hurried down the street to catch the streetcar back to my office.

CHAPTER 8

CAMBRIAN DREAMS

Captain Nitwit and the Wild Gypsy Woman

After I packed up Adora's belongings, I delivered them to her mother and sister. Then I called the landlord and told him I had to give up the cottage. I knew in that moment I would more than likely never dwell in a common abode again...that I would live like a vagabond bachelor out of the back of my office, hitching a ride with the stars on balmy nights and listening to that lonely sax wend its way across the city I belonged to.

The other thing I knew was, I had to get out of town for a few days. I gave Zelda an extra key and asked her to watch after my office while I was gone. I knew she wanted to come with me—wherever I decided to go— but she was a smart lady and knew I needed to have some quality time alone to heal the grief that was just now beginning to set in. I was one of those brave types who don't react to the layers of sorrow up front. The delayed reaction gave me room to function until the worst was over. Eventually, I decided I'd go to the ocean and kill two birds with one stone by dropping by to check on Cassie, Saturnalia's little alien daughter. She was supposedly now in human form, living in Cambria Pines-by-the-Sea and working behind the counter of a local pharmacy. Elisa Moreno owned a 1924 Ford coupe and she was happy to let me borrow it for my long journey to San Luis Obispo County. And so it came to be that

I set out on yet another bizarre adventure in the life of one Cable Denning, Private Detective.

I got into town late on a Wednesday afternoon. I found a little motel called *The Bluebird* right on State Route #1, which was Main Street of the tiny hamlet. The layout was a large two-story home where the owners lived, and about a dozen separate little cabins with varying capacities around the perimeter of the area with parking in front of each one. Before settling in, I went outside and found a little trail behind my cabin that led to a charming little creek, called the *Santa Rosa*. The wonderful smells of vegetation and water filled my nostrils and I could breathe more deeply than back home in the smog-choked metropolis. Around dusk, I ambled over to the office to inquire about Arthur Beatle. Johnny Anderson...Hungarian, energetic, well-built and completely bald, was the owner-proprietor along with his very pretty and slightly plump wife, Barbara. Seems that Art Beatle, sometimes known as *Captain Nitwit*, was a local pariah, and not the most welcomed citizen of Cambria and its environs. In fact, they told me plenty, maybe more than I needed to know.

His real name was Arthur Beatle. And according to Johnny Anderson, he was a legend in his time. Few said that they had ever met a hardier or more physically powerful man. He wasn't particularly tall—sinewy and bright-eyed, his face worn where life's experiences cut their paths. The silver running through his black hair, belied a face that looked smashed against the world, his nose bent to the side, his eyebrows thick, his forehead furrowed, his eyes a twinkling blue. He chewed tobacco and spat accurately, so they say, and his nickname was *'Spit Beetle.'* Some say he palled around with Jack London in San Francisco in the days when one could ride horseback into town from the Valley of the Moon. He must have been eccentric to begin with, for when I found him, he had built a castle of stone and mortar inset with abalone shells and toilet seats for windows—no glass. The front gate was an ancient bedspring that hung on rusty hinges and moaned when the wind blew too hard. Old water pipes served as railings as one chugged up the steps inlaid with shining abalone and beach pebbles. Some stairways went nowhere, others led into long troughs of spinach or kale in stone beds with local soil thrown in for good measure. Jeffery Pines stood sentinel around the massive monstrosity while a rickety metal stove pipe penetrated the roof of the fourth story where Art lived.

Legend has it that he was a construction foreman in 1918 during the fiasco they called *the war to end all wars* in Europe. I hope they were right, but I doubt it. Humans always find a way to aggress on their neighbor's real estate or want something they have. Anyway, already in his mid-thirties, Arthur emigrates to San Francisco after World War I and becomes a fry cook in some dump on Mission Street. There he meets Maria Contelli...a fiery young gypsy woman. Pretty soon they get together and Arthur tells the completely uncontrollable hot-tempered babe that he bought a few lots near the ocean on the Central California coast and is building a 'honeymoon' cottage near the top on a flat postage stamp of land. So Beatle builds the edifice where no electricity, indoor plumbing or running water exist and invites Maria to come visit. She loves the pine tree forests with a hint of fog and sunshine. The passionate twosome quit their San Francisco jobs and she moves in with him. But soon ominous signs betray the fact that both of them are highly tempered individuals and after the 'honeymoon', things get pretty rough as Maria begins to get cabin-fever, starts throwing things at her dearly beloved and adding salt to the wound, takes up with a younger, hard-drinking friend of Arthur's!

Now the plot thickens as Arthur's Genevieve betrays his trust and leaves the happy nest he had provided her with. In a rage of unparalleled madness, Arthur destroys the cabin, board-by-board, tile by tile, tossing whatever furniture there was out into the thickets and busting up anything that might remind him of 'that woman.' Then one day Maria Contelli leaves town, never to be heard from again.

Venting his pent up hurt and anger, Arthur Beatle begins his gargantuan project. Using only his hand shovel, a makeshift wheelbarrow, and willpower second to none, stone by stone, nail by nail pounded into the used wood edifice, the four-story fairy tale rises from the ground. *Nitwit Ridge* will never be finished and the emotional pain he feels can only find solace in ceaseless labor, bent on forgetting what might have been and glossing over the possible reality that the couple was never compatible in the first place. In a way that reminded me of Joe Lorena, an alien who fell in love with a human woman and lost her. And that...was the legend of one Arthur Beatle, known to many as *Captain Nitwit*, philosopher extraordinaire!

223

It was hard for me to figure this guy as an alien, though. And Saturnalia's lovely young daughter was living with him? Some of it didn't make sense, but who could figure these damn aliens? If *Cassie* was anything like her mother, I'll bet she was a dish. As Mr. Anderson finished his story, I inquired about a young woman who might be living in his home. "Shambles is more like it," Mr. Anderson said. "How could any attractive young lady like Cassie Olson live in that filth and disarray? Of course, there is rumor that she lives in sin with Art Beatle. I couldn't say. But I know she never goes to church." I was wondering how she got the last name "Olson" when I knew that Saturnalia *had* no last name. Maybe she made it up.

"Well, thanks, Mr. Anderson—Mrs. Anderson...I'm going to turn in, it's a long drive from L.A. to your little paradise here by the sea."

"Oh, you must visit the ocean, down by the community park there are lots of rocks to climb at low tide." Then he studied my face. "May I ask, Mr. Denning, what it is you do—I mean, professionally?"

"I'm a private dick—you know, a private investigator. I used to be a cop but moved up in the world."

"Is Cassie in any kind of trouble? Despite her horrible living situation with Art Beatle up at Nitwit Ridge, I would say she's a wholesome and beauteous young thing."

"No...I'm here strictly for pleasure. I promised her mother I'd drop in on her—make sure she's okay."

"Maybe okay, but look out for Jane Slaughter."

"And who, may I ask, is Jane Slaughter?"

"A bad influence, I'd say. A reckless young woman without scruples, no visible means of income—and sleeps until all hours."

"Now how would you know that?" I asked.

"Well...." He looked at me and then at his wife. "Jane lives here. She rents a room permanently from us. I'd refuse her, but we need the money. You see, Cambria is an off-the-beaten track community—and very seasonal. We depend on summer trade and therefore rent out whatever rooms we can on a weekly or monthly basis during the off-season months. I'm sure you can understand that."

"Oh, I sure do. Especially with the Depression on and all. Well, good night, now."

I walked down a little lane that led to my cabin, a little one-room and bathroom affair with a blue roof. It was getting on to about eight o'clock when I turned the key to my door. When it got dark out here in the boonies, it was pitch black. Only the sound of crickets and frogs could be heard coming from the little creek down the way. Then I thought I saw out of the corner of my eye, a figure dashing into the shadows and the snap of twigs beyond some trees not far away. I ran in, grabbed my coat off the bed and went for my .38. I waited until I thought the coast might be clear and quickly slipped out of my cabin. I crept toward the trees, but approached from behind, doing the old Indian trick. In a faint light coming from the reflection off the motel sign out on the highway, I saw a man smoking a cigarette. A twig popped under my foot and the man instantly spun around, drew a knife and threw it at me in the dark! I dodged and fell to the pine needles and shot once, hitting the man in the chest, probably right through his heart. It wasn't hard to guess that this was probably one of the tails the *Oculus* liked to send my way, just to keep things from getting too boring in my life. I approached the body. Then I heard a voice behind me. "*Now* what are you going to do?" a fairly rough-hewn female voice chirped out.

I spun around with my revolver still in my hand. "Where did you come from?" I asked.

She didn't seem too excited about the whole thing. "You won't need the gun, Mister. I'm not the kind that chases guys, anyhow." She studied my face as she approached. I put my gun away. "Looks to me like you've used it before. Well, at least this breaks up the monotony. You don't look like the killer type. Who's the mug you just creamed? He looks like a well-dressed hoodlum to me. I saw him hanging around here earlier, before it got dark."

"He's a messenger from some people who don't happen to be very fond of me just now. Because I'm the guy at the other end of the law—you know, the one who's supposed to clean up after thugs like him."

"That figures. Yeah, you look like one of those guys." She extended her hand. "I'm Jane Slaughter—and it looks like I'm your neighbor—at least for tonight."

"Good to meet you, Miss Slaughter. And thanks for keeping this on ice. I'm—I'm Cable Denning. I'm a private dick—supposed to be on vacation, but I guess *that* hasn't worked out so far."

She snickered out loud. "A private what? I'm not sure I heard you right, Mr. Denning."

"A private detective—*dick* is short for that...you know..."

"Well, that isn't how I remember it—at least not in East L.A."

"You come from East L.A.? I was born there. Bred and born in Boyle Heights, across the river from Little Italy."

"Yeah—well, what a coincidence. I know exactly where that is. Small world, eh?"

"We've got to get rid of this body, Miss Slaughter. Can you help?"

"Sure, we can dump it out at Leffingwell. Let's drag it to your cabin around the back way and onto the seat of your car."

As we were doing that, we spotted a flashlight coming down the lane toward us. We dragged the body behind the cabin and I told Jane Slaughter to stay put with the corpse. I quickly took out a Lucky Strike and lit it. "Oh, Mr. Denning, did you happen to hear a gunshot or something like it earlier? My wife swears she heard something. I was listening to the radio—the 'F.B.I. in Peace and War'—so I didn't hear a thing."

"Naw, Mr. Anderson. Maybe a car backfired on the highway or something," I lied, puffing away on my cigarette. "I just came out for a smoke. I don't like to sully nice clean motel rooms with cigarette smoke. And I don't like to sleep with those clouds hanging around all night," I fibbed again. I did it all the time in my office, my bedroom, wherever I lit up. I was the all-time air polluter wherever I went. Filthy habits like smoking take part of your life away, I knew, but when you're addicted at age 13, it's hard to stop the momentum toward the early grave.

"How considerate. Well, then, Mr. Denning, have a pleasant night."

He ambled off with his flashlight. I went around to the back of the cabin. Jane Slaughter and I finished pulling the creep's body into Elisa's little Ford. I was careful to check for any blood that might end up on any of us, on the car seat or where I shot the bloke. I'd have to check again tomorrow. We hopped in with the body on the rider's side while the young lady sidled in tightly next to me. Quietly as possible, we drove out of the gravel driveway and on to Highway One, heading north.

It turned out *Leffingwell* was a small creek that emptied into the sea about five miles north of Cambria. We were on our way to a county garbage disposal site and bumped up and down over a rutty gravel road, the corpse constantly falling over onto Jane Slaughter's shoulder. After about fifteen minutes, our headlights shone on a clearing, strewn with all the remnants from unloaded garbage trucks.

"Don't you think the body might be discovered if we just toss it on a pile of debris?" I asked, beginning to enjoy the hard-nail gal in my company. She seemed compatible with my kind of man, maybe because we both grew up the hard way and appreciated what it was like to be out of the ghetto of East L.A.

"Recently, I was out here with Pinter, my boss at the bar. Someone cut down a huge pine tree and there are jillions of branches, over there at the far end. We can throw the stiff on the ground and then cover him with branches. Probably a better burial than the son-of-a-bitch deserves. I hate people who go around killing other people."

"Yeah, me, too. That's why I became a cop when I was twenty-four. I had this ideal dream that the good guys went after the bad guys and the good guys won. Well, Miss Slaughter, I found out it wasn't always that way."

"Jane to you. So what way did it go?" she asked.

"One side is just as crooked as the other. Hell, in L.A., you want someone killed? Pay off a cop a few bucks and the job gets done."

"Yeah, figures." We pulled the car to the edge of the chasm where hundreds of branches lay strewn in a dry creek bed. We took out the corpse, rolled it over the embankment, then jumped down and covered it with branches, the headlights of the little Ford lighting up the gulch. We made it look as natural as we could and high-tailed it out of that smelly maggot infested area as quickly as possible.

"By the way, Jane, you can call me Cable. How in the hell did you end up out here in nowhere land?" She was about five-foot five or so, reasonably slender with fair breasts filling out a light blue sweater. Her dark, nondescript hair flowed just below her shoulders, and a face that was a bit hard, as if she were wearing a mask. Underneath the facade, I saw a handsome young woman, who, with a little make-up would light up any man's evening, I thought. Her eyes were washed-out blue and her thin lips were covered with something clear and shiny, but with no color.

"How does anybody end up anywhere? I guess I'm a drifter...here, there, everywhere..."

"How old are you, if I may ask?"

"Twenty-two. Like my friend, Cassie, she's the same age. What about you?"

"I'll be thirty-two soon. Can't believe it...just yesterday I was twenty-seven...time flies whether you're having fun or not. Uh...about your friend—?"

"—Yeah, you can say that again." She studied me. "You've got a handsome face, in a rugged sort of way. I'll bet the babes really go for you, eh? With some guys, you can just tell."

"I don't know about that, but I guess I've had my share of beautiful dames. But I think they come in a close third to chasing down bad guys and listening to The Great American Songbook in some smoky dive with a dish in a revealing sequined gown singing Porter or Berlin or Mack Gordon. Yeah, kid, I think those are now my priorities in this world."

"You're quite a guy, I can tell," she said, punching me lightly on the shoulder from the rider's seat. "I may not have the sequined gown, but I'm a singer, though, and pretty good too. That's what I do at *The Bucket of Blood*."

"Bucket of wha...? You're putting me on? What the hell's that? Son-of-a-bitch, and you're a singer, too?" I was getting the willies inside. It seemed the fates kept throwing babes who could sing at me. So I had to make sure I didn't make any advances on this lady, not to mention I was still mourning Adora a hell of a lot—and what was supposed to be a getaway rest for me so far had ended up being a series of strange occurrences under a series of strange circumstances. For example, where did the goon come from who threw the knife at me? Was it or was it not rather strange that this Jane Slaughter should happen to be staying at the same motel I chose—and did she say that she was a friend of Cassie's?

"*Bucket of Blood*...a dirty, filthy tavern in downtown Cambria, west of the post office. Being it's Prohibition and all, these places should, by rights, either be closed or serving soda and non-alcoholic beverages. But there are three fully stocked bars in Cambria. On the south-side of Main Street, there's *Camozzi's*...then *Reali's*, which is on the corner opposite the Bank of Cambria—and *The Bucket of Blood*, located down a small street where residences start to blend with businesses. Believe me, if I didn't need the work, I wouldn't be caught dead in the place....which, by the way, is what happens to a lot of guys who hang out there. Or might just as well be..."

"Now whatta ya mean by that?"

"Hard-drinking men come in, gamble, whore around, shout, yell, spit and pinch my rear for kicks. A certain other group of men, however, slip a Mickey to some poor bloke, and when he passes out, they conk him over the head, take his money and clothes and toss him aboard a vessel waiting off shore in Pirates Cove sailing for China—"

"—or maybe Siam," I interjected. "In other words, these guys get shanghaied to unknown ports of call for an unlimited duration, right?"

"Yeah, how'd you know?"

"When I was a cop, we busted up a ring of these hijackers at San Pedro. But for every one you arrest, there

231

are twenty more to take his place. So, in the end, very little gets accomplished."

"That's how I kind of figure it. Anyway, I sing there with an old beat up piano playing old beat up tunes three nights a week, mostly for tips." She looked over at me with a very faint smile, but probably it took Jane a long time to even come up with that. "I think I'm gonna like you, Cable. You're not like the other guys. You're rough and tough, the way I like a man to be, yet sensitive and observant. And I like your voice—the way you talk..."

"Thanks, Jane. Truth is, I'm supposed to be on leave of absence, healing up from a recent tragedy. It just hasn't worked out that way so far..."

She looked over at me as I lit up a Lucky Strike and she could see my face more clearly by the match light. "So that's the pain in your eyes. You've lost someone dear to you—I mean, more than just a break-up—"

"—I'm sorry, I really don't want to talk about it. Just know that I lost someone I can't replace—and let's leave it at that, okay?"

"Okay," she said, settling back into her seat.

"So...you mentioned before that you have a friend named Cassie. Coincidentally, I am here to see a Cassie Olson at the request of her mother. Any chance your friend is one and the same? And, if so, can you maybe introduce me to her tomorrow? I promised her mother I'd drop in on her before I mosey on my way."

"Well, I'll be...! Sure...Cassie Olson! She gets off work at five or so. Mother? She's never said a word about a mother—are you sure?"

"Yep. Her mother and I shared an interesting adventure together."

"She was pretty good in the sack, huh?"

"No, not that kind of adventure but something a bit more out of the ordinary. But I don't want to talk about that, either."

"You sure carry a hell of a lot of secrets, Cable. Don't you trust anyone? You can't go through life like that, you know...sooner or later you gotta let go and find yourself in the here and now—like I have to do—and realize things ain't necessarily gonna be better tomorrow."

"And maybe meet someone along the way you can trust?"

"Yeah, that's it...sometimes we get lucky—it can still happen, you know. I don't depend on luck or fate or that shit, though."

"Well, Jane, it's not finding someone you can trust— it's life *itself* you can't trust. Settle in with someone and you're bound to experience hell and damnation, some good laughs and a lot of tears along the way. Show me a couple who after two years of marriage aren't either disinterested or at each other's throats and I'll show you a pipe dream."

"Damn, I like the way you talk, Mister. Are you that intense in the bedroom? I'll bet you are. Women love you because you seem unattached—and that makes 'em clamor for you, doesn't it?"

"Well, for now, Jane, I've about had it with the romance department of my life. So I really don't want to talk about it. I don't know where I am anymore. Ever get to that place when you have to play it day to day, otherwise you might jump overboard?"

"Oh, yeah, try every other day or so. So...what does a private detective do to bring him to the brink of—of destruction?"

"Try life in L.A., for one. The Depression makes me depressed, and it seems like I'm jinxed to lose a lotta people in my life—especially those I dare to love. Add to that—I've seen some things I...I wasn't supposed to—and you've got one screwed up guy."

She reached over and grabbed my arm. "Seen things? Like weird stuff that doesn't make sense?"

"You might say that."

"Whoa, Nellie! So have I, Cable. And it has to do with—with Cassie Olson, my friend. I still can't get over that you came here to see her, met me and....well, anyway, finish what you were saying."

"Yeah...strange how things sort of fall together like that. Well, it doesn't really add up to much. Most of what I do to make ends meet is pretty boring. I snap photographs through bedroom windows of unsuspecting husbands or wives in the throes of some erotic tryst. They get used as evidence when I present the photos in divorce court to a bored judge. It's all about money, Jane, that's what I've learned about this fucking world. Follow the money trail and that's where the action is. Whether it's about a wife getting everything she can from a philandering husband or a gangster in a speakeasy—it's all about dough. Toss in the yen for power and control, add some sex and you've just described human existence for the folks upstairs who run the world."

234

"As I said, I sure like the way you talk, Mister. It's kind of a cross between your tough upbringing and what you've forced yourself to become in order to survive the L.A. jungle. Hell, I'd like to leave this area and maybe join you in the city. Got room for a female private investigator? I could be your undercover assistant..."

The more I was in the company of this rough-hewn young woman with a good head on her shoulders, the more I liked her. I laughed. "You could get killed, lady. I wouldn't like that. I forgot to tell you about the seedier parts of my job. It's a violent world out there."

"Ha! Tell me! You don't have to go to the city to see that. Just spend a night at *The Bucket of Blood* and you'll get a craw full."

We drove up to the front of my cabin. I turned the engine off. "So what about Cassie? You said she was strange?"

"I've just seen things, that's all. I should let you be the judge. How about if we all meet tomorrow night at *The Bucket of Blood*? I'll even sing for you, if you don't mind a rickety old piano that's out of tune and a drunk piano player--me." Then she studied my face there in the dark with only the light from the street sign to go by. "I think I like you, Cable. And I'm serious about being a female detective. Maybe you could teach me. I have really good instincts about things....if you know what I mean."

"Yeah, I do...you gotta have 'em razor sharp to survive out there, Jane. And it takes guts. Maybe your L.A. school of hard knocks chiseled you out a bit, eh? But I don't know if you can teach that kind of thing. You're going by the seat of your britches most of the time."

"I like the danger, Cable. I always have. Three punks cornered me when I was about sixteen. I had hitchhiked to Bakersfield to visit an uncle and they picked me up. Somewhere along the way, they turned off the highway and found a secluded spot and forced me out of the car. I could feel the fear and excitement in me. I knew they wanted to rape me—and maybe either kill me or leave me abandoned and bleeding out in the fields off Highway 99. What they didn't know was that my brother Chester taught me some Chinese martial arts stuff—you know, how to defend yourself with some fast moves? Well, when the first two guys came at me, I started to unbutton my blouse as if I knew I couldn't fight off all three of them. Then, when they were about to grapple me, I chopped one of them on the neck with a lethal blow, kicked the other in the groin really hard and they fell. The third guy got scared, got into the car and took off, leaving his buddies to their fates with me."

"Damn, Jane, that's a hell of a story. You're a brave babe. I wouldn't wanna tangle with you. Thanks for the warning!" I said, admiring this doll who could take care of herself.

"You wouldn't have to worry about tangling with me, Cable. I like you. I would probably *want* you to tangle with me. It's been a long time between guys for me. You'd better watch out," she snickered.

"I've heard of this Chinese stuff. What's it called?"

"*Kung Fu*. It's some kind of training for 'unarmed' self-defense. It's a martial arts thing.

"Crap, I'm so old-fashioned—I'm still punching guys out like Tom Mix cowboy style. Maybe you could teach me a few moves..."

"Oh, yeah, Cable...I could teach you a lot of moves..." she said in a very seductive voice. I knew then I had to keep my margins tight with this gal. I couldn't afford to get mixed up sexually with anyone just now. There were few times in my life when I didn't feel sexual desire. This was one of them. I guess being in love with Adora, still smarting over Honey's death, all messed up my desire psyche or something. "Well, that might be nice sometime. I'm—I'm, uh, gonna hit the hay, kid. It's been a long day—and night. Thanks for helping me out with the dead guy."

She looked at me curiously. "You're used to it, aren't you, Cable?"

"Used to what?"

"Violence, dead guys—and saying good-bye to people?"

"Yeah, I told you...so we don't need to cover that anymore, okay?"

"Yeah, sure." She opened the car door. "Well, good-night, Cable. I'll see you at *The Bucket of Blood* about 8:30 tomorrow night? What are you doing during the day—maybe we can—"

"—taking a walk along the beach—*alone*—and then making a call on Art Beatle up at Nitwit Ridge."

"Good luck. He's strange, but he's an okay guy. Smart. He's also the garbage man around here. He won't get back until around two or three in the afternoon."

"Thanks, Jane. Oh, and by the way, I think I'm gonna like you, too," I said, getting out of the car and smiling over at her.

"Good-night, Cable," she said as she walked away into the night.

Terror at 'The Bucket of Blood'

The morning fog lifted about ten a.m., like a misty curtain from the land, and withdrew to the sea revealing a fairyland of coastline meeting the pine tree forests. The Santa Lucia Mountains glowed in the distance, reflecting brown tones in the morning light and I knew just nine miles to the north, Hearst Castle stood glistening white in the sunlight of another day. Cambria was dissected into three residential hills, subdivided recently by the Cambria Pines Development Company out of San Francisco. Lodge Hill, Happy Hill and Park Hill comprised the subdivision settled in amongst the Monterey Pine trees. Twenty-five by seventy foot lots were postage stamp properties for retired folks to build their dream cottages and live out their final days. Few paid attention to the fact that the local soil was a sticky clay and sewage percolation would be a difficult process. So the morning air also held a certain odor of leaking septic tank leach lines. Ah... for the sake of the all-mighty buck!

The local community park was located along the shoreline at the base of...you guessed it...*Park* Hill. I walked along the shore, listening to my feet crunching in the pebbles and watching the waves break against the rocks dotting the shoreline. There didn't seem to be any sand on these beaches....just the tiny pebbles. The northwest wind had begun blowing by eleven o'clock and a chill came to the air. I spotted an old-timer with a cane making his way toward me. He looked tanned and was singing at the top of his lungs. He wore only an undershirt and trousers. "Top of the mornin' to you, stranger!" he bellowed out in a big, healthy voice. "Every day's a good day for it—now isn't it true? I'm known as Tarzan of the Pines, my good lad."

"Good for what?" I asked as he came closer. "My name is Denning."

"Breathing in clean, healthy air and scouting the beach for vibrant, healthy young things. We never lose our need to ogle, in case you were wondering how it'll be when you get older."

"No, I guess not. You...you live here long?"

"Yep. Ray Tyson and I are probably the longest living residents except for Pop Lyons, and Fidelio Fiscalini. Gus Cosso and Spider Bianchini come in a close second, I'd reckon." Then he looked at a clump of rocks a little south of us. "Those rocks—see 'em? A few years back a world-class swimmer drowned in the undertow over by those rocks. See how the waves come right up to the shore, then curl under with a violent action and spin back? That's because the sea is so deep here, almost up to the tide line...treacherous. I learned long ago to respect Mr. Sea."

"May I ask, what you know about a guy named Arthur Beatle?"

He looked at me with a different expression than he had heretofore. "Beatle? Ha! A quintessential quack! A big talker, a dangerous man...cynical, criticizes everything, from abalone poaching to our magnificent U.S. Government. Why do you ask?"

"I, uh... I was wondering about his character. I'm supposed to look up a young daughter of a friend of mine who's staying with Arthur Beatle. Just trying to get some inside information."

He scrutinized my face and narrowed his eyes. "You some kind of detective or something?"

"Yep. Exactly. Only I'm acting in an unofficial capacity during this visit. I'm supposed to be on vacation."

"I see. Well, stranger, if you're talkin' about Cassie Olson—Art Beatle and she are two birds of a feather—that's how I'd describe the young lady. On the other hand, she's almost too beautiful to be here in Cambria. She carries herself like she belongs in Hollywood in the movies or something. I've watched local boys destroy themselves trying to get at her. But she is either very persnickety when it comes to the opposite sex—or maybe doesn't prefer them—if you get my drift."

"Yeah, well, it's hard to tell about those things sometimes, isn't it?"

"If your friend is her mother, shame, shame...she shouldn't have abandoned the young woman—I think she's barely over twenty—in a remote community where there's little to do for young people. Unless you become a slut like that Jane Slaughter and warble a few songs to the drunk sailors at *The Bucket of Blood*."

"Well, you've been very helpful, sir. Thanks and I'll bid you good day." I walked away from the rather opinionated bloke as he continued his way down the beach toward the jagged rocks he was speaking of earlier. I could still hear his singing voice on the wind as I got in Elisa's little black coupe. Funny how prejudice people become, how they judge before knowing the whole story. Maybe it was to protect their own little moral comfort zones, or maybe they simply didn't care enough to take it any further, but remained content to rabble rouse and let the partial truth or the lie remain. I don't know, maybe Jane Slaughter was a whore, but it wasn't any of my business.

Nitwit Ridge and Arthur Beatle's creek rock castle was everything people had said—and a few things more. I parked across from the four-story monstrosity and walked across the little dirt road to the bedspring gate. A sign read, *"Professor Nitwit Is In…"* and so I took the liberty of entering. About fifteen steps took me to the first landing. Each step was hand crafted with cement, inset with pebbles of all sizes and abalone shell pieces. I wandered about for a few minutes, marveling at how a man's frustrated sex drive could have built this edifice in a decades-long frenzy of building and rebuilding.

Finally, I found a sinewy man with dark, curly hair shoveling in a patch of garden on a terrace about three flights up. "Mr. Beatle—I hope I'm not intruding. I wanted to speak with you for a minute, if I may."

He eyed me suspiciously. "You from the political piggy bank in San Luis? If you are, you ain't gettin' my blood, no siree!" he exclaimed.

"No, I was an acquaintance of Miss Olson's mother—she asked me to check in with her daughter if I should pass this way. Well, I'm passing this way…"

"Pshaw!" he exclaimed. "Name ain't no more Olson than mine is Charlie Chaplain, says I." He put his shovel down and walked over toward me. He spit on the ground. "Why didn't the mother come to visit her kin? A strange bunch, Professor Nitwit is thinkin'."

"I—I guess she might be dead by now, Mr. Beatle."

241

"Dead, you say? That's piteous news, now, ain't it? Call me Art—and who might I be exchanging verbiage with?"

"Denning...Cable Denning."

"And may I inquire precisely as to your personal interest in Cassie? You see, many a man has turned the rug over for that gal, got fit to tie themselves into the woman-snare, but she isn't about to succumb. So how did the mother get dead?"

"It's a long story...but I think she's gone by now."

"By now? You knew she was going to be raising turnips?"

"A short while ago. Let's just say I had advance warning. You see, her mother was rather eccentric, sort of—"

"—one of *them*, eh? Why didn't you just come out and say it?—mother's a stranger to these here earth climes, now wasn't she? Just like that taunting daughter of hers with alabaster skin and yellow-green eyes—with little fire-red specks in 'em. But Professor Nitwit knows a thing or two."

It puzzled me how he sensed that Saturnalia was not a native species to the earth. "I wouldn't go that far—"

"—why not? I would. Like mother like daughter, Denning. Cassie be strange, no matter how you look at her. She's *too* everything. She's too intelligent, too good lookin', too cautious, too isolationist, too perceptive, too mysterious and too desirable. Pshaw! We're two grown men and we know for a fact that little lady ain't local!"

"What makes you say that?" I asked, having no real clue as to the answer.

"Besides all the features I just described she's abnormal sexually. She has no men friends, never has since I've known her. Second, old sly fox Beatle here sees her with Jane Slaughter, a raw at the gills little hang-around down at *The Bucket of Blood.* Why would a beautiful young woman like Cassie choose an ex-delinquent from L.A. to fraternize with, I asks myself?"

"So, what'd you come up with? I met Jane Slaughter last night and found her delightfully rough around the edges. I grew up in East L.A. just like Jane. I saw what happens when you don't get your hinges oiled when you're young and your door gets kicked in when you're not looking. I've seen a lot of dames like Jane Slaughter get raped in a dark alley or killed in a knife fight with their own sex, just as I've seen them fight like helpless kittens tossed into a bag and thrown over the bridge into the waters below. Most of 'em can't swim, so they drown before their time, they get stuck in the ooze society created to keep the poor and down trodden at arm's length, keep 'em from polluting you so your shit won't stink and you can pretend after a while these kinds of people don't exist—as long as they stay in their part of the jungle and pay up when Uncle Sam comes calling for the property taxes."

Art Beatle looked at me curiously, then spat again on the ground. "Damn now, Mister if that ain't expressive! You won't get no argument from me, no siree. You've just been espousin' my central philosophy." He extended his hand out to me. "I am gladdened to make your acquaintance. How would you like some of Professor Nitwit's favorite kale soup that's always on tap and a cup of java?"

"Yeah, thanks...I haven't eaten anything all day. Mind if I smoke on your premises?"

"Hell's a poppin'—no! I chew it, you puff it—what's the frickin' difference?"

We spent much of the afternoon chewing the rag. I discovered Art Beatle was indeed a literate man, a published author, a hard-drinking, gambling man with no longer an eye for the fairer sex, due to his calamity with the young gypsy woman some years back. I also learned that he suspected Cassie to be other-worldly and he confirmed that in his own mind when she asked him if she could live in a certain small room up by the chicken coop. Trouble was that each time he went to check on her well-being, no matter what hour of the day or night, she was not to be found. Where did she go? Then eventually it dawned on him that the young woman was definitively not native to the earth and he had seen other things earlier in his life he would not divulge, but I got the idea that he had witnessed some unidentified flying objects or had had a definite encounter with their inhabitants.

We parted in good spirits. I had shared a small bottle of English gin with him before I left and he relished it. It was about nine p.m. when I pulled into the post office parking lot across the street from *The Bucket of Blood*. I had this feeling in my gut this would turn out to be a memorable evening. It was the kind of sensation that wound up in your stomach like the spring of a grandfather clock and at some undesignated moment, the whole damn thing would unravel in one terrible moment, ripping and tearing your insides out.

I crossed the street and even before I opened the faded maroon swinging doors, I could hear the din of the joint, mostly men's voices spitting and cursing and laughing, yelling or shouting. As soon as I sidled up to the crowded bar, a little weasel of a man came up to me. "Would you like to buy a quicksilver mine? Up San Simeon Creek road, it lay. One thousand American greenbacks and you stand to make a million—all she needs is some good grubstake money to make 'er go...."

"No thanks," I bellowed out at him. "I live and work in Los Angeles. I'm not the prospector type. Sorry."

He gave me a disgusted look and staggered away. The bartender finally asked me what I wanted. He had none of what I customarily drank. So I ordered just straight lousy whiskey. Of course, everything was supposed to be water, soda pop and non-alcoholic drinks. But, as Jane said, no one in this town seemed to care about Prohibition and its far-reaching arm.

Just then I noticed Jane Slaughter come in. She was dressed in a tan leather coat, a long black dress that went to her ankles and black shoes. As soon as the local gentry saw her, there were whistles and cajoles from the rather vulgar men who frequented the joint. Her hair shone and fell straight to her shoulders. She came up to me. "Hello, Cable. Welcome to *The Bucket of Blood*."

"Hi, Jane. I'm looking forward to your songs. This rowdy group needs a gentle female touch, don't you think?"

"I don't know about the gentle part, but I can punch it out with the best of them, I guess, if push comes to shove."

245

Right behind her, in walked a beautiful young woman with the whitest skin I'd ever seen. Her hair was a glowing red and fell half way down her back. She wore a full burgundy dress with a tiger tooth neckpiece and very nice white shoes. She stood where she was. As the crowd saw this infrequent visitor to their less than sanitary environs, the room began to quiet somewhat. I left the bar and walked over to greet her, as if she needed me to protect her or whatever stupid thing I was thinking. "Hello, Cassiopeia, I'm Cable Denning. I knew your mother before—"

"—yes, Mr. Denning. I know...she told me..."

"*She* told you?"

"Would you like to go outside with me for a moment, please?"

"Yeah, sure," I said, glad to get out of the joint. I waved to Jane that we'd be right back and she nodded as she approached a well-used, old upright piano and sat down to play. She started a fast version of *Why Don't You Do Right?* as Cassie and I walked out into the fresh, cool night air. "I—I, uh, promised your mother I would drop in on you if I was ever up this way. So here I am, supposed to be on a vacation— but things haven't exactly turned out that way, so far. Anyway, I'm honoring your mother's request. I kind of liked your mother. She had a way about her..."

"Thank you. What little she knew of you, she felt you were an honest man who could keep a secret. How did mother die? She doesn't tell me—even now."

"Even now? Ah.... then she's gone. But how can she communicate with you if she's dead?"

She studied my eyes with her beautiful, warm reddish-orange orbs. "Didn't she tell you? We're goddesses—remember? We can't die....not really."

"Yeah...I forgot that part. Well, the last time I saw her alive, your not-so-good father punished her for helping me escape the *Evening of the Purple Mists* as one of the breathe-able participants." She laughed and I smiled at her. "I accidentally found her banished to a filthy alley in skid row L.A—an aging old lady with boils all over her body, brought about by your loving Dad. She told me then that she would be gone in a few weeks at most. She also told me not to worry, it was only a physical body and she'd eventually pick up another one through a regeneration process back on her native planet, Saturn. Did she ever use the name *Saturnalia or Rhea*?"

"Yes, of course. I was with my mother for many thousands of your years. But when my father's anger began to worsen, as my mother continuously stepped out-of-bounds from what he decreed, she sensed I would soon be in danger. As you know, to avoid competition, my father ate my mother's first seven children, but when I was born, my mother hid me, took my swaddling blanket and put a large stone in it. When my father discovered an undevoured child, he immediately gulped the rock down, thus disgorging all my brothers and sisters. When my brother Zeus grew up, it was then that he beat out my father for control of the earth. But that was many thousands of years ago. When Cronus discovered mother's deceit, Cronus swore vengeance. So she *mortalized* me, gave me earth-money under the assumed name of Cassie Olson. You called me by my real name.

Please call me Cass or Cassie, though." She studied my face. "Mother tells me I can trust you. Can I?"

"Well, that depends on what department you're talking about. But I'd say in general, yes—I'm solid and dependable, drink and smoke too much, don't swear too much, keep late hours and used to chase skirts a lot, until lately." I was thinking about how Adora would have loved the adventure of this balmy night on the Central Coast of California.

The human woman in Cass started up those dangerous brain waves—the thinking process that the female instinct is prone to. "If I may ask, why until lately? You're a young and handsome human male animal—mother thought so."

"Well, she was quite a looker herself, a fine dish with a good head on her shoulders. As I see it, her only weakness was goodness—and your *father*—or at least avoiding catastrophe whenever she could."

She looked—what I perceived to be—directly beside me. "Thank you for allowing me to experience this life…"

"What do you mean?" I asked, perplexed as hell.

"My Mother is standing beside you—she is pleased and told me she wanted you from the first night in her little cottage by the firelight—but that her desire would lead to your destruction. You would be killed."

"So instead, Gor killed her."

"Sort of…but not really…she misses her physical body just now, but we can still communicate. She'll get another one."

I turned around to look for Saturnalia. I saw nothing.

"I guess that special kind of sight is reserved for your kind, eh?"

"I usually don't like earth males. So I will share this with you now. I think they are crude, rude, pushy, focused only on the lust of the moment, to breed and consider the female gender a lesser form of life. Or at the very least, males in general consider females as worlds apart to their 'superior' status, in many aspects."

"Well, Cass, you're welcome to your opinion, but there are always two sides to a story. For example, look at it from a man's perspective. As a rule, he's got a short time to sow his oats with all the babes he wants to bed down. All too soon some gal comes along with that certain twinkle in her eye, she gets pregnant—or they get married and then she gets pregnant—either way he ends up mowing the lawn on Saturday mornings, supporting a bunch of brats who will grow up to pretty much forget him."

Cass just stood there checking out my eyes. "You still didn't tell me why you gave up 'chasing skirts,'…..your term for pursuing women." Then she did an unexpected thing. She took my hand and we walked back into the tavern to listen to Jane Slaughter sing at that little upright, that was somewhat out of tune, clanking away all mixed up with the din of the joint.

We walked over toward Jane. "Did she try to seduce you or something?" Jane tittered in a dry tone. "Just like her." Then she looked at Cass. "You fight off guys at the drug store daily—and now you're suddenly friendly toward a mug who's a private eye in Los Angeles? You must know he's got lots of women—"

"—Remember? Let's not discuss it, Jane," I said, admonishing her. "We came in here to hear you croon a tune or so. Ready?" I got out a Lucky Strike and lit it up. Cass watched me intently. "Either of you two want something to drink?"

"Yeah, I'll have a beer, thanks," Jane said.

I looked at Cass. "Oh, I can't touch alcohol. Ruins my head. I don't even see how you can smoke that terrible stuff—inhaling it like that into your lungs. I think smoking is a kind of suicide—a death-wish when people secretly want to hurry along their demise."

"Well, aren't we particular and judgmental? Look, lady, I pick my poisons, you pick yours, okay? What made you think I'm all cozy and happy with my life? Maybe I *want* to hurry things along a little."

She winced a little and then looked away. "You're right, I'm sorry. It's none of my business."

Jane launched into a medium tempo version of *Keepin' Out of Mischief Now* and I wanted to make her stop. It was a song Honey had sung one night not all that long ago—in fact, Jane Slaughter had certain tone qualities and inflections that reminded me of Honey a lot. Anyway, the rowdy men in the Bucket of Blood loved it. In sixteen measures of music, Jane had 'em eating out of her hand.

The music ended and the men went wild. But Cass had noticed my face as Jane sang. "Who was she? Did you break up or—"

"—I told you earlier—I don't want to talk about it. What the hell's the matter with you girls? I'd appreciate it if you would just...I have my reasons. Let it go at that, okay?"

"Okay…" Cass had a tone in her voice that made me think for an instant, that she could easily be jealous of other women in my life. Or maybe it was just a crazy notion I got from her voice when she spoke, or the mood I was in from being here in Cambria and standing in a room filled with mostly noisy men who couldn't give a shit about Jane Slaughter's singing, in the long run. They just wanted to ogle the face, tits and hair as she sat there at the piano. A pretty girl will do it every time!

Jane sang a few nice tunes that night. I told her so and she was very grateful that someone had noticed her talent instead of just her body. It was about eleven-thirty when we left *The Bucket of Blood* and I was thinking how glad I was we didn't get shanghaied—when I spotted three men in the shadows over by the parking lot. I told the girls to go back inside the tavern, but they refused. I backed them up against the outside wall of *The Bucket of Blood*. "Now look here," I whispered firmly. This can go several ways…but I've got a feeling those goons over there intend to give us some trouble. They're the kind of gangsters who play for keeps, you two, so don't tell me I didn't warn you."

Quickly Cass grabbed both our hands and we fled back into the tavern and out the back exit, almost unnoticed in the crowded, smoke-filled room. Once in the alley she asked us to follow her. "Where in the hell are we going?" Jane asked.

"Into Roc Rava's vegetable garden," Cass answered. We ran down the alley until we came to a back gate to a little house with a metal stovepipe and a rickety old greenhouse beside it. We got to the back door and Cass

251

knocked. It looked to me like it was made out of match-sticks. A shaking little man with a wonderful smile came to the door. He was wearing black britches, old leather shoes with dirt all over them, an olive green flannel shirt with suspenders and a hat.

"Cassie! Com-a visit old Rocco...come in," said the nice old man with the shaky voice. It appeared as if he had a palsy of some kind and his hands trembled as he stood there welcoming us. "I have a bigga Zucchini for you, eh?" He got out a pocketknife and before anyone could say anything, he led us to the middle of his garden patch. He deftly clipped a large green zucchini squash from its vine. "Now...dissa guy...you tak-a him-a home. Gonna tast-a real-a good!"

"Thanks, Rocco." Then Cass finally said, "There's someone chasing the three of us. Could we hide out in your place for an hour or so?"

"Dat's-a nice-a. Rocco need-a sleep. Get uppa early. Stay...as-a long-a you wish-a, eh?"

We thanked him and we sat in the dark of Rocco Rava's little kitchen. Then something strange happened. The front door swung open quietly, squeaking on its rusty hinges. Then the room began to have an eerie glow about it as an orb about the size of a cantaloupe entered under its own power and approached us! It seemed to be brass or some similar metal and glowed more around it than within it. Jane and I were rather startled, but Cass stepped forward to greet the suspended object. There also seemed to be a slight hum to the orb. "Hello, Mother," Cass said. "Yes?" There was a silence as Cass was obviously receiving some kind of communication from the orb. "I see. Where can we go,

252

then?" Another silence filled the room. "I can—but they won't be able to tolerate the vibration. And I won't leave them behind. Cable and Jane both deserve to live. Why should I be responsible for their deaths?"

Things weren't sounding too hot for Jane and me. "Whatta ya mean...deaths?" I whispered to Cass.

She glanced at me quickly. "Oh, nothing. We're just trying to figure out a way to keep from being captured by those men out there. Mother wants to help." Who was I to say, but I thought 'Mother' was near dead some time ago on a Los Angeles street. So maybe the disembodied spirit of Saturnalia was on our team and seeing things from a different perspective. Who in the hell knew anymore? I noticed that Jane wasn't any too comfortable with the unfolding events, either.

Then Cass registered surprise in her voice. "What? Let them do that? Oh but Mother, that's taking such a chance. You know humans—you just never know—yes, I see...Oh....I'll ask them, that's the least I can do."

The orb reversed its direction and exited as it had come, leaving us once again in the darkness. "Mother thinks we should let ourselves get captured—I'm not too clear on her thinking about the situation—"

"—Shit, Cass—those mugs will rape and kill us both—you know that! And God knows what they'll do to Cable. I say we make a run for it. And does anybody know just who in the hell *they* are?" Jane exclaimed.

"My father's people—hirelings, sent to do his bidding."

"Oh, that's swell—just what I need—to be back in the loving arms of your Dad. Ol' Cronus-Gor won't be mild or neglectful this time, I suspect. Yeah, Cass, I agree with Jane—let's make a run for it."

"Okay, I'll go along. We've all got to agree or it won't work."

"What won't work?" I asked.

"Synergetic compliance—our agreement will form an energy with no opposition—and it becomes much more powerful when going in the same direction with the same purpose."

"Oh, why didn't you say so?" I laughed, not under-standing a whit of what Cass was trying to explain.

There was a long wooden stairway that led up to a grade school at the top of the hill at the intersection of Bridge Street and route 1, Main Street. We decided to take it. It was very late and the local environs felt like a ghost town after dark as we sprinted out of Rocco Rava's garden. But our efforts were for naught, for as we exited I could feel a hard object hit my head and I was out on the pavement, hearing only a little outcry from Jane before I totally blacked out.

The Monster of Piedras Blancas

"Probe him," I heard a cruel sounding male voice echo. I tried to open my eyes. Everything hurt. "Tell me what he really knows. And if he knows nothing, we'll throw him to the sharks—as I promised our leader." I sensed there were two presences in the room. Then they proceeded to walk down a corridor that echoed their footsteps. I felt helpless and didn't have a clue as to where I was.

Then I heard a voice calling to me. "Cable...Cable! It's me, Jane. Where are you?" She was speaking through a pipe vent from some other location. "Are you okay? Please...talk to me...how can I ever grow up to be the first female private eye if you're dead? I heard what that terrible man said."

I crawled toward the sound of the pipe that came out of the wall about four feet above an old sink that was no longer functional. I boosted myself up to get my mouth close to the pipe. "Jane...! It's me...I haven't got much time...are you okay, kid?"

"Yeah, they haven't molested me yet—or beat me up. They seem to want you. I don't know why they're keeping me."

"Because you know too much already...where's Cass?"

"I don't know, Cable...I fear the worse...and I've got menstrual cramps."

"I hope she's okay...her father wants her back, now that Saturnalia is gone. I think old Cronus-Gor wants me, too. I don't know what the hell the probe thing is— but it doesn't sound good—and something doesn't make sense."

"Yeah, why would they want to kill you if you're still valuable to them? Maybe this creep that does the talking is talking out of the side of his mouth. You know some lunatics—power-mad because they want to take things into their own hands."

Just then I heard someone coming down the corridor towards me. "Talk to you later, babe. Hang in there..." A big man in a light-blue outfit came in with a large syringe needle spurting its stuff on the floor. I was weak and he grabbed me and plunged that thing into my arm. Soon the room was spinning and again, I hit the floor. I don't know how long I was out, but when I finally did come to, some guy was making me drink some water and wiping my perspiring face at the same time.

"You are a strong young man, Mr. Denning, and defiant. My name is Paddy Straight—and I'll get straight to the point, if you'll pardon the pun. I'm here to help cure your insanity. You see, you've lived under delusions for quite some time. Frankly, we've made very little progress with you over these past months."

"What in the fuck are you telling me, Straight? That I wasn't with two beautiful women tonight, or I wasn't at *The Bucket of Blood* or staying at the Bluebird Motel in Cambria?"

"Not only is none of that true, but you've had nightmares, other delusionary imaginings, such as experiencing some creature you keep calling *Saturnalia*, or fearing an imaginary husband-god of hers—and even further back, you have fantasies about lovely young women who don't exist. Let me see...there was this wonderful fantasy you dreamed up named Honey Combes—now what an inventive name that was, wasn't it? And to fulfill your lost mother's love and passions, you conjured up a little Latin number named Adora Moreno. There is a long list, but you get the gist—I enjoy rhyming—don't you?"

If I didn't know myself better, I would think I really was going nuts! But they hadn't heard Jane's voice through the pipes. I did, didn't I? Yeah, and there was Jane and I burying the thug at the Leffingwell dump. Oh, yep, no one could fool me. "So just where the hell am I, if you don't mind divulging that little bit of information."

"Not at all, Mr. Denning. You are here at Shady Oaks in Los Angeles, not far from where you grew up. You've been here for some time."

"How did I get here?"

"Well, as we blend fact with fantasy, your recognition of yourself and your real life ends with getting hit on the head while you were a policeman, inside a vault...by some deranged mortician's assistant, one Dr. Sandor, who unfortunately has since passed away. You were honorably discharged from the police force and sent here to be with us. It seems the concussion you received with your injury, damaged parts of the systemic brain areas that strangely affect your ability to divide reality from fantasy. In other words, you have become a marvelous storyteller, Mr. Denning. The other side of that, though, is that you *believe* your stories to be true— when in fact, they are very detailed, colorfully portrayed fictional adventures, produced by a very fertile imagination."

This guy was starting to get to me as the crap the other guy had injected me with began to do its trip on my head...spinning me around the world in five seconds or less. "Damn you're clever, Straight...clever and cagey as hell. Talk about being...a—a professional...I'll bet old Gor loves *you*."

"There is...one peculiar item, however, that has us stumped here at Shady Oaks. In one of your dreams, just before you became unconscious, you have repeatedly spoken of a golden capsule, part of another adventure shared with a Chinese fantasy, one Lei-Tao. You attributed many special properties to her, but for whatever reason, we cannot discover why you stop when it comes to your unveiling the *content* of this magic capsule. I think you called it *The God of Our Fathers* or the like."

"Of course this is all part of my fantasy, right—I mean, just another imaginative trip to dreamland, right?"

"Of course. That's why it's curious that you should conceal—or shall we say, not *reveal* the simple content of that clever dream. The best we can get out of you is the supposition that you learned from Dr. Sandor, that the golden capsule contained not only the constituents of cosmic Creation itself, but also the *why* of it. Now, wouldn't that be fun to hear you espouse on? Delightful, I say..."

I was getting more and more into the effects of the drug they had injected me with. "Delightful...yeah, delightful..." Then I pretended to completely fade away. Straight lifted my eyelids to see if they were pulled up and away. I learned to fake that pretty well in the police academy.

"Hempstead, make sure you record every word of this dummy's blabbing under the influence of the *dormitine*. If he knows nothing, then Gor has got to know it as soon as possible so we can dispose of him."

"But why not just kill the women now?" Hempstead inquired.

"Because, you idiot, the redhead is Gor's flesh and blood daughter—presently—and he wants her back. The girlfriend knows too much, but Gor feels she may be useful to us—later. In the meantime, no person is to

258

touch either of them without my permission. Is that understood?"

"Yes, Mr. Straight."

That night I found myself at the *Bella Notte* listening to a dazzling Honey Combes sing *My Heart Stood Still.* How the audience and I loved her, craved and raved for more as her music climbed the stairway to the stars. She had made it, she had ascended, reached the places where few go and did it before she was thirty. But now her heart *had* stood still. It was always harder to imagine a young woman gone than someone who had lived out her years. I didn't want to do as Ralph Waldo Emerson had done. A few months after the death of his beloved young wife, he entered the crypt to view the corpse. The realization that exterior beauty could fade so easily, shocked him and stayed within his psyche as a traumatic moment for the rest of his own life. I listened to Honey finish and went up to her and held her, telling her how wonderful she was and that I missed her sassy wit and pert smile, bubbling personality and sensual female nature. Then I was pulled away and she faded into the mists of an also fading din of music and applause.

I awakened in the same dark room with no windows. It was hard to tell whether it was day or night and I no longer heard Jane Slaughter's voice coming through the pipeline. That worried me. Then Straight came back in to continue to pound at my sanity. I was on to his trick, but the damn drug kept me punchy enough to allow enough of a margin for self-doubt whenever Straight interrogated me. Was I really nuts after all—

and had the last three years been an injury caused frenzied fraud? And of course, that was their ploy. So Straight began his daily tirade. "You are insane, Denning—nuts—crazy! You've got to come to it—realize you're a nobody from nowhere and that the taxpayer foots the bill for your sickness here at Shady Oaks via the police department. For all intents and purposes, your life is over. So that we might help others who follow you with a similar malady, I'm hoping you might tell all that you've experienced. For example, did you dream last night?"

"Oh, yeah, Straight—I dreamed you are the real dipshit you are—how's that for openers? I also learned that your approach is old-fashioned and creaks with lousy attempts to veil your real agenda here.. Your drugs dope me up alright, but it's not going to get you where you want to go with me—to the revelation of the *Fen de Fuqin*. A lot better men than you have tried and failed, you slimy hireling."

"I'm sorry to hear that, Denning. The depth of your illness may require much more powerful doses of the *dormitine*. Have you become friends with it yet?"

"Yeah, like I've become friends with you, fuck-face!" I tried to get out of bed and hit the bastard, but I was still too drugged. "Oh, there was another dream I had last night. Honey was singing at the *Bella Notte* before Frank Laggore killed her. She was singing *My Heart Stood Still* and guess what? It did...her heart stood still because crumbs like you are still out there in the jungle, vampire predators who *themselves* are the sick and emotionally degenerate of this world."

He thought carefully and then drew up a chair closer to my bed. "You see, Denning, these dreams—your insanity, that dark world your poor soul dwells within—these dreams are nothing more than that. *You are insane. You are demented. You are a crazy man. You are so nuts* that you have nightly dreams of people and things that never existed. There never was a Honey Combes, or a silly nightclub called *Bella Notte* or perhaps even a song called *My Heart Stood Still.* It's rather like getting your dimensions mixed up. You cannot tell me what dimension you exist in anymore, can you? Dimension number one? Dimension number two? Or is there possibly a number three?"

"Get me a 1929 phone book, Straight, and I'll set you straight, pardon the pun. And another thing, Jane Slaughter and Cass better be okay or I'll turn you inside out and grind you up myself."

"I'm sorry, we cannot provide you with any outside material that might negatively influence your dementia. During your drug-induced *confessions*, it is easy to see the pattern. Your sickness is expressed in traits such as sexual addiction, not to mention alcohol and tobacco. The fantasy of so many young and beautiful women lead me to observe how repressed and empty your early life must have been, battling for survival in the ghettos. The wretched misfits of this world such as yourself, are probably born a tad demented anyhow."

"No, Straight, do you wanna know what makes people like me crazy? It's idiots like you pretending to be someone at the expense of—"

Before I could finish my sentence Jane Slaughter rushed in with a pipe and conked Straight on the noggin. "Gees, Cable, fuck! Let's find Cass and get out of this place!"

"Am I glad to see you!" I said, as I tried to get up. But I realized how dizzy the damned *dormitine* had made me. "Give me a hand, babe."

We left Straight on the floor out cold and made our way down a dark corridor. Jane led us to a flight of descending stairs and I held on to the railing as she helped us both down. As we reached the bottom I could smell the scent of the sea. "Where in the hell are we?" I asked.

"Put your ear to the wall, Cable." I did, and was astonished to hear the crashing of waves, and in the distance the sound of a ship's horn blast.

"A ship's horn? Are we off shore—shanghaied from *The Bucket of Blood*?"

"I don't think so. I think it's a fog horn and we're underground near a lighthouse or something."

I chuckled. "Damn, you're thinking like a private dick, kid," I said, slapping her on the fanny.

"As long as you don't think with *your* dick we'll be okay, Cable. I told you I might make a good female detective." She looked around. "I was above you. I worked that piece of pipe loose and I clobbered that terrible man with it, then waited my time. I have a feeling they took Cass to a more secure, protected place."

"I'm surprised they haven't shipped her off to Dad yet—or have they?"

"I don't know. Let's follow my instinct first, okay?" We wound around a few cave-like passages until we came to a large red door. Above the transom were the letters *Initus Mortis Domum*. She whispered to me. "What does it mean, Cable—how's your Latin?"

262

I studied the words. I knew enough Latin root in Spanish and Italian when I grew up to at least decipher the intended meaning. "I think it's something about *death when you enter here* or something like it. It ain't an invitation to a family picnic, that I can tell you."

Jane snickered under her breath. "Damn, Cable, you're just like me—cool under pressure with a sense of humor."

"Well, that's to keep my knees from shaking," I confessed.

"Shall we?" She nodded and I turned the knob and the large metal door gave way. We could hear the crashing of the breakers and the roar of the sea much closer now. There was a barred window up ahead and we could hear seagulls shrieking in the distance. We approached an intersection with three doors. We instinctively headed for the center door. But before we could reach the handle, two goons came out from the door to the left and seized us. I was too weak to fight much, but Jane starting punching, kicking, biting and using her Kung Fu. Then one of the goons clunked her over the head with a sap and down she went. They dragged us through the door on the right and down some stairs into a huge cell that smelled of rotting flesh and seaweed.

Just then a still woozy Straight entered with his Dr. Injector henchman. "Foolish—foolish...and this is even more evidence that your insanity is at its maximum—in fact, as maximum as you can get. For now, I will continue to drive you insane, in case you felt you were not yet indeed over the edge. The young woman will die for striking me—and you will watch."

They pulled Jane to the wall and chained her. They came back and shackled me to the bars near the entrance, so I was facing Jane. Then two men turned a crank in the wall and a door-sized portion of the wall lifted. Then Straight took out what seemed to be a whistle. But when he blew it I heard nothing. "Higher frequencies than the human ear can hear, Denning. But not so with *Godfrey*...he has many superhuman capacities." Then there was a deep, horrible growl that echoed from the passageway behind the wall-door. Slowly it came closer and each nerve in me twitched with anticipation as the hair raised up on the back of my neck, like an ancient response to a danger so threatening as to freeze me where I stood. Jane's eyes widened in terror as a human-like monster appeared at the transom. He was covered with seaweed from head to toe and must have stood about seven feet. "Godfrey is an experiment," Straight announced from the other side of the bars. "Albeit, a failed one...we were trying for the perfect synthesis between land and sea creature. But Godfrey's mind couldn't take it and he went berserk. You see, Denning, Godfrey really *is* crazy."

Immediately I was thinking of Lexie and Zephyr. I was thinking how this same so-called "Order" without pity, compassion or sympathy, created a boy-dolphin with the mind of a human but the body of a fish. "You're really the worst kind of sub-human, Straight, the scientific type who plays at being God. People like you are what's wrong with the world—and who in the end wind up being a victim of their own stupidity. The crime is *you*—and you take so many with you on your way down."

"Entertaining, Denning. But really not true. We *are* God—those like me who dare to probe into the minds and bodies of things human—*and* otherwise."

I shouted at Straight. "You're still a worthless piece of shit, no matter how you slice it, Straight—and in the end, even if you kill that poor innocent girl over there—or me, there'll always be someone else who sees the true degenerate that you are, and who will step in to defend human kind from bastards like you!"

"Human kind? Ha! ha! ha! Who cares about human kind, Denning? They are leeches, parasites on the planet, contributing nothing to the welfare of the earth. Do you think I care about *human kind*?" He laughed loudly. "If I *did* care, I could not stand by and witness two of my own kind getting ripped to shreds and eaten before my eyes, now, could I?"

All the shouting seemed to rile up Godfrey. He put his nose to the air. I think he was sniffing out Jane. "I'm sorry, Jane...damn, I'm useless here to help. Thanks for trying to rescue me anyway."

Godfrey went into that low, forbidding growl as he eyed Jane and started towards her. "I started bleeding this morning, Cable—and I didn't have anything—"

"—I knew he was smelling something in your direction—maybe it'll repel him—what do you think?"

"I don't think so—especially—especially if he's—he's mad—I mean nuts kind of mad." Jane was brave as hell, but I could see her starting to break down.

"Yeah. I get it." I pulled at my shackles.

The seaweed creature now towered above Jane. In a flash he ripped her blouse off along with her brassiere. I hadn't noticed before, but Jane was very nicely endowed. What a hell of a time to think of that! Godfrey then tore her dress off, leaving only her panties, now stained with fresh blood from her menstruation. Almost gently, he peeled her panties off until they were at her ankles. Then he ripped them off her legs and brought them to what must have been his nostrils hidden behind all that seaweed. He growled again, put his head up high into the air and let out a roar. He started for Jane, she began to scream as the monster began to tilt back and forth stretching his arms out. Then he lunged for Jane. Suddenly I heard a gun report from behind me and Godfrey staggered. As the monster turned toward me and began to topple, another two shots were fired and all seven feet of him came crumpling to the ground. I looked around. The gun was still smoking in Straight's hand.

"One can only see so much..." Straight said with a low, resigned tone. "Perhaps...everyone has a ceasing point ...besides...he was a failure..." Then he brightened up. "And I just remembered, I promised Gor I would not do in Miss Slaughter until I got orders to do so. And just think...now we may resume your 'treatment' for the cure of acute insanity. In the meantime, you were treated to a little nudity show, were you not? Miss Slaughter, minus the blood of course, has quite a comely woman's body, wouldn't you say, Denning?"

I was still reeling from the shock of Straight shooting Godfrey. I was also suffering from the effects of the *dormitine* that had made my brain wobble. "Yeah, I guess, Straight. Look, give Jane some clothes and clean her up. That's the least you can do." I felt hopeless, despondent. "Then you can continue to work me over until

I'm dead, Mister. Thirty-two used to be a ripe old age once upon a time, eh?"

"I like that attitude, Denning. It shows resignation, surrender to your superiors." Soon one of the goons returned with some clothes for Jane, entered the cell and covered her. Then they led her away. She glanced at me with tears in her eyes, too frightened to speak. "Don't worry...for the moment Miss Slaughter will be kept safe—but this time under lock and key. No more surprises."

I watched as Straight put his revolver back into the side pocket of his coat. He had three bullets left after the three he had emptied into Godfrey. They unshackled me and we started up the stairs. There were four of us, myself out ahead of them, the goons walked directly behind me and Straight took up the rear. About half way up the stairs that orb which I remembered from old Rocco's house a day or two before, suddenly appeared above us and floated slowly in our direction. It began to emit a very bright light, almost blinding. I took advantage of the moment as I pushed the two goons down the stairs, thrust Straight against the wall with all the strength I had left in me, grabbed his gun and started firing at the goons below. I hit one, but missed the other. Now I had only one shot left. The remaining shooter got down on his knees and focused his gun up toward me. I fired at him and hit him in the chest. At the same time I yanked Straight over in front of me as a shield. Sure enough, the wounded idiot fired back and hit Straight square in the middle of his face as he yelled and went tumbling down the stairs. And that was that. The orb had dimmed and hovered at the top of the stairs, as if waiting for me. I clamored up the remaining stairs and went in search of the girls. It led me to the central door in the little corridor Jane and I had first come to. "If that's you, Saturnalia," I said, talking to the orb, "thanks...I owe you one." The swirling brass ball led me to a yellow door and hovered. I went in with my gun drawn, even though I had no remaining bullets. I found a half-naked Jane and a completely clothed Cass.

"Cable!" Cass exclaimed upon seeing me. She ran up to me and kissed me hard on the mouth. "I thought you were—were—"

"Hey, that's supposed to be my kiss!" Jane crackled.

I managed to unwind Cass's arms from around my neck. "We've got to get out of here, ladies!" I said. "I'm a bit weak, but I dispatched Straight and his henchmen. I don't know where Mr. Injector is, but let's not wait around to find out."

"Thank you, Mother...I know she's around. I can feel it."

"Yeah, I know. I already thanked her." We ran out and kept running, until we found a door that looked like an exit. As soon as we opened that door we found a long ascending flight of stairs. We scampered up as fast as we could until finally we were out onto a short grassy meadow on a cliff overlooking the sea. A few hundred yards to the south stood the gleaming white tower of a lighthouse.

"Piedras Blancas Lighthouse," Jane said. "I visited it one day. It used to be gas-powered. Now it's electric."

"How far are we from Cambria?" I asked.

"About twenty miles or so," Jane answered.

"So now what are we going to do? I know for sure those terrible people wanted to take me back to my father," Cass observed.

"How about a car?" I inquired. "Where can we get a car?"

We ended up hitchhiking into town, picked up by a delivery truck returning from a little tiny hamlet called *Gorda*. We checked into our rooms at the Bluebird Motel. The girls went to take showers and clean up. I did the same, but walked around the outside of my little cabin just in case some of Straight's goons were staking out my place.

It had been a hell of a day or two. I had lost track of time, but my room was still intact and Elisa's little Ford coupe was still parked where I'd left it the night I walked to *The Bucket of Blood* to meet the girls. Paddy Straight tried to convince me my whole life had been an illusion. What if it really was? What if everything we perceived as real was just another show put on for the gods—and we were the hapless players? What if life *was* an illusion, a kind of hologram projected and suspended like Saturnalia's orb? What if our attributes were like *spiritual forces* and we magnetized them to us by our behavior? I don't know. But if I told anyone about the adventure the three of us had just endured, they wouldn't believe me. After all, it wasn't every day people came up against the *Order Oculus* and *The Monster of Piedras Blancas*—and lived to tell the tale!

CHAPTER 9

'THE CABLE DENNING SHOW'

Life is a sideshow and you're your own star. Yeah, the one in the spotlight for that instant of eternity when there is still enough self-importance in you to take life seriously.

It seems like life and death are unlikely traveling companions. For humans, one's not fulfilled without the other. For other-dimensional beings, however, death doesn't seem to be part of the equation. Ever meet a woman so exquisite you felt she didn't belong in this world? Well, that's how I felt when I first laid my eyes on Cassiopeia. Death wasn't part of her equation for me, like her gorgeous, naturally sensual mother, beauty like that could never fade because there was a timeless essence to it and whatever quality that was, it would never be pulled into a grave like Honey or Adora or Rusty Wilson and all the other mortals who would molder in a coffin six feet under. Or was I missing something? Was I missing the possibility that even us "mortals" were made of an essence that out-lived the physical body? Hell, look at Saturnalia. Seeing a withered old broad with festering boils all over her face, her once-lithe body shrunken along with drooping breasts and faded hair sure reminded me that one of the *immortal's* bodies was headed for the old scrap heap. If they could conceive of immortality, why not us? Or maybe we were messed with biologically—long ago—and we don't remember what a splendorous ancestry we have!

When we got back to the *Bluebird Motel*, both Jane and I were exhausted, plus I was having some anxiety shit running through my body like the front line in World War I due to the now deceased Paddy Straight's *dormatine*. One never knew about Cass. It was hard to figure what these "mortalized" immortals might be feeling at any given moment. She didn't seem any the worse for the wear regarding the *Piedras Blancas* horror. Of course she hadn't been in that cell with Godfrey, either. Jane must've been petrified, thinking her life would be over in seconds as that growling, hovering giant approached her. And there she stood, chained to a wall naked, menstrual blood leaking down her leg. What a hell of way for a person to go! Whatever it was that prompted Straight to fire on his own piteous experiment, I might never know. Suffice it to say he had reached an absorption point and like Mary Shelly's Frankenstein creature, felt it best to put Godfrey out of his misery......maybe. More likely, it was his own fear that if he didn't obey Gor, he'd be cooked meat anyway. After all, brilliant and sick animals like Straight were self-preservationists. Naw, in the end I think he acted to save his own butt.

That night the three of us agreed we'd meet on the morrow and I told them I'd delay my trip back to L.A. an extra day in order to recap our adventure and sort out what the next steps ought to be. After a hot shower, I collapsed into my little bed in Cabin #7. I had the window open and I could hear the happy little bubbling creek nearby, the sound of crickets and frogs, the mournful call of a foghorn.

But my body could not go down to that deep and peaceful place nature commanded of it. The *dormatine* had wormed a hole in my psyche and all kinds of crap was leaking out all over a movie screen in my brain. I was falling down into the beam of a huge spotlight and my body trembled as I could feel things wind down to a slow-motion snapshot of me watching myself. I was dressed in a bright yellow suit, wore white shoes and hat with a red tie! Seems I was a master of ceremonies on a stage somewhere and in the back of the auditorium lights flashed the words, *'The Cable Denning Show'*, and an invisible audience started applauding. Or maybe it wasn't an audience after all, but one person sitting in the middle of all those theatre seats clapping very slow-ly. The show must have stunk!

In the wings I could see all the babes I'd ever known waiting for their turn to go on. They were dressed in glitzy, very sexy outfits. Amanda Baxter, Lei-Tao, Honey Combes, Ginny Fullerton, Zephyr and Eden Royce, Rusty Wilson, Zelda Blodgett, Sarah Mapleton—even Misty Sheridan waited in the wings for her cue. Only Adora was missing. I somehow knew each one sang and danced and I was the beneficiary of the proceedings. Except for the man in the audience. Who was he? The energy I got from his presence was dark and somber. What was he doing here in my dream? What was he waiting for?

Then a weird thing happened. Out from the other side of the wings came a short little man with a thin, an-imated face and bright brown eyes. He was wearing a brown-checkered suit with brown gloves and very shiny brown shoes, topped off with a very large-brimmed brown hat. He wore a yellow tie, almost matching the color of my suit. "Well, are we having a good time?", he queried to the audience of one. "Funny Charlie wants to tell you a joke. But first, the stock market tip of the day—*toilet paper*! Futures in *toilet paper* and you're a millionaire tomorrow by wiping your butt today!" Then he launched into a ridiculous song.

"*For the show I wrote a joke or two*
and I found out without a doubt
Mr. Denning...the joke's on you!
So won't you sit...?"

Then the chorus took on a kind of bluesy style.
"*You can be sure...you can be certain*
the babes in his life, wait for the curtain
for when he's through loving you,
you'll just die from over-exposure
from thighs to shoulder as he takes off your hosier.
no one is bolder than this dick
with the crick in his member
so in December, when, baby, It's cold outside,
You can be sure, you can be certain,
you'll get the blues when the curtain—rises
for you will turn yellow from loving this fellow
so run away, run away
or baby, you'll pay, pay, pay
cause the Devil's got him in tow...
on the Cable Denning...the Cable Denning...stay tuned...it's the Cable Denning Show....!"

When he finished I glanced at the women staring at me from the wings. They were silent and watching me like I was on trial or something. There was only the sound of that single presence in the audience slapping his hands together in that unnerving.....slow...applause, that gave me the willies. I could just barely make out the shadowy figure appearing to pulsate in and out of form, with his pale face mostly concealed by a dark hood. Then Funny Charlie took me by the hand and yanked me into the wings as the babes entered the stage with a perfectly choreographed chorus line number. They were reprising *The Cable Denning Show* song and at a certain juncture, Misty Sheridan went back stage, grabbed my hand and dragged me onto center stage with the rest of the girls locking arms in back of me and finishing the production number. Each doll kicked up her feet and at a certain cue, kicked me in the butt as some kind of punishment for loving them. They had changed the finishing lyrics to:

"'cause his mischief call was he loved us all—at the same time!
Cheaper with a foursome thinking us a whore-some four—or more
but it ended like it started
leaving us down-hearted,
on The Cable Denning...Cable Denning...The Cable Denning Show!"

Again, from out of the darkness, came that deliberate....foreboding applause. Then, one by one, the girls departed, kissing me on the cheek and placing a black rose in my hand. Funny Charlie came out and added a final rose to the bouquet. Now I had a dozen black roses as Charlie stepped out in front of me to face the one in the audience.

"I once had an Auntie named Flo
   who so loved the Iceman, Joe.
But he couldn't play nice
   without putting her on ice,
with her ass astride a block of H₂O!

He seduced her in her shanty
   in her panties very scanty.
And they slipped around with much enthusi-ásm.
Though they very nearly fell,
   It all turned out just swell.
For she still had a full or-gásm!"

Funny Charlie took off his hat and bowed deeply, almost reverently to the audience of one. Again, those lifeless hands came together five times, then ominously stopped. I stepped forward, put an open hand over my forehead as a visor so I could see out there in the dark theatre. But now, I could see no one!

Then, beginning to feel apprehensive, I turned to Funny Charlie, who was perspiring and wiping his brow with a handkerchief. "Why was there only one person that came to see my show? Who is it out there?" I asked.

He snickered. "Only *Death* will see your final show, Denning," Charlie spoke, but his voice had suddenly grown ominous and dark. "You are the fool who knew too much...and lived too much...but dying,...*that*...you can only do once..." So.......it was the Grim Reaper who came to see.....my show! My....FINAL show? Then the applause started up again, along with the most terrifying laughter!

I woke up on my bed tossing and turning with Jane and Cass holding me down. "Cable! Cool it!" Jane cried out. "It's me—Jane—everything's okay, you've just been dreaming!"

I opened my eyes, my skin on fire, my eyes feeling like two eggs fried sunny side up. "Jane! Cass! Crap—it was so real...the whole damn thing. The shit that Straight injected me with—had—had long lasting side effects. I took a dope trip in full color."

Cass looked down at me, her beautiful face half-hidden by her magnificent shiny red hair. "Cable. Can you walk to the creek with me? I think I can help."

I was naked and the two girls helped me get dressed. I was so weak I could hardly stand up. Cass suggested to Jane that she needed to do what she had to do with no one else watching.

Jane gave her a strange look. "Now, you wouldn't do anything I wouldn't do, would you?" she ribbed Cass.

"I might. Depends on how urgent the situation," Cass answered.

"Are you urgent to *cure* him —or just urgent for *him*?"

"Jane! He's ill...please understand...come along if you really want to. I was hoping I could work alone—"

"—you're right. I'll stay behind. I always do. I'm a stay-behinder, or didn't you know? Especially when it comes to men."

"We'll be back soon." Both of the young women helped me to my feet and got my legs circulating. Jane accompanied us to the head of the little trail that led down to the creek. There she stopped while Cass put her arm around my waist, held my arm and we walked to the creek side.

As before, the smells were fresh and revitalizing. Cass had me sit down at the edge, took my shoes off and put my feet in the cool water. It felt good. Then she went searching for something. Soon she came back with a small bouquet of herbs. She handed me a root of this and leaf of that and had me wash it down with water each time I chewed it. Then she pointed to a large plant that looked much too prickly to me. "We must take the seeds and boil them and have you drink it while it's still hot."

"What the hell is it? Are you sure it won't kill me?

"Yes. It's milk thistle and will help remove the poison. What is inside your body now *will* kill you if it remains." Just then I began to feel the worst nausea I'd ever felt in my life. No hangover ever came close to the violent urge to barf I felt now. I got on all fours by the side of the creek and began to heave up my insides. But Cass held me tight and helped me through fifteen of the worst minutes of my life. Then she had me dip my head into the waters and suck up as much water as I could. I was almost too weak to walk, so Cass ran for Jane and the two of them practically carried me back to my cabin. I sat up in my bed because to lie down would have begun the writhing nausea all over again. Then Cass disappeared to fetch the nettle plant parts that she would boil into some kind of potion, I guessed.

Jane came and sat beside me. "I'm surprised you're not dead—that shit those guys injected into you and all..."

My voice was still weak, breathy. "Maybe I am dead, Jane. At least, according to my dream, Death is my best audience."

"What do you mean?"

"My dream...it was so vivid and nuts—I was a guest or master of ceremonies or something like that, in this theatre—and Death was the only audience. He clapped his hands slowly together after each musical number or joke—"

"—Cable, don't push it. You've been under a lot of stress." She took my hand and held it. "I wish you were mine, Cable. And I could take care of you...in all ways. But I know it could never be. Even if I were your proté-gé private detective, no one can ever have either of us. That's what makes us so unique and maybe why we like each other. We're both damaged—hard to reach."

"I like you, Jane. You're my kind of tough," I mum-bled at her. "People...who—who have never experi-enced the sharp end of the stick don't get it. But I know you do..."

"Yeah, Cable, I also have a tender side. That's the one that gets left behind. I've had enough tough for the rest of my life."

I went in and out of a kind of stupor as Jane held my hand. Finally, about an hour later, Cass came back with a steaming pot and a large mug. She glanced at Jane's hand holding mine. She seemed to ignore it. "Now, you need to drink this as hot as you are able. It won't make you vomit anymore, but you may feel a bit ill as the poi-sons are processed out of your body and it will cleanse your blood."

"How in the hell do you know so much about local herbs?" I asked, impressed with Cassie's knowledge.

"Your herbs here have biochemistries that grow everywhere on any terrestrial plane. I have studied herbs for thousands of years. I know their medicinal properties."

"I didn't think you needed stuff for your physical bodies where you come from—I mean, immortal or perpetual—or is it other-dimensional? I get it all mixed up," I said, a bit frustrated.

Jane looked at both of us with surprise. It was the first she got it driven home to her that Cassiopeia was truly not an earth native—and that I had experienced some of the other dimensions. "So it finally comes out..." She carefully looked over the beautiful Cass. "Even though you look human, you're not really—and lover man here knew your mother in another dimension? Is that right or am I just pretending to have my own version of a breakdown here? I've seen mother's radiating orb and all, and I know something's going on—"

Cass handed me a cup of the hot thistle water. I winced at the thought of drinking it in, but I trusted the alien sister. She watched me sip a bit and then turned to Jane. "—Mother's going to *un*mortalize me tomorrow. Somehow she's going to sneak me back to Saturn without my father finding out—at least not right away."

I was wondering. "How's she gonna do that—being only an orb with some kind of silent communication with you? Ha!"

"Don't do it," came a voice from out of the bathroom. Suddenly there stood the short little elfin from the *Cave of the Seven Truths.*

The women pulled back in fear at first. "It's okay, girls—this is Toggth—a buddy of mine, and I think after tonight, a buddy of yours."

Toggth came forth and extended his warm hand. Hesitatingly, each girl took his hand and acknowledged him. "I am pleased to meet both of you." He smiled a mischievous smile. "I can see Cable has been concealing you—no doubt for himself."

I snickered. "Yeah, right...I'm lucky I'm still glued together after what we've been through the past forty-eight hours or so. Why didn't you come help us out during the underground thing by the lighthouse?"

"Sorry...I was busy with something else and didn't tune into you until you were retching by the little stream with a patient Cassiopeia beside you."

"You know my name?", Cass said. "Did you know my mother?"

"No, but we spoke tonight. That's why I'm warning you not to go for the *un*mortalizing process she wants to put you through. It's fraught with pitfalls, she isn't strong enough to do it in her present state—plus your very mean-spirited sire is lying in wait for you—and ready to pounce if you go the direction Saturnalia suggests."

Cass was thinking. "Oh, dear, I see." Then she looked at me and checked out my eyes.

"Yep, Cass, I've never known Toggth to be wrong about these things. Remember, he's like you, an other-dimensional creature, very familiar with the goings on of what has to take place with—"

"—well, I guess that leaves me out," Jane interrupted. "Hell, what chance does a plain ol' ordinary earth gal have against the likes of you guys? How did I get into this nest of alien crap with you, Cass?"

"Because you liked me. And I liked you. I still do, Jane. You've been my one companion all these months, ever since Mother planted me here."

Then Jane softened. "Yeah, I guess I still do, too. I'm sorry. I have a complex about being left out. I feel so ordinary around you guys. Gees, a beautiful alien friend I can never compete with, a private detective I have a crush on who isn't available—and now a little magical creature who zips in and out whenever the whim strikes him."

Toggth laughed. "Jane...Jane...take heart, little one. We are all of equal stature in the cosmos. No one is greater than the other. I think the biggest problem comes when people forget they have to *earn* consciousness, immortality, perpetuity, beauty, grace, wit—and above all, love. Do you think it comes free? How do we lose the good that was given? By stepping out of rhythm with our own Source."

Tears had come to Jane's eyes. "I don't know...when you talk like that, you make me feel better about myself. Is that part of your magic—?"

"—no, child, it is part of *your* magic that you can hear and understand me, respond to me and be honest about yourself and your feelings. Saying you like and desire Cable is natural for a pretty young woman like yourself—accept yourself, Jane Slaughter..."

She felt a little embarrassed. She looked over at Cass. "Don't look at me. I never said I wanted Cable. I don't want any mortal man. I've told both of you I can't stand them. I belong with my own kind. But it doesn't mean I can't like you..." Then she looked over at me and her words slowed. "...or love you...that's something that is found everywhere in all the universes..."

"I'll second that," Toggth tittered. "Now...we've got to figure a way out of this mess with your Mother and Father, Cass. And not involve these mortals or at the very least, not endanger them."

I was feeling well enough to accompany Jane and Cass to *The Bucket of Blood* that evening. It would be my last night in 'Cambria Pines by the Sea' and the girls were decked out and looked great as we meandered into the tavern around 8:30 p.m. Toggth had decided to remain behind while he pondered the dilemma we all faced together and the impending danger of Gor's inevitable next assault.

An unusual phenomena happened that night as Jane finished an up-tempo song and began to play and sing a poignant version of *Among My Souvenirs*. The ordinarily raucous men and women quieted down as Jane's song told an age-old story. By the time she had reached the bridge of the song, even the bartender had stopped what he was doing to lean across the bar to listen. "*A few more tokens rest within my treasure chest, and though they do their best to give me consolation...I count them all apart, and as the teardrops start, I find a broken heart among my souvenirs...*" A hearty applause followed and Jane cracked a half-smile as she turned in her chair to acknowledge the audience. Maybe everyone in that smelly, smoky room could relate. I don't know. Maybe everyone had shrapnel from a broken heart stuck in their guts that they were still trying to pull out, the kind that tells of memory and regret, an uneasy aching that never quite lets go until maybe you're pushing up daisies at the local cemetery.

Jane got up from her honky-tonk piano and walked to the bar where Cass and I stood still silently applauding her. "Hey, babe, you nailed their heartstrings with that one. I never heard this mob so quiet."

"Yeah, neither have I," she replied. She looked at Cass, then at me. "Cable, could I talk to you privately—outside for a minute?" Cass nodded her head in understanding and Jane led us out into the back alley, not too far from old Rocco's little zucchini garden. We stood under the light of a near full moon and Jane looked lovely, but her face had a wrinkled brow and her eyes a sad perplexity. "Cable...I know you're leaving tomorrow. I've really been fighting something inside—whether I should come to L.A. or not."

"I told you the truth, Jane. I'm not sure you're cut out to be a female detective—but then again, I never met one, so I can't say."

"It's not that. It's you—and me. I've got these feelings for you, Mister. I don't think I could be around you too long without wanting to hop in the sack with you."

I had seen this one coming. "Damn, Jane, I'm really flattered. But I told you up front that I was healing up from someone—someone I was in love with. We were together only a couple of years when she died a terrible death."

"I thought it was something like that...there was too much pain on your face for it to be just a breakup—"

"—and as for you and me—as you said, we're too much alike, tough, embittered, walking around with an axe to grind against the world—I don't think it'd be a good match."

"Goes to show how two people see things so differently. Here I was thinking that would be a good reason we could make it. Two old battered souls on the roadway of life, you know."

"I don't think it works that way. Old wounds have a way of flaring up and you always blame it on the one who's closest to you. Besides, I really ain't the regular kind of guy—I wouldn't want a dame who's always hanging around—I like to drink and smoke and hide out in my office, waiting for the phone to ring so I can pay the bills. I'm a loner, Jane, when you really get down to it."

She looked at me with a pained expression, like an animal trapped between two places. "I kind of thought so. Now that I'm naked and embarrassed standing here in front of you, I'm asking myself, what am I going to do with my life? I can't stay here plunking out-of-tune keys and warbling songs forever. I'm still young, I want to live, Cable!"

"You can ride with me back to L.A. Don't worry, I'll keep an eye on you so you don't go off the deep end and get swallowed up by that city—"

"—Cable, it's past that! I'm in love with you—for God's sake—*love me or kill me*—but don't let me suffer like this!"

I looked away and took a deep breath as I retrieved a cigarette from the pack of Lucky Strikes in my breast pocket. I didn't know what else I could say. Jane had painted herself into a corner. I lit up and took a deep drag. "Again, thank you, Jane...that you should care that much...but as I said, I'm still nursing that thing in me that holds on to my heart like a bulldog's grip and the only way I can numb it is with booze and smokes, evenings spent in memory and regret—"

"—what about a good woman? I think that's a hell of a lot more healing than alcohol and cigarettes—which will kill you anyhow."

"I can't do it, Jane, maybe if you'd come into my life later—"

"—fuck it, Denning! I don't need you or anyone! I never did!"

She turned and ran down the alley. I ran after her and caught up with her, grabbing her by the shoulders. She wriggled out of my grip. She was crying, her body rigid and she avoided my eyes. "Let me go, Cable. I'm gonna walk home to the Bluebird. I'll be okay. I always am. Good luck, in case I don't see you tomorrow." Then she broke away and ran down the alley, the sound of her heels grinding the dirt under her feet as she disappeared around a corner.

I went back inside to *The Bucket of Blood*. Cass was waiting patiently and I saw a knowing expression on her face. "She confronted you, didn't she? I mean, about you and her."

"Yeah, something like that." I looked around at the motley, noisy customers in the joint. I knew I would never step foot in it again. "Let's get out of here," I said.

She took my arm and we went out into the cool night air. "Since this is your last night, can we—can we take a little ride—maybe down by the cliffs near Pirate's Cove?"

"Sure, why not?" We walked in the moonlight, this exquisitely beautiful young woman clinging to my arm. I opened the coupe door and let her in. I got in on the driver's side and sat back, exhaling all the tension I had felt with Jane Slaughter. "Crap, Cass, why does life always have to do with sex, one way or another?"

"Maybe it's not just sex, Cable. Maybe Jane really loves you—in her way, the best way she knows how. I feel she's sincere."

"I don't want to talk about it anymore. She ran back to the Bluebird after I told her I couldn't be her bed partner if she came back to Los Angeles with me."

"Oh, that must have hurt. A woman never likes to hear that—especially if she's got her mind set on one particular man."

"Let's just drive for a while," I said, heading onto Main St.

We drove to the cliffs of Pirate's Cove, got out and stood at the edge, looking down at the shimmering sea in the moonlight.

Cass turned to me and held my arm firmly. "I suppose it's my turn now, isn't it?"

"What do you mean?"

"Jane had a turn to pitch her ring into the arena of love. Now I guess it's mine. I might surprise you, though. I might be bolder than Jane was." Suddenly I was thinking of a way to escape, just run, anywhere, away from the emotional cat-and-mouse games people play. Even this spectacular babe holding on to my arm couldn't stop that instinct in me from wanting to bolt, disappear into the night where no one could find me. I calmed myself by realizing it would all be gone tomorrow. I'd be on my way back to the city that bred me, turned me over daily like a bad coin, chewed me up, spat me out and took me back again the next day as one of her sons. What man had a greater love-hate relationship with that City of Angels than I had? Then I came back to the present.

"Uh...bolder? I'm not sure what you mean, Cass."

"I want to be with you, Cable...while I'm still a mortal woman...to experience those feelings, like the helplessness that physical intimacy causes, taking over my heart, my life. I've always been so much...in control."

I took her hand and looked into those fire-warm eyes of hers. "As I told Jane, I'm very touched—not to mention flattered. You know, Cass, I'm kind of young in earth years, but I've learned a few things along the way. I learned that a man can never possess beauty—and you, young woman—you are too beautiful for words, too lovely for mortal men to know how to handle—I would get lost in you."

She reached for me and put her head on my chest. "Would you? Please get lost in me, Cable! So I can be lost in you and never want to know another man. Spoil me, seduce me, touch me...everywhere."

I broke away from her embrace as if what she said hurt me. But what it really did was bare my own nakedness and vulnerability. "If you were my lover, wherever we'd walk, men would salivate over you and plot ways to remove me from your life. Your exquisite looks would drive men mad from wanting to possess your body. And if my emotions and heart caught up with my body's desire for you, I would only want to make you stay, possess you myself, own the essence that is you, that elusive wisp of warmth and mystique that makes men fight and die."

"So what's wrong with that, if I felt the same? What if I fell in love with you? What if my own feelings became so human I would *want* to stay here on earth with you?"

I took out a Lucky Strike and lit it up. I took a deep drag and let the smoke out slowly. "Then I would pity you......pity you, because I would grow old and die right before your eyes and the young virile man who seduced you, brought you ecstasy in the night would become a creaky old man who complained about everything, and worst of all, he will have forgotten what it feels like to caress that beautiful, young dream who once upon a time slept by his side. Plus this guy you're talking about, he's selfish, insecure, unreliable—and looks long and hard at a pretty skirt, especially one that looks great in a low-cut sequined gown and sings romantic songs in the middle of the night in some smoky cabaret."

"But if I chose to stay mortal, I would grow old beside you—I would never leave you, Cable. There would always be something wonderful about you. The heart and spirit never grow old—do they?"

"You don't get it. In truth, no man wants an old broad hanging around him as he ages. His memory isn't *that* bad. It's a private world he retreats to, isolates himself from the outside chaos of youth and kids and war and trouble and pain. He's had enough. He'll fantasize about some young thing in a magazine or a signboard or someone in the last movie he saw." I reached into my inner breast pocket and got out my silver flask of gin. I offered Cass a slug, but she refused, so I took a big gulp myself and put the flask away.

She turned her face to the sky and moonlight lit up her perfect profile there on the hillside overlooking the sea. "I guess it's like the sound of the surf. The waves are constant and seemingly forever. But it's different water and different winds that cause it all to happen. Is that what you're saying? Things look constant but they're not?"

"Yeah, sort of. Nothing is as constant as change, it is said...at least here. Even your mother would tell you that. Look what she's gone through."

"I know my mother wanted you. But she knew that falling in love with someone is an illusion. She told me she could never possess you, so why start loving you?"

"Smart woman. You see, I rest my case in front of you and the whole damn cosmos. I thought she was beautiful, intelligent, and sexy as hell. But I also knew she had a plate full of complications, not to mention eight kids who were now many thousands of years old."

"So...getting back to the present...why wouldn't you want me?"

I looked at her, touched her, saw her fine figure there in the moonlight. "I already told you. It has nothing to do with not desiring you, Cass. It's my own weakness as a human. Who's to say I wouldn't fall in love with you and really get lost? I can't afford that. I've been married to my career since I joined the police force. There's no room for a full-time doll." I looked out to sea. It shimmered in the moonlight, endless undulations rolling toward the shore. "Just recently, I buried the on-

289

ly woman I will ever be in love with—I mean really *in love* with. And that still hurts a lot, Cass."

"I'm sorry. I knew you were here to do some healing. May I ask you about this unique woman you loved? What was she like?"

I put out my cigarette. "Adora was beautiful and simple, devoted and sexy, quiet spoken yet adventurous. I would have lived out my life being happy with her by my side. Sometimes, if you're lucky, someone comes along and they just *fit*. Adora just *fit*. She was like taking in a fresh breath in the middle of a spring night, or walking into Paradise with the only person you'll ever need. I don't know...how do you explain these things?"

Tears were trickling down Cass's cheeks. "I see...thank you for telling me, Cable. I would never have known. No woman could hope to come close to what you felt for her, I can tell. So...I guess that puts me out of the running, doesn't it?"

I looked at her and squeezed her arm. "You were never in it, Cass. I knew up front you were the personification of the elusive dream men dream, that illusion they keep hoping comes true in every sense so they can own it. But as I said, it always disappoints. It's far better to appreciate beauty from a distance than to complicate both lives by trying to possess what can never be possessed."

She looked luscious there in the moonlight and I was powerfully tempted to take her in my arms and forget everything I had just said. But it would not be true for me, and in the end, I was a truth guy. She turned to me and looked longingly into my eyes. "It's been hard for

290

me here on Earth. There just aren't many Cable Dennings around—and you know how selective I am. Wouldn't you know it, the only man who doesn't pant after me and sell all he owns to have me—is the only man who refuses me. You're right, this earth life thing is a perverse irony." Then she sat on the grass and pulled me down beside her. "Could you not enjoy me as an appreciation of beauty—as I would appreciate you as intelligent, passionate, virile, aggressive, muscular and handsome? Why must we look beyond the present moment?"

"Because, as I said before, your beauty is exceptionally rare...exquisite. I don't know how I'd react if I was intimate with you. What if I went berserk or something? And why would I take something so beautiful and grind it out in the dirt like every other lusting man does?"

She laughed. "Put a sack over my head and pretend I'm ugly and make love to my body. I would give you that willingly, Cable." Then she studied me carefully, sensing what was going on at the root of it all. "You're afraid, aren't you?"

"Yeah, maybe I am, lady. Even with a sack over your head, your voice, your sighs, your cries and moans, the smells and tastes of you, your swollen and wet womanhood, your heaving breasts—no, I couldn't separate you from you. Would you want me to do that?"

"No...I would want you to look into my eyes when you bonded with me and say nothing you didn't want to say, do nothing you didn't want to do."

I was getting a bit uncomfortable. "You know what I think?"

"What?"

"I think we're talking each other into making love."

"Yes. And things are beginning to go that way for me, too. What choice do we have, Cable?"

I got up, grabbed her hand and pulled her up to me. "Every day when the sun shines, Cassiopeia, I would think of this ideal woman who loved me and who one night I held in the palm of my hand, preciously. But the memory will not even be about something that might have been, but about that perfect beauty that glows—like the first time I saw you walk into that tavern. Sometimes those first snap shots are enough to last a lifetime, Cass. It's like the star system that's named after you—look into the night sky and long for it, Cable Denning, but you can't touch the stars. And for me, I think it's going to have to be...like that..."

She put her arms around my waist and her head onto my chest. "How can I live without hearing that voice? When you talk, it comforts me, Cable. I can't explain—but that's the way it feels." Then she unwrapped herself and brought her gorgeous face closer to mine. "So I'll be this *beauteous ideal* locked up inside you—like—like some unattainable creature you just dream about when you get lonely?"

"Well, not exactly. But close enough. Actually, that's the biggest complement a girl can get...that I hold you so high that I would never want to despoil the perfect vision I have of you since the first night I saw you. That will live in me in a way no sensual earth experience can. That single vision of an ideal object of desire will still be in me beyond these years. And in my imagination, I'll make love to her—like a god, lady."

"But in the meantime you'll make love more easily to someone like Jane, won't you? I know she desires you."

"You know I like Jane. I owe her one. She helped me out that night when I really needed someone to come along. But Jane's wounded, sort of like I'm wounded, Cass. Two wounded people are unhealthy for each other. Before I can be with another woman, if you want to know the truth, I have a lot of healing to do—especially after Adora. What I didn't tell you was that two years before losing Adora to leukemia, I lost my fiancée to a mad killer's gun. So you can see, my romantic road hasn't exactly been an easy one to hoe. I'm sorry, Cass, but I know the higher part of you understands."

"Oh, so does the lower part, Cable. It's just that I can't shut off desire like a switch. It'll take some time. It's the way I'm made. But thank you for being so honest with me and sharing what I realize you simply don't tell just anyone."

"Yeah, you're welcome—and thanks for understanding." I took her hand and we walked back up the hill to the coupe. In my head I was fighting with myself, hoping against all the stupid hopes in the world that hid out deep inside me there, that I had made the right decision. Experience with babes had taught me a lot. We don't always make the right calls for ourselves. Sometimes you get lost in thoughts that aren't even you and find yourself going back and forth like a ping-pong ball being batted by a mad player trying for a grand slam. Sometimes you make bad decisions. You might end up regretting a decision made years before. Hell, life's a dice game anyway.

CHAPTER 10

LOVE ME OR KILL ME

Jane Slaughter was nowhere to be found the next morning. From all that I could gather, she had checked out the night before and disappeared into the ethers of life. I was sorry. I liked Jane and would have been happy to help her find her way in Los Angeles. I knew dames like her would probably slip between the slats of society, falling further until either men or drugs or prostitution—or all of them—got a hold of her and she would die early in some dark alley one night, destroyed by the very society that bred her into the world. Or maybe not. There was always the hope that some secret stamina survived inside someone like Jane, an intelligent knowing that you could rise to better things. It was just that the Great Depression had taken away hope from so many. It was little less than a toss-up. And that was the lighter side of it. What if Gor's thugs got a hold of her first?

My destiny with Cassiopeia was another story. I kept hearing the music of Honey drift in and out of my head as we got ready to depart for L.A., like she was calling me back and when I got there, she'd still be singing at the *Bella Notte* as if nothing had happened. It was beautiful, nostalgic—and painful. But I had to hear her again, otherwise my heart would wrap up too tight and then shrink into nothingness. And that ain't me, no matter what else. So I listened and cried inside and suffered.

After Cass said good-bye to Art Beatle up at Nitwit Ridge, an unlikely trio rode back to L.A. with me. Cass sat next to me in Elisa's coupe while Toggth rode in the back seat, mumbling all kinds of possible solutions to our current predicament: how to keep Gor off our trail and protect us from his widespread goon squads. Or worse, the inevitable confrontation I would have to have with him one day. I knew in my gut I couldn't avoid it. But I didn't want to get Cass more involved than she was already. I knew also, that staying with me extended the possibility I might fall in love with her one day before she went back to her home planet—and she would fulfill that human young woman's longing for sexual fulfillment by loving someone who could love her back in a way that was suited for both of them. On the surface, we made a great looking couple. I could never get over her beauty, day or night, she always looked naturally fetching, the kind of face you want to adore and kiss twenty-four hours and day—let alone the rest of her!

"Now...your office is a deathtrap, Cable," Toggth was saying. "If not for you, then for Cassiopeia. I'm sorry that Miss Slaughter has decided to go her own way. I fear for her. She's a walking target for any of Cronus-Gor's killers. Now they *will* kill her if they catch up with her. She's no longer of use to them, and she knew just a little too much to be allowed to live. That's how they think. Primitive, I know. But they are what they are."

Just then the rear half of the automobile lit up with a warm, yellow glow. Saturnalia's brass orb hovered immediately next to Toggth,. "Mother!" Cass blurted out.

"Good day, Saturnalia," Toggth said. "Good of you to join us to help solve our strategic puzzle."

There was a silence. "Mother says hello, Cable," Cass reported. "She says you're brave and gutsy—or ignorant and bull-headed to go back to Los Angeles. But either way, she'll support you."

I laughed. "Thanks a bunch, lady!" I grinned. "Seems unfair, though, that I'm out-numbered—three aliens to one gringo."

Again, a long silence put me into a state of feeling left out. What in the hell were they saying? I was wondering if I could develop that skill, when Toggth spoke up as Cass was nodding her head in the affirmative, quite excited and sad at the same moment. "I agree with Saturnalia's plan—in most every detail. Here's how she's suggesting we proceed. We transfer the specific knowledge of the *Fen de Fuqin* directly into Cassiopeia's consciousness. Then you, Cable, will no longer have it stored in your brain cells. Secondly, we'll teleport Cass temporarily to a unique location near the *Cave of the Seven Truths*, in my dimension. Now, it gets sticky because we cannot *hold* the energy of either that information or Cass's multi-dimensional body in that state indefinitely. At some point it will all revert. The *God of Our Fathers* knowledge will come snapping back into your brain because it is organically magnetized there— and even more risky, Cassiopeia will be shuttled out of my dimension—to an unknown destination. All we do know is that she must for now re-appear in a physical mortal body until Saturnalia has the strength and form to transmigrate her daughter into an astral state—and send her home in that vibrational form."

"How's that sounding?" I asked Saturnalia. The glowing orb came to the back of my seat and conked me gently on the head.

"I think that's a 'yes', Cable," Cass chuckled.

"So before we decide for sure here, let me recap as I understand it. First, we extract the specific brain cell knowledge of the golden capsule from my noggin, right? Then we invest it temporarily into Cass's brain and send her to Toggth's temporary dimension, not her own, mind you—but one comfortable enough for her to hang out for a while. But none of it will stick very long and one of these unsuspecting days, all of a sudden I'll know I've got the knowledge of the golden capsule in my brain again—and at the same time know Cass is back—but where?"

"Well, frankly, that's one of the more dangerous risks. We don't know," Toggth remarked.

"Mother is suggesting to me, since I must first be teleported to earth in a physical body, that I set my mind to what she taught me as a child."

"And pray tell, what was that?" I asked, my tongue in my cheek.

"*Wish-ports* was a game we played when I was very young. It's all about mind focus... using your mind to direct your body to be where ever you wish it to be...if that makes sense."

"Oh, like Phillip K. Dick—I've read weird things like that in his way-out-there books—but it's science fiction."

"Who says it's science *fiction*, Cable?" Toggth returned. "All things are shades and shadows of what's true. Manifesting something from the mind or imagination state to the three-dimensional state is simply the art of *knowing how.*"

"Easy for you to say," I said. "Okay...let's assume we all agree to do this thing. Where and when? You know, you guys gotta remember, I'm still a private detective. I go on facts—show me the *facts* and I can act on them. We can't have speculation about—"

"—fact number one, Cable, is you will be in great danger during this time. As soon as we teleport Cass, Gor will know. He will be angry. He will have you summoned and brought before him. He will want to kill you—but he will realize the knowledge of the *Fen de Fuqin* has been transferred to his daughter's consciousness. He'll be even more angry. Then he'll express some kind of revenge on you. Not enough to kill you yet, but enough to make you suffer."

"Oh, that's swell. Why do I always end up being the fall guy?"

Cass grabbed my arm and squeezed. She didn't say anything, but I could feel a surge of love go through her right up to my heart and down to my groin at the same time. "So...are we agreed?" Toggth continued.

We all concurred this was the best way to stave off the monster of Gor and the *Oculus.* But we were now confronted with two things: one, that time was of the essence and two, we needed a facility to do the sending of Cass into another dimension. *A very powerful magnetic field* was how Toggth put it. We were all puzzled at this one.

"Mother says to go visit a grave—I'm trying to decipher—oh! It's your Honey—the one who was murdered? That one."

A sinking feeling went through me as I thought about re-visiting Honey's gravesite. Although it seemed ages ago, it really wasn't—and I wasn't sure I was up to it. "Honey? Are you sure Saturnalia hasn't got her wires crossed?"

"Trust it, Cable," Toggth said. "The sooner the better."

The Moldering Embers of Love

We got back to L.A., but by the time we arrived, Toggth and Saturnalia had gone back into their respective dimensions and only Cass and I remained. "Now, where are we going to put you up where it's safe? Your father has tentacles all over this city. And I'm not so sure he doesn't sense when you're not too far away."

She put her hand on my leg and squeezed gently. "Let me stay with you. The closer I am to you, the safer I feel," she purred. I knew exactly what the female in her was thinking.

"Forget it, Cass. That would be jumping right into the fire—for both of us. No, we've got to find a safe place for you to stay until this thing is resolved. I'll go visit Honey's gravesite tomorrow. I sure in the hell hope those guys knew what they were talking about."

"I'll go with you, Cable."

"I'm not sure how I feel about that, Cass. It's kind of a private thing, you know."

"She's gone, Cable. My energy will be good for you. I can help."

Women have a way about them, even if they happen to be extra-terrestrial in origin. So that night I stood guard at my office desk with my .38 on the desktop along with a pack of Lucky Strikes and a bottle of cheap gin. After a change of sheets, I put Cass in my bed. I was thinking what a comedown that must be to a Saturnalian princess, to bunk out in a smelly old bachelor's lair. But she didn't seem to mind. In fact, during the middle of the night, the scrumptious Cassiopeia came out to check on me. She was wearing only my bathrobe and her perfectly shaped breasts were solidly outlined beneath the cotton material, her nipples exalted and inviting. Had I not been so exhausted from the trip from Cambria, the intricate conversations and the all-night vigil, I might have sprung up and taken that exquisite creature into my arms and thrown her on my bed and tossed all caution to the winds by making love to her. "Are you alright?" she asked as she approached. She sniffed the sleeve of my robe. "I love your smells, Cable. Your whole bed smells of you. Masculine, independent, like you."

I had to make light of things. "If you think that's potent, you ought to sniff out my laundry. Why aren't you sleeping?"

"I rarely sleep. When I was staying at Art Beatle's, I would walk the pine forests all night sometimes."

"Ah, that's why he said he'd check up on you once in a while and find you absent from your little garden house."

"Yes. Sometimes I want to sleep. But I have no human dreams, there's not much to connect with in my earthly experiences. I've been here such a short dura-

300

tion." She studied me. "If we made love, I would have beautiful dreams, I'm certain. Then I'd have a worthy human experience—and a lovely, positive one at that."

"How do you know it would be worthy—or lovely?"

"I know. I can feel it. You have more inside you than you realize."

I took a deep breath. "Well, you know the score, Cass. Believe me, I could say I should...but I can't...hell, woman, you're thinking about making love while I'm dreading that visit to Honey's grave tomorrow. Have a heart!"

"I'm sorry. That is rather selfish of me, isn't it? It's probably a human woman trait, don't you think?"

"Yeah, it's called *territorial*. You see, you want to be the next female to stay in my cave. That means I *mark* you by breeding with you. Then I become territorial, possessive of you. Then I fight off other guys in some kind of pecking order, a survival of the fittest ritual in which nature demands only the strongest survive to perpetuate the species."

She thought for a minute. "Offspring...children...I never thought of that. Can my body bear you a child if we made love?"

"I don't know. Do you have monthly menstruation periods?"

"Like Jane did? No. I think Mother left that part out of me."

"Consider it a blessing, lady," I said, relieved to hear it. "That means you can make love without conceiving a child—or worry about your 'offspring' for the next twenty years or so."

"I don't know. My mother conceived from my father's seeds. I don't know why I can't. I'll have to ask her."

"In the meantime, Cass, get some rest. I need some, too. Hell, it's already four in the morning. We'll get going around eight or so."

She smiled at me with those fire-warm eyes of hers. "This opportunity may never come again, Cable. Are you sure?" She came over to where I sat on my comfy chair behind my desk. She grabbed my head and kissed me hard on the mouth until I could feel it curl my toes.

"You did that once before, in Cambria," I said, trying to downplay the sexual stimulation the babe had injected into me with that kiss.

"So I did it again. I'm only twenty-two of your years, so it's only natural to have those feelings. Do you blame me?"

"Naw, kid, but I can't take you up on it. Please...go lie down, Cass. You're not helping things, you know."

"I'm sorry. Good-night...I won't come out again." She moved away from me, gliding back toward my bedroom. How stupid can a guy get! I was thinking.

Some realities never seem real. "*Fly Home to Your Song*" was the epitaph Honey's foster parents requested for her tombstone's legend. With Cassiopeia standing next to me, part of me was lost in the memory of that vivacious little blonde who loved me when she was sparkling with a song and rising in the world. I was recalling the night when she paid me tribute by saying, "A couple of years ago I fell in love with a young policeman," she had said. And when she finished, she lifted her glass and toasted me. "So here's to the boy in my man...I dedicate this song." I remember the song was Al Jolson's *Sonny Boy* and it brought tears to my eyes then, just as it was doing now as I heard her again in my reverie.

Cass jerked me out of it. "She's not here, Cable."

"What do you mean?"

"Beings don't hang around their bodies. There's only discarded chemistry down there, moldering like mulch, to return to the soil."

"Yeah, so what? It's a place to remember someone you cared about, Cass. Doesn't your kind do that?"

"You know what else? You didn't tell me. Honey was an alien—like me, just a different species."

I was shocked by Cass's revelation. "Now just how in the hell would you know that?"

"I can feel it—pick it up in my senses."

Just as I was wondering what the hell I was doing here with this psychic extra-terrestrial, I spotted a familiar figure standing a few yards in back of us. It was Joe Lorena! I turned and motioned him to join us. I went up to Joe and shook his hand. I could see his eyes had been tearing. "Good to see you, Joe," I said.

"Likewise, Cable," he answered. Then he looked long at Cass.

"Oh, this is Cassiopeia—a friend of mine—"

"—well, not exactly—she's a Saturnian. I can see her color orb. Aliens can spot aliens a mile away, detective." He took Cass's hand. "Good to meet you, Cassiopeia. She...she was my daughter, you know..."

"I am pleased to meet you," Cass said diplomatically. "No, I didn't know. And her mother?"

"She was an earth woman I fell in love with. She died shortly after Honey was born." Joe was sizing up the two of us.

Cass smiled gently at Joe. "I'm very glad you're here, because we have another reason for seeing you...other than Cable visiting Honey's gravesite."

"Reason?" Joe queried the young woman. "I just felt called to visit Honey's place of entombment, that's all."

"Well, it goes deeper than that, Joe," I chimed in. "You see, Cass here needs to get out of town fast, so to speak—she needs a powerful magnetic boost to teleport her to Toggth's land near the *Cave of the Seven Truths*. Saturnalia, Cass's mother, suggested we come here today and we'd meet someone who could help us get her there." Then I drew him closer. "You see, Joe, she's Gor's daughter and he's on a rampage both for her and my hide. But Toggth and Saturnalia assured us they can extract the exact knowledge of the golden capsule from my brain and temporarily put it into Cass's head somehow. Thus when Gor comes on to me like a killer plague, I'll have nothing to share with him. So at best we're buying a little time."

"You do know, it *is* temporary and this young woman will be drawn back out of that vibration within a fairly short time? And the magnetized knowledge of the capsule will be zapped back into you."

"Yeah, we know. But what other options do we have, Joe?" Joe Lorena thought quietly.

"Cable, bring Cassiopeia tonight. Here." He took out a small notepad and wrote a number and location. "Destroy this by setting a match to it the minute you make this phone call. I will be at the other end and give you a pick up address." He gave Cass a pleasant look. "I think we can help. You are beautiful and intelligent, like my Honey was. Cable's a lucky man. How does he do it?"

"Oh, we're just ships in the night, Joe, Cass is gonna be moving on back to Saturn as soon as Mom can get her energy hopped back up."

"That isn't what *I* see in her eyes, Detective Denning. You need to learn a thing or two about us aliens." Cass flushed. "Sorry, Cass. Earth men can really be dense."

"It's alright," Cass said softly, glancing at me and then away.

"What time tonight, Joe?"

"Oh, say about nine? I'll make sure to be at that number."

I took his arm and walked him a few feet away from Cass. "How are you really doing, Joe? Have you been restructured or whatever you needed to have happen after the Laggore thing?"

"Oh, I don't know, Cable. I'm kind of a ship without a rudder these days. I think I'll go home someday soon, like Cassiopeia. She's absolutely stunning. Where did you find her?"

"Long story, Joe. Met up with her gorgeous mother— the one who had eight children and Cronus-Gor, her husband, ate seven of them?"

"Oh, that one...no wonder you're in hot water." He waved to Cass and started to walk away. "I'll see you tonight, Cable..."

Most of that evening seemed like a blur to me. Cass and I reached the public phone Joe Lorena indicated, and made the call. We were picked up and driven to the bottom of a steep hillside just north of Altadena. We were blindfolded and led into what I assumed to be some kind of underground facility—one I'd heard Joe speak of during Honey's time. It was very quiet except for some deep hum in the distance. We were brought to some kind of waiting room and, still blindfolded, helped to sit down on some pretty comfortable chairs.

Cass was nervous. She reached for my hand, directed by the sound of my voice. "Cable, what—what if I never see you again?"

"I don't know, angel. I try not to think about it." Secretly, I loved holding this captivating young woman's hand. "Even though my gut tells me you'll cycle back into my life. Seems I've been tossed into a mixer with your family. First your mother, then your dad, and now you. Who's next, I wonder?"

"Well, if you must know, I'll tell you a secret." She squeezed my hand and tittered a little. "My sister, *Hestia*, is really—really—oh, another word for angry I've heard you use—"

"—*pissed*—"

"—Yes, pissed...at my father. She's going to challenge him for the earth. Our brother Zeus would still have been here ruling over you mortals if he hadn't gotten bored with it all. But there's never been a female ruler over your planet that I know of."

I was rather confused, but delighted at this prospect. "How do you know this—and can she do it? Overthrow your unredeemable father?"

"I don't know." Then she took a big breath and a sigh came to her voice. "I just wish...I just wish you and I could have been lovers...I mean, just to experience the bonding—to feel what it feels like—to know and trust a human man inside me, holding me, mating with me—"

"—come back to reality, Cass. This is the eleventh hour here—let's stick to the task at hand. I'm sorry if I sound hard, but I've learned not to get too sentimental. It always comes back to bite you."

She withdrew her hand just as Joe Lorena came back in the room with a couple of other men. They led us further down a hallway and then removed our blindfolds. We were in a gigantic room where the hum I had heard earlier was now obvious and we had to speak loudly to be heard. "We need to leave you here, Cable," Joe said. Immediately Cass threw her arms around me just as Toggth showed up through the portal of another room.

"Hey, I was wondering if you were coming," I said just as Saturnalia's brass orb came in behind him. I unclenched myself from Cass's arms. "Nice work if you can get it, kid—and it looks like you've got a great team on your side. Hell, you keep having these kinds of adventures and you'll be the talk of the town," I kidded her.

They pulled the beautiful Cassiopeia away from me and disappeared down a hallway. My first impulse was to follow and yank her back and tell her I needed her to help heal the pain she had stirred up inside me, the one that had my name on it and I had hoped to the heavens was healing up. But when a babe like Cass kisses you

307

and throws that body of hers onto yours, curves and all, it's hard because the instinctual need of the moment is to hold on to the beauty and covet it as long as you can, take that exquisite body and pound it into the sheets of a luxury bed somewhere on a tropic isle.

I stood there for what seemed the longest time. Soon Joe came back. "It was successful, Cable, thanks to Toggth. That little guy knows his stuff. Cassiopeia is now safely ensconced in his dimension. For the time being, that is."

"What about my head thing?" I asked. For all I had felt was a little stab of pain while I was waiting for Joe earlier.

"It's done." He took my arm and led me back to the waiting room where he blindfolded me once again. "For your own protection." We began the walk back up to the surface. "By the way, that stunning redhead is in love with you. Just like my Honey was. What's your secret?"

I laughed a strange laugh. "Ha! Probably base, primordial sexual instincts mixed with a little appreciation for art and beauty," I answered.

"It seems when alien women are *mortalized*, they take on a response to those primal sexual instincts. It's almost the less you care emotionally, the more they want you—it's perplexing to me."

"Don't try to figure it out, Joe," I said. "Incidentally, strictly speaking from the curious mind of a private detective, Cass mentioned in passing that one of her sisters, *Hestia*, wants to challenge Dad for number one position in the earth hierarchy."

"I've heard that rumor, too. I don't know. I've learned that despite all the dimensional levels of possible experience, there's still some kind of divine hand in the cosmos, Cable. It's *just*, but not moral in the sense you are taught as a youngster. Humans are allowed their folly, hate, despair, endless violence and political-religious struggles and pragmatic crystallization because they believe they are divided from their fellow beings—and what you perceive as free will is part of the experimentation to discover how lessons learned, *stick* and ultimately elevate the individual consciousness." We reached the entrance to the facility and he removed my blindfold. "Anyway, I'm not sure what Hestia is up to. To unseat Cronus-Gor would mean she'd have to pretty much destroy his present—and considerable—network...which is worldwide and controls just about every branch of human endeavor, from banking to planning elections to starting wars. Art and music they don't bother with.....yet. But who knows? Maybe one day they will suck the essence out of that, too."

"Well, that's not a rosy picture you paint, Joe. What's your role in all of this? I can't imagine you standing still and not working for the side of good and triumphing over evil, as they say."

"I don't know, Cable. I'm tired. I think I might go home for a while. There are other younger creatures of my own species who are anxious to fight the good fight. After Honey—and my killing Laggore and his strong arms—I rather lost my taste for it. I don't think anyone can last long without love. It was my hope that you and Honey would bring me that delight, and maybe a grandchild or two—"

"—Joe! Please! It's hard enough that we're two grown men standing here with tears in our eyes, lamenting what might have been. Let's get on with it, Mister. You know you can call on me anytime. I'm not so sure about the love thing, but I like you a lot, Joe."

He wiped his eyes with his sleeve. "Thanks, Cable. But I think I'll disappear for a while."

We embraced and his driver let me into the back seat of the waiting car. "Thanks again, Joe, for helping out...I know Cass's challenges aren't over yet."

He looked after me and smiled. "Even the gods have challenges, Cable. See you around..."

That night I was so exhausted that I collapsed on my bed with my clothes on. Bright and early the next morning I heard a key slide into the lock outside in the office. I drew my .38 out from under my pillow and crouched on the bed. Soon I heard a whistle and a feminine voice humming. It was Zelda Blodgett. She had come to check on things and water the plants that she maintained would help cheer up my rather bleak surroundings. Then she peeked around the corner and saw me lying on my stomach on the bed with my gun drawn. "Cable! It's me! I didn't even know you were back."

I lowered my gun. "Hi, Zelda. Yeah, got back a couple of days ago. I had to do a few things before I jumped into business as usual."

"I'm happy to see you." She came up to me and hugged me. "God, you smell of tobacco and alcohol. Where have you been?"

"Oh," I laughed, "with some beautiful redhead in a cave, making mad, passionate love and then sending her back to her native planet."

She smiled. "Oh, you! I might believe the redhead part—because I know you never give brunettes like me a chance. But I'm still glad we're friends and all. I don't know how many times your phone has rung.... but a lot. I took down a few messages while I was here. There's been one persistent lady who really wanted to know where you were. I told her I didn't know. She left her name. *Florida Heston, HOllywood 6411.* How could I forget? She's been a nuisance. Anyway, the plants are fine."

"Thanks, Zelda. I'll tell you what. Soon as I get a few bucks ahead, I'll take you out to a nice dinner—and if you behave—maybe a few spins around the dance floor, eh?"

Her face lit up. "Really? That would be swell, Cable! Thanks!"

"It's the least I can do for you, keeping up the joint like you do and bringing in the little touch of greenery."

"So when can we go?" she asked anxiously.

Just at that second there was a commotion at my front door and in ran three women, clad in white leather jackets and black slacks with high heels! One of them pulled a gun on Zelda and me. "Who's the female twerp, Denning? Lose her. My business is with you!" she demanded.

I was sitting on the edge of my bed with Zelda standing above me. "I guess you'd better go home, Zelda. Don't worry. I'll call you later for that date."

"Gees, Cable—I don't know about you—I mean, your life is exciting and all—but so dangerous and scary! Who are these people?"

"I haven't got a clue, kid. C'mon, go home, we'll talk later."

311

Zelda walked slowly toward the door, the gal with the gun watching her. Then she turned to me. "Surely, you can do better than that. My mother tells me you're the ladies' lady's-man...they just can't get enough of you. And I understand my sister is smitten with you." She looked me over. "Well, you're alright for a youngish earthman, I guess. But you're no Ramon Navarro, either."

I slowly got up from the bed and walked into my office, still trying to shake the morning. "Want a cup of coffee?" I asked the women. I didn't know what else to say. "By the way, that's a pretty fancy gun you're toting there. I don't think I've seen anything quite like it."

The three women looked at each other. They were all good lookers, one a blonde, one a kind of reddish hair and the boss woman who did all the talking had dark brunette hair. She had a hell of body on her, while the others were more modestly endowed. "No—no, uh, I don't drink coffee. I get too excited on the drug. The gun? It's a new design, from Germany. It's called a Schnellfeuer. Produced by Mauser with its own select-fire, detachable magazine."

I looked at the other two women. "And you ladies?" They simply shook their heads in the negative, staring at me in amazement that I wasn't frightened of them. "So...you aliens get the latest, I'll say that." I said as I placed some ground coffee in my old percolator. I walked slowly into my bathroom, filled the coffee maker with water, went back to the corner, turned the little hotplate on and then stood to face my company. "So what can I do for you rather energetic ladies, this early morning?"

312

"I am *Hestia*, but I prefer being called *Vesta*. I am the virgin goddess, first-born daughter of Cronus-Gor. I am also the first one he jealously devoured—and the last one he disgorged when my mother tricked him into— well, you know the story. I know Cassiopeia has told you a lot—maybe too much. But so has mother. Some thousands of your years ago I gave up my seat in the hierarchy of the pantheon of the gods on Olympus over to Dionysus. Just like my brother, I got bored playing Miss Home and Hearth and praying at the votary every day ad nauseam."

I tried to control any humor I might reflect back to the dame. I found her very funny. Her dress, her mannerisms, affectations, the nervous way she presented herself, rattling on and on. "I see...so let me guess. You've come to good old planet earth to sight see and maybe look at taking over Dad's operation—how's that for starters?" I said, doing my best to wake up.

Vesta looked very surprised. "How did you know? Yeah, that's what I've been thinking for a long time. We're tired of male-dominated tyrannical rule."

"To be sure, you'd rather see female-dominated tyrannical rule."

"You have a smart mouth, as your gangster films say. How would you know that?"

"Because you Titans are war-like, aggressive, and when your kind gets bred with a mad-dog lineage like your father's, all bets are off."

She looked at me strangely. Then she whispered something to the two other women and they left. "Leave the parking meter running?" I joked. But she did not take kindly to my humor.

313

"You are a typical human male, your self-importance and monumental ego is drooping—errr—dripping from your conversation. Self-assured, aren't you? You think you have your life in control, don't you?"

"No...I wouldn't say that, Vesta. But my patience with you *is* running a bit thin. So how can I get rid of you? You see, that doesn't quite explain what you are doing in my office before ten in the morning when sometimes I'm only just getting to bed! So, I would urge you to declare your business with me—or kindly leave and play your little gangster gun scare tactics else-where. I'm a busy man with plenty going on just now."

"Okay..." She thought for a minute. "Okay...so I'll spill it to you. You are about to be summoned to my father's not so kind presence."

"So, tell me something new. I knew that was going to happen a few days ago when I agreed to help teleport your sister to an undisclosed hiding place, along with certain information I had previously possessed."

"I know all about it, Mister. What I was really think-ing...was that...at least I was hoping...we could help each other... I am not as clear in the earth ways as you are. You can help me overthrow my father—and I can help you protect whatever it is you are protect-ing....keep Father off your back—and even throw in my sister Cassiopeia for good measure, since I know she's just dying to experience one of you primitive hormone-driven earth males."

I thought for a minute. Even if the babe was nuts, she had a point. If we could keep Cronus-Gor preoccu-pied for a few hundred years defending his *Oculus* from a powerful rival, I would sure breathe a lot easier. That would also take some pressure off Toggth and the *Fen de Fuqin*. I wasn't sure of the Cassiopeia part. I just wasn't ready for a doll between my sheets yet. I'd have to wait that one out.

"So, maybe you've got a point there, Vesta."

"I know I do. But I can't do it without—as much as I hate to admit it—without a strong male influence and a knowledgeable earthling to guide us. I have a complete order of my own already set up, modeled somewhat after my father's."

"But why would you think I'd help you continue this cruel and terrible trick you play upon the human race? Why would I support you in bringing misery through selective control to millions of lives?"

"Because I would change things. Just because my model is secretive and it's functional and multi-tiered like my Dad's, the *methods* would be different. I would introduce a very different content of procedure. *Education...not indoctrination*, that's how you change things for the better. Educate *everyone*. Law and order are maintained because of universal rules—the self-same equity for everyone—must be observed. In this way, your species will outgrow ethnic cleansing, martial aggression over regimes and real estate, political or religious causes being the reasons for bloodshed—the individual could then assert his or her rightful place in the scheme of things."

"You sure make a lot of sense, sister. I'd vote for you. But I think it's a tad unrealistic. You don't know my species the way I do. There are elements within the nature of humans that would scare off your grandmother. Humans stand on slippery ground. I'm not sure why, but I suspect they've been tampered with by 'aliens' other than yourselves. You see, there's a fault line that runs the length of the species, nothing in them is deep enough, real enough, sincere enough—a few can really love, but a whole mess of them can really hate and destroy, take what the earth offers free and put a price to it. One minute they'll kiss you and the other they'll slap your face and put you in front of a firing squad with no regrets. Governments will lie, bankers and stock brokers cheat and defraud you until they've broken the back of the spirit that kept any ideals alive." I stopped and realized my coffee percolator was running over. I turned off the burner and poured myself a cup of java. Vesta said nothing, but put her gun into her coat pocket.

"No, Vesta, honesty, truth, integrity, long-running loyalty without avarice or ulterior motive are still pipe dreams for humans. They set up puppets to give the illusion that someone out there cares, but in fact are too busy feathering their own nests to worry about the next guy. Everything's dependent on business and the corporation; the new world of the *consumer* is upon us. Creatures like your father prey on this weakness and not only validate it, but increase it, turning brother against brother, who may never even meet in this world...so those flaws cracking the human psyche in two can be exploited until dooms day!" I stopped and breathed in. "And then nothing will have mattered, will it? Because when you're dead the only calling card you left behind is pain, misery, memory and regret, that you met someone, maybe had a few kids and slaved the rest of your life to support what you yourself never had in the first place: fulfillment, creativity, peace of mind, true spiritual awareness that there really is something beyond this piece of shit we call man's world. And in the meantime, you gave nothing back to the earth.....she who fed you, sheltered you, clothed you, and loved you through the dark night of men. You give nothing back to the Great Mother because humans are sponges, leeches, suckers, vampires whose only directive is to *take, take take*— none of us have a clue as to what it's like to really give, balance out the world with good stewardship, honoring what we did not create but have the pleasure of enjoying." I coughed and lit up my first cigarette of the day. "A perfect blue sky, a breath-taking sunset, a windy hot night on top of a hill listening for the sirens of eternity, the moon traveling slowly across the sea's shimmering surface, an autumn walk when the leaves are so brilliant with reds, gold, yellows and oranges you have to believe you're walking down a lane in some unending fantasy."

Vesta stood there, her eyes wide with the wonderment of my words. "In all my thousands of years, I never heard someone speak like that, Denning—"

"—call me Cable—I hate formality..."

"Okay, Cable." Then her body became very animated as she came toward me. "You could be the *voice to end all voices,* the human who thinks like a god. Join my cause and we'll be ten times more powerful unseating my father. Someone from a higher place gives you those words you speak, Cable. I know that as fact. No one can speak like that unprompted by higher forces. You are special."

"I don't know about that. Look at your Dad. He's a god and he ain't doin' that great in the positive department. Don't you see, it's what my friend Toggth once

317

said...you've got to *earn* the best attributes that you can be. And frankly, I don't even trust my *own* human nature. It stinks, it's treacherous, deceitful, scheming—if given half a chance."

"I don't know if I believe all of that. If what you say is true, then there's a stalemate in creation. Maybe nothing will ever quite evolve beyond whatever is endemic in its source. And we don't know what the source really invested into the original seed."

"No, we don't," I said. I was impressed with the brilliant head on this alien woman. She seemed sincere and maybe she would succeed in deposing old pop on his Cronus-Gor throne. Who the hell knows? "So we leave it at that. All the rest is speculation, the quest to build a better mousetrap with your own take on life and how the world should be run. But you've got to remember, a philosophy is just that—it too, has its terms of limitations. Just like your sister's imminent return back to this dimension as humanized woman—plus the *Fen de Fuqin*."

"Yeah, I've heard of that. That's what the whole thing's about, isn't it? Some silly coded capsule or something? And funny, it was my mother who taught us many, many thousands of your years ago that everything we ever needed was right here—inside. Why didn't my father remember that?"

"Because greed and lust for power are a disease, Vesta. And I suspect old Daddy Boy's got it pretty bad."

She began to walk toward the door. Then she turned back to look at me. "Be careful, Cable. You can only fool Cronus-Gor as long as he can't read your mind. So say nothing about anything you might image, because he'll

318

trace the energy of the story right back to its origins. And then he'll be really angry."

"Thanks for the tip, Vesta," I said, waving my hand from behind my desk.

"How old are you, Cable?"

"Well, by all accounts of weights and measures, I'm going to be thirty-three next September."

"I think it's more like thirty-three million. You've been circulating in the universe a long time...a long time...I'm sure we'll be seeing each other soon. I'll visit you after you get back from Father's." Then she was gone. The day had just begun, yet I was exhausted. The weight of these days was heavy on me and for whatever reasons I was missing Adora really bad just about now. I was hearing her gentle voice with that charming Spanish accent and maybe the radio was on and I could hear Honey singing. Oh, yeah, nothing says it like music and good memories............

The next day was busy with phone calls and getting new cases lined up. I had called Zelda and told her everything was okay with me. I didn't happen to mention that the three female personages who visited me were of alien origin. That may have been pushing the envelope, even with Zelda. This was Wednesday. We had made a date for me to take her out to dinner Friday night.

CHAPTER 11

'PLAY ME ON A MISTY NIGHT'

That night I got restless and felt like getting lost in one of those dark and noisy cabarets, where a pretty thing in a sexy dress and a good voice held court with a microphone and a few great tunes. I checked the paper and was reminded that Misty Sheridan was still out in Santa Monica at the *La Monica Ballroom*. I had returned Elisa Moreno's little black coupe and so I took the trolley out to Santa Monica.

By this time, Misty Sheridan was a pretty big draw. Of course she didn't rival Honey in her heyday, but nonetheless, Misty was good and coming up in the world of entertainment. I wouldn't be surprised if at some point, she'd get a recording contract, and like Honey, show up on a radio show or two. I walked in and the place was noisy with the usual din of people pretending to like each other, lots of laughter, drinking, smoking and a few couples out on that huge dance floor, smooching as they twirled around to Misty's song. When I came in she was singing a nice version of Jerome Kern's *They Didn't Believe Me*—and believe me—the way Misty sang it, there were probably very few men in the room who didn't have a bulge in their pants! Misty had the gift of sincere and steamy, the kind of gal you wanted to take home and ravage without mussing her makeup! I know that sounds strange, but it was the feeling I had. Her large, welcoming full breasts were having a coming out party in that wonderful black-satin dress of hers, the sensual lips and flowing hair, those blue

320

eyes that looked at and through you before she even opened her mouth to utter her first notes. Yeah, that was Misty Sheridan. Even her voice was misty, a kind of breathiness that could melt you like a popsicle on a hot summer afternoon.

As soon as she saw me she brightened up with a smile and then directed one the verses of the song toward me: *"And when I tell them....and I'm certainly going to tell them...that you're the man whose girl someday I'll be...they'll never believe me...they'll never believe me...that from this great big world...you've chosen me...."* I applauded and whistled when she had finished. She took her bow and came down to greet me. "Hello, there. Long time no see. I always remember you, for some reason. The gumshoe detective who loves music—"

"—don't forget the pretty babes part. That goes along with it, you know, the kind who sizzles underneath and comes up as a real woman—but—well, good to see you Misty Sheridan," I said as I greeted her.

"Of course...I hope I fit the bill now and then." She extended her hand. It was warm. "Uh.....let me see...you know, I still have a card of yours right by my telephone—in my bedroom. *Cable*—that was it, wasn't it?

"Bingo! Thanks for remembering. I guess I should feel privileged—I mean, being in your bedroom and all."

"Yes...no *man* has ever shared my bedroom." She looked around. "Last time you were here, you were with a lovely little Mexican number." I winced. "Are you no longer an item—you seemed—well, you seemed very much in love with her."

"She...uh, she died...some time ago," I uttered, a stab of pain cutting through me.

Misty Sheridan registered shock on her face. "Oh, Cable! How could I have known? I'm so sorry..."

"Don't worry, kid, it's nobody's fault. It wasn't even her fault. She got a lethal dose of leukemia and it took her out pretty quick."

I didn't know why I could talk so freely to Misty about Adora's death. For whatever reasons, it just seemed okay. "If there's anything I can do...or be...for you..." She started falling into my eyes, as if the news of Adora's death opened up a channel for her to walk inside me. "I always thought we would be good friends, Cable. I think I even suggested that once. But you were with some other lady then. I think she was a singer?"

"Yeah, let's not talk about my past anymore, okay? Tell me, how have *you* been. I see you're still packin' 'em in here."

"Lucky, I guess. I think a lot of single men like you come in here to the bar and think I might be available—and they tell friends, and some of those friends turn out to be couples and before long, wow! I've got a nice following."

"All based upon your sex and talent..." I said, looking over that wonderful body and face of hers.

"Sort of, I guess. Say, it's Wednesday night and I get off early. How about a sandwich somewhere together afterward?"

"Sure, if you can stand my rough edges and private dick personality."

"I kinda like your rough edges, mister...and as for the dick part, unfortunately, I have to pass on that. So, it looks like friendship to me..."

"Will you sing a song for me before you call it quits for the night?"

"Sure, if I know it. Which one?"

"I need something happy just about now—and a little make-believe. How about a nice version of *Wrap Your Troubles in Dreams*? I've had a lot of those, lately—troubles, I mean."

"Absolutely, Cable—good choice, one of my favorites."

When Misty began the song, I could feel a new resurgence of life in me. Her energy was positive, unique and warm, as if it poured all over me like a bucket of melted sunshine. Even her feminine sensuality reached me in a new way, as if it were saying, "Wake up, wake up, you sleepy head..." A big burst of applause followed her song and I was proud to know this young lady who would figure in my life in ways I couldn't yet know.

Misty's friendship was ideal for me at this juncture of my life. We walked to a little bar on Santa Monica Boulevard called *Sam's* because Misty loved the pastrami sandwiches Sam served late at night. We sat in a semi-lighted booth and she looked so pretty there with her fresh complexion, light-blue shimmering earrings and that low-cut black gown that bulged out her cleavage in a most appealing way.

After some idle conversation, I dared to ask her a personal question. "I've never met your lover, have I?"

"You mean my partner?"

"Yeah, I guess I mean that—I don't know, I get them mixed up. After all, they are sort of one and the same, aren't they?

"Well, in our case, perhaps a bit different. Her name is *Edie Clason*. She was my very first—and only—singing tutor. I was seventeen and she was thirty-seven. I can't believe it, but now I'm twenty-eight and she's forty-eight. She's beautiful inside, like starbursts of love, energy, music. She was born in France and became a cabaret chanteuse when *she* was seventeen. She was an older woman's protégé like me. But those days when economic bad times happened—even worse than we're having here now—Edie turned to alcohol, cocaine and abusive men. She became this hard-looking woman, wrinkled with a low growl of a voice—but always full of genuine emotion that—that would make you cry." Misty took her napkin and dabbed her eyes. "I had experienced a very violent sexual assault by a step-father when I was thirteen. From that day on I swore off men, that not another man would ever touch me again."

She paused while the smiling Sam placed our pastrami sandwiches in front of us. Then Misty looked into my eyes. "Are you okay with this—I mean, the gory details and all? I don't even know why I'm telling this to you, I hardly—"

"—it's okay, Misty. I'm a good listener—and remember, I'm also a private investigator and hear that kinda shit all the time—and you can trust me," I said, putting my hand on hers across the table. "I think we're going to be friends, which I admit is rare for man and woman—especially as young as we are—anyway, go on."

"There isn't much more, really. Since Edie and I had similar experiences with the opposite sex, we talked it over and she told me she had found far superior sexual satisfaction with women. So we tried it, I liked it—and

324

we committed to each other. And here we are," she concluded, taking a deep breath and letting it out before taking up her sandwich.

"And obviously Edie Clason is an excellent singing coach, because she did such a fine job on you. I even like your sensual interpretations."

"Thank you. Yes, the best. She understands nuance and color in the tone. She says your heart can be in your—your, uh, between your legs sometimes as well as in your chest and head. What are we communicating when we sing? Every song can't be sexual-romantic. But most of the stuff I do is because that's what sells to all the horny, anxious men in the audience fantasizing about me singing in bed to them. And it makes money for the club."

I laughed. "Yeah, you got that right, sister! I was watching them tonight. I'm sure there were a lotta bulging trousers. Lust comes in a lot of different colors, doesn't it?"

"And what about you? Were you out there lusting for me tonight?"

"You bet. Yep, the old Cable Denning was thinking all the things every other man was thinking and I still kept my pants on."

She tittered slightly. "Is there a *new* Cable Denning that makes him think differently?"

"Let's just say a *healing* Cable Denning. I'm not sure how I'm going to feel about my sexual self down the line. I've heard it can be a long journey. I've also heard that sometimes it ends up on the rocks early because the psyche has suffered such trauma that it doesn't want to go there again. Sort of like your experiences that shunted you from male to female."

"Somehow I can't feature you as less than sexual with women, Cable. It's in your voice, the way you touch, the way you carry yourself and your self-assured manner."

"All that, eh? Thanks, Misty—even if only half of it is true, I consider myself a lucky man. So what else do two intelligent people talk about beside sex in 1933? Politics?

"Ugh!"

"Religion?"

"Give me a break."

"Travel?"

"Maybe a little warmer..."

"Philosophy, metaphysics?"

"Could be closer..."

"Reading poetry to each other?"

"Only on a cold night cuddled up by the fire."

"Hmmm...what about...what about *music!*"

"Bingo!" she laughed.

We were having a good time and I could feel Misty warming up to me. "Okay, now...what category of music?"

"Well, my earliest exposure was Uncle Charles. Through him I heard Beethoven, Mozart, Tchaikovsky, Brahms, Bach—you know, the big guys with the big sounds. I love classical music to this day."

"How'd you get interested in Tin Pan Alley music?"

"There was a black lady who came and cleaned our house twice a month. Gracie Munson Applebee was her name and she was in love with jazz and blues of the teens. She'd be in the kitchen wailing the blues or a spiritual of some sort and I loved her sound. I must have been eight, or maybe ten, when I fell in love with all those oldies. Then one day I was walking by a record shop and I heard Irving Berlin's *Always* and I knew I would sing the rest of my life until I couldn't anymore."

I started singing in my low, irregular baritone. *"I'll be loving you always, with a love that's true, always...when the things you plan, need a helping hand, I will understand, always..."*

"You've got a good voice in there, Cable." She seemed enchanted. "Do you know any more of the song? Nobody ever sings to *me*."

I continued as best I could. *"Days may not be fair always...that's when I'll be there...always...not for just an hour, not for just a day, not for just a year...but always..."*

Misty Sheridan's eyes were misting. I could tell I had reached a place deep inside that was new to her. Her intense blue eyes softened. "If I was ever going to—to love—or care for—for, uh, a man, I think it would be someone like you, Cable."

I looked at her as she reached her hand for mine in that semi-dark little booth in *Sam's* joint. It was one of the moments you took a snapshot of, one that would live with you maybe the rest of your life. "Ehhh...you're just sentimental, like me, a sucker for a good song," I said, trying to get my ship back upright because it was starting to capsize with me in it. "And that's quite a story you told me, babe. I kind of pegged you for the real thing. But, now that we're on the precipice...one other category we kind of skipped over..."

327

"And what's that?" she chortled, taking a sip from her soda.

"Love...even some guys have the ability to talk about that."

"Who knows what that is? We sort of talked about romantic love—which is sex hopefully attached to a little deep caring. What else is there? Yes, you can love a relative, a friend, maybe even someone from a distance. But I'm still not sure what love is."

"Well, let me see here..." I said, conjuring up a crystal ball on the table. "The Great Dennini sees three possibilities...first there's *falling in love*, then there's *being in love*, and last but not least, *simply loving someone*. What rings a bell with you, my little daisy?"

She chuckled. "I don't know. I guess you and I could simply love each other someday. I don't think it's instant. But *falling* in love is scary, I feel. You can't control it and it sneaks up on you. I've seen it when it crashes and burns. It hurts like hell. *Being* in love is probably the most wonderful. Then there's this perpetual state of being happy together because you wake up with that person beside you and you know you're still in love with him—or her."

"Is that how you feel about Edie?"

She suddenly drew serious. "Relationships change through the years. Ten years ago the erotic thrill of Edie teaching me new things was exciting. I loved it and she loved teaching me." Then she stopped. A sadness came upon her face. "Now...? Now I don't know...I don't think I've ever fallen in love, Cable—or really been in love with someone. I had a short affair with some gal some years back. But when I saw how much it hurt Edie, I—I ended it."

"Hell, let's be honest here. You're in love with your music like I'm in love with being a private eye—now ain't that right?"

She smiled. "Yeah...I guess that's really it. Music...singing...I've always been in love with singing. And the great songs that very professional men and women wrote."

"Where do you live?" I asked as I glanced at my watch. It was getting on to 1:00 a.m.

"Near 38th and Crenshaw. Wanna ride me home?"

"Sure, why not?"

We hopped aboard the streetcar and jabbered away until we got off at 38th Street. I walked her to a decent apartment complex. "Come in for a quick nightcap? I've got real alcohol—not the bathtub crap."

"If you've got some English gin, I'm your customer."

Misty Sheridan lived in a neat and modest apartment. She poured me a gin, then she boiled some water and had a hot whiskey with honey in a heated snifter. "Good for the voice," she said as we toasted. "Here's to friends, Cable."

After about three or four of our drinks of choice, we were feeling no pain and telling all kinds of wonderful stories about our lives to each other. I trusted her and she trusted me. When I first came upon the extraterrestrial possibility, she said she believed we were not alone in the universe, but had never seriously entertained the thought of meeting an alien. When I explained they can look just like us, she got a shiver. "You mean they can be that devious? So how do you know who's who?"

"They usually volunteer that info so you'll know up front, once they come to trust you, you know."

She sat opposite me on a sofa. "Trust...that's it, isn't it, Cable? We've got to trust each other. If not, all there'll be left on this planet is debris and a few fish. Maybe not even the fish."

"Yeah, you're right, Misty Sheridan," I said, feeling in my cups a bit more with each drink. "I'll tell you what...someday...someday I'll introduce you to an alien—would you like that?"

"Yes! I'd love it." She crossed the room and came to sit next to me on the love seat I was sitting on. "Now don't get the wrong idea, Cable, but I'm going to kiss you."

"What for—to shut me up?"

"Oh, no, no. To tell you I'm glad you're here and that you're becoming my friend." She slugged down the rest of her honeyed whiskey and leaned toward me. She kissed me gently on my forehead. "Now...that's for being my fan at the club." Then she kissed my left cheek. "That's for treating me at *Sam's*." She went around to my other cheek. "That's for being such a wonderful conversationalist." Then she brought her warm, full lips onto mine and stayed there, tenderly, for the longest time. It was as if she were a beautiful vampire, sucking out whatever essence she derived from kissing me. It also felt damn good. I think that kiss surprised her, too. "And that...that's...for...being a gentleman...."

"Ahem! My—my pleasure," I said, recovering from the warm, loving kiss Misty Sheridan had just planted on me.

She felt her lips. "I think my lips are a little numb from the alcohol. I don't drink much." Then she looked at me with that face which launched a thousand songs into the land of romance and sensuality. "I've never—never kissed a man...like that before, Cable..."

"So why now?" I asked, genuinely curious.

"I—I don't know, maybe a lot of things. Maybe because you're brand new in my life. I'm excited that you're here, or it's the alcohol—or maybe I just like you. May I do it again?"

I was rather bowled over. I didn't expect the dame to pull this one out of her hat—at least not on our first outing together. "Why not? I can tell you now, *my* lips gave your kiss a definite affirmative—but I warn you, it might start reaching places...uh, uncomfortable for you."

She giggled. "I'm like a tease, aren't I? Do you mind?

"Not if the going price is right..."

"I love the way you talk, Cable. Please...just sit there...still, with your eyes closed, okay?"

I did so and Misty's lips ever so slowly clasped onto mine again, only this time she increased the pressure until we could both feel sparks fly between us and I knew in that instant—maybe not today or tomorrow—but one day Misty Sheridan would kiss me like that and take her clothes off and take my hand and lead me into her bedroom.

Just as slowly she pulled her lips back, but they kind of stuck together and it was hard for both of us to release from that kiss, as if lips had minds of their own. "Oh...!" she exclaimed as she finally pulled free. "Cable...I don't know about you...who *are* you? Are you one of those aliens you were talking about? I feel dizzy."

I laughed. "Yeah, babe, I'm from Planet X, meaning 'X' marks the spot where you just kissed me. Uh...that, by the way, felt great."

"Yes...for me, too. I didn't expect this tonight, Cable. You caught me by surprise. I'm usually cold and aloof toward men. And you would never have gotten into my apartment in the first place."

"Want me to go now?" I asked. She was kneeling on the rug beside me. She grabbed both of my knees with her hands and clutched them.

"No...but I think you'd better. I'm afraid...I don't know—I sound crazy—but if you stayed, I might do something I'd regret tomorrow."

I got up from the love seat and pulled Misty up until we faced each other. "We gotta be clear, Misty. It's either a platonic friendship—or—or the other thing, the thing that 'lifts you high to heaven and lets you fall to hell' all in the same breath, the thing that most humans succumb to because they're too weak to explore the next chapter in human experience....the one that says maybe, just maybe, a man and a woman can become good friends and not fuck their way to oblivion." I took her hand and shoved it into my crotch. "You tell me, Misty Sheridan, why would a woman desire a physical appendage that brings her ecstasy at the price of agony and heartbreak? Why would she risk her safety—even pregnancy—because her passions lead to instincts she can't help, or toss her alone on the rocks below when

332

it's all over because a guy can always move on—and often does. Yeah, look at me, doll, you're my love object of the moment, my prize singer for the night, the altar I go to when the world out there is too much to handle. So I go into the smoke and laughter to hear your music, your siren call of notes strung on longing and regret, calling my heart and my balls to your side, calling me like all the other poor blokes panting for you out there in the audience, making us juvenile chumps longing for the great elusive fuck—the one he'll only dream about for the rest of his life, because he finds out that woman is an *illusion*, that sooner or later a babe will come along and put a collar around his neck and make him a slave from eight to six to bring home enough bacon to support her and three demanding brats in the nest." I stood there looking at her, not sure why I was unloading all of this on poor Misty. "So what is it going to be, my beautiful Miss Sheridan? Keep me as a friend—set the tone now—or run the risk of falling in love and being lost to eternity, so one day someone might scrape you up off the Boulevard of Broken Dreams."

She was shaking and walked over to the other sofa and sat down. She couldn't look at me. "I think...it's too late...Cable...I think I fell in love with you over—over the second bite of my sandwich at *Sam's* tonight. Then I kissed you...and my whole world changed...suddenly I could feel the woman in me stir...in a brand new way I've never felt before..." Then she looked up at me, yeah, me, standing there like a pompous prince in the middle of the floor. "No, Cable...I don't want to go back, I want to go forward—with someone like you, strong and resilient to the world, yet loving and sensual. Maybe—

333

maybe it's time for me to experience life as a woman who was designed to love a man...what do you think? I'm a little drunk just now—and maybe acting stupid."

"I told you what I feel, Misty. Those are the odds. Most couples have a shelf life. Sooner or later they break up and the party's over. I can promise you nothing. I live on the edge of a risky blackness, one I could fall into at anytime. My career owns me...I didn't intend it to happen. But at any time a bullet, a poison slipped into a drink, a car running me over in the street—any of it---could end it for me at any minute. You'd want to live with that roulette wheel spinning around in your love life?"

"Yes...if it was you...because as you said, I didn't intend for this to happen...but it did...and it happened so quickly...I'm a different girl than I was just a few hours ago. Do you understand that? That's why I can't go back. There's nothing to go back to anymore."

"What about Edie Clason? You owe her something, don't you?"

"Owe her? I've given her ten years of my life—and my youth as well. I love her—for all the good reasons and the love she poured into me, for the years she protected me from men like my step-father, for her believing in me and allowing me to excel when her own singing career diminished. She was never jealous, always supportive."

"Well, that's worth a lot." I took a deep breath. I wanted to smoke really bad, but I didn't want to pollute the singer's immediate environment. "So...where are we now? Where do you want to go, Misty Sheridan, singer extraordinaire?"

She got up and came over to me, clasped her arms around my neck. "Wherever you take me, Cable. I've always been the one in control. But now I want you to allow me to be the soft one, the one who surrenders to giving that part of myself. Will you give me that chance?"

"Well, lady, I'll tell you what. I'm gonna take off now. I want you to sleep on it. Think about it...let it settle in, okay? And if tomorrow or the day after that you still feel the same, let's talk about it." I reached into my breast pocket and took out a card. "Call me."

"Will you kiss me one more time before you leave?"

"No, Misty—if I do, I'll stay...I'll grab you up in my arms and carry you off to your bedroom, toss you on the bed and take your clothes off like the same kind of animal who raped you when you were too young to defend yourself. Plus I don't think I'm ready yet......you understand."

"I guess so," she said, her face a little sad. "But please...just one more kiss...something to remember you by, so when I think it through tomorrow I can feel it below my belly button, too." She pulled my face toward hers and planted those luscious lips on mine. I could feel my manhood begin to surge. "Like that..." she whispered.

I left Misty Sheridan's feeling like that lonely sax had moved from the early morning breezes into my chest and started a new tune...one I hadn't heard before. But I also knew that sooner or later, despite whatever happened between me and Misty, that *sound* would come back to haunt me, like it always did, restless through the night, always there in moments when I was alone, counting out the hours that I might have left. We go through life taking for granted that it will always be there tomorrow. But surprise! It isn't always. Nothing is for always. Just like Misty Sheridan. She hadn't been there...down that trail of joy and tears with someone you love and lose. But one day she would.

Hands Across the Table

Late the next morning I was catching up on some bookwork when the phone rang. "Yeah, Cable Denning here..."

"Mr. Denning! I'm so glad I finally got hold of you! I've been trying for days—and Harry isn't getting any—any—well, I need your services—I've lost my husband—he's just gone! Gone, Mr. Denning!"

"Hold on there, lady—first of all who am I talking to? And second of all, get a grip on yourself. I'm not a talking post. Just the facts. Tell me the facts and I can respond, okay?

"Okay. I'm Florida Heston—your secretary or house cleaner or whatever, told me you were gone a few days. I really needed you more a few days ago, you see, because Harry's —Harry's—"

"—Harry's what, Mrs. Heston? Unless you're honest with me up front, I can't help you. So what's going on with Harry?"

"Can you come out to my house and meet with me? I'm afraid to go out...afraid they'll come for me."

"Who are you afraid of, Mrs. Heston? You're not making much sense. Do you need to check yourself into a hospital or something?"

"No! How much do you charge? I'll double it if you come to my home—I just can't leave the house!"

"I get twenty bucks a day plus expenses, like carfare, meals."

"I'll give you fifty dollars if you'll come out."

I could really use the bucks, I thought. "Where do you live, Mrs. Heston?"

"2000 Highland Avenue. Please...come...will you?"

"Yeah, okay. I'll drop what I'm doing and be there within an hour."

"Oh, thank you, Mr. Denning...thank you so much!"

We hung up and I grabbed my coat, hat and gun and figured the best way was to walk up Cahuenga. When it merged with Highland Avenue, I walked south a few blocks to the address. It was a nice neighborhood, fairly new homes built of brilliant white stucco and terracotta roofs. 2000 North Highland Avenue was a two-story affair in flamingo pink with the Spanish style roof and set back from the street. I walked up the path and rapped on the door. A short little woman with hazel eyes and a pageboy haircut answered. She was busty and carried herself a bit stiffly. "Mr. Denning? I can tell it's you—by the way you dress. Exactly like a private detective."

"Hello, Mrs. Heston." I took my hat off and she led me to a large front room. I noticed a strange odor permeating the room, as if someone hadn't emptied the garbage for a while. She went to her purse and handed me the fifty smackers she had promised. She invited me to sit down on a very comfortable light-grey sofa.

"Now...what can I do for you? You seemed rather unsettled on the telephone."

"Well, I don't know exactly where to start, now that you're here. You know how it is, sometimes we get desperate about things...and then we realize we don't have to be desperate anymore because things seem to work themselves out on their own."

"You mean your husband's come back?"

"Well, not exactly. But I know where he is."

"And?"

"Well, he's in the bedroom."

I was starting to put two and two together. "Is he okay?"

"I guess so, but one never knows about these things." She took a big gulp of a sherry she had in her hand. "You see, I killed Harry several days ago. He had embezzled all my money and invested it in the stock market—we lost everything. When I complained he threw it in my face that I was stupid and couldn't handle the money anyway—and the stock market would recover and we'd be even richer than before. But I didn't believe him."

"This is a matter for the police, Mrs. Heston, not a gumshoe."

She ignored me because I realized a screw had gone loose inside her head and she had to tell the story to get it out. "And to add fuel to the fire, Harry was seeing his petite—young—secretary, a cunning little bitch, who I found out had been in heat for my husband for months. So one night when Harry did come home early from the office, I confronted him. He denied everything. So I killed him."

338

"I see," I said, rubbing my chin. "May I ask what you killed Harry with, Mrs. Heston?

"He bought me a wonderful culinary knife set for Christmas. It contained a very sturdy meat cleaver, so while Harry was sitting up in bed reading, I chopped him—and chopped him—and chopped him until he fell over, gurgling blood out of his betraying big neck!"

"You do realize there are laws against killing your husband, even if you found him out in his little tête à tête and he turned out to be a lousy embezzling husband."

"No! There are no penalties for a justified wife! I know my rights. Harry was definitely in the wrong. He confiscated my inheritance and diddled his female employee. Of course I killed her, too."

I started! Now I knew the dame had really gone over the edge. It's strange, when an ordinarily sane woman snaps and she can kill in cold blood without remorse. Probably things like that accumulate inside like a festering canker that has to come out one day. And it does. This time it was expressed with the ultimate violence. I'd seen it a lot of times when I was a cop. Going to people's homes in the middle of the night to find one partner lying dead. More times than not it was about money and sex. This one was no exception. I tried to keep the conversation calm. "And where, if I may ask, is the dead young lady?"

"In the trunk of my car". She said rather matter-of-factly, "I chopped her up after a liaison with Harry. It was late at night and I had to drag her from a little house Harry had rented for her—with *my money*—and heave her into my trunk! You see the justification there, of course, Mr. Denning. Totally justified...I am completely guilt-free in this case...don't you agree?"

"Well, *I* might agree, Mrs. Heston. But I doubt if a judge and jury will. A double homicide is a pretty tough rap to beat—unless it was self-defense—and even that can get sticky."

"Will you defend me, Mr. Denning? Will you tell them the truth? We can't let scoundrels like Harry and Miss Fancy Ass live now, can we? Otherwise, there'll be too many of them, won't there? And then where would society be?"

"You've got a point there, I agree, Mrs. Heston. But you see, the laws vary from country to country. Like in Saudi Arabia, a man can kill his wife with impunity for going to the store without her head being covered. In Morocco, wives are sold to slavery if they don't work out so well. But in these so-called civilized countries, like the good ol' U.S., lawyers have to make their big bucks and spousal murder is kind of discouraged, if you get my drift."

"Such a pity, Mr. Denning. But surely a smart lawyer will defend me properly and I will be acquitted justly."

I got up from the spacious gray sofa. "I'd get rid of the body as soon as you can, Mrs. Heston. It'll smell up the nice home you've got here. Harry's already beginning to stink up the place"

She giggled. "Oh, Mr. Denning! Thank you for making me laugh! I think it's funny, too. Doing Harry in wasn't too hard because I had planned it for a long time. So doing it didn't make me fret a lot."

"I do have one question...why did you call a private detective and not the police right away?"

She thought for a minute. "Oh, well, you know...I didn't want to bring in a whole gang of people traipsing through my lovely home. After all, Harry says he'll get a new gardener next month and we'll take out the old hedge and put in a new one—Holly Berry, my very favorite. But Harry is treating me to that. We won't get the bill for at least a month. Then maybe he'll pay it without complaining. He's always complaining about spending too much money on the house." Then she flipped again and got angry. "But he doesn't care how much he spends on that whore secretary of his—oh—no, let's keep Florida in the dark, let's keep her guessing..." She ran to her kitchen sink and grabbed the ol' cleaver and came after me. "And you, too—you seemed so nice—but you're a wife killer, too, aren't you? You screw all kinds of women on the side and never let the little woman at home know about it." As she came screaming at me I drew my .38 and as soon as I had an opportunity, I dodged her and conked her on the head with the butt of my gun. She went down, sending the meat cleaver across the room.

I called the cops and waited until they came. Jimmy Swinson was the lieutenant in charge of the case. I knew Jimmy from earlier days when he was a Swedish punk drowning his girlfriend's newborn kittens in a huge pot of Mrs. Murphy's leek soup. When Jimmy looked at a dazed Florida Heston with a little lump on the back of her head, he threatened me with assault and battery. I told him to shove it, that I was doing his job for him and went back to the office. The day hadn't started off so well. But there was one silver lining to this Thursday. About 2:30 p.m. the phone rang and I picked it up, hoping it wasn't another Florida Heston or some other nutty fruitcake wanting to hire me.

"Yeah, Cable Denning here."

"Well, you don't have to shout. I'm right there...in your heart," a lovely, sexy voice intoned into my ear.

It was Misty. In light of a day that had already gone bad, her voice was like the fresh air right off the seashore. "Hey, babe...and how are you this fine afternoon? Did you sleep in? You were a little snockered last night, you know."

"Yes, Cable....I slept in and dreamed about the most special man I've ever met. I was fantasizing about what it would feel like if I woke up and found myself wrapped around him."

"Whoa! Wait a minute, Nellie! This isn't a done deal yet....I didn't stay because I'm giving *both of us* an escape clause in this contract."

"I don't know about you, but I have no desire to run, you handsome Private Eye. My only desire is—is...for a wonderful guy who my heart's been introducing to my womanhood."

Misty's words poured into me like hot chicken soup when you're recovering from a bad case of the flu. "Sounds like a pretty lucky guy to me, doll. It all happened so damned fast last night. Have you had it happen like that before?" I asked, not being able to recollect too many magnetic relationship beginnings in my life outside of Honey and Adora. They were like that. And look at them, they're gone....out, kaput, disappeared from my life, dead. I took a deep breath of dread, thinking what if my death-jinx was now going to fall on Misty? What if my presence in a beautiful dish's life meant her imminent death?

"No, remember me? I'm the *Sleeping Beauty* who just now woke up to her Prince. I've been asleep, Cable...all this time, thinking one man was all men. What a fool I've been. How much time I've wasted."

"Well, look at the good side. It could've been worse. You could have gone through a dozen guys by now, all with the wrong brand on their boxers."

She giggled at the other end of the line. "God, you're funny, too, Cable. How do you manage a sense of humor in a grim and thankless job? I can't imagine dealing with some of the people you must see."

"It's like your singing—you have to love it and realize at the end of every rainbow there may not be a pot of gold, but there'll be *truth*....and I'm kind of a truth guy, Misty."

"I like that—truth...it was the truth I was speaking last night, wasn't it?"

"Maybe. Or was it part fascination with the evening and part eighty-proof honeyed whiskey?"

"No, it was *me*, Cable. You're really something, you know. Here I'm feeling like a woman for the first time in my life and you're on the other end of the phone still trying to find reasons why I shouldn't fall in love with you. Well, Mister, as I told you last night...it's too late for that. You shouldn't have sung to me across the table. That, plus my second bite into the pastrami sandwich, was all it took."

I laughed. "Damn, but I think you're a special lady, Misty Sheridan. That last kiss is still hanging around on my lips, you know. I have to admit it was hard not saying to hell with it all, taking you up into my arms and carrying you off to your bedroom."

"I wish you had. We only delayed what's going to happen anyway, you know."

"You sure of that?"

"Yes. All of me says 'yes,' Cable. There's a song I want to sing for you some night at the club. It's called *That's My Desire*. And right now, Mr. Detective man, you're my desire. When can I see you again?"

"You're a true romantic, kid. I like that. Your softness contrasts my everyday life fraught with human debris." I thought about when I could commit to seeing her again. I knew I'd be stepping into a new chapter of my life with this babe. "I—I, uh, have a few things to do this week. Maybe Sunday? We could have a late lunch or something. What's your schedule look like?"

"Oh, I don't know...by then it may be too late. Who knows, I may have forgotten the man who aroused me last night. If you come in Saturday night late, I'll sing that song for you...entice, entice, entice..." she kidded.

I chuckled. "Okay, I'll do my best. Oh, one other thing. I need to take it slow, Princess. I don't know how soon I can—can, uh, *swell to the occasion*, if you know what I mean. But once I'm there—"

"—you leave that up to me, big boy," she said in her most seductive voice. "But I've waited at least ten years for you, Cable. I guess I can wait a little longer. See you Saturday...?"

"Yeah, babe—so long!" We hung up and I was thinking how it felt to have the world lifted off me when I talked to Misty Sheridan. Feeling that young woman's legs wrapped around me would feel like knocking out Dempsey in the first round in a world title bout!

The rest of the day was like a lack-luster football game with amateurs playing on a soggy field. I slogged through bookwork and conversations on the telephone like a bookie who'd lost interest in horses. And talking about horses, Misty Sheridan had made me feel like a wild stallion hot for some young filly who came up over the hills of my life and reared up, tossing her beautiful head so I could see her. And I did.

By day's end I was tired and sat back in my chair with a Lucky Strike and a large shot of gin in my usual unwashed glass. Sometimes you wonder how much of life is pretending because you *want* it to be better than it is, or how much gold dust falls out of the heavens and covers you long enough to experience something really good and lasting, like maybe love or a beautiful sunset you can't forget, or some babe singing a song that rips your heart out but replaces it with a better one. Maybe I stood at that threshold right now, feeling the warm naked breasts of Misty Sheridan against my skin, her wet, pulsing womanhood thrust against my crotch, those incredible lips clinging to my own like an abalone on a rock at high tide. I could see her wondrous blue eyes looking into mine, my nostrils buried in her hair, the smell of her neck as my teeth nibbled it, sending rivers of shivering nerves up and down her beautiful body. Yeah, that's what I do with her in my fantasies already, spinning out all that pent up passion that I'd saved for Adora and thought I could never release again. But now I could, thanks to this dish— a singer who came into my life out of nowhere, to rescue a thirty-two year old ex-cop who had begun to fall through the grating of a street gutter. And I would give back to her what she had denied her natural woman all these years, because of a vulgar man's degenerate lust.

I was almost dozing in the twilight of early evening when I happened to see two figures approach my office door through the opaque glass. I opened my center drawer and took out my .38. My intuition was working overtime and adrenaline began pumping through my body. I hadn't turned on any lights yet, so whoever it was wouldn't even be able to see if I was in. I heard the sound of the door lock being picked. Then two goons entered slowly, creeping around like the slime they were. They looked Asian to me. "Can I help you, boys?" I spoke up, surprising the two idiots who now whipped around to face me. We were at a standoff, both of us with guns drawn at each other. "I can probably kill both of you before you get me," I said, still a little groggy from the gin.

They seemed Chinese, although who in the hell knows with Asians? They all looked alike to me. One spoke English. "We have orders not to shoot. We take you. Now. If you please."

"Well now, since you're asking so nicely, I guess I'll oblige." I knew this was the summons from Cronus-Gor I'd been expecting and Hestia/Vesta had told me was coming. I put my gun down on the desk, went over to the coat rack and got my London Fog and hat—put them on—picked my gun back up and joined the two smallish men awaiting me. "By the way, if you damaged my office door lock when you gained entrance, I think

I'll kill you, just for the hell of it," I joked. But Orientals don't seem to have much of a sense of humor, so instead they put a couple of gun barrels into my ribs and moved me out of my office, down the stairs and into a waiting car.

The local headquarters for the *Oculus Pyramis Mandatum* was a pretty classy affair. Of course I didn't know where it was located because the mugs who'd kidnapped my person, had blindfolded me once they shoved me into the automobile. Large rooms with high, domed ceilings painted with angels and cherubs, gods and goddesses were framed with excellent hand-carved woodwork. I was led to a rather large banquet room and made to sit at a very long table with maybe twelve chairs. Only one item was on the table. A very fine Sheffield silver server, the kind with the tray and huge domed lid and handle. It sat in the center of the table. The lighting was subdued with one particular light focusing on the domed platter. Then I heard the unmistakable voice of Cronus-Gor.

"So we meet again, Denning..." the low rumble of a voice spoke.

"No, you got it wrong, Gor—*you* meet *yourself* again—I don't recognize a being I can't see or speak to one-to-one."

"You...you...are an impertinent, human!" There was a sound like a clap of thunder. "I am patient with you only long enough to get what I want. First you all but seduce my wife—whose familiar and appealing body I regrettably had to destroy...then you all but seduced my daughter, who is unaccountably enamored with you. Then you employ the services of those weak, inept aliens, fruitlessly attempting to defeat me—by sending my Cassiopeia off to some dimension I cannot trace, abetted by Saturnalia as a silly, bouncing orb of energy consciousness."

"Well, you brought it all on yourself, you piece of cosmic crap! Creatures like you make the big mistake of assuming superiority—god or no god—not knowing this is a big universe and all who are born in it have equal right to its intelligence. So guess what? You're *not* smarter than other beings. You treated Saturnalia like a tramp after you stole her, took her virginity and made her bear you eight kids—seven of whom you devoured because you couldn't take the competition. Then your clever wife tricked you with Cassiopeia to disgorge your consumed children, bringing forth Zeus, your own son, to unseat you for the domination of the earth. You then force Saturnalia to *humanize* your daughter for fear you will kill her too—again, Gor, you can't stand to be challenged because you might lose the game after all, you invisible coward!"

Again, a roll of thunder filled the room. "Silence! You impudent human! I have a gift for you, a reminder that I am playing this game you talk about *for keeps*, as you humans say. So thus, I give to you in remembrance of me. Lift the domed lid, Denning, see the puny weakness you humans are bound to, your sentimental nothingness."

I looked at the silver server in the middle of the table. I got up, leaned over and slowly opened the lid. The horror that greeted me made me sick to my stomach. There on the serving tray were two feminine hands, cut off just above the wrists. "What the...? What unspeakable cruelty have you done here, you worthless piece of shit!"

"She played the piano and sang to you, didn't she?" Gor continued. "Look...at the delicate hands—she loved you, Denning—the hands even loved you and she gave up her life—if not willingly, then...painfully. She didn't run away from you, she would have come with you to Los Angeles. But we captured her and read her mind, and I thought...what better gift could I give you, than the hands that played for you and almost fondled you with passion in the dark of night?"

I replaced the lid and sat down hard on my seat. When cruelty without a trace of conscience takes over the world, then I no longer want to be in it. Jane had more right to life than that son-of-a-bitch who hid himself from me out of cowardice, afraid to be seen so he wouldn't have to face another being one-to-one. "How do monstrous things like you get born, Gor? What terrible perverted element is there in the cosmos that gives birth to dark, irredeemable creatures like you?"

"Ah, this is a world of dualities, Denning...you cannot have light without darkness. You cannot have goodness without evil—or regard for life or conscience, as you say...without the lack thereof. You little striving mortals whose moral codes bind you to your own prison, have no understanding that they are the very reasons I *can* rule over you." Then there was a pause. "Now...to the subject at hand, so to speak. Last time we encountered one another, my errant wife assisted you in escaping from me. Not this time. I will now extract the knowledge of the *Fen de Fuqin* from your otherwise stupid brain and then shrink you down into a piece of dry dust on my floor."

"Too late again, asshole. I don't have that memory in my consciousness. It's been removed, along with your daughter. Search as you will, you won't find her, because we're discovering your secret—aren't we?—you are *not* all-powerful, Gor!" I was struggling not to picture Cassiopeia or the *Cave of the Seven Truths* because I knew he could read my mind if he chose. Instead I concentrated on the picture of his ailing Saturnalia, sitting in a shadowed alley with boils all over her face, dying from *his* hand.

Another clap of thunder filled the room. "Ahyrrrrr...!" Gor shouted in frustration. "Suck his head dry!" he commanded. Instantly two men in white coats came in with a little machine with rubber sucker pads on each end of a couple of tubes. They put the pads to my temples and turned the little machine on. I heard a high frequency that hurt my head. "Probe first...let me see it on the mind-screen!" Gor demanded.

The two men then told the invisible creature they could not find the sought after knowledge in my memory banks. "Go, idiots!" Gor exclaimed. I could tell the god-Gor was really pissed. "Now! You...Denning!...I am beyond patience with you, yet I am forced to concede...for the moment. Cassiopeia shall be forced to return—whatever spell has been cast on her—she'll come back along with your knowledge of the *Fen de Fuqin*. Then I shall extract it from her humanized brain cells and put an end to *you*—once and for all!"

"Maybe...maybe not, you pretentious egomaniac! You know, Gor, I'm not afraid to die, but I always wonder how in all the universes there can be beings like you. Why? Because I keep looking for one scrap of something good or decent in you that might tell me you have a heart. How can one being fill himself with only avarice, greed, lust for power and control—and not have one redeeming quality? *Why did you choose to vibrate so low*—when you so-called immortals could do so much *good* in the world—any world*?*"

There was a silence. Then the voice was slow and deliberate. "Go now, Denning. I will be watching every move you make—and hoping you make a false one..."

"For all the good it'll do you. It's payback time, Gor. Your days as supreme ruler of the earth and those of all your minions are gonna be over soon. You'll have your hands full as your past comes back to haunt you... you worthless scum!"

The thunder clapped again and I heard the god Cronus-Gor laugh as I never heard him laugh before. "Ha! Ha! Ha! Ha! No matter if I am detained with minor distractions...I will destroy Cassiopeia once I extract the knowing of the Golden Capsule from her. Then I *shall* be all-powerful with all the knowledge of Creation at my disposal. You might know, also, Denning, I am grooming a *new evil* to rule over the world in my stead, just in case. He will rise from Europe and I will empower him with every darkness in my divine cells. No man shall oppose him and he shall carry the seed of my conquering nature within him. *Hister, the God of Evil* shall rain fire and destruction upon the earth until he has cleansed you and your weakened kind away. Ha! Go now, leave me!" he roared.

In came the two Asian goons and whisked me back to my office, leaving me in peace once again. Every encounter with Cronus-Gor took a hell of a lot outta me. It was almost as if I lost years from experiencing his presence, even if I couldn't see him. It was like I found myself fighting *the intention of his energy*. And I was thinking of poor Jane Slaughter. Were some people slated for an early death? Or was it a matter of bad timing? These were mysteries that still baffled me on the playing field of human existence. If it wasn't a moral universe, and no inner governing mechanism within the individual to be positive existed—you know, the one where you do good and decent acts, and simply heed *The Golden Rule*— what was it that caused order, then, in the cosmos?

It was getting on to dawn. I shed my clothes, took a shower and fell onto my bed, exhausted. The world would have to wait.

CHAPTER 12

ANOMALIES CAN BE LONELY

Zelda the Warrior

Life is often a strange harmony of contrasts. Things you think would never fit into your life suddenly do. Somewhere in the Christian Bible it talks about *the least shall become the most, or the meek shall inherit the earth*...and like that. Zelda Blodgett was one of those anomalies. As Honey's housemate, she seemed the perennial bookworm, the studious aspiring botanist, following in her father's footsteps. She had had a brief romance with only one young man I knew of, otherwise Zelda's life was bereft of male companionship. I knew she looked to me as a kind of friend, maybe-could-be-lover type. Women can have crushes for years. I fear such was Zelda's story.

But one has to hand it to her. She went from a slightly frumpy young thing with thick glasses to a far more streamlined version. Now, an attractive young woman who had slimmed down, lost the glasses except for reading and looked great in a low-cut dress. She was always a bit busty, I guessed, but in losing weight, her bosom was definitely one of her standout features. I liked Zelda. She was honest—and real, the kind of woman who would be a girl for a long time without the assumptions of sexual experience and how it transforms the female nature into a competitive, seductive creature. Not that it's all bad, mind you—but on Zelda, seduction would at best be an awkward attempt at becoming a sexually active woman. Somehow I couldn't feature that as being high on her list of priorities.

We met up at seven o'clock Friday night. She lived a couple of miles from my office and I had chosen *The Wishing Well*, a respectable dinner house with a nice dance floor. But I had failed to make reservations in time and when we got there, the line was interminable. On a lark, and perhaps not the best decision I ever made, I suggested going out to Santa Monica to the *La Monica*. Could be it would be less crowded, but mainly my manhood was aching for Misty and I had this thing inside that kept itching to see and hear her again. Her Wednesday night kisses were still playing chills up and down my spine when I thought of her. Funny, I thought, most dames don't even come close to doing that for me, including beauties like Cassiopeia.

Zelda didn't mind. She was just happy to be with me. We made our way out to the *Ballroom* about 8:30 p.m. The plan was for Misty not to notice me in the crowds. By a stroke of good luck, I slipped the waiter a fiver and he got us a secluded booth quite a distance from the bandstand—and the bar.

It was nearly nine when we finally got seated. It was only then that I realized how good Zelda looked. She was wearing a low-cut black-satin dress, tight around the middle. It came up to just below her knees and she wore shiny black heels with a fine set of white pearls around her neck. Her face was a good face, ruddy cheeks, thick lips, a very sexy chin and very graceful looking hands. Suddenly, Jane Slaughter's hands came to mind and a chill came over me.

"Gees, Cable, this is exciting. Thanks for bringing me here. I like it." She looked around. The band was playing a lively version of *Keeping Out of Mischief Now* and I was beginning to think I had just stepped into a big pile of it.

"Yeah, Zelda, I'm glad you like it. It's a jumpin' place, isn't it?"

She started tapping her fingers on the table to the music. "I love music. I always wished I could sing well. When I was little, my mother would let me stay in the bathtub as long as I wanted on Saturday nights. I liked singing in the bathroom because my voice reverberated in there. I thought I actually sounded pretty good. But now I'm too shy to even attempt it."

"Singing's good for you, kid. It cleanses the psyche, you know."

She looked at me and smiled. "You say the darndest things, Cable. But I get what you're saying. I always felt better when I sang."

Then I saw Misty emerge from behind the bandstand and my heart rate went up. She was wearing a light-blue sequined dress and I thought if it was cut any lower she could get arrested. What a figure the babe had! She joined the band and took a chorus of *Keeping Out of Mischief Now,* that sounded wonderful. She had a pertness about her, and add to that, her naturally sexy, sensual nature and you had a recipe for a hell of dish who just happens to entertain people with her voice, emotions and body. Yeah, she was a deadly combination for any unsuspecting chump in the audience who might fantasize about Misty when she sings.

As soon as she finished the lively number, I had this funny feeling she could tell I was in the room. Don't ask me how. Then I saw her eyes searching around in the crowd. She left the bandstand, drifted up to the bar, and got a drink. Some obnoxious character was hitting on her and I could tell she was irritated as hell but trying to be polite. The guy had a buddy with him. They both had been drinking and the buddy tried to pull his friend away from Misty. But the jerk pushed the other guy, which got him mad. Instinctually, I told Zelda I'd be right back and made my way through the noisy throng until I got to the bar. "Hey, buddy, the lady's the entertainment here, not some dame you can maul. I hate pushy guys on the make." Misty was shocked to see me, but also delighted. I could feel it. I was her knight in shining armor come to rescue the damsel in distress.

He turned to look at me, that half-drunk glaze in his eyes. "Who the fuck are you? Shove off, buddy or I'll floor you." Then he turned back to bother Misty. "Some dumb turd trying to horn in on us."

Now I was mad. "I don't think you heard me, Mister. If you don't stop bothering Miss Sheridan here, I'll yank you outside and teach you a lesson the hard way."

He was bigger than I was and looked to be in pretty good shape. But so was I. "So...you don't wanna buzz off, eh, buddy?" He took a swing at me. I didn't want to start a brawl on Misty's watch, so I grabbed the man's arm and twisted it around behind him."

"Owww! That hurts—okay, okay! I'll leave the lady alone!" Then he turned to Misty again. "I just want you to know...you're the prettiest little pussy they've ever had in this joint—and you can actually sing. I used to play the trombone, so I know—"

"—move, buster, or you'll be having your teeth for breakfast."

Misty had stayed out of it until now. "I think he'd do it, too, Mister. He's been in here before. He's a professional boxer—and you wouldn't want to be at the other end of his punch," she said with her tongue-in-cheek.

Wisely, the bandleader had his boys start up a lively song and the incident got buried somewhere between the din of the room and the music. "You think I should leave, huh? Only if you—hic—say so, Miss Sheridan. You can call me Pip. My real name's Peter, but my friends call me 'Pip' because I'm a good guy—a real pip! Ha! ha!"

"Yes, if you don't mind. Come back another time when you're sober—and bring your nice friend."

"You're also built like a brick shithouse, lady," he continued. That was enough for me. I winked at his friend and together we escorted "Pip" out of the club.

I came back and found Misty waiting for me at the bar. "Cable! You're not due until tomorrow night! What happened? Why are you here tonight?"

I took her arm gently and put my lips close to her ear. "The damned truth is I was aching to see you again—I know it's stupid—"

"—oh, Cable...I was aching for you since last night. I'm so glad you're here. I do have to get back and sing my next song in a minute."

"I'm—I'm also not alone. There's a young lady with me—we're over there—in the rear booth by the potted palm."

Her eyebrows lifted. "Young lady? Is this new or old, someone in your collection or someone you're considering?"

"No, babe, nothing like that. Zelda Blodgett was Honey Combes' roommate before she—she—well, anyway, it's a long story, but come over later and I'll introduce you to Zelda."

"Zelda? You bet I will. I'm sure there's an explanation why the two of you happened to show up here."

"To be sure, babe, there is. But....uh, later, okay?"

She left me and walked back to the bandstand and I went back to join Zelda. "Gees, Cable, you sure helped that lady out. You're gutsy and strong. Did you know her?"

"Well, sort of." I sat back down next to my little plant lady. "I've—I've heard her sing before in other clubs. We're kind of getting to know each other, if you know what I mean."

Zelda frowned. "Oh, yes, I *do* know what you mean. How come it's always some other woman you get attracted to? Me? Ha! I don't even count, do I? Or at least not in that department of your life." She folded her arms. "Humph! Men! They're all alike."

I chuckled to myself. "You're right about that, Zelda. I didn't bring you here to see Misty though, but to enjoy the evening with *you*."

"Yeah...I'm grateful for that. Do you have any of that gin you usually carry around in your flask? I could sure use a swig just about now."

"Sure, kid." I reached inside my coat pocket, took out my flask, and poured a generous amount into Zelda's lime soda water. She drank the whole thing down in one gulp.

"Whew! Now I feel better."

"Cheer up. As I just said, I'm with *you* tonight. It's not like I'm going home with her or anything."

"You might just as well—the way she looked at you when she left. Gees, why doesn't anybody notice *me* that way?"

"You're wonderful, Zelda. And did I tell you, you look stupendous in that sexy black dress you're wearing. I even like the way you have your hair up."

"Really? Thanks, Cable. I'm sorry...I don't know why I go on thinking you and I might be an item someday. You've been up front with me, and I appreciate that."

"I like you, Miss Blodgett," I said, taking her hand and patting it like a friendly uncle. "I wouldn't want to lose you. So, try to keep in mind, no matter who else is in my life, no one can take your place."

She cheered up. "I wouldn't ever want to lose you, either." Then her eyes brightened. "May I have another little shot of your gin?"

By the time Misty went into her next song, Zelda and I were back to normal. It's funny how you have to smooth things over so a dame can feel something exclusive with you. As I watched Misty, it was easy to see how lost men can get obsessing over a woman. A different man than myself would have caved in to Misty's charm and ended up with a ring through his nose, if she let him. But I was tough and independent and my breathing didn't depend on some broad bestowing her favors on me.

Misty was singing *Don't Blame Me* and I knew she had a message in that song for me. *"I can't help it if that doggone moon above, makes me need...someone like you to love...blame your kiss, as sweet as a kiss can be, and blame all your charms that melt in my arms, but don't blame me..."*

She finished to great applause and started to make her way over to our table when a slight, older woman stopped her and began to converse with her. The exchange seemed a bit heated. I could tell Misty was frustrated and ended up bringing the woman with her.

I stood up to greet them. "Damn, I never heard the song done that way, lady. You sure can deliver a tune, Misty Sheridan."

"She had a good teacher," the older woman said with a thick French accent. "I taught her to enunciate and cross her T's."

"Cable, this is Edie Clason, my one and only vocal coach—and my long-time, uh...special partner."

That really sounded strange coming from Misty's lips. And even my little botanist companion acted surprised. "Pleased to meet you, Miss Clason." I acknowledged Zelda. "And this is Zelda Blodgett, plant lover and botanist extraordinaire."

"How do you do...?" The older woman mumbled a response to Zelda and Misty was giving her the once over. I guess seen from the perspective of another woman, she looked pretty damn good and it could easily have been said—which happened to be true—that Zelda dressed that evening to impress me—or who knows? Maybe women dress to parade their feathers to

360

other women as well. Men are damned if they do and damned if they don't, I thought.

There was some minor chit-chat and Misty excused herself and went back up to the bandstand. Edie Clason started to walk away and then returned to our table. "Would you 'ave a moment, Mr. Denning? I would like to speak to you...privately, if you don't mind."

"Sure," I said, knowing what was coming.

She guided me outside into the cool oceanic air. She was short and very skinny, with thin lips and dark, but warm eyes. She wore an all-black outfit with pants and black patent leather shoes. Her hair was a dirty brown-grey with a touch of Henna in it. Her face was worn and her teeth were discolored a pale yellow as she spoke. "I'm sure you know what is going on, Mr. Denning. My Misty is smitten...a passing thing, I assure you, but I cannot afford to 'ave her—what would you say?— *detoured* or derailed from her career."

"Hey, I'm her number one fan. That's how I met her, admiring her talent and beauty. And isn't that her choice, lady? Nothing stays the same forever, you know. Misty's a beautiful young woman with a lot of mileage yet to be traveled—"

"—please, Mr. Denning. I don't want some man to wear her out on ze road, so to speak. I would like you to come to my *Chateau Briand Club* tomorrow evening. I want you to see *our world*, Misty's and mine. Zen maybe you will understand. Will you do zis?"

Of course, I didn't mention I was seeing Misty late that night. "Yeah, I guess I could pop over for a while. When do you start and where is your club—I'm sorry, I've never heard of it."

361

"Underground, ze true underground, where zose of us who are not accepted by Christian society go. Is located on Los Angeles Street, below Broadway. Is right under ze Woolworth Building 'eadquarters, 811 Los Angeles Street. Per'aps around ten o'clock?"

That was one of the seediest places in the city, only the lost and lonely, the disenfranchised and the forgotten, like Crazy Jack, hung out there. "Okay, Miss Clason, I'll—I'll be there. But don't expect me to be a *yes man*— I'm known to have my own take on things."

"Yes, Mr. Denning. I beg of you not to tell Misty. Understandably, she would be upset wis me. Sank you." She tucked her little purse under her arm and walked away.

I went back inside and rejoined Zelda who had been sitting on pins and needles. "Did she take a swing at you?" she joked, bright-eyed and curious. "If looks could kill...Gees, Cable, that older woman is your new friend's lover? I don't get it."

"Sometimes it's not for us to get, doll. Let's do some dancing."

Zelda and I went onto the floor. I hoped Misty wouldn't see us in the semi-lit room. As large as that ballroom floor was, everyone was there to dance and you had to really hold on to your partner, or you might lose her. Misty was singing another 'message' song to me. The tune was called *It's the Talk of the Town*, a kind of lament of a broken love affair. I was wondering if that was meant as a swan song for Edie Clason or for her frustration with getting started up with me. But Zelda was having a good time. "Gees, Cable, having you all to myself—at last—feels so good."

362

"I'm sorry about the interruptions tonight. I had no idea—"

"—that's okay. You didn't know. But I wish you had told me you knew Misty Sheridan, I would have come naked or something—I mean to compete with her, you'd really have to have something special."

I laughed. "Naw, I like you just the way you are, Zelda." She snuggled those large, warm breasts into my chest.

"I hope so. Maybe I could be your back-up girl, you know, the one the detective novels talk about. A kind of Girl Friday with a twist, you know."

We had a good time the rest of the evening. As we were leaving, I waved up at the bandstand to Misty but she couldn't see me, so we left. We took the trolley to Zelda's little place. I had never seen it before, and as expected, the damn place looked pretty much like an apartment-greenhouse. She opened the door with her key. "Now," she kidded me, "I want you to know I'm not going to try and seduce you—although I'd like to." We got inside. "You didn't say, but what did that Edie lady want?"

"She wanted to talk to me privately tomorrow night—late."

"She's going to try and discourage you from pursuing you know who, isn't she?" Zelda put a low lamp on in the corner near a sofa and lit a votive candle.

"I suspect, something like that."

"Well, maybe if she persuades you, then there might be room for me. You just don't know how much I enjoy being with you, Cable."

"Zelda—if I made love to every girl I met and liked—well, hell, I'd be dead by now!"

"I'm just not any other girl, Cable. I'm special...because...because I've loved you from the first day I met you when all you saw was a homely overweight prude with her nose in plant books." She went to a cupboard, got out a bottle of gin and poured us both a large shot. "You see, you've tainted me already. I'm a private drinker now."

"You gotta watch that stuff, it'll creep up on you."

"You can creep up on me anytime, detective."

"I know you're not just anybody, Zelda. But you've got to have the *initial attraction* for a babe, you know—"

"—like you have for Misty Sheridan, and maybe you had for Honey. Or that cute little Mexican lady you told me about who also...died. But what happens to girls like me, Cable—what happens to sensual young women who may not look like the tall, perfect model in the latest version of some fashion magazine?"

"You find someone who *fits*, Zelda, someone who wraps around you like a soft red ribbon on Christmas morning and glows with you like the lights on the tree. You should know, Adora Moreno was the only woman I was ever *really* in love with. I don't know if I could ever allow myself to let that happen again. It's hurts too much. I loved Honey, but it was different. Being *in* love with someone—well, you can't describe it, you've just got to experience it, live it out...feel it with that other person."

She reflected a minute, then spoke slowly, looking down at the floor. "Funny...that's how I feel about you... but isn't it perverse...life...that only one of us feels it?

"Yeah, it is, kid. I don't know what else to say about it...things are what they are. We can't help the way we feel—or don't feel."

"So I guess that's it, isn't it?" Then she brightened up. "Can we still be friends? I promise I won't drag you through my own whining anymore. I realize you've got a lot going on in your life. Maybe you can use a secretary who will keep your files straight, take your phone calls when you're not in the office and tidy up after you. With the Depression and all, I don't think I'm going to be getting a botanist's position anytime soon."

"That'd be swell, Zelda. Thanks for offering. I can't pay you much. How much is your rent and food and other expenses?"

"About fifty dollars a month. I can live on that if I have to."

"Well, I'll tell you what. Let's give it a go and when I get a good paying case in, I'll give you a bonus. How's that sound?"

"Perfect!" she said. I also knew that part of her enthusiasm was the knowledge that Zelda Blodgett would still be around Cable Denning fairly frequently. But I let it go. "When do I start?"

"In a way, you've started already—while I was gone. Come on in Monday and I'll show you the ropes. Files, phone directory listings—even where the dust mop is," I kidded her.

She smiled at me, standing there looking loving and sexy in her tight-fitting black-satin dress with that ample cleavage. "You make me laugh, Cable. I'll always be grateful, I mean, even to be just your friend."

"Sometimes friendship is more powerful than the roller coaster of intimate relationships. Passions come and go, but a good friendship lasts through the years. Who knows, we may even spend a Christmas together somewhere one day."

"Really? I'd love that. I've really got no one else. I have one girlfriend who's a bookworm like me. Lynne is hopeless. She's skinny as a rail, got nothing on top, if you know what I mean. I don't think guys even look at her. But then again, they don't much look at me, either."

"Well, I'd better get going. Need to catch up on some sleep," I said, checking out Zelda's pretty face.

"I didn't tell you, but you looked so handsome tonight. I could sense right away that the older lady was jealous of you when that singer of yours came over to our booth and started to chat. Anyway, any girl with half a brain would love you, Cable. I do..."

I hugged her and kissed her on the cheek. "You're the real thing, lady. And I'm proud to call you my friend, Zelda Blodgett."

"Is that all I get? Not even a little smooch on the lips?"

"Now...office rules, begin here and now. No overly affectionate displays during working hours."

"And after working hours?" she said in a very sexy voice.

"We can have a gin tonic and talk about the day, if I don't have to go out and get killed or something."

"Please—don't joke about things like that. I know your work is dangerous, but I realize you'll never tell me all the things you do. And maybe that's good, because I think I'll feel better not knowing."

I walked to her door and turned back to look at her. "You're a hell of a girl, Missy."

She ran to me, threw her arms around me, and began to laugh and cry all at the same time. "Cable! Let me love you in whatever way I can! Even if it can't be as the woman I would like it to be—but please let me love you—and don't be afraid of my love. I promise, I won't smother you."

"Thanks, Zelda..." I said that, seeing the pathos in her eyes, the disappointment when the man she had her sights set on takes a left turn. But I knew she had cooked up that fantasy long ago. Even when a guy is on the level, women think what they're gonna think.

Little Boy Blue

I got back to the office thinking how much deep shit a guy can get into in one night. I sat back in my comfy chair smoking my last cigarette for the night when the phone rang. "Yeah?" I said in a disgruntled voice.

"Well, don't bite my head off, but you didn't say good-night. Familiarity breeds contempt, you know."

I snickered. "Actually, I have a love-hate relationship with women. I did wave to you on the bandstand, but you were still singing."

"Oh. I'm glad you did. Thanks. I hope Edie didn't upset you."

"Naw, I'm gonna drop in to her little smoke den tomorrow evening around ten or so and I'm sure she'll level her guns at me with both barrels. But don't tell her I told you."

"Tomorrow evening? God, I know she's going to try to keep you away from me. What are her chances?"

"Not too good. That'll be pretty hard, babe."

"I hope so. You do remember you're supposed to see me, don't you? I'm sorry I reacted to your little friend the way I did. I found myself being jealous, Cable— definitely not like me. When was I ever jealous of another woman because of a *man*?"

"I don't know, when were you?"

"Never 'til now. And whether you know it or not, your little Zelda is quite taken with you. Are you sleeping with her? I just want to know where I stand."

"First things first, lady. First of all, you said not until late tomorrow, right? So I'm coming late. Second, Zelda's my little plant friend and she's going to be working as my secretary beginning Monday. Zelda's not my type, doll—*you are.* Just remember that. If we don't trust each other up front, there's no use beginning."

"I know you're right. I don't know why I'm so insecure. Maybe with the Edie thing and all—and I'm tired. Long night. And thanks for helping me out with that drunk guy." She paused. "I—I, uh, think your little Zelda's quite attractive and would probably love you to death if you gave her half a chance."

"She said you were so pretty that she'd probably have to come naked in order to capture my attention away from you."

"Smart girl. I think I might like Zelda."

"She's the real thing. I don't want you to worry about us before we get started, so let's leave it at that, okay?"

There was another pause at the other end of the line. "Okay..."

I didn't want the conversation to have a negative or fearful overhang. But we find chinks in the strongest armor, and Misty had a few that were already apparent. "I just want you to remember, doll, I came over with Zelda because the original joint we were going to was jammed, so I suggested yours. I had promised her I'd thank her for watching my office while I was gone by taking her out to dinner. But down deep I wanted to see you, even if it meant watching you from a distance. It's that simple."

"Forgive me, Cable. I felt the same—and still feel the same. I promise I'll be in a better place tomorrow night. Will you stay over?"

"I don't know…that kind of depends on the babe I'm with and how she treats me."

"Oh, I'll treat you real well, Mr. Private Detective. Some special part of my anatomy has been pulsing for you since that night in my place. It's new to me, Cable, please be patient. I'm a bit nervous about Edie. I haven't told her yet. But I promise I will…soon. Good night, my prince."

We hung up and I sat back on my chair. It's the shits, you know, that nothing in life quite works out the way you planned. It seems a glitch always appears in the works somewhere. With Misty I already had two glitches—and we hadn't even made love yet! I knew I'd have to deal with the Edie Clason thing, plus Misty's insecurities. Oh, well, tomorrow would be another day…

Saturday morning, May 22, 1932, dawned with a warm, yellowish sun filtering into my bedroom. I got up around nine or so, showered and shaved. By the time I put my clothes on and wound my watch it was after ten. The phone rang a couple of times, but I wasn't ready to answer it yet. My brain needed a shot of gin with a little orange juice. That was always a nice breakfast before I had my first cup of coffee. It seemed the whole country was addicted to something or other. Maybe the world, for all I knew. I had opened all my windows and the front office door to air things out. As I was sitting at my desk toying with a pencil, trying hard to focus enough to get the day started, when a small boy stood at the threshold of my office. "What is it, kid? Can I help you?"

He seemed like the Fisk Tire Boy, sleepy-eyed but present. Only he wasn't carrying a tire. He had a paper bag in one hand. He didn't say a word, but cautiously walked in and came to sit in the client's chair opposite me. "So...what's your story, kid—everyone has one. You need some dough for breakfast?" He looked forlorn, his clothes were rumpled as if he'd been sleeping in them and he was very thin.

"I—I'm lost, Mister." He began to cry. "They left me on the highway. They just left me there."

"Who left you where?"

"My—my Mommy and Daddy—because there's seven of us and they don't have no money to feed us anymore. They said if I walk on the sidewalks people would give me money. But nobody has. And now I'm just lost!"

"You mean your folks deserted all of you kids to fend for yourselves? I know times are rough, but you don't throw your own child to the wolves out here on the streets—"

"—they kept Laurie and Lorna, my sisters. But Joey, Frankie, Butch, Buster and me—well, they wanted us to make our own money and stuff."

"I see." It was hard for me to conceive that parents could ever go that far. The Depression had spawned many such stories, so I was told. But this was my first encounter with one of its casualties. "So what's your name?"

"Dickie—Dickie Overton. I live—used to live—in Bakersfield, California. Mommy and Daddy picked stuff—in the fields. But now there's no work for them. I was born in Arkansas."

"So, here you are...so what do you think we should do with you? There are authorities who take care of runaways and abandoned kids. Should I contact them? Maybe your brothers are already there."

"No...thanks. I don't like my brothers."

"Oh. So how old are you, Dickie?"

"I'm eight going on nine. I'll be nine in September."

"Oh, yeah? That's my birthday month, too. What day?"

"The 13th—my Mom told me I was born on Saturday night."

I was floored. The kid had the exact same birth date as me! Different year, that's all. "That's kind of spooky, young man, because I was born on the same day you were, too."

"But how could you be? You look a lot older than me."

"Same month and date—different year, that's all."

"Oh."

I got up and went into my icebox and got out some bread I'd been chilling. I handed the boy the whole loaf. "Here, if you're hungry...I'll get you some water." I filled him a glass with tap water and handed it to the kid. He had consumed half of the bread and crumbs lay all over my office floor. "You're hungry alright, kid. I'll say that for you. I don't have much here in the office, even though I live here."

"You don't have a house to go to?" he asked, his mouth stuffed with bread.

"Naw...I did, but the lady I shared it with, died. So now I live here. It ain't much, but it's better than nothing—and nothing is what you've got just about now. That should never have happened."

"My Mom and Dad didn't mean for it to happen. They live out of the car now. They have the front seat and Lorie and Lorna live in the back seat."

I was thinking how a life filled with misery can come from a few minutes of pleasure in the sack. There had to be something perverse about human desire and breeding cycles, not to mention being accountable to your children. But I knew that wasn't the way the world worked. There is little forethought in parenthood, for the most part. Screw and someone gets born. That's about the gist of it.

So...what do we do with you? Is it the street or an orphanage?"

"What's that?"

"I told you, a place where they take in young kids if there's no one to take care of them."

"Well, I guess. Can I stay here with you?"

"Sorry, kid, but I'm not the Daddy type—plus this is an office and I have a dirty and sometimes violent job."

"What do you do—are you a bank robber—or gangster?"

I snickered. "Well, not quite—you see, I'm at the other end of that. I go after bank robbers and gangsters and bring them to justice."

"What's that mean—kill 'em? My brothers and me play gangsters and cops a lot. I have this neat wooden gun my Dad carved out of an old box and—"

"—what's it gonna be, kid? I have a busy day ahead of me. The street or an orphanage?"

"Can I think about it?" he asked with such an innocence I couldn't refuse the lad.

"Yeah, I guess you can stay here tonight and think it over. But by tomorrow you need to decide, okay?"

He made a meek gesture, as if someone had just put a small blade in his ribs and it hurt. "Okay..."

By nine p.m. Dickie Overton was sitting next to me on the streetcar on our way downtown to see and hear one Edie Clason. I couldn't very well leave the lad in my office. Lord knows what he might get into—or was he totally honest and not part of some theft ring? You never knew these days.

The Chateau Briand Club turned out to be on the edge of Hell's Half Acre, the dumpiest part of the city, near San Pedro. Crazy Jack's not-too-fancy *Panama Hotel* was just a few blocks down on 5th Street. The place turned out to be a real dive that you could smell long before you reached the walk-down entrance. The odors of booze, cigarettes, saw dust saturated with beer and mixed drinks, urine and God knows what else permeated my nostrils as Dickie and I walked into the dump. As soon as we entered some dyke with very short black hair spotted us, and I realized we were the only men in the joint! She told us I couldn't take the boy past the little corridor leading to the bathroom. So I asked him to sit while I was escorted to a table. The place was crowded with women of every size and dimension. It seemed like everyone smoked and a dirty blue spotlight shone on a piano. Little candles flickered at each of the twenty or so tables, giving the place an eerie, surrealistic look.

Soon I saw Edie Clason approaching me. "I appreciate zat you came, Mr. Denning. Who is ze boy?" she asked, looking out to Dickie Overton sitting quietly on the cement floor in the tiny hallway.

"Oh, some kid who wandered into my office this morning. Says he's lost. I've given him overnight to make his mind up—the street or an orphanage."

"'Ow cruel!" Edie complained. "'e 'as a right to live a decent quality life, Mr. Denning—ze same as you or me ...no?"

"Call me Cable...it's easier that way."

"Per'aps for you, not for me. If you don't mind, I shall address you by your surname."

"As you wish. Not all of us are gonna have a decent life, Mademoiselle. I came up on the rough side of the tracks, and I know what poverty does to kids. Most of 'em never make it out of kindergarten—in their brains as well as in the circumstances they have to live."

"I do know. Ze world is 'orrible—a horrible place to live." She glanced down the hall. The boy had fallen asleep leaning against the wall. "Especially a fine young boy like zat needs an opportunity—to—to live and grow up into someone special. Like my Misty. Which is why you are 'ere, Mr. Denning."

"I was wondering when you'd get around to that."

"I cannot permit you to abuse 'er, take 'er for your sex playzing of ze moment. Look around...many of my audience are women who one way or anozer 'ave been abused by ze treacherous male animal. Certainly, some women are born wis a predisposition of homosexuality. But not most. I know zese women. I 'ave watched zem writhe and wiggle in zeir roles with zeir own sex. I, too, would be a man's woman 'ad I been treated right when I was young and beautiful. But I was deflowered by an older bastard of a man, one who took and picked ze flower but once—and zen left her zere, bleeding."

I winced. I knew of such stories, had heard them before. Police work taught me a lot about the lesbian community. They expressed the same traits as hetero-sexual couples do: loving, fighting, feuding, fussing and making up. That was about it. "I'm sorry those scars remained with you. I was a cop once upon a time. I attended many a knock-down-drag-out battle between women over women."

"Zen you know...so back to Misty. Per'aps I can show you what I mean—illustrate her world from ze eyes of my world, Mr. Denning."

She motioned for a piano player to come up out of the audience and with a cigarette on her lips and a drink in her hand, Edie Clason began to croak out an incredible performance. The song had a fragmented melody that haunted me from the first forlorn notes. Then she climaxed the song, higher and higher until a tear born from the highest note filled the room! Then the singer was at peace again, ending as she had begun, in a growling, guttural sound that came gurgling from her worn throat. I'm sure there was not a dry eye in the house when she had finished. I had had a truly moving experience. And you know, even better than the big clubs I usually hung out in. The absence of shouting, yelling, swearing, drinking, smoking and competing for space was a welcome relief. Everyone was reverently silent during Edie's moving delivery. But my little boy in the hallway slept on, oblivious that a life had just declared itself, took all its pain, all its sorrow, its past joy, ecstasies and hopes, declared the twisted irony of romantic love and shoved it into a song, sixty-four measures long.

Edie Clason returned to the table at which I sat. I was wiping my own eyes. "I've heard a lot of songs and a lot of dames sing them, lady, but I never heard anyone *live out* their song as you just did. Thank you."

She cracked as much smile as she could muster. "I 'ope, Mr. Denning, you 'eard my many years of punishment for choosing to be an artist...and my ten years of joyful reward in loving Misty."

"Yeah, somehow I did. But you know, neither of us can decide for Misty. *She* has to know when to turn that page in her book. The cold reality is either or both of us may lose Misty. Nothing lasts forever, lady. Truth is, I could get killed at any minute. I've got some pretty serious players wanting to take me out."

"All ze more reason, Mr. Denning, for letting Misty be. If you set 'er up for tragedy, it will affect 'er rise...'er performance."

"Life is a tragedy for humans, Mademoiselle Clason. I respect you for surviving this long. You're French, you ought to know, from cradle to grave, life is one emotional roller coaster after another. Yet, what is it you say, *'C'est la vie'*?"

"Yes. Very good, Mr. Denning. Under different circumstances...I may even 'ave liked you. You are a good man and fearless."

"Well, thanks, but I wouldn't go that far. But since we're playing 'to tell the truth' just about now, are you interested in my truth?"

"I suppose I must...or else I shall not be reasonable to myself."

"I think you're gonna lose Misty, if not to me, someday soon to some other bloke. You see, I've been around a lot of dames in my thirty-odd years and a guy like me can spot a man's woman a long way off. A couple of years back when I first met her, I was knocked back when she told me she had no interest in men. At the time my plate was full, so I didn't think much of it. But as the tragedy of my own life crashed me into a cement wall, I began to see things in Misty and hear things in her songs that made me believe that whoever was keeping her, had kept her beyond her graduation day. The rest of the story is simple...we talked, went out for a sandwich, felt the magnetic attraction intensify—well, I don't want to hurt you anymore than you will be—"

"—you are right!" Edie Clason interrupted. "But I will fight you every moment. What if she becomes wis child from a careless liaison wis you? What if you two-time her wis someone—like the buxomly young tsing you were wis at ze *La Monica*?"

"That's life, lady, it kind of gets under your skin after a while, leaves you with a restless itch that something isn't quite right. So you spend the rest of it trying to fit together pieces of dreams, things you want to make right. But it never works out quite the way you planned. So you grab what happiness you can along the way. Isn't that what you did? Didn't you take a gorgeous young doll like Misty and groom her for yourself—and then break her in as your lover so no man could ever have her?"

She had tears in her eyes. "You are *gauche, vulgaire*—and *cruel*! What gave you ze right to break up a happy couple? Why did you not leave well enough alone? Fate would come in its time...not you—"

"—I *am* Fate, Mademoiselle, the catalyst in the mix, the guy who came along and disturbed the status quo. That's part of who I am in this world. You can't stop the world from turning, lady."

She took out a cigarette from a side pocket. I lit it for her. "No, we cannot stop ze world from turning. So...at fifty we realize we cannot compete any longer wis twenty-seven." Then she looked up into my eyes, not with malice, but a pleading silent voice that begged me, *'Please don't take my happiness away!'* "But I must hear ze intention from Misty's lips. So far she has said nozing."

"That's between the two of you."

She glanced down the hallway to the sleeping boy. "What do you intend to do wis him?"

378

"Bring him down to the orphanage in a couple of days. What the hell else can a restless, short-lived gumshoe do?"

"You can give him to me. Let me take him home. I 'ave no children. When I was very young, I wanted a boy and a girl. I promise I will take 'im to ze authorities. But if I truly like ze boy, I will ask to be his surrogate Mama. Zat would be nice in my older age..."

"That's swell of you, Edie Clason. Okay, it's a deal. I'll tell him. I'm sure you have a better place for him to sleep than my dirty, cold floor."

"*Mon Dieu!* Considerably, Mr. Denning. He will sleep in a nice bed and eat some of my French bread and onion soup."

It felt awkward getting up. I wanted to reach across the table and shake her hand. But I didn't. Neither did she. Instead, I thanked her and left Dickie Overton fast asleep on the floor of the *Chateau Briand Club*...to face his new fate.

It was getting on to midnight when I walked into the *La Monica Ballroom*. Misty had just begun singing. She looked so great on that stage bathed in the warm spotlight that I wanted to kidnap her off the platform, shove her in back of the curtain and take her right there! I don't know what it was about the babe, but she got feelings going on in my male member that I hadn't experienced in a while.

When she finished to tumultuous applause, she smiled, bowed to the audience and came off the stage, looking for me. She found me at the bar nursing a honeyeyed whiskey in a snifter of boiling water. I loved to smell the aromatic essence steam out of the glass. I could tell she was nervous. "There you are!" she pronounced, coming right to my lips and planting a warm, wet kiss on them. "I was worried. You're late—but you said you'd be. So...how was it with Edie?"

"Hiya, babe. She just became a proud mother," I laughed.

"What?" she asked in a perplexed tone.

"A young boy came meandering into my office today—the kid had been abandoned. I was stuck with him so I took him to Edie's smoky den where he proceeded to fall asleep in the hallway. Well, she took a shine to him and wanted to take him home and care for him before she went to the authorities."

Misty nodded her head in a knowing way. "That's just like Edie. She always wanted children. A boy, you say? Hmmm...I think that's a good thing for her, Cable, maybe even healing for her."

"That's kind of how I saw it."

"So? What did she have to say?"

"You didn't tell me she sang with her heart and soul. Her rendition of something called *Marée Basse La Mer* made me cry, along with everyone else in the damn joint."

"Oh, yes...that song is her life signature. I'm glad you heard her. No one I ever listened to has even a fingerfull of the emotion she's capable of."

"I'll second that. Anyway, she's convinced I'm not good for you. That you might get pregnant in a careless moment with me or that someday I might leave you—"

"—will you? And if I carried your child? Would you still leave me when the next woman lures you back into your old life style?"

"I don't know. I can't answer that, doll. Who can? Can you?"

"No, I guess. For all I know, someone else could walk into the club and sweep me off my feet. Maybe someone who isn't as carefree with his life on the edge of danger all the time might come along. I don't know if I could live with that terrible sense of danger hanging around us all the time."

"Well, you'd better make up your mind pronto, kid. Time's a ticking away for both of us."

She looked into my eyes and kissed my nose. "My womanhood is still panting for you, Mister—so I guess that's a 'yes.' What can I lose except you and my heart?"

I laughed. "Now you're being realistic. Good...that's life on the other side of the eight-to-six grind of nothingness and boredom."

"I have that song I want to sing for you. Are you ready?"

"You bet. I'm a sucker for your songs, babe, you know that."

She left me and went back up to the bandstand. She began singing a haunting version of *That's My Desire* and confirmed in my heart and mind—not to mention my crotch—she really wanted me, that she was willing to live on the edge of life and death, breathe in the danger and uncertainty that plagued my professional life. *"To spend one night with you, in our old rendezvous, and reminisce with you, that's my desire..."* That was all I needed to feel my manhood surge inside my pants and realize this beautiful babe was singing the song exclusively for me.

When she finished, again an enthusiastic audience told this beautiful young woman how much they appreciated her and how she spoke for so many of their erotic dreams and longings. Misty Sheridan was the true Troubadour of Romantic Love. She came up to me and I embraced her. "Damn, babe, you got a mattress on the floor back there?" I joked.

"No, but you can have me the minute we get home." She kissed my lips. "Maybe I won't even take my clothes off first...you'll have to unzip me, Cable, then undress me stitch by stitch."

That comment brought a wave of you-know-what throughout my body and I must have flushed a couple of shades of passionate red. "So when can we go?"

"Now," she said.

We walked out of the club into a balmy Santa Monica night. We were heading for the street car stop when all of a sudden three goons stepped out of the shadows and before I could react with my .38, they rushed us at gunpoint into a nearby alley. Quickly they confiscated my gun and tossed me up against a wall, one of them holding Misty with his hand over her mouth. But she kicked the idiot in the shin and broke away. "Run, Misty—back into the club, fast!" I yelled. She dashed away, the mug limping after her. One of the hoodlums was the Asian who had done the talking before they escorted me to the headquarters of the *Oculus*. The second ape stood about six-six and must've weighed three hundred pounds, and he sported a nasty grin with a couple of silver teeth on the upper bridge. He also possessed a couple of serious brass knuckles and smiled as he approached me. "This is a serious message from Mr. Gor, and he told me to say to you, that he regrets he cannot do it personally."

With that the little Asian hit me hard in the stomach so many times that each time I bent over in pain, he slugged my gut again and sent my body reeling back into the brick wall I was pinned against. Then Mr. Tall and Ugly's right hand came smashing into my face with those brass knuckles and I felt the flesh rip open on the left side of my face. I went down, the pavement coming up to meet me like a fast moving freight train. Then I was out.

I woke up in Misty Sheridan's bed. It was daylight and she sat beside me, dabbing an open wound on the side of my jaw. Everything on my body hurt. My stomach felt like I had done a thousand pushups on Mount Everest and my face was swollen. The brass knuckles had ripped open a three-inch cut on the left side of my face and I had a big bruise on my forehead where I'd hit the pavement full bore. "Poor darling....Cable...can you hear me?"

I opened my eyes to a squint. "Yeah...where am I?"

"You're in my bed. Not exactly in the way I planned, but I'm here for you. I didn't know what else to do. I realized calling the police wouldn't be a good idea, so I had Mr. Garson and a dishwasher from the club help me bring you here."

"Thanks, kid. Sorry about...about the evening...it didn't quite...turn out as—as we planned, did it?"

She chuckled. "No, I had to take care of myself with a cold shower. But what about you, you poor dear...do I need to take you to a hospital?"

"No...if I've got...no...no broken bones...then I'll heal up...okay."

All that day Misty attended to me. Kept my wounds clean, helped me to the bathroom, fed me some chicken soup and sat with me whenever she could. By early evening I could speak a little better and we conversed. I knew she would have to try and understand the deep shit I was in with Gor and the *Oculus*. And after last night, maybe she'd decide she didn't want to risk being around me. After all, the bastards had threatened her as well. Sometimes people die because of someone else, being at the wrong place at the wrong time...sounds a lot like my story. I was thankful it wasn't Misty's turn last night.

"I need to tell you something," I said when I was sufficiently recovered to speak with an even voice. My gut muscles still hurt when I talked, but at least my head was clearing a bit and the lump on the back of my head where the goon had slammed me up against the brick wall of the building in the alley was starting to go down. "A lot of people I've known are dead because of me, Misty. I don't want you to be one of them. I'm telling you this so you can make your mind up...whether or not to be with me. Inadvertently, I got mixed up in this fouled up thing when I was about twenty-seven."

Misty sat on the bed with me and held onto my arm, putting it in her lap. "I like good stories, Cable. I have a feeling yours is going to be a hell of tale. So I'll be quiet and you talk."

I patted her on her leg. "I was a cop then. My police patrol partner and buddy, Mario Angelo and I, got assigned to check up on some stiffs at the county morgue. They were gangsters, assassinated gang style in a takeover by a Mafia boss named Joe Dragna. One of the dead guys had a hollowed out place behind the back of his tongue—like something important used to be there. It turned out to be a *golden capsule*, encoded with how creation was created and even more important—*why*. It had been stolen from a place in another dimension and brought to our world to accommodate the greedy whim of a very nasty being who headed out an Order that basically ruled the world and called the shots in politics, banking, warfare and social education."

"Well, that pretty well covers all of it, doesn't it?" Misty commented. "Now...Cable...all of this is true...you're not just entertaining us because you're convalescing..."

"True to the best of my knowledge, doll. I even saw the damn thing, an object about the size of a walnut called the *Fen de Fuqin.* Anyway, through too many adventures to recount, I was instrumental in getting the capsule to a Chinese babe who was the overseer for it. She guarded it along with another multi-dimensional lad named *Toggth*, who I happen to be quite fond of. For the present we have kept this monstrous creature from getting a hold of the capsule. But he's after me, because I possess the image and knowledge of the *God of Our Fathers*—another name for it—and wished to hell I didn't."

"So why doesn't he just extract the knowledge and kill you?"

385

"He would in a heartbeat, but Toggth and others healthfully extracted that knowledge from my memory cells. But it's kind of on a timer and one day, not too long from now, it will come popping back into my brain. That's when this creature who-would-be-God will want to dispatch me. It was his goons that hit us last night. But only as warning that they were playing for keeps."

"Lord Almighty, Cable. I wish you'd told me all of this—before I fell in love with you."

"That's why I'm giving you an out now, Misty. Indirectly, they killed my fiancée Honey Combes in her prime—"

"—*the* Honey Combes? She was your fiancée? God, Cable, I didn't know. I loved her. I learned a lot just by listening to her records! No wonder you're leery of singers—as I should be of *you*..."

"Yep. And there are others who now lie six feet under because of me. I don't want to get into *that*—just take my word for it."

"Poisonous, passionate bait—that's what you are, huh?" Misty said in a light-hearted manner. But I knew deep inside she was running scared. And I didn't blame her. She needed to hear the truth.

"Something like that. So I want you to think it over, doll. If you can arrange to have me driven to my office tomorrow, I can be out of your hair and get on with earning a living, which I've still gotta do."

"Sure, I can get Eddy to drive you over in the morning. Are you sure you're going to be well enough to get around?"

"Well, I'll stay in and out of bed for a few days—and nothing strenuous...Zelda can take care of a lot of the office stuff."

"Oh, I almost forgot about Zelda. That's good. You'll need someone. If I could get off from work, Cable, I'd really like it to be me."

"That's okay, babe, you gotta make a living, too."

She held my hand and spoke softly to me. "It's so strange. Just last night before we ran into those terrible men, I was feeling so much desire for you—that our lives would begin a new chapter and I knew that I would continue to fall in love with you more deeply, that you'd satisfy me as a woman—and I felt I could make you happy. Now it's all topsy-turvy. Truthfully, I'm even a little frightened. What if there really is some kind of death-curse hanging around you?"

"I'm the first to say it, baby. When I saw what they were going to do to you last night, I realized a pattern was repeating itself. I didn't want you to become part of it. I would never want to risk you. I hope you know that, no matter how selfish or horny I was for you."

"Yes, I do know, Cable. And I love you for it. But what will we do? Here I am pushing thirty and maybe throwing away the most important man in my life."

"The story's not over 'til it's over, Misty Sheridan. Let time heal a few things—including my body. And then let's look at us again, okay?"

She leaned over and kissed the undamaged cheek. "I don't know how falling in love can be arrested midstream—I mean, right in the process. But here it is, and here we are, having second thoughts."

"It's okay...that's life sometimes. You look and long over the next hill until maybe if you're lucky, someday you find him or her. And life is going to be fine and dandy with happy dreams and Christmas spent before a warm fire. And one day you wake up and it's all gone. The person beside you is a stranger and that ache inside, that longing that kept you a restless, searching wretch returns because there's still something missing."

"Oh, Cable...when you talk like that, I remember why I was hypnotized by your voice and style—and brilliant mind. How can someone so bright turn out to be just a private detective?"

"Because being a private detective takes a lot of 'bright' and flexibility. I think my profession and I fit. Just like you and your singing fit, babe. Now all we need is for *us* to fit."

"Wouldn't that be perfect? Funny, but when I hear you speak, I'm hearing someone familiar I know—but at the same time I'm feeling there's a complete stranger in my bed...a man I was willing to give myself to."

"It's known as *history*. You need a history with someone so you can build those vital, essential bridges, things two people share. I've seen it before...after six months of great sex, who would we be? What would we really have in common? And we'd have very separate careers."

"And I still don't know if I can believe those fantastic things you were telling me about, like creatures who rule the world, other dimensions and all that stuff. If it's true, and you've really lived those things, then nothing common—a common love, a common relationship, a common woman, a common life style—none of it could even compare to the incredible, out-of-this-world experiences you've had."

I looked over at Misty with a lot of admiration in my eyes. "You know, babe, you just put your finger on it. Yeah, you're right. Unless a woman was willing to love me and have great sex with me while she teetered on the edge of risk and danger—none of it would work. Thanks for that—you're very astute."

"I still want you, old man, as beat up as you are—and as strange as you are. I can't help that. I still think that is meant to be. But it's a choice we both have to make—whether or not the risk of my safety is worth the wild, passionate love making I sense we'd have together."

"Ah, don't forget the music. As I told your Edie, you are a born Troubadour, just as she is. That is your first allegiance. Who is in there?"

"In where?"

"In you. Once I went to hear the Robert Schumann *Piano Concerto in A Minor* and when I listened to the music and how incredibly one man could write such power and depth and romantic feeling, I was taken up into it and carried away. But even more than that, that night I fell in love, not with some woman in the audience who happened to look great in a revealing gown, jewelry and with a flirtatious manner, but the *elusive ideal*. Someone you have loved all of your life but haven't met yet. As I left the theatre that night, I asked myself the questions, '*Who's in there?*' Who is that soul I know so well and why is he buried so often behind a personality in a careless, violent world? Then I got it. The art and beauty Schumann brought through came from another place, another dimension. It wasn't something his restless balls produced because of Clara, the wife he had the hots for, but he was a medium for something far more powerful and lasting. That piano concerto will endure because it is a vibration...a vibration of Will in the universe, expressing itself because it loves itself."

Misty was in tears. "I *do* love you, Cable. I'm in there somewhere. Don't throw us away—quite yet. Please...give us some time..."

I opened my literally aching arms to Misty Sheridan and she gently slid into them. "Sleep in my heart tonight, babe, will you?"

The next day Eddy the waiter drove me to my office on Franklin and helped me upstairs. I must have been quite a sight, for when I came in, Zelda dropped everything on the floor. Her eyes widened to see my limp, beat up face with a couple of bandages and a stranger helping me to my bedroom. "Cable! What happened?" She helped Eddy and me by walking me into the bedroom and sitting me down on the bed. I thanked the kindly waiter and gave him a fiver for driving me.

I explained to Zelda what had taken place the night before. She was alarmed and felt I needed to hide out pronto. But I assured her the goons wouldn't be back for a while. At least not until Cassiopeia returned and the knowledge of the *Fen de Fuqin* had been restored to me. Then I looked into her loving, concerned face. "I'm glad to be back, Zelda—and I'm glad you're here."

"Zowie! When you came in I thought you'd died or something—I mean, you looked so bad. But if it's just a bunch of bruises and things like that, I'll make you some of Zelda's super-duper plant broth. Some of it's made from the plants I grow, like the aloe vera cactus and some other herbal plants."

I shuddered at the thought of it. "Sounds great to me—when do we start? I'm actually not too hungry, so don't hurry."

"Gees, you were supposed to teach me the ropes of the business today. You know, the files and all that stuff? But I think it's going to have to be Zelda's day to wait on Cable."

"Yeah, I'm afraid it'll have to wait a day or two."

"I'll go home and make up some soup for you and bring it over later. Will you be okay until I get back—and what else can I bring you?"

"You're thoughtful, Zelda. Nothing...just bring my little plant pal back—that'll be enough."

She left humming and I knew Zelda would be happy tending to me as I began the long, hard road to recovery.

At some point I fell asleep and began to dream. I dreamed I was about eight or nine, maybe about Dickie Overton's age, running through a field of tall, green grass. It was a perfect day and the blue of the sky gave you the feeling you could see all the way to forever up there. Then I came to a little brook going through the middle of the field. I stopped because I didn't want to cross and get my shoes wet. On the other side of the stream I saw a little girl in a sky-blue dress with big yellow buttons going down the front. "It's me, Cable...come on over," she said.

I was puzzled. I didn't know her, never saw her before in my life. "Do I know you? Maybe you got me mixed up with someone else."

"Of course not, silly," she said. "How could I know your name if we were strangers. You can say my name, if you want. Go ahead, say it."

I thought for a minute. It didn't come to me. "I'm thinking—but I can't find it—is it supposed to be in my head?"

"It's everywhere. In the air, across the fields, in the water, flying across the sky like birds, croaking in the marsh over there, it comes from the sun, the moon, my words...come on now, say it...you *can't think it,* Cable, you have to know it."

All of a sudden I let myself out of my head and her name came to me! "*Love!* It's you! You're right, I do know you."

"See? I told you. Now will you come on over and be with me? I get a little lonely when you're not with me."

Bravely, I forded the stream and came to join my little blonde friend with the twinkling blues eyes and blue dress. "Now I'm glad I'm here, Love, and I didn't even get my shoes wet...look!" She giggled and we walked off together, hand in hand.

I woke up in the dark. I slowly opened my eyes and saw Zelda... sitting on the floor, asleep, leaning against the bed with her head tucked by my left arm. I stirred but she slept peacefully on. In the scant light from a neon sign across the street, I could see her warm, generous face. I took my index finger and slowly stroked her forehead. She was startled. "Oh! Cable! Gees, I'm sorry...I must have fallen asleep...are you okay?"

"Yeah, Zelda, I'm fine. How are you doing?"

"I was dreaming. I was waiting at a little stream for a boy I knew. But I guess I never really knew him because he didn't show up. So I started back home, a little sad. But it was such a beautiful day..."

I was shocked and puzzled to hear that Zelda and I had similar dreams. They were very much alike except her little boy didn't show, maybe she didn't know his name—and most important she didn't mention her name, *Love*. I thought the dream was special and had a message for me in it. But I wouldn't tell Zelda. At least I wouldn't tell her today. "You know, kid, I need to take a bath. Can you help me?"

"Sure, Cable. You—you, uh, don't mind if I have to peel some of your clothes off. I know your ribs are sore, you can't bend very much."

"Yes, please...help yourself to my beat up and bruised body—just don't hit my schlonger with anything."

"Your what?" she asked, truly perplexed.

"My family jewels—and the appendage that accompanies—think plants and reproduction, Zelda..."

"Oh, Cable!" she said as she put the bathroom light on. "Now you're embarrassing me. I was hoping you'd undress around me someday, but not exactly under these conditions."

I tried to laugh but it hurt. "So, go ahead, peel off my pajamas, my tee shirt, my shorts, kiss my tummy, slap my buttocks and throw me in the bath!" I chortled.

Zelda looked very strangely at me. "Gees, I think you're a little crazy, Cable. Or maybe all that physical abuse you took loosened up some screws in your head or something."

"Yeah, that's it. Well, at least help me get these flannel pajamas off." She helped me out of my nightwear and with my shorts and tee shirt still on my sore and bruised body, we ambled our way into the bathroom. "I can probably get into the tub okay, but I might need you to help me out."

"Shall I look at your naked body when I help you out?"

"Do you want to look at my naked body? It's pretty beat up, but I'm still in pretty good shape for a thirty-two year old."

She blushed. "I've never seen a guy's—what is it you call it? —"

"—*schlonger, prick, penis, cock, pee-pee or hi-diddle-diddle*—take your pick, lady."

She laughed heartily, finally getting it that I was ribbing her all the while. "Oh, Cable...I never know if you're joking or not."

"Didn't you ever have a brother?"

"No, I'm an only child."

"What about your Dad—ever see him naked?"

"Nope. I've never even so much as looked at girls in the locker room in high school. I'm really a prude, I guess."

"Well, you didn't look like a prude last Friday night." She helped me ease into the tub. "Are you looking?"

"No, my eyes are closed."

I wanted to make her feel good about herself. Of all the people I knew, I think Zelda needed it most. "Tell you the truth, if I didn't have designs on Misty Sheridan,

I might even give you a romantic spin around the block—check out your pistons, fenders, engine and all..."

She snickered. "Oh, Cable Denning. I don't believe you. You've convinced me I'm not your type. And that's all right. I'm strong. I told you I'd be a good friend. After all, a girl can't spend the rest of her life living a fantasy about some guy who's hopping into bed with beautiful young singers—"

"—uh—uh—not yet..." I teased her.

"What do you mean not yet?"

"Well, Misty and I were on our way home to—to have a late evening of romantic titillation when we got waylaid by those bums."

"Really? You mean you haven't slept together yet?"

"Nope. Not exactly as I had hoped, but it's true. Now I think she's got cold feet. Have you noticed so many people around me die?"

Zelda opened her eyes and looked at me, forgetting her reserved nature for the moment. "I never thought of it...but you're right. I mean tons of people. Your friend Mario Angelo, Honey, the Moreno woman, I saw the Rusty Wilson case, and the young woman you met in Cambria—gadzooks! The list goes on and on, Cable!"

"I warned off Misty. I guess I should do the same for you. Except, for whatever reasons, they never seem to bother my secretaries."

"I wonder why that is?" she inquired to herself.

"Maybe a secretary is like the mail—it just has to get through."

"I never thought of that. Gees, what if that were true?"

"It is. Certain things are protected for posterity. Ever notice that?"

Zelda thought it over. "I really learn so much from you, Cable. Well, I'd better let you soak."

"Can I call you when I need my back washed?"

She hesitated. "Wow...I've never washed a man's back."

"What if you have kids someday—shouldn't you know how to scrub and rub and use the soap sparingly...or in case the brats misbehave and you have to wash out their mouths with it?"

She giggled. "I always thought those things came naturally once you were a mother. My mother never taught me any domestic anything. She was into books, books—mathematics, church—and books. I think she liked me, but it was my Dad who I loved to be with. He was the adventurer, the plant trailblazer—yep, the Blodgett giant strawberry."

"That's nice, Zelda. So can I call on you to wash my back?"

"I guess...if I don't get too embarrassed. If I do, I'll just have to throw the sponge in and leave. Is that okay? You won't be offended?"

"Nope, now that you explain it that way. I'm okay with it." Eventually my little plant friend did a good job scrubbing my back. My sore and pain-ridden body truly enjoyed *that* bath!

Nightmares and Bathtubs

After I got settled in and I sent Zelda home with her promise she'd return by nine in the morning, I began to doze off. But this time my dream was startling and vivid. I was in India in some kind of dark hut. There was a lovely Indian woman rubbing me all over with some kind of salve that made my body shine. Then a crazy doctor entered the hut and pushed the young lady away from me. He sounded like one of those mad scientists in a couple of talking movies I'd seen lately. Whatever it was that the young woman had rubbed me with had completely weakened me and I was helpless while the doctor shackled and led me out of the hut to another building at the edge of a clearing. There were torches on the walls and a stairway descending. The doc grabbed a torch and we went down about fifteen feet until we were in a passageway. It led to a huge wooden door leading to a room that had been dug out of the earth. Everything smelled musty and like damp dirt. But there was another smell that caught my primal instinct response and raised hackles on the back of my neck. A shiver went through me. The doc opened the door and pushed me inside, then quickly slammed the door behind me. It was pitch black. I spoke, but there was no response. Then I heard a deep, unearthly "hiss" that seemed to be accompanied by a growl of some kind. How could some primeval creature hiss and growl at the same time? I backed up to the door. My fingernails were digging into it out of trepidation. Then I heard a movement. In the blackness, something even blacker moved slowly toward me. I was perspiring and shaking.

Nothing unseats the nervous system with fear like the unknown in the dark. I took a deep breath and spoke again to the unknown something in the darkness. I heard the growl-hiss again, only this time it was much closer. I could sense something looming above my head now and I picked up an odor I had never smelled before. It was the one I had detected earlier, musty but animal in origin. I was still shackled and helpless to defend myself, so I closed my eyes and wished myself somewhere else.

Suddenly I was in a coffin. I lay there inanimate when something woke me, pounding on the top of the wooden box. Then I saw a glint of light above my head. I shouted, but no one responded. I shouted again and this time I was rattled out of my sleep by the phone ringing and Zelda's voice calling to me. "Cable! Cable! You're having a nightmare! It's me, Zelda—can you hear me?"

I was dripping wet with sweat and shaking uncontrollably. It was like I had a palsy and I couldn't stop shivering. Instantly Zelda ran to the bathroom and started the bathwater. She ran back to me, pulled me up out of bed, and began to remove my sopping wet clothes. Then she pulled me up and we staggered together into the bathroom where she helped me into the tub, the hot running water and steam waking my body somewhat. Then Zelda Blodgett quickly took all of her clothes off and got into the tub with me, holding me close to her with her naked body clinging to mine. She held me and rubbed me and the combination of that wonderful care and affection and the hot water started to bring me around and my trembling began to subside. In fifteen minutes or so, my nervous spasms subsided to a minimum. "Zelda...I had a terrible nightmare...I'm okay now...thanks, babe..."

"I'm here, Cable, I'm here," she comforted me. My eyes cleared up sufficiently to see this lovely creature attending me was completely nude!

"Is this your way...of...of seducing me?" I asked, still a shiver in my voice.

"Not today, Cable...I was really worried. Your night-clothes, your bed—they're all soaked with perspiration. I don't know what you dreamed, but I'm sure it has to do with your body going through some kind of shock from the way those people beat you up!"

"Yeah...you're probably right. I guess I took more of a licking than I thought. You ripped off your clothes...and jumped in with me—do you realize, young lady...you...you're completely naked—but then again...so am I...."

She laughed as she hugged me tight, her cheek up against my one good cheek. "Gees, and somehow I'm not afraid or embarrassed anymore—at all. It's almost like I wanted you to see me naked anyway—someday—I just didn't know it would be this way!"

"Life is full of surprises, Zelda...now...isn't it?"

"Gees...who could have known? Oh, by the way, your girlfriend Misty called. And a very nice man with a deep voice phoned. He said his name was Jedediah Penn, a friend of yours. He wants you to call him as soon as you can."

"Okay...if you can eventually get us out of this here bathtub."

Zelda helped me out of the tub and she dried me off, from head to toe. I was a bit embarrassed when she skirted around my shrunken balls and penis, but I was too sick and in pain to let it bother me. But I *was* looking over her fine curves, those large breasts dangling in front of me when she bent over, wonderful dark-pink nipples standing to attention and a dark patch of pubic hair dripping with water. "I don't think you should sleep in your wet bed tonight, Cable. I think you should come over and sleep in my bed—and I'll take the little love seat or something. I'm going to have to wash those sheets and air the mattress."

"Are you sure?" I asked, feeling all of this was something Zelda might have imagined in her wildest dreams had I not looked like a prizefighter who got beaten to mush in twelve rounds. But taking me in this way proved to me what a good sport and caring person she really was.

"Of course. Gees, Cable, I'm all you've got right now." I thought for a second. Yeah, she was right. With Honey and Adora gone, Misty a big question mark—who else was there? Cass was never a real romance candidate since she'd be returning to her home planet one day soon.

"I guess you're right, Zelda. You are all I've got—I mean, someone to really be there when the chips are down."

"What happened to your pretty singer girlfriend?"

"I told you, it never quite got off the ground. She got frightened when I told her the truth about the babes in my life ending up as stiffs at the local morgue. And this latest attack, where they grabbed her too, might have sealed it. Besides, I don't think Misty's the domestic type. She's a showbiz pro and that's her life."

"Well, I'm no domestic either...I just care about you." She looked up at me as she helped me with my last sock. "Gees, Cable, think about it. A year ago I wouldn't have dreamed I'd be taking care of you, let alone jumping naked into a bathtub with you."

I needed to change the subject. "Okay...as best I can today, I'll teach you some of the ropes around the office. You saved Jedediah's phone number—I think I've got Misty's somewhere."

"Yes—and yes you do. You've scribbled her name all over your desk pad," she said a bit indignantly.

I started Zelda on the fundamentals of being a good Girl Friday for a gumshoe and left her with the files. I got to the phone and called Jedediah Penn's number. A gruff voice answered at the other end of the phone. It was a familiar one, a sound I liked to hear when the world lost its sense of direction. "Jed Penn, old boy, it's me, Cable Denning here."

"Am I glad to hear your voice, Cable. I've got some important things to tell you. When can we meet?"

"Well, to tell you the truth, Dr. Penn, I'm kind of laid up at the moment. You see, I ran into some pretty rough thugs and they worked me over pretty good."

"Oh no...Cable...I'm sorry...but it's the nature of your work. Tell me who you go with and I'll tell you who you are, I say."

"It's better than selling lead pencils on street corners these days. I gotta catch as catch can, Jed."

"So when can you see me? It's pretty important that I see you, Cable. You know me, I wouldn't call unless—"

"—but I wish you would call, doc. It's been a little lonely on the male end of things without your patter.

After all, we share some pretty unique history, wouldn't you say?"

"Yes, Cable, oh, yes...which is part of what we need to talk about."

"Being this banged up and all, I can't hobble around alone." I glanced over at Zelda, who I knew was listening. "I need my nurse-secretary to be my third leg." Zelda smiled and turned back to her business. The more I was around this gal, the more I liked her.

"Why don't you commission that wonderful little Latin number who obviously adored you?" It hit me then that Jedediah Penn didn't know about Adora's death. "She's...she's...no longer with us, Jed. She contracted leukemia and went out like a flickering light bulb."

There was a silence at the other end. "I—I don't know...what to say, Cable. My condolences. When did she—she—"

"—some while ago now. I've been doing okay, Jed. Whatta ya do, except trudge on? You don't stop breathing, but try to find some reason to keep going, even if some days you don't want to." I didn't even want to tell him about Honey. "So, when can you come see me, my friend? Why can't you crank up Polly Parker to bring you over to see *me*, old boy? You are in Los Angeles?"

"Yes, but I am immobile these days, I'm afraid, Cable. So I'll need you to come *my* way."

"Truth? I'd say three or four weeks."

"Is that the best you can do?"

"I'm afraid so, doc. I'm sorry, but I'm in a lot of discomfort and moving up and down stairs more than I have to right now is a painful experience. I hope you understand."

"Please, Cable, don't forget me. We have important things to discuss. If you can make it earlier, give me a ring. Polly will set up a little lunch or something."

"How is Polly Parker?" I asked, remembering his assistant.

"Eh, she's ornery as ever—and twice as nice. I could never have made it without her. Make it sooner than later, Cable...good-bye for now."

We hung up and I looked out across my desk at Zelda who was busy bending down putting away some files. She straightened herself and turned to me. "It's hard, isn't it? Talking about your ladies who died. Gees, Cable, when you think of it, what a strange life you have lived so far. If I didn't know these things to be true, I would never have believed them if someone told me."

I smiled. "Yeah, like someone I know stripping her clothes off to jump into the bath with some weird private detective."

"Are you going to keep carrying on about that?" she queried.

"You bet. Once a day and twice on Sundays."

She laughed. "I bet you would, too."

I went back to the task at hand and called Misty. She seemed a bit aloof but concerned about my state of health. When she learned that Zelda was still caretaking me, she seemed even a bit more frosty. I don't know what it is about dames, but at the slightest hint that someone might be in their territory, they back off and cool down. But I guess guys are the same way. Why bother if someone else is taking a place you couldn't fill anyhow? And my truth was Zelda was here and Misty wasn't.

I tired early that day and Zelda suggested we go to her place and she'd fix us a little to eat and that I should go to bed early. We staggered down the stairs and I limped to the streetcar stop with the aid of Zelda's arm. I must have looked like a street fighter as people glanced at us riding along. But what the hell, sometimes you get smacked for being in the wrong place at the wrong time and not having any premonition of it. I knew I had to work on that.

Zelda made us a couple of olive sandwiches with a pickle on the side and a gin tonic for desert. We were happy together and laughed a lot. She brought a down-to-earth plainness with a slight hint of smoldering sensuality. A hell of a combination, I thought. As she spoke to me, I was still picturing her lovely naked body leaning over me, wiping me down after the bath that morning. Yeah, the little babe had a lot going for her.

About eight o'clock she helped me into her bed. I owned only one pair of pajamas, so I crawled in naked. Zelda turned the radio on for me and sat at the edge of the bed. There was a nice sentimental version of *A Ghost of a Chance* playing and suddenly my little plant lady looked sad.

"What is it, babe? A memory?"

"No, it's just the way I feel about you, Cable. I know I don't stand a ghost of a chance with you, just like the song says. You know, it's funny...a girl gets stuck in a place...somewhere inside of her, a long time ago, when she idealized a man she was attracted to. Then, if she's not careful, she gets frozen in time. She watches her life go by. She doesn't go out with other guys because in her heart she doesn't want to. And in my case, no one would even look at me twice to care, anyhow."

"I wouldn't say that, kid. After all, didn't you have a serious guy hanging around for a while?"

"He turned out to be queer, Cable—remember? That's how bad my judgment in men is." The tune ended and a bouncy little song came on the radio entitled *"Let's Do it, Let's Fall in Love."*

"Damn, Zelda, we can't always fly the minute we jump out of the nest—be patient with yourself!"

"I'm going to be twenty-six in December! Do you know what that means for a girl? No husband, no house, no children?"

"Hell, if it's children you want, doll, just hop into your bed with me—I'll pump as many kids as you want into you," I crackled, probably for the shock value of jolting her out of her lethargy.

"Cable! That's crude!" Then she checked my eyes out. "Damn, I know you're joking. But to me it's serious. Plus I really need to love someone—not just lay down and spread my legs like Jacqueline Conklin used to do. And she did end up pregnant. To this day, I still don't think she knows who the father is. I can't be like that."

"Nobody says you have to be. Just be you." I had a slight headache. "I—I, uh, need to get some shut-eye, hon. You can leave the radio on for a while. It kind of soothes me. Where are you sleeping?"

"Out on the love seat. It's pretty comfortable."

"Well, then, good-night babe, and thanks for everything today. You've been a lifesaver, Zelda Blodgett."

"Don't mention it, Cable," she said softly.

She started out of the room. Her gait was listless and I knew she didn't really want to leave and maybe would've liked to chat a while longer. I didn't feel really great about kicking the babe out of her own bed either. "Oh, Zelda?" I called after her.

She came back into the room. "Yes?"

"I'm a bit cold, a little shaky. Do you think you could warm me up a bit before I fall asleep?" I said, knowing she would jump at the chance.

She lit up like a Christmas tree. "Gees, Cable, really? I'd love that." Unabashedly I watched as Zelda Blodgett, the bookworm from Plant World, took off her clothes and slipped under the covers next to me. She sidled in close until our skin was touching. Actually, it felt good. "This is the second time today I've been naked with you. Who would have thought?" She snuggled closer to me. Then she shocked me. "Can I touch you? I've never touched a man before. I promise to be gentle. Think of it as an educational process for me—if you can see it that way."

"Educational? Come on, Zelda, you just want to get laid, admit it."

"Well, yes, but not exactly like that. So, is it okay with you?"

"Sure...but do be gentle...all of me hurts right now. And don't expect anything else. Even if I wanted to, it'd be impossible tonight."

"I promise." I closed my eyes and smiled to myself as I felt Zelda's tentative hand carefully take up my balls and massage them. Then she stroked my other member warmly and gently, getting a little rise as blood surged into it. "Am I doing something wrong?" she asked.

"Oh, no...you see the—the, uh, penis normally responds to touch, if it likes someone. Of course, since it has a mind of its own, I can't control these things," I answered with tongue-in-cheek.

"Then he likes me—I think," she said, her voice sounding like that lethal combination of little girl and a young woman exploring her own sexuality. She continued to massage me until I was at half-mast. "Gees, Cable, he's growing so big—do you want me to stop?"

"Well, maybe for tonight. I don't want us to start something we can't finish, if you know what I mean."

"Yes...but now that I felt it—I like it. Crazy, isn't it? It's like touching me down there, or on my breasts. I just know I'd respond with a lot of—of good feelings..."

"I think we should try to sleep, Zelda. Please...give me a couple of aspirin, if you will, and let me drift away."

"Sure." She got up out of bed immediately and came back with two aspirin and a glass of water. "Here you are..."

As she handed them to me, I took her hand. "You know what, lady? You're a warrior in this world. I'm glad I know you, Zelda Blodgett."

"I love you, Cable Denning...and that's all there is to it."

CHAPTER 13

TENDER IS THE NIGHT

It was July 6th before I was up and around sufficiently to go see Jedediah Penn. Miraculously, Zelda and I had slept together for a few days without having sexual intercourse, before my returning to the office living quarters. She was a trooper and we laughed a lot. She had become a companion of mine. So finally my sheets were clean and my bed aired out, and I resumed life as usual. Well, sort of. Usual for me was the next surprise around the corner, the next gun in my ribs, the next babe walking into my office whose problems resemble the national debt, or the little boy lost, seeking love and shelter.

"So, Zelda, when is that appointment with Dr. Penn?"

"Wednesday. Today's Tuesday, Cable," she said with her head in an account book. "Mr. Richelle owes you eighty dollars, by my accounting. Should I bill him?"

"Always try the personal touch first, Zelda. Phone him."

"Okay."

That's sort of how our days went. Zelda was fast, efficient and learned the ropes quick. Every once in a while when she bent over and she was wearing a particular white blouse, I got an unsolicited full-blown view of her marvelous tits. Some days it was hard not to touch them. But then I knew that would open up a whole can of worms. But now and then I wondered how she might be when the both of us meant business in the bedroom. I had a good feeling about it.

It was a slow Tuesday night and after I sent Zelda home, I decided to go and catch Misty's act. The place wasn't as crowded as usual. It was predicted by some that 1933 would be the lowest economic year in modern U.S. history. The Depression had hit everyone, except the rich and powerful. But the little guy like me got it in the shorts and business was hard to beat out of the bushes. I barely had enough to pay Zelda let alone my own meager bills.

When I walked in around 9:30 p.m., Misty was singing a medium version of *I Cried for You* and maybe she was telling me it's my turn to cry over her. I don't know. Dames live in another sphere of thought, I conjectured. When she finished the song she spotted me at the bar and came over and greeted me. "Well, well, well, the one-time invalid. How are you feeling—all pasted together?" She hugged me, but it was a so-so hug, perfunctory and without much feeling.

"Okay, babe. I'm walking around with most of my head together, no headaches and a slight limp. How about you?"

"I'm on a break. Can we find a table and talk?"

"Sure."

She led me to the very table Zelda and I shared the night I brought her here. We sat. "I'm sorry, Cable, I've been aloof lately, haven't I?"

"Aloof? I'd try totally absent, living on another planet for starters. Am I not worth a phone call now and then anymore? What ever happened to 'I think we can be the best of friends'?"

"I run when I'm afraid, Cable. I ran after that Sunday we took you back to your place and I knew your little plant lady would be there to adore you and look after you. But it wasn't just that. You really scared me about those people dear to you ending up dead. I'm too young to suffer that fate, or even walk in that direction. There's something else. If we became lovers—I really wanted you, Cable, and I still think about it—I realize I would be on pins and needles day and night worrying if I'd ever see you alive again, or be waiting for the next knock on my door that some terrible person you offended would be out for revenge on me." She licked her lips and reached across the table for my folded hands. "And...I've gone back to Edie. I felt she was right. Not just because I owe her so much for the sacrifices she made to get me where I am today, but because she's safe. And now we have a little boy at home with us. Dickie Overton is a delight. No one ever claimed him and the authorities are too jammed to even consider providing for him at this point. So Edie and I are going to adopt him."

I winced at the thought of losing Misty Sheridan. "That...makes me happy. I always thought the kid needed a break. As far as we go, you and I....hell, I gave you the options and you took one of them. It's okay. We nipped it in the bud before it even got started. Now I can admire you from afar and always wonder what it would have been like. That's enough in itself to keep a guy's libido active, isn't it?"

"I guess...putting it crudely. I guess I've always told my life stories in song, haven't I? When I sang *That's My Desire* that night for you, I really meant it. I *had* been aching for you all day. I don't know why frightening statements like the ones you made later, threw a bucket of ice water on me. I guess I was also afraid that I wouldn't satisfy you—or be satisfied by you intimately."

"What do you mean by that?"

"Well...when you're with a woman, certain nerves and parts of a woman's genitals get—get, uh, 'trained' and used to a certain stimulation. To be blunt, vaginal intercourse would do nothing for me, I'm afraid."

"Have you tried it?"

"No...I mean, not since I've been with Edie."

"Then you really don't know now, do you?"

She seemed flustered. "I don't want to talk about it, Cable. I'm sorry...please...let's be good friends...I'll always be happy to see you come into the club. I love singing to you."

I gave her a weak smile. "And I love hearing you sing to me. So, toots, I guess that's it. I'm glad I came tonight. Do you have another song for me—I was thinking, if you knew *I'm Getting Sentimental Over You*—that'd be swell. I thought that might be a good song to remember you by on a rainy night. One never knows when a special evening comes along and you can tear open the wrapper on an old memory."

Her eyes were misting. "Yes...I do know that song...I'll sing it for you. I warn you, though, my arrangement might be a little too sexy for Hollywood private detectives."

I laughed. "I like sexy—I think I can handle it."

She excused herself and I meandered back to the bar. She was wearing a red sequined gown and with her reddish hair and blue eyes, topped off with a thin, black choker, she looked like a million. The spotlight hit her and she launched into the song. As she was singing, I

411

was wondering just how many storms love affairs can weather. Life has a way of twisting the plot so what you thought you had ends up sawdust in your hands one day. Nothing holds together forever. Lives are lost by crossing a street, love is lost through the wrong words at the wrong time, fortunes are lost by bad judgment and nations are lost through greed for money and the self-serving of a few despots. None of us get out of this world alive. Misty's safe decision to mend things with Edie Clason was right for her. For me? I had the hots for her, sure enough, but would it have lasted very long? Maybe, maybe not. Who knows? That kind of passion usually comes with a short fuse and desire explodes the two of you into smithereens, and by the time you're able to gather your pieces back together, it's over. It's almost as if, where love's concerned, there's a third party in love...when it decides to leave, that part is missing and neither of the remaining parties can fill the gap. So people either limp on with the emptiness, or leave the relationship. Heartache is a crippling disease. I was still doing flip-flops in my stomach when I thought about Adora Moreno—or precious times with Honey Combes. All the *might-have-beens* in the world can't compensate for what you lost, that can't be regained.

I went over and thanked Misty for the song. She took my hand and led me into the shadows behind the stage curtain. She put her arms around me and kissed me deeply. As once before, that kiss zoomed from my shoes up to my head and on the way back, hit my groin at two-hundred miles an hour. "What was that all about?" I asked, quite puzzled.

"Desire...it's what I always have for you. Even if I can't find love, I just realized as I finished my song and looked at you standing at that bar, I'll always find desire with you. Maybe love hangs you up, and desire doesn't. What do you think?"

"That's why guys hire whores, doll, to feel desire without love."

Her eyes widened and she slapped me on the face, pretty hard. She walked away, leaving me there in the dark. As I said, you can never figure a dame!

I had just gotten off the streetcar at Gower and Franklin when something hit my head like an electric shock from touching a power pole. I staggered for a minute and came to rest against a building. Suddenly I knew two things. One, I had the knowing of the *Fen de Fuqin* back in my brain cells—and two, Cassiopeia had just come back from *The Cave of the Seven Truths.* I ran to my office just in case she had returned without knowing that her mentally disturbed father was hot on her trail, thinking she had what I had. I found no one and it looked like nothing had been touched. I sat at my desk rubbing my head when all of a sudden I heard a slight hum sound. Then through my outside window came a small brass orb. Saturnalia! She was frantically doing all kinds of movements, gyrations, spins and circles. I wasn't an alien, so I couldn't read her transmissions, but she was obviously agitated. Finally, I started to tune in on some of what she was pulsing to me. The orb moved my note pad in front of me and scooted a pen from the right side of the desk. I took the pen and let the orb take over my pen hand. All I could get were some letters. First, all I could distinguish were P – A – R—what the hell did that mean? Then after I quieted myself, the letters began again: 'P – A- R- K—the park! "Is that it, Saturnalia? Bronson Park?" She weaved a big, slow circle in the air. I took it to be a yes.

I flew out of my building and as luck would have it, I spotted a taxicab without a fare, hopped in the back and had him take me to the park entrance. It was closed after dark, so I jumped a fence and went running down the trail that eventually led up to the Bronson Caves. I don't know how I knew, but I did—*she* would be there somewhere. The moonlight lit my way as I stumbled up the hill. As I approached the caves I saw a figure lying on the ground. I ran up to it. It was Cassiopeia! She was face down on the dirt, so I turned her over. "Cass! Cass! It's me, Cable! Your Mom clued me in—and I just got my head-stuff back a little while ago—can you hear me?"

She opened her eyes, recognized me and instantly reached up for my neck, bringing my face crashing down onto her lips. "Cable! Oh, Cable! I wanted to be close to you! I missed you so much..." she cried in a shaking voice. There in the semi-moonlight she held me so tightly, I couldn't move. Then she opened her legs and put my body in between them. She reached inside my pants and pulled out my erect male member and thrust it between her legs. She let out a cry of pain and joy as I entered into a warm, blissful, mysterious and electric world. It was like a kaleidoscope of colors and sensations, as if the aliens had additional powers of light and color and titillation which was all but overwhelming to a human. She pushed on my buttocks harder and harder and I went deeper and deeper until it was as if my whole body had entered her beautiful world through her humanized vagina. She brought me to a climax and we both exploded into bits of stardust, glowing, rising and falling through a night of endless stars. It never seemed over and it was as if she wanted me to rise even higher. But human males can't do that, for once the orgasm has released his sperm, the male requires a rest period. But not Cassiopeia! She continued to rock me until finally I had to stop.

"Cass! I've got to stop! You're gonna kill me!"

Finally her body came to a trembling halt. "Oh, by the gods and eternity, Cable, I was so *ready* for you. I could think of nothing else except you during my absence. Did I hurt you?"

I glanced down at my wet and glistening penis, which now drooped and dripped just outside of my pants. "I don't think so." I cleared my throat. "So how are you? And how long can you stay?" I didn't know what else to say.

"Was it good, Cable? Did I please you? I could feel you come with me. Your spirit was willing...you mated with me. Too bad I can't have your child. That would absolutely complete my earth stay."

"It was super-great, doll. I never went to so many wonderful places." I laughed and looked up at the moon. "Do you think the man in the moon helped?"

She giggled. "I feel so good, Cable. These human nervous systems are so sensitized. I could feel all of your energies—even your confusion—but I couldn't wait. I knew it had to be now."

"Well, I'm glad you asked me first," I said a bit sarcastically as I got up, put my schlonger away and picked Cass up from the dirty roadway.

"I know, in human standards, that's naughty. Actually, it's even naughty in Saturnian standards. But wanting is wanting—and I could not actually proceed with my life until I'd had you. Do you understand any of it at all?"

I took in a big breath. "I'm not sure, Cass. All I can say is I enjoyed it immensely. And wouldn't mind a rematch sometime."

"Can I sleep with you tonight?"

"Well, it's actually morning. But yeah, you'd better come back to my place with me. But now both of us are in deep shit, babe. Your Dad is about to come down on us with everything he's got."

She smiled. "Oh, I wouldn't worry too, too much."

"And what gives you this sudden confidence?"

"Hestia—Vesta, my sister—and her small army of invaders have already blocked off my father's headquarters and have engaged him in combat."

"Well, that's good news! She came into my office—but you knew—well, she was talking about in imminent invasion then. I'm glad she's going to lambast your very cruel and tyrannical father. I hope he loses and gets banished a thousand light-years from here."

We began to walk back down the road. "*That* might not happen. But I can see Vesta keeping him engaged for a few hundred—or thousand—of your years."

"So...what do I do about the *Fen de Fuqin* knowledge?"

"Toggth showed it to me back at the *Cave of the Seven Truths*. What a wonderful dimension. He told me about your Chinese lover—Lei-Tao. She was naughty too, like me, huh? She got turned back into a lotus flower pod. Mother told me she's almost ready to send me back home. I'm excited, Cable. I'm going home...!"

"Yeah, babe, and I'm glad for you. Just out of curiosity, do you—do you, uh, have any emotional feelings for what we just did—I mean, in making love and all?"

"Emotional feelings? I know what you mean. We discussed them and I allowed myself to feel them when we were in Cambria and I stayed with Art Beatle—and I stayed with Art Beatle—and I stayed with Art Beatle—and I stayed with Art Beatle—and I stayed—"

I hit her shoulder. All of a sudden I got this feeling that Cassiopeia wasn't Cassiopeia anymore. "—your gear's stuck!" I exclaimed. What the hell's going on with your brain?"

"—with Art Beatle," she concluded. "But I think they just translate to pleasure and joy for me, Cable."

I was really stumped about her behavior. "Are you all right? I mean, the teleportation trip back and all—it didn't fry your brain or anything, right?"

"Fry my brain—fry my brain—fry my brain—fry my brain—"

Now I knew I was dealing with a humanized mannequin. There never was a Cassiopeia human woman per se. Their version of humanization was a trick, an anatomical illusion. I had just ejaculated my sperm into an organic machine! "—okay, stop, Cass! Just say nothing for a while, understand?"

"Yes." She quieted and we rounded the last bend before the trail descended into the little park area where the bubbling little brook trickled. There stood Toggth and Saturnalia's orb awaiting us. "Saturnalia apologizes for her daughter's behavior, Cable, even though there are worse things to experience, I'm sure."

"Yeah, Toggth. Why didn't you warn me you guys were coming—and that the beautiful redhead here with all the energy is in reality a replicant?"

"Well, it wasn't intended that way. Saturnalia could only conceal the spirit of her daughter in an organically synthesized bio-pod, not an actual human woman. Besides, we're all cranked up to go now. Our two wayward female Saturnians may now return home."

"That's good news, Toggth." I glanced over at both the bobbing orb and Cass, who stood motionless with a mechanical smile on her face. "I suspect some of the bio-pod went haywire on the last teleportation...her rationality quotient has dropped along with her intelligence quotient—she repeats herself a lot."

"Not to worry. We'll destroy this bio-pod as soon as her soul-journey begins."

I walked to Cassiopeia, daughter of Rhea-Saturnalia and Cronus-Gor, the creature who would be God. "I wish you the best, Cass. Wherever you end up or whatever you want to be in your real life—up there, on the 6th planet out. I sure learned a lot, kid."

"Thank you, Cable...thank you, Cable...thank you, Cable...thank you, Cable...thank you, Cable...," she continued on and on like a broken record. I asked Toggth to get a hold of me when the mission was accomplished and walked down the trail into the cool early morning.

418

I had asked the cabby to wait and I knew exactly what I wanted to do. I didn't stop by my office. I went directly to Zelda's little place. I knocked on the door. A very groggy but pretty lady in a see-through nightgown opened the door. "Cable! Wha—what—?"

I put my hand over her mouth. "Zelda—please, don't say a word. I want you to take me to bed right now and make love to me—human style—fuck me like a human woman, love me with all that feeling you keep saying you have for me—but do it now—before I go nuts any more than I am—or change my mind!"

She immediately took me into her arms. "Cable..." she sighed, caressing me all over. "Oh....Cable...yes! yes!" She took my hand and led us into her bedroom, slipped off her nightgown, helped me undress. I pushed her onto the bed, my lips and fingers touching and caressing every living human female part of Zelda Blodgett. When her legs parted and she brought my head powerfully into her breasts and I could feel my manhood enter her warm, wet womanhood, I knew how great it was to love a real flesh and blood being whose capacity to share and give and love was endless! This would be my legacy to myself...my joy of love.

Epilogue

Sometimes the sound of that melancholy sax isn't so sad. Sometimes a little happiness finds its way through the registers as that breathy, sensual tone ascends to a high E-flat or an F. Those are nights when the breezes blow in cool from the coast and there's a girl beside you who likes a lot of the same things you do. She sits with you at the Friday Night Fights, not because it's her favorite thing to do, but because she loves you so damn much she wants to bathe in your company as much as she can. And you don't mind, because your desire for her has become a nice habit and she lies down on the bed with you quietly and opens her arms because you're the best thing that ever happened to her. And that means a lot to you, because someone good and honest is worth a thousand dames full of pretense and lies, booze and an easy trick on a sultry summer's night.

Every once in a while love is good to us and we should mark down those priceless times on our calendar of broken dreams. Red-letter days are rare because they're a recess from the school of hard knocks and they tell you that somehow on a particular day or night, you won't have to fight the unbeatable foe or pretend you like the human race. No, love exempts you from the guilt of what came before that you lied to yourself about. It elevates you to mattering in the world, first to yourself and then to others. And you know, it's catching---like a good cold, because when someone else thinks you're wonderful you pass it on to others. And in my case, I gave praise and respect in like kind to Zelda Blodgett—the least likely young woman to succeed in

420

romantic love, the one who thought no one in the world saw her, who felt being a plain young woman *sans* the glamour of pedigree, social station, great clothes, jewelry and lots of dough was a death sentence on being popular with the opposite sex. None of it's true, because social protocol is an illusion created by a commercial media to sell commodity. You are who you are. There's nothing in front of that, nor behind it. It's like life...it just is.

Some nights my addiction to smoky joints with great music pouring out of the door, draws me to a mystique I've never quite figured out. Almost thirty-three years old...yet I smoke, drink and chase skirts like it's a ritual of conduct, a rite of passage in a cave of din and madness. Some babe in a low-cut sequined gown with full breasts and a wonderful smile still turns me into a fan of the late night club scene, especially if she sings well, and the music is Porter, Gershwin, Berlin, Mercer, Kern or Harry Warren—when the lights are low and the spotlight on the sequins of that slinky dress, draws you right into their reflection, and you can see her lipstick shine all the way from the back of the bar—you know you've arrived to bathe in your dreams and get healed from all the garbage upstairs there, on the street. Being there also means a world beyond the perpetuation of the species, the empty busyness of survival coupled with the empty promises our leaders heap on an ignorant public, that tomorrow just might be a better day. The drinking, smoking, talking, whoring, listening and dancing on a crowded floor, puts a lie to all of that. Nothing matters except today and spinning your own tale or listening to someone else's—and if you're looking for love, aha! the cabarets are the great classrooms of humanity, made of dreams and lies and perfume, under which wait the empty longings for someone you haven't met yet...when all the time it was *you* you were looking for.

No, as I hear that sax waft up the airshafts of my brain, I think today's a lucky day. After all, I'm a gumshoe with a spacious office, enough business to pay the rent and food—and a great little secretary who takes dictation in the afternoon and takes me to bed at night, makes great herbal vegetable soup and attends me when I'm sick. Now, tell me something that's gonna beat *that*—in this world?

The End

Acknowledgements

Cover Images:
Cable Denning: Kenneth A. Cox Photography
Adora Moreno: © Can Stock Photo, Inc/disorderly
Zephyr's Cove: Photographer – Vladimir Kondrachov
Saturnalia: © Can Stock Photo, Inc/fanfo
Alien eye: Original art – Frances Walker-Moss
Zephyr: Provenance unknown
Dolphin: Provenance unknown
Conch shell: Provenance unknown

Original cover designs: Frances Walker-Moss

Editing and Research Consultant: Frances Walker-Moss